BRENDA NOVAK

BEFORE WE WERE STRANGERS

Recycling programs for this product may not exist in your area.

ISBN-13: 978-0-7783-0907-9

Before We Were Strangers

For questions and comments about the quality of this book, please contact us at CustomerService@Harlequin.com.

www.Harlequin.com

Printed in U.S.A.

Praise for the novels of Brenda Novak

"Riveting drama and suspense from a master of the craft. I loved this twisty tale of friends, enemies, lovers, liars, and a family fractured by secrets. It's the perfect read to cozy up to on a long winter night."

—Susan Wiggs, #1 *New York Times* bestselling author

"Teeming with riveting, hold-your-breath suspense... Novak is at the top of her game with this gripping thriller. Prepare to be up all night!"

—Heather Gudenkauf, *New York Times* bestselling author of *The Weight of Silence* and *Not a Sound*

"Novak's fans will devour this one, and the relentlessly twisty plot will win her some new fans, as well. This is the kind of book best swallowed in one sitting: suspenseful, surprising, and 100% addictive."

—Kimberly Belle, national bestselling author of *The Marriage Lie*

"What a book! *Before We Were Strangers* is dark and compelling, an excellent thriller with heart-pounding twists, full of secrets and lies, and all too real. This is Novak at her sweet and sinister best in a story that could be happening in the house next door. Who is telling the truth? You won't know until the explosive end..."

—J.T. Ellison, *New York Times* bestselling author of *Tear Me Apart*

"Brenda Novak's seamless plotting, emotional intensity, and true-to-life characters who jump off the page make her books completely satisfying. Novak is simply a great storyteller."

—Allison Brennan, *New York Times* bestselling author

"The best romantic thriller I have read... Novak has a raw talent for bringing her novels to life. Realistic, suspenseful, and an edge of your seat romance that will have readers coming back for more."

—*The San Francisco Book Review* on *The Secret Sister*

Also from Brenda Novak and MIRA Books

UNFORGETTABLE YOU
RIGHT WHERE WE BELONG
UNTIL YOU LOVED ME
NO ONE BUT YOU
FINDING OUR FOREVER
THE SECRETS SHE KEPT
A WINTER WEDDING
THE SECRET SISTER
THIS HEART OF MINE
THE HEART OF CHRISTMAS
COME HOME TO ME
TAKE ME HOME FOR CHRISTMAS
HOME TO WHISKEY CREEK
WHEN SUMMER COMES
WHEN SNOW FALLS
WHEN LIGHTNING STRIKES
IN CLOSE
IN SECONDS
INSIDE
KILLER HEAT
BODY HEAT
WHITE HEAT
THE PERFECT MURDER
THE PERFECT LIAR
THE PERFECT COUPLE
WATCH ME
STOP ME
TRUST ME
DEAD RIGHT
DEAD GIVEAWAY
DEAD SILENCE
COLD FEET
TAKING THE HEAT
EVERY WAKING MOMENT

Look for Brenda Novak's next novel
CHRISTMAS IN SILVER SPRINGS
available soon from MIRA Books.

For a full list of Brenda's books, visit BrendaNovak.com.

To Dana Kelly. Sometimes life surprises us
in the most pleasant ways. I feel fortunate
to have had the opportunity to get to know you.
You are one of the most capable, generous,
kindest individuals I know. So glad you're my friend.

BEFORE WE WERE STRANGERS

CHAPTER ONE

Bayside Cemetery
Queens, New York

As far back as Sloane McBride could remember, she'd been told she was an ice queen. Even the people closest to her, *especially* the people closest to her, complained about her reserve. Her height, her physical appearance and her vocation didn't make her any more approachable, so what served her well professionally worked against her personally. She heard people mutter words like *stuck-up*, *aloof* or *distant*—and knew they were referring to her. No one seemed to understand that she hadn't *chosen* to be standoffish. That was simply a by-product of what she'd been through.

She never talked about what she'd been through, however. If she could help it, she tried not to even *think* about her childhood. But she'd always known she'd have to go back to the small Texas town where she'd been raised eventually. And now that Clyde was gone, she didn't feel as though she could continue running from the past. When she lost him, she'd lost her emotional safe haven here in the Hamptons, her excuse for remaining in New York.

"God, I'm going to miss you," she whispered and squatted as gracefully as she could in her black dress and heels to rearrange some of the flowers decorating his grave. Everyone who'd known him had lost a friend, and his funeral, which had packed the church to overflowing, proved it. But no one would feel the loss of his presence more than she would. He'd taken her under his wing from almost the first moment they met, when she was barely eighteen, and he'd never tried to change her, never criticized her, either. He'd just accepted her for who she was. Whenever she withdrew from one of his many parties, he'd often come find her, but he wouldn't drag her back to the crowd she'd left. He'd simply squeeze her hand and say, "What are you thinking about?"

Sometimes she'd tell him and sometimes she wouldn't, but he never pressed her, regardless. That was one of the things she'd loved about him. He'd say, "Still waters run deep" or something else that gave her permission to be comfortable in her own skin, and then he'd return to his other friends, where he would continue to talk and laugh until late in the night—simply winking at her if she happened to come into the room again.

She wasn't ready to leave the cemetery, to leave *him*. Forever was much too long a walk to take without him. But his five children and their spouses—those who had spouses, anyway—stood nearby, whispering among themselves under the pavilion, and she guessed from their expressions they were growing disgruntled by the fact that she was lingering so long. They'd never approved of her relationship with their father. At the funeral, she'd heard Camille, the youngest, murmur to a family friend, "They *had* to have been sleeping together. He was *so* devoted to her. I got the impression he loved her as much as me or any of the rest of us children."

"Of course they were sleeping together," the friend had agreed.

Sloane had been tempted to inform them otherwise. Instead, she'd slid her sunglasses up higher on the bridge of her nose and tried to ignore them, along with all the other people who were, no doubt, speculating about the same thing. Chances were they wouldn't believe her even if she told them, but she hadn't been the younger woman trying to take advantage of the rich older man. Yes, there *had* been twenty years between her and Clyde and, yes, they'd been very close. He'd been her friend, her confidant, her mentor, her modeling agent and even her landlord. She'd been living in the small cottage behind his mansion ever since he'd talked her into walking out of that coffee shop in Portland where she'd been working when he'd come to town for his ex-wife's funeral. But he'd never been Sloane's lover. He'd never even hinted at any romantic interest, and that wasn't what she'd felt for him, either.

The size of the lump in her throat threatened to choke her as she straightened. But she had a lot to do, couldn't focus on the loss or the pain. She'd survived thus far in life by always looking forward, never back, and the next few days would be busy. She had to pack up her belongings and move. Clyde's estate would go to his heirs, the same group of people who were waiting for her to leave. They'd given her notice months ago that they planned to put the place up for sale as soon as he died.

She gripped her purse a bit tighter with her left hand while turning so that she could wave with her right. Facing Clyde's family even for that brief moment wasn't easy. She could feel the gale-force wind of their disapproval pressing on her back, threatening to blow her right out of the cemetery.

Only a couple of them bothered to acknowledge her in return. Even then, the responses were half-hearted.

Doesn't matter, she told herself. Clyde had loved them, which meant she'd always treat them kindly. She'd also abide by their wishes regarding the house. Even though she'd earned plenty of money since coming to New York and had tried to talk him out of it, Clyde had left *her* part of his vast fortune. Not nearly as much as each of his kids but some. That was probably the reason they seemed to hate her even more since he died, but she was going to accept his gift just as he'd wanted her to. He'd said he was grateful for the hours of thoughtful conversation she'd provided over the years, the scuba diving trips they'd taken together to Hawaii, the atolls of the Maldives and Australia, the late-night laughter and all the hard things she'd had to do in order to care for him over the past fourteen months while he battled bladder cancer. None of his children had been able to help for longer than a couple of hours here and there. They were too busy with their own lives. They'd suggested hiring a nurse, but Sloane had refused to leave his care to a stranger in case he'd feel as if, now that he was no longer able-bodied, he was to be cast aside while the rest of the world moved on.

To avoid that, she'd given up her career. She'd hated knowing that his days were numbered, had wanted to spend as much time with him as possible. She probably wouldn't have worked for much longer, anyway. Modeling wasn't any fun without him. He was so good at shepherding her from one pinnacle in the high-fashion world to the next, she couldn't imagine continuing with someone else, couldn't bring herself to replace him. It was his intervention that had pulled her out of her desperate circumstances in the very beginning and had given her some semblance of a life—a life, as it turned out, that many people now envied. Representing brands like Prada, Gucci and Dolce & Gabbana certainly sparkled on the outside. Sloane was grateful for what she'd achieved, but in this moment, it felt as though that chapter of her life—the New York chapter—had come to a close with Clyde's death. So she'd decided, finally, to close the chapter she never had—the Millcreek chapter. The one she'd run away from so many years ago. She owed it to her mother.

And who could say? Maybe Sloane's instincts had been wrong all along. Maybe she owed it to her father and brother to find the truth, too, and dispel all suspicion.

Her phone rang as she climbed into her Jaguar. Caller ID revealed a Texas area code.

She frowned as she stared down at it.

It had to be her new landlord. Other than Paige Patterson—Paige Evans now—her closest friend from high school who'd reconnected with her last year on social media, her landlord was the only person who knew she was returning to town.

Her finger hovered over the talk button. Just thinking about going back to Millcreek twisted her stomach into knots. Was she ready to return?

No, but she wasn't sure she'd ever feel ready, and she doubted there would be a better time to do battle with her father. She'd come to a natural break in her career. She had the financial wherewithal to be able to live without an income. And thanks to the strength she'd received from Clyde's unwavering support, she now had the determination to *finally* achieve the answers she sought—no matter what it meant.

At least she hoped she had the determination. Her father had trained her and her older brother to believe that loyalty mattered above all else—even truth. Would she be able to cross him?

After drawing a deep breath, she answered. "Hello?"

"Ms. McBride?"

"Yes?" In the distance, she could see Clyde's family gathering around his grave as though they'd been waiting for her to leave so they could approach.

"This is Guy Prinley."

Her new landlord, as she'd assumed. Sloane willed herself to calm down. She'd have to cope much better if she planned to hold her own in Millcreek. "What can I do for you, Mr. Prinley? Don't tell me you haven't received my first and last month's rent and security deposit. I sent it through PayPal yesterday morning."

Two weeks ago, she'd gone online hoping to find a place to live in Millcreek when she returned. Clyde had been so weak. She'd known he was down to days, maybe hours, and that she'd have to move soon. But there hadn't been much available in her hometown and nothing set off by itself; space she would need if she planned to retain both her resolve and her sanity. She'd thought she might have to buy a house—or build one—which would take so long and be such a hassle. But then she'd spoken to Paige, who'd mentioned that Hazel Woods, Sloane's former piano teacher, a woman now in her eighties, was going into assisted living, and her son-in-law—this Guy Prinley—was planning to rent her secluded Spanish pueblo-style, two-bedroom, two-bath home, which also had a large music studio. Sloane was sold the minute she heard the place also had a newly designed kitchen and wide patios that were heavily shaded by the same vines and trees that all but hid the house.

"I have," he said. "I'm just calling to let you know that I've sent it back."

"*Sent it back*?" she echoed.

"Yeah, I'm sorry. I didn't realize that my wife already had someone else who was interested."

Sloane stiffened in her leather seat. Being interested didn't necessarily mean the house had been taken in advance, so why would he back out on her? "Excuse me? I signed the lease you emailed to me before I sent the money. You got that, too, right?"

He cleared his throat, seemed uncomfortable. "I got it, but look, I don't know what to say. I can't rent the house to you, okay?"

"You already have!"

"You signed only yesterday. It's not as though you've even had time to pack. You can find something else. I'm not sure those electronic signature things are legally binding, anyway."

"I don't want to find something else. And those electronic signatures are definitely binding, Mr. Prinley. No one in real estate would be able to use them, otherwise. So please, tell me what's really going on. This doesn't make any sense."

"I'll have to call you back," he said and disconnected before she could express her full outrage.

Sloane dropped her phone in her lap. She didn't have the emotional fortitude to deal with something like this today. She'd just buried her best friend!

She pressed a hand to her forehead as she sat there, wondering what to do—until she noticed the way Clyde's family kept glancing over at her. Apparently, they were bothered to see she hadn't left.

"Oh, for God's sake! I'm going, I'm going," she grumbled, and used her Bluetooth to call Paige as she backed out of the parking space.

"Hey, are you in town already?" Paige asked.

Sloane adjusted her air-conditioning vent to hit her more directly. They were in the middle of a terrible heat wave. "No. I'm still in New York."

"Then you're coming this weekend?"

"Actually, I'm not sure when I'll be able to come."

"What do you mean? You rented a house here."

"That's the problem. It's not clear whether I have the house. I just got a weird call from the guy who leased it to me."

"Weird in what way?"

"He was basically telling me I *don't* have it, that his wife already promised it to someone else."

"Has the other person also signed a lease?"

"I have no idea."

"Because if you're the only one who's signed, it's yours. He can't change his mind."

"That's what I told him!"

"What'd he say then?"

"Nothing. He got off the phone really fast."

There was a slight pause. "So what are you going to do?"

Sloane rubbed her left temple as she drove. The tightness in her throat and chest, the pressure of unshed tears, was giving her a headache. "I don't know." She recalled the dirty looks she'd received from Clyde's kids and couldn't help feeling hurt. "I have to be out of the place where I'm living as soon as possible, but I'd rather not move twice in one month. Moving is hard enough as it is."

"Why don't you come here? Lay over at my house? You can deal with that stupid landlord—or find another place, if it comes to that—after you get to town. It'll be much easier when you're not trying to do it from so far away."

The lump in Sloane's throat swelled even bigger. She was tempted to jump at Paige's kind offer, but she also felt guilty. Once she'd graduated from high school, she'd walked away from Paige the same as she'd walked away from everyone else—without a backward glance. She'd had to cut all ties to Millcreek, or she knew she'd never really escape. Her father would use those she cared about to manipulate her if he could.

But Paige and any others she'd hurt didn't understand the terrible choice she'd had to make or why she'd made it. Paige could have *some* inkling, since they'd talked about Sloane's mother on occasion, but she could hardly identify with the deep-seated suspicion that'd eaten at Sloane ever since she was five years old. "Are you positive you have room for me?"

"Sloane, I'm divorced. Micah left me the house. He gave me everything—far more than I asked for."

Mention of Micah Evans made Sloane's hands tighten on the steering wheel. She couldn't help but feel his name right in her gut—even after all this time. He'd married Paige only months after Sloane left Millcreek. Her boyfriend and her best friend—such a cliché, and yet, she'd never seen it coming.

She should have, she supposed. She'd known that Paige had a thing for Micah, could tell by the way she'd acted whenever he was around. But a lot of the girls at school had had a crush on him. Why wouldn't they? He was the boy who had it all—looks, personality, intelligence and athletic ability in a state where football was everything. It was just that Sloane had never imagined he'd suddenly take an interest in Paige; he'd seemed so indifferent to her before.

So what had gone wrong in their marriage? Sloane was curious, but she couldn't ask. That was one subject she was fairly certain she and Paige would *never* be able to discuss. She'd left them both without a word and without ever contacting them again, so they'd moved on with their lives. Sloane couldn't fault either one of them for getting married and even having a child together, no matter how much it hurt. But considering their history, wouldn't they all feel a little—or a lot—uncomfortable?

"I can get a hotel," she said. "I wouldn't want to invade your son's space."

"No way would I ever let you go to a hotel," Paige said. "Trevor's nine. He'll see it as a grand adventure. And I would love the chance to spend some quality time with you. I've missed you," she added more softly.

Since she was stopped at a light, Sloane allowed herself to close her eyes for a brief moment in an effort to stem the tears that were finally trickling down her cheeks. She'd missed Paige, too. Terribly. Because she'd never been close to her father or her brother, and her mother had disappeared when she was so young, Paige had been almost like a sister. But Sloane couldn't allow herself to feel that longing, to acknowledge the pain of their extended separation, because it could and would influence her ability to stand strong against her father.

Someone honked behind her. The light had turned green. With a quick glance in the rearview mirror, she gave the Jaguar some gas. "I wouldn't want to put you out," she said to Paige. She wouldn't want to come to depend on her friend's support, either. She needed to be able to leave again, when she was ready, couldn't allow herself to fall into the kind of emotional quicksand that could so easily suck her in and make it that much harder. Leaving ten years ago had been the most difficult thing she'd ever done; she wasn't interested in making that hurdle any more difficult to clear.

"Life is short," Paige said. "What matters are the people we care about. Come stay with me. Let me help you get situated here."

Sloane could almost feel Clyde nudging her to embrace the opportunity. He'd always been so much better with people, always ventured forward when she held back. She needed to gamble more often, perhaps, but it wasn't wise for her to risk making tight connections, especially in Millcreek where her future was so uncertain.

Despite her reservations, she heard herself agree. After what Paige had just said, it would be rude to insist on getting a hotel, and she was glad for the chance to possibly rebuild their relationship, at least to the point that she no longer cringed when she remembered how difficult things had been between them their senior year. Besides, with Clyde gone, she didn't want to stay in New York any longer.

Once the decision had been made, she felt an exciting yet frightening blend of anticipation buoy her spirits. "I can't wait to meet Trevor," she said, and that was true, even though she understood it would also be painful. Had she stayed in Millcreek, she might've married Micah and been the one to bear him a child…

"He's such a sweet boy," Paige said, her voice filled with the affection she felt for her son. "I predict you'll love him."

Did he look like his father?

She'd soon find out.

"It'll take me a few days to get packed. I'll rent a storage unit in Dallas for my stuff and will bring only a suitcase to your place. Then, when I figure out what's going on with the house I supposedly rented, or I'm able to get a different one, I'll have everything delivered."

"What will you do with your car?"

"I'll drive it."

"All the way to Texas? That'll take forever!"

"I don't have to do it in one or even two days. I'll stop and spend the night whenever I get tired."

"If that's what you want."

Sloane could use all of those hours to prepare for what lay ahead. "I really appreciate you helping me out."

"It's no problem. You're welcome here. You'll *always* be welcome here."

"I should arrive in a week or ten days. I'll call with the exact date as it gets closer."

Sloane was about to hang up when Paige stopped her. "Does your father know you're coming?"

"Not yet." *She* hadn't told him. But she had a sneaking suspicion that word might've traveled back to him. Her father was an important man in town—the most important. That she'd run away at eighteen and hadn't been seen again, except in the pages of various fashion magazines, would be big news in such a small place. Her father had probably told everyone she was just like her mother—flighty, undependable, selfish, vain. He'd characterized Clara that way so many times; Sloane knew "being like her mother" wasn't a positive thing.

Anyway, if someone in town had learned she was coming back, it was likely Ed would be informed. Guy Prinley might even have been the one to tell him. That could explain why Mr. Prinley was trying to back out of renting her the house. It would be like her father to do all he could to punish her for "turning against him" in the first place.

"Then I won't mention it," Paige said.

Sloane turned down the long drive that wound around Clyde's sprawling French Tudor to her own Tudor-style bungalow. "There's nothing he could do to you for letting me stay with you, is there?"

"Excuse me? Why would he do anything to me?"

Paige owned Little Bae Bae, a boutique downtown that sold toys, clothing and furniture for infants and toddlers. She wasn't beholden to Ed for her job or anything else that Sloane was aware of.

"He wouldn't. Never mind. Clyde's funeral was today, and I'm not myself. Let me call you later."

"Okay," Paige said and Sloane disconnected. She hated to think her father might've tried to stop her from getting the Woods house, but now that she'd acknowledged the possibility, she couldn't quit mulling it over.

Especially because there'd always been something about Ed, some lack of feeling or conscience, that frightened her.

CHAPTER TWO

It took two weeks to get everything packed up and sent to storage in Dallas, an hour and a half east of Mill-creek. There weren't any storage facilities in Millcreek itself. The movers were driving a big, lumbering truck almost the size of a semi and yet they delivered Sloane's belongings before she got there. She stayed in several states along the way and lingered in Dallas for two days.

She was procrastinating her final return to her home-town, and she knew it. She'd lost Hazel Woods's house, wasn't going to get it despite how perfect it had seemed. She had a legal claim, could've pressed her right in court. But as angry as Mr. Prinley made her, he'd re-turned her money, so she didn't get ripped off in that regard, and she wasn't prepared to file suit. She had enough negativity to contend with, didn't see the point of forcing him to provide the keys. She'd decided—at Paige's urging—that she would stay with Paige and her son for the first week, until she could more thoroughly investigate her housing options.

In deference to the heat, she was dressed in a sleeveless taupe sheath dress with white polka dots and white sandals. The air-conditioning in her Jag was doing its job, and yet she felt moist with perspiration when her GPS guided her, on a Thursday, to a one-story brick house with a black door and matching shutters, behind the baseball park where her father probably still played in a men's league.

It was almost dinnertime. She'd wanted to arrive after Trevor went to bed. She felt it would be wise to get reacquainted with Paige first, to have a chance to talk and catch up with her old friend before meeting her son and facing whatever emotions he might evoke. But Paige had been so anxious to see her she'd talked Sloane into joining them for dinner.

As Sloane parked at the curb and turned off her engine, she eyed the picture window in front with more than a little trepidation. She didn't get the impression that Micah and Paige had been wealthy while they were married, but she could tell they'd been comfortable. They'd had Paige's income from the store, and Micah had become a police officer. According to Paige, he was hoping to make chief one day, and it looked as though he had a great chance. Paige said he was the frontrunner in the department for when the spot became available in the next decade or two, which didn't surprise Sloane. She'd always expected Micah to do well. He'd been so capable, even when he was only eighteen.

She saw the curtain move. She'd been spotted.

Steeling herself for the onslaught of memories that were already beginning to assail her like arrows, she gathered her purse and the bottle of wine she'd brought and got out.

The front door opened and Paige hurried down the walkway. "Sloane! Welcome back!"

Sloane resisted the urge to return to her car and drive away. She loved Paige, had missed her, but her feelings toward her best friend had grown murky before she left, and after so long, they were mixed with her residual feelings for Micah and her reluctance to embrace Millcreek in general. "Hi. Thank you for letting me come."

Paige gave her a warm hug. "*Letting* you! Of course! I'm so happy I was able to convince you. After leaving the way you did, you must be hesitant to see your father and brother, or you would've gone to one of their houses. This will give you a friendly place to hang out while you set yourself up in whatever situation feels most comfortable to you."

"I appreciate that. I won't need to stay long."

Paige took the wine Sloane proffered. "You'll be in town at least a year, though, right?"

"Maybe not quite that long. We'll have to see what happens." She'd leave earlier, if possible. She was only here until she could determine what'd happened to her mother twenty-three years ago. She had no idea how hard solving that mystery would be but guessed it wouldn't be easy. Not long after she'd moved to New York, she'd hired a private detective who'd searched using every database available to him and found nothing. He'd said it was as if she'd disappeared into thin air. He'd wanted to come to Millcreek and talk to everyone she knew, see if he could track Clara that way. He insisted it was the logical next step. But it had been a step Sloane hadn't yet been willing to take. It crossed the line from searching for her mother to investigating her father, so she'd stopped him. And he was about the only person who'd ever really looked.

Ed claimed she ran off, and he was seen as such a rich, upstanding and important member of the community that, to Sloane's knowledge, no one here in Millcreek had ever pressed him, least of all anyone in the police department. Now that he was mayor and could influence whether the officers on the force kept their jobs or received a promotion, she doubted that was likely to change.

No one had ever asked Sloane what she'd seen and heard that night. Since she was only five at the time, they probably didn't expect her to have anything of value to contribute. She wasn't convinced she would've spoken up even if they had asked her what she remembered. She'd been too afraid of her father and too unsure what the sounds she'd heard signified. Heck, she was *still* afraid—afraid that her father was as dangerous as she thought he might be, or that she'd come out in open opposition to him only to learn that her mother was as flighty and undependable as he claimed and had, indeed, abandoned them.

Being wrong would be almost as bad as being right, at least when it came to her relationship with what she had left of her family. Her father would never forgive her for voicing the deep, dark suspicion that lurked inside her, let alone doing more. Maybe that was why it had taken her ten years to come back. If only her brother possessed a memory of that night. Then she could've gone to him for clarification and illumination, would've had someone whose opinion she could lean on. But Randy had been spending the night at a friend's when their mother "left." And he was so close to their father, he would never entertain the possibility that had given her such terrible nightmares, nightmares in which she saw her father digging a grave in the backyard and then heard him slowly climbing the stairs to come get *her*.

"At least we'll have a few months together." Paige took her hands and squeezed them. "You are so beautiful. Look at you. You only get prettier with time."

At only five foot two inches, Paige was considerably shorter than Sloane, who stood over six feet—the All-American Mary Anne to Sloane's more sophisticated Ginger. Paige's mother used to tease them about resembling those two characters from *Gilligan's Island*, except Sloane had dark brown hair, amber eyes and olive-colored skin. Thanks to her mother's Greek heritage, she didn't look like Ginger, and Paige had sandy-blond hair and freckles, so she didn't look like Mary Anne. Paige's mother had been referring to their general sizes, shapes and personalities, Sloane supposed. Sloane had always gotten the impression that Mrs. Patterson wished Paige would elicit the same amount of attention as Sloane, but Sloane felt the Pattersons should be grateful Paige didn't. Paige was pretty, and yet she could blend into a crowd if she preferred to be anonymous for a time, or go to a mall, a movie or a nightclub without being unduly noticed. Sloane stood out, had never been able to disappear in a crowd.

"Motherhood seems to agree with you," Sloane said.

"I love it." As if on cue, Paige turned, drawing Sloane's attention to the entrance of the house, where a boy who had to be Trevor peered out at them.

"Come here." Paige gestured to him. "Come meet

your mother's best friend. You know how you and Spaulding hang out together all the time?"

He nodded as he drew closer.

"Well, I grew up with Sloane. We were inseparable all through elementary school, middle school and…and most of high school."

Until Paige had fallen for Micah after Sloane was already dating him. Micah had put quite a bit of stress on their relationship. The way Paige's tone weakened at the end of that statement told Sloane she, too, remembered, and it made Sloane slightly uneasy. She feared she might've made a mistake coming here, but it was too late to change her mind.

"You are such a handsome boy," Sloane said and felt her heart melt the second Trevor's big blue eyes, so much like his father's, met hers.

"Wow!" he said. "You're *tall*!"

She got that reaction a lot. People often stared as she walked by or whistled or mumbled about her height. "Yes, I've always been tall. Looks to me like you are, too—for your age, anyway."

"Yes." Paige tugged on his ball cap. "He's the tallest boy in his class."

"My dad's six-five," Trevor said proudly. "He's even taller than *you*."

Sloane nodded. "Yes, he is."

He squinted as he gazed at her. "My mom said you went to high school with her. That you know my dad."

It took some effort to keep her smile in place. She hadn't expected such an acute pain in her chest. "Yes, that's true."

Trevor twisted his neck to look up at his mom. "So can we invite Dad over for dinner, too?"

Paige cleared her throat. “Not tonight, sweetheart. I’m sure he’s busy.”

“He’s not. He’s about to leave the station. I just talked to him.”

“Maybe another time,” she muttered and propelled him along as they started for the house.

“I’ve made chicken enchiladas,” she told Sloane. “I was craving a good margarita, so I decided to go with Mexican food.”

“Sounds wonderful. You can’t get good Mexican in New York, not like you can out here.”

“I’ll give you the recipe.”

Paige led her inside to a living room/dining room area that had a kitchen off to one side. Sloane poked her head into it to see white subway tile, gray granite countertops and white Shaker cupboards. “Your home is lovely.”

“Thank you. I’m happy that it’s close to Trevor’s school and the ballpark. Makes it possible for him to walk both places.”

“You like baseball?” Sloane asked Trevor.

“Yeah. I’m a pitcher.”

“Do you also play Pop Warner Football? Or does that start when you get a bit older?”

“Some of the guys play now, but my mom won’t let me.”

Paige motioned for her to have a seat at a glass-topped table set on a wooden trestle surrounded by chairs with white cloth seats—a brave choice for someone with a kid. “He’d like to play football, but we’ll focus on baseball. Fewer head injuries,” she added ruefully.

“I’d probably make the same choice if he were my

son," Sloane said. But football was such an important part of life in Millcreek. She guessed Trevor would feel left out when, in a few short years, all of his friends tried out for the high school team and began making that the center of their lives. She wondered how Micah felt about having his son not play, since he'd led their team to state. "Does Micah agree with that decision?"

"Not entirely," Paige replied.

"My dad says it should be up to me," Trevor volunteered. "I think so, too."

"Except you're not old enough to make an informed decision," Paige said.

He groaned. "Mom, everyone plays football!"

"Not everyone gets out of the game without serious injury."

"Dad did!"

"Your dad was lucky."

"I'm not going to get hurt!"

"You could."

Sloane hid a smile as Paige gave him a quelling look for mouthing off.

"Parenting can be as challenging as it is fun," Paige grumbled as an aside.

"Is he close to his grandparents?" Sloane asked.

"He is. He's lucky. Both sets still live in the area, so they attend his games, school plays, birthday parties, et cetera. He has it pretty good."

Except for the divorce. Trevor couldn't have been happy to have his parents split up, but Paige didn't address that. The longer Paige went without mentioning Micah, the more Sloane began to relax, especially once dinner started. The margaritas they drank helped, too.

After they did the dishes, they watched Trevor play

a few video games in the living room. Then Paige sent him off to do his homework. At nine, he went to bed and they moved out onto the patio, where they talked above the cicadas that serenaded them from all sides.

In those moments, Sloane was glad she'd come. Despite the loss of her mother and the questions that constantly filtered through her mind about that night—not to mention how overbearing and controlling her father had been, especially of her because she was a girl—she'd had a decent childhood in Millcreek. She loved the town, and Paige had always been a good friend, even if they wound up loving the same boy in the end.

They discussed only the pleasant memories and steered clear of their senior year as much as possible. Sloane learned that Paige's father still owned the brewery that'd been his livelihood when they were kids, her mother was now on the school board and Yolanda, Paige's older sister and only sibling, had divorced her husband after her last child left for college and was living in Millcreek again. Apparently, Paige and Yolanda were finally developing a relationship. They'd never had a chance when Paige was younger. Since Yolanda had been born fourteen years before Paige, she'd left for school, married and then moved to California with her husband when Paige was four.

It wasn't until Sloane put down her glass, stretched and said she'd better get to bed that Paige brought up Micah. No doubt the alcohol had loosened her lips.

"He's going to be surprised you're back, you know," she said, staring off into the darkness at the edge of the patio.

Paige could've meant Sloane's father or brother, but Sloane could tell by the gravity in her voice that she wasn't talking about Ed or Randy. Suddenly eager for that last drop of margarita, she reclaimed her drink. "You didn't tell him I was coming?"

"No. You asked me not to tell anyone." Paige pulled the tie from her hair and used her fingers to comb it into a fresh ponytail. "And to be honest, I was afraid I'd see a little too much excitement in his face—the look he used to get whenever you came into the room."

Suddenly, Sloane felt she couldn't breathe. She'd been doing her best to avoid thinking about Micah, but the scent and feel of home made that impossible. Since she'd driven into Millcreek, the levee holding back those memories seemed to be cracking. At first, only the most poignant snatches of conversation or images slipped through—the softness of his mouth on hers, his voice whispering that he loved her, the tangy taste of his sweat when she kissed him after football practice. Soon, however, there was much more. And now Paige was taking a bulldozer to what little of that levee remained. "It's been ten years, Paige. He won't be excited to see me. After what I did, he probably hates me."

"He *does* hate you, in a way. Or maybe it's not hate exactly. He resents you for hurting him. No one else has ever treated him that way."

Although Sloane couldn't help flinching at this bald assessment, she tried not to show how much that comment stung.

"He was devastated when you left," Paige added. "You can't bug out on people and expect them not to be angry, not to feel any pain."

Obviously, Paige had been hurt, too. Hearing the sharp edge of bitterness in those words, Sloane considered explaining why she'd left, but she doubted Paige would understand. Paige would say things like, "You could've at least stayed in touch with us. We would've been supportive." But there was no way Sloane could've remained in touch without wanting, desperately, to return. And if she'd returned too soon, before she was strong enough to hold her own and before they could move on without her, she knew she'd get caught here in Millcreek indefinitely. "I'm sorry that I hurt you both."

Paige gave her ponytail a final, tightening tug. "That's all you're going to say?"

"That's all I *can* say." Surely there had to be a part of Paige that'd been glad she'd left. Sloane's leaving was what had given her a chance with Micah.

Paige's laugh sounded sad. "I guess you're just a hard person to forget."

"I didn't forget you, either," Sloane said. "I had to leave for my own peace of mind. I had to figure out who I was without my father and my brother, without you and Micah, and without this place." She gestured around them with her drink.

"And did you find out who you are?"

"In ways." Again, she was tempted to tell Paige the real reason she'd come back, but the less people knew, the less chance there'd be that she'd have an ugly confrontation with her father before she was ready. She and Paige had only recently resumed their friendship; she had no idea how much Paige might've changed, or who she was close to these days.

"I'm glad. I hope it was worth it, because it was damn hard to compete with your ghost."

Sloane put down her drink. "What do you mean by that?"

Paige stood. "Nothing. I think it's time we turned in, don't you?"

As Paige gathered the dessert plates they'd brought out with them, Sloane studied her carefully. There was a deep reservoir of feeling beneath Paige's last statement, something turbulent and passionate enough to make Sloane wonder if Paige liked her even half as much as she pretended. It was almost as if Paige blamed *her* for the divorce.

But when Paige looked at Sloane again, all of that animosity was gone. She was even smiling. "Come on," she said. "I'll show you to the guest room."

Micah had owned this house at some point, Sloane thought, as she stared up at the ceiling above her bed. He'd lived here with Paige, as her husband. He'd made love to Paige in the master bedroom—maybe even in *this* bedroom. He'd showered here, eaten here, helped raise his son here. He'd probably even walked around in his underwear occasionally, or come home tired from work to relax on the couch and watch TV. Sloane didn't *want* to imagine him moving through this house, living in this place; she couldn't help it. She'd shoved him from her thoughts so many times over the years it'd become habit, but she couldn't seem to deny him tonight. He seemed so present in this space, even though he was no longer *in* this space.

What was Micah like now?

It wasn't easy to imagine him in a police uniform. She could only picture him as the boy he once was—tall with overly large hands and feet, no beard growth and the same blue eyes he'd passed on to his son. She thought about the country song "I Got the Boy" by

Jana Kramer and felt a familiar pang. She could identify with those lyrics, even though they didn't fit her situation exactly.

Was Micah seeing anyone these days? Had he met someone else? Is that why his marriage to Paige had ended?

And...if Sloane bumped into him, would he even speak to her?

She wouldn't blame him if he gave her a dirty look and turned away.

With a sigh, she rolled over. She'd been lying there, wide-awake, for two hours. The glowing digits on the alarm clock beside the lamp mocked her struggle to get to sleep by marching relentlessly on. She had so much to do before she was ready to confront her father and brother, needed to rent a place of her own and get moved in *soon*. After tonight, she feared the overtures of renewed friendship Paige had made in the past year via Instagram and Facebook weren't as sincere as she'd assumed. That they'd fallen in love with the same man made it difficult for both of them, but Sloane got the sneaking suspicion Paige blamed her for more than leaving. She couldn't be responsible for the divorce, though. She hadn't spoken to Micah since she'd slipped out of the RV where they'd made love for the first and last time on graduation night.

Although Sloane had had sex with a handful of other men since Micah, he'd been her first, and she'd never experienced that same powerful connection—ironic since neither of them had known what they were doing. It wasn't the best sexual encounter by many standards, and yet she'd never forget how hard her heart had pounded—or how his hand had trembled—when he first touched her.

The toilet flushed. Someone was up. It had to be Trevor; Paige would've used the bathroom off the master.

Sloane waited for Trevor to go back to bed, but when the water kept running, she began to worry that he'd neglected to turn it off.

She got up to do it herself only to find him standing at the sink, letting the water cascade over his fingers as he stared at himself in the mirror. He hadn't bothered to close the door, but why would he? He was used to having only his mother in the house, and it was the middle of the night. Obviously, he hadn't expected to run into anyone.

"Are you okay?" she asked.

He seemed startled by her voice, hadn't heard her approach over the sound of the faucet. "Um, yeah." He turned off the water and pivoted to dry his hands on the towels hanging behind him.

Sloane had caught a glimpse of the sad expression on his face when he was gazing into the mirror, so she was fairly certain he wasn't as okay as he'd just indicated. "Are you having trouble sleeping?"

His hair was mussed, making him look younger than he had before. "Not really," he mumbled.

"Okay. I won't pry." She offered him a smile and started to walk away, but he stopped her.

"Sloane?"

She turned back. "Yes?"

"Can I call you that? Sloane? Or do I need to say Ms. McBride?"

"Sloane is fine."

He glanced over his shoulder, as if he was afraid they might already have awakened his mother. Apparently, he didn't want Paige to hear what he was about to say. That became even clearer when his voice dropped to a whisper. "Are you *really* the reason my father left my mother?"

Sloane sucked in her breath. "Is that what your mother told you?"

"She said we'd still be a family, if not for you."

"I didn't have anything to do with it," she said.

He checked the hallway again. "Then will you...will you talk to my dad and see if he'll come back? I miss him. I want it to be the way it was before."

While her mind raced to find an appropriate response, Sloane tucked her hair behind her ears. "When did your parents divorce?"

"A year ago."

Right about the time Paige had reached out to her on Facebook. "So you were in third grade?" He'd told her earlier that he'd just started fourth.

He nodded.

"That's a tough thing to go through, Trevor. Sometimes parents can't get along well enough to live together. But I have no doubt that both your folks still love you deeply. Your father leaving doesn't mean that has or will ever change."

He stared down at his bare feet. "That's what he says. But it's not the same."

While her own folks hadn't divorced, Sloane had been raised by a single parent. Her mother had either run away or...

She wasn't convinced it was even fair to consider the alternative. That was the tough part. "I'd fix things for you if I could," she said. "But I haven't seen your father in ten years. Haven't talked to him, either. That's why it can't be my fault—the divorce, I mean."

His shoulders slumped. Sloane got the impression he'd been hoping otherwise—because then she might also have the power to undo what she'd supposedly done. "My mom wants him to come back, too," he said. "I've heard her crying on the phone to him when she doesn't think I can hear."

Sloane was willing to bet Paige wouldn't be happy that Trevor had revealed so much, but children his age didn't understand the concept of saving face. The truth was simply the truth. "The Micah I remember from high school was a great guy. But your mother will eventually get over him and find someone else."

"That's just it," he said glumly. "I don't want her to find anyone else. Spaulding has a stepdad, and he's mean."

"It doesn't have to go that way for you."

"It could."

Although Sloane wished she could say more to comfort him, he was right. It wouldn't be wise for her to get involved, regardless, to become emotionally attached to anyone or anything in Millcreek. The problems the people faced here were simply not something she'd be able to fix.

She wouldn't be around long enough to even try. And until she left, she'd be lucky to hold *herself* together.

CHAPTER THREE

Someone was in the house.

Sloane shut off the shower so that she could hear well enough to determine more about what was going on around her.

Steps sounded in the hallway, so she got out and grabbed a towel. She was supposed to be home alone. Paige had gone to the shop shortly after Trevor left for school. Paige had said that Trevor would be walking home with a friend this afternoon. That she'd be back shortly after five and he'd return then, too.

But it wasn't anywhere close to five. It was only ten fifteen when she'd quit searching the internet for rental properties and decided to get showered for the day. So what was going on?

Surely, Paige wasn't being *robbed*...

Heart pounding, Sloane pulled on her panties and her silky animal-print robe—what she usually wore while getting ready. It was all she had in the bathroom with her.

Once she tied the belt, she cracked open the door so she could peer out. She couldn't see anyone, but she heard more noises. She wasn't alone.

"Paige?" Damn it, she didn't even have her cell phone handy. She'd left it in the guest room along with her suitcase and purse.

Hoping she could get to it before she came face-to-face with an intruder, she gazed down the hall. But all the noise was coming from much closer, in Trevor's room.

"Hello?" She leaned around the doorway to see what was going on.

Someone was there, all right. But not Paige. It was Micah. And he'd obviously heard her, because he was striding toward the opening, moving so fast they nearly collided.

His jaw dropped when he recognized her. *"Sloane?"*

Her wet hair had soaked the back of her short robe, but she knew that had nothing to do with the prickle that ran down her spine. "Micah…"

His gaze ranged over her. "What are you doing here?"

"I—I'm staying for a few days until…until I can rent a house of my own."

"Not in *Millcreek*."

He didn't sound pleased. She swallowed against a dry throat. She'd known it wouldn't be easy to see him again, but did she have to run into him when she wasn't fully dressed? "Yes, in Millcreek. I don't plan to stay long, though. A year, at the most."

"I wish you'd been that up front with me before. A 'by the way, I'm leaving in the morning' might've come in handy. Maybe it wouldn't have been such a mindfuck to find you gone if I hadn't been blindsided right after making love to you for the first time."

She tightened her belt. "I'm sorry. I… I had to leave."

"Because..." He raked his fingers through his hair. "God, I've waited so long to hear your reason. Please tell me you have an answer."

He was wearing his uniform and somehow, even though she couldn't picture it before, the cop look seemed natural to him. "Because of my father."

"You've always had issues with him. But what about *me*? I didn't matter?"

"Of course you *mattered.* It's just…we were eighteen years old! What were we going to do? Get married right out of high school?"

"Maybe! I would like to have been given the choice!"

She sighed. "My father would never have allowed it. He would've made our lives miserable. So what then? We marry in spite of him and move away from Millcreek? Leave your family and the cattle ranch you'll eventually inherit? I wasn't sure I'd even be able to find a place to stay or work. I didn't want to drag you down that path with me. Your life is here. I knew that even then."

"Yeah, well, thanks for making the decision for both of us. I can only imagine your surprise when leaving turned out so well for you."

"Meaning…"

"You had to have made a lot of money, lived quite a life in the big city. Far better than I could ever have provided. And to think I was so worried about you in those first months. Good to know you didn't need me."

She curved her nails into her palms. "It's not that I

didn't need you, Micah. I caught a lucky break, made a good friend who opened a lot of doors. That's what turned everything around for me. If not for Clyde, I could still be a struggling waitress."

"Clyde? That's his name?"

"The name of my modeling agent, yes. My late agent."

A muscle moved in his cheek. "So that's why you're back. The man you were with is gone."

"I wasn't with him in *that* sense. I didn't leave you for another man, if that's what you're thinking. Clyde isn't the reason I stayed away, either."

Their gazes locked for several seconds. She wished she could read his inscrutable expression, wished she could get some idea of what was going on behind those blue eyes, but his face remained shuttered as he lifted the paper he held in one hand. "Trevor needs this, or he won't be able to go on the field trip with the rest of his class on Monday. I'd better get it over to the school."

She stepped aside so he could get around her, but he stopped when they were only inches apart, making her so self-conscious about her state of undress she pulled the V closed at the top of her robe.

"You really screwed up my life," he said as he stared down at her. "I just want you to know that."

So many things went through her mind, including the fact that she'd been trying *not* to screw up his life. She'd wanted to leave him untouched. He was the homecoming king, the starting quarterback, the cherished youngest son of honest, hardworking parents. He belonged here. She had little doubt he'd live his whole life in Millcreek, hadn't wanted to drag him down with her.

But of all the retorts that flew through her brain, only one came to her lips. "I screwed up your life so much that you had a child with my best friend only a year later?"

She nearly gasped at her own words. Where had *that* come from? She'd been trying so hard not to be hurt by his defection, since everything that'd happened had been her own fault. But there it was…

His eyes flared wide with anger. He had plenty of stubble on his jaw and chin now, she realized. And he'd filled out. He'd always had broad shoulders, but the muscle he'd packed on in the past ten years made him look powerful.

"Don't even go there," he gritted out. "You don't have the right."

That was true, but he stalked out before she could admit it.

"Oh God," she muttered when the door slammed, and she fell against the wall. She was shaking. His words had stabbed her like a thousand tiny darts, even more accusatory than she'd expected.

Living here was going to be worse than she'd thought, especially if she had to run into him.

That was why she couldn't hang around Paige's, contemplating the choices and sacrifices she'd made in the past, she told herself. She had houses to see and then some very important questions to answer. Only when she knew for sure what'd happened to her mother could she leave.

She pushed off the wall and went back to the bathroom to finish getting ready.

Micah sat in his patrol car, trying to let some of the adrenaline pumping through his body subside before starting the engine.

He couldn't believe it. After ten years, there she was in the house he'd shared with Paige—in the house he could've shared with *her* if only she'd stuck around instead of running away without any warning.

Drawing a deep breath, he ran a hand over his face. Talk about getting sucker punched. Why hadn't Paige told him that Sloane was in town? Why wasn't anyone else talking about it? Nothing happened in Millcreek that didn't immediately whip through the gossip circles. They had only seven thousand residents. So how had the return of such a famous model gone unremarked?

"Shit." With a glance at his watch, he started his car. Trevor was waiting for him. He needed to get the permission slip over to the school before recess ended, but he called Paige with his Bluetooth while driving.

"Really? You weren't going to tell me?" he said as soon as he heard her say, "Little Bae Bae Boutique."

Silence.

"Paige?"

"I assume you're talking about Sloane."

"You're damn right I'm talking about Sloane!"

"I thought you wouldn't care either way. After all the times you swore to me that you weren't in love with her anymore, I guess I decided to take you at your word."

If that were true, it would be the first time she'd ever taken him at his word where Sloane was concerned. He'd tried so hard to love Paige, to convince himself *and her* that Sloane had nothing to do with his inability to fully embrace her and their marriage, but Paige had never believed it. She'd hounded him, poured on the guilt and played the martyr, always pressing him to say something that would make her feel secure. And he'd failed miserably, which was why he'd asked for the divorce. If he couldn't fulfill Paige, and she couldn't fulfill him, why stay?

He'd lasted eight years for Trevor's sake, but as their son grew older, Trevor was becoming more and more aware of the emotional distance between his parents, mostly because Paige couldn't accept the mild affection Micah had been able to offer. She craved the all-consuming passion he'd only ever felt for Sloane—she'd *demanded* it—and that set the bar too high. He'd felt nothing but inadequate when they'd been married, destined to let her down again.

"Why?" she said as he turned into the schoolyard. "How do you know she's back? Did she call you?"

That underlying suspicion never went away. Paige had been convinced that he and Sloane were keeping in touch. She'd peppered him every so often with accusations that they were secretly communicating—or that he was cheating with someone else. She'd known he was locked in a situation where he couldn't be happy.

"Trevor called me," he said. "He forgot his permission slip for the field trip on Monday and asked me to bring it to school, so I swung by the house to get it."

"Why didn't he call *me*?"

"Because he knows you're at the shop, that you can't leave it unmanned during business hours and that you'd probably just ask me to do it, anyway."

"I need to get the locks changed on the house," she grumbled.

He stiffened at her response. She'd had a whole year to do that. She hadn't bothered because she was confident he'd never abuse the privilege of having easy access to her home and their son. If she started dating someone, that could change. But for now, she was hoping he'd come back even if it was only to satisfy them both sexually. She'd hinted that she'd be open to letting him stop in after Trevor was in bed; he'd been the one to decide that using each other would only cause them both more pain. "If that's what you feel you need to do," he said.

"That's what *most* divorced wives would do."

Which, again, proved that she was somehow more generous than other exes. Almost everything she said was geared toward making him regret leaving her. "Then most divorced wives wouldn't be able to rely on me to run this errand, right?"

"If you hadn't had a key, you couldn't have been caught off guard by finding Sloane at the house."

He pulled into a parking stall and jammed the transmission into Park. "If only you'd said something, we could've avoided that, too."

She seemed stymied that he hadn't asked her *not* to change the locks. But he hated to be manipulated, honestly didn't care what she did so long as she didn't try to bar him from being part of his son's life.

"So...what do you think?" she asked at length.

"What do I *think*?"

"Was it difficult to see Sloane again?"

Not unless Paige categorized having all the pain Sloane had caused his boyish heart ten years ago rush upon him all at once as "difficult."

"Don't start probing, Paige. We're divorced. I won't put up with you continuing to badger me about Sloane."

"I was just curious if you felt as over her as you've always claimed you were."

He'd only claimed he was over her to try to make Paige happy. What good would it do to tell the woman who'd become his wife that he'd only married her because she was pregnant?

He turned off his car. "I'm at the school. I'll talk to you later."

"You could join us for dinner tonight, if you like."

The taunt in her voice made him grit his teeth. "I'm hanging up," he said and disconnected.

He wasn't going anywhere near Sloane McBride.

The house Sloane decided to rent was far too big for one person. It was also in the exact area she'd been planning to avoid—near a lovely bend in the Brazos River but within a quarter mile of her father's home. As soon as Leigh Coleman, the leasing agent she'd called off the internet, showed her through, she'd known she should take it. By returning to this exclusive and tight-knit community and becoming a member of it in her own right, she'd be able to relate to the neighbors in a different way, would have a certain amount of credibility she wouldn't have otherwise. Hopefully, that would make them more willing to talk when she asked about her mother. Driving over from somewhere else in town in order to go door to door wouldn't be well received, especially given the amount of power her father wielded in this town.

"I'm so happy you like the house." Leigh shook Sloane's hand in the foyer of her new place just before they both walked out into the bright sunshine. "As soon as I run your credit, I'll email you the paperwork." She took two steps, then turned back. "It's such an honor to meet you, by the way. I've heard about you, of course. You're the mayor's famous daughter, Millcreek's own celebrity."

Sloane was also the black sheep of the mayor's family, but Leigh wasn't insensitive enough to mention that.

"I've seen you on the cover of *Vogue*," she continued. "I usually only buy magazines that have to do with houses and interior design, but I think everyone in town ran out and bought that issue. It must've been exciting to do that photo shoot."

It would've been more exciting if being a model had been her lifelong dream, but she'd always wanted to paint—something that was even harder to make a living at and nothing her father had respected or supported, for exactly that reason. "It was. Thank you."

"Are you finished with modeling?" she asked. "Or are you just taking a break?"

"I haven't completely decided."

"Well, we're excited to have you back either way. I didn't live in Millcreek before, when you did. I moved here only five years ago. But I've heard about you all the same."

"Thank you."

After Leigh left, Sloane pivoted on the stoop to stare up at the imposing brick structure, which had been painted a nice ecru. She liked the ivy scaling the walls and the many arches that'd been used in the architecture. Somehow this place reminded her of an estate in England. But what was she going to do with six bedrooms? She'd also have a study, a library, a drawing room—as if anyone even used those anymore—a family room, almost as many bathrooms as bedrooms, a gym and a massive family room and kitchen area with a wall of windows that looked out on a gorgeous garden. In the back, she'd have a guesthouse and a barn, which was, thankfully, empty. She'd had a horse growing up, and a dog, but she didn't want to worry about taking care of any pets while she was in Millcreek. She was going to remain as unfettered and ready to leave as possible.

Maybe she'd move into the guesthouse instead of the main house, she thought. It would be big enough for her. But if she was going to pay to live in such luxury, she might as well enjoy it. She'd end up rambling around, feeling out of place, but she was grateful she could afford something like this, something her father would respect. It was well beyond anything he would've expected her to be capable of getting, even as a rental, at only twenty-eight years old.

"I can only do it because of you," she told Clyde. She couldn't help thinking of him; wishing he were still alive.

She wandered around a bit more to be sure she'd made the right choice, and decided that, yes, this home was her best play, even if it meant she might have to pass her father on occasion.

She needed to call him, let him know she was in town. It was the polite thing to do, what any daughter *should* do. He hadn't physically abused her, hadn't neglected her, either. The damage he'd inflicted had been far subtler than that.

Still, she decided to put off making that call until tomorrow, when she hoped to feel more capable of handling his response, should it get ugly. Thanks to the number of hours she'd tossed and turned last night, she was exhausted.

She was just climbing into the Jag when her cell phone rang. She dug it out of her purse right away, in case the leasing agent had remembered something she'd meant to say or was suddenly going to change her mind, the way Guy Prinley had done. Sloane didn't care to lose a second house, didn't want to be forced to continue her search tomorrow.

She sighed in relief when she saw that it wasn't Leigh. It was Paige.

"Hello?" Sloane checked the clock on her dashboard and held the phone with her shoulder so she could buckle her seat belt. She still had to pick up the wine and dessert she'd insisted on contributing to dinner. Since Paige had cooked last night, she'd offered to be responsible for their meal tonight. She'd known she wouldn't have much time but figured there had to be some good takeout she could get. She'd once loved the Texas BBQ place that sat on the corner of Brazos Boulevard and Third. But Paige had refused the offer. She'd said she was a mother, that she had to cook every night regardless, and it was no trouble to feed one extra person.

"Hey, how's your day?" Paige asked.

Sloane tilted her head to be able to see her new house through the windshield. "Good, so far. I think I've found a place."

"Where?"

"In the River Bottoms."

There was a slight hesitation. "That's a little different than the place you chose before."

She situated her purse in the passenger's seat. "No joke. It's a lot less secluded and a lot more pricey."

"Not to mention super close to your dad."

"Beggars can't be choosers." Sloane started to back out of the drive. "There isn't a lot available. I can't believe Guy Prinley bailed on me. That was so unethical."

"That's why I'm calling. I was curious as to why

he would suddenly back out of the deal, so I did some checking."

"And?"

"His wife works at city hall."

Sloane stomped on the brake. "You've got to be kidding me."

"No. One of my customers belongs to her church. Pamela Prinley is the deputy city clerk."

"Wow. That means he probably told her not to rent me the house."

"That's my take, too."

Sloane let the engine idle while resting her head on the seat. *Great.* Her father knew she was coming back. But did he know she was already here? "It's nice to feel welcome."

"If he had any idea you might rent a place closer to him, I bet he wouldn't have sabotaged you," Paige said with a laugh.

Sloane finished backing into the street. "Exactly. He might live to regret it."

Just having her close wouldn't be the worst of it. Not for him. Her father was going to hate having her back if she found proof of what she suspected.

And she was certainly going to look.

"Do you need me to pick up anything else for dinner?" Sloane asked.

"No. I've got what I need."

"Okay, I'll see you in a few." Sloane tossed her phone in her purse as soon as she disconnected. After running into Micah this morning, she was hesitant to spend another evening with Paige. The hard look on her ex-boyfriend's face, the steel beneath his words, the anger and distrust she'd felt rolling off him hadn't left her. She'd been carrying that negative energy around ever since he appeared at the house, didn't feel capable of pretending that encounter hadn't knocked her on her ass should Paige ask about it.

"I'll have my own house soon," she muttered. She needed a private and safe place to go when she could no longer subdue her emotions. But if her father learned she was renting a home so close to his, he could try to block her again, and he might easily succeed. It seemed like he always got his way these days. If anything, he'd gained *more* power since she'd been gone.

She could only hope he'd never expect her to be bold enough to choose his own neighborhood. That she'd first tried to rent the Woods bungalow might help her in that regard, might make him think she was looking for something much smaller and on the other side of town.

She was making her way out of the neighborhood when she passed the street leading to his house and suddenly stopped, right in the middle of the road.

CHAPTER FOUR

It didn't look as though anyone was home, so Sloane pulled to the curb a little ways down and let the engine idle. So much had happened in that house, both good and bad. For the most part, she'd loved the property—until it began to feel like a prison, of course. The older she got, the stricter her father had become, and the more claustrophobic she grew as a result. As she entered her teen years, she also began to see her father in a different light. That was what had allowed the suspicion she'd buried to become an obsession of sorts, which made it impossible to remain under his roof after high school graduation.

Although the house wasn't quite as big as those that had been built in the area since, like the one she was hoping to rent, the yard was almost three acres instead of two, and the estate as a whole spoke of timeless gentility. Her father had taken great care of the place; he'd always been exacting (of himself and others), which was why his home, his collectible Corvettes and other vehicles, even his suits, were immaculate.

But the fact that he could afford to buy such a property so soon after he married her mother didn't speak to his own accomplishments. He'd succeeded in business and small-town politics since then, but just before he graduated from college, an intruder bent on robbery had broken into his parents' home in Dallas an hour and a half away and shot his mother, father and younger brother. He'd lost them all at once, which was beyond tragic. She'd often wondered how he coped with such a horrific thing, if that was what had made him so aloof and unable to really care beyond the incessant need to control everyone close to him.

She didn't know because he rarely talked about the past, and that incident in particular, which was understandable, but that was how he'd come into so much money at such a young age. His dad had been an oil tycoon.

Sloane often wished she could've known her father's parents. It might've made a difference in helping her understand *him.* She'd known and loved her mother's mother, but Grandma Livingston had lost her husband, due to an infection that went undiagnosed until it was too late, before Sloane was born, and had died herself a decade later, thanks to a blood clot after having elective surgery to help her lose weight.

Ed had always treated Grandma Livingston with disdain. To him, she was fat, sloppy and disorganized. But she'd always had plenty of love for Sloane, and to Sloane that was all that mattered. It was Grandma Livingston who'd helped her cope with the loss of her mother, even though Grandma Livingston was also hurt to think Clara would walk out on her and everyone else. Although she'd mostly kept her thoughts to herself, there was one time she'd hinted that she didn't believe what had happened had gone the way Ed claimed. Grandma Livingston had been drinking that night, which was probably why she'd said what she did, but she'd seemed strangely lucid when she'd stated that Clara would've been in touch with *somebody* if she were still alive. As soon as Sloane questioned her, however, she'd quickly masked the strange look on her face and said not to listen to her, that she was just an old woman crying in her beer.

That was one of the memories that most troubled Sloane. She needed to find Clara for Grandma Livingston, too.

After glancing up and down the street to assure herself that no one was taking particular notice, Sloane got out of the car. If her father still lived by the same routine, he had the gardeners come on Friday mornings, but they were gone by now, and a lady who spent all day Saturday getting him ready for the coming week with groceries, a few meals and all the housecleaning.

Sloane's heels clacked overly loud on the cement, drawing her nerves taut, as she marched, matter-of-factly, down the sidewalk. She was self-conscious, would rather not be seen, which was probably why it seemed as though she was making too much noise. It was getting late in the day. If her father didn't have a chamber mixer or some other plans for dinner, he could be on his way home. That was why she was moving so fast. She knew she was crazy to be doing this right now. But it'd been so long since she'd been home. She just wanted to take a peek, to see if it still looked exactly as she remembered.

The deep woof of a big dog rose to her ears as she reached the front entry. A wave of nostalgia caused her to hesitate as her thoughts segued to Scout, but she understood it probably wasn't the same dog they'd had ten years ago. Scout had been eight years old when she left.

A narrow tan-and-black face appeared in the window, and she decided for sure that it wasn't the dog she'd known. Her father must've gotten another German shepherd, since that was his favorite breed.

They're the smartest, most loyal dogs in the world. I could tell him to attack you right now, and he would. There'd be nothing left of you, not unless I called him off.

Sloane shivered at the memory. After her father had told her that—while he was sitting at the dining room table one night, drinking a scotch and water, angry because she'd come home a few minutes after curfew—she'd begun to view Scout with more fear than love. She'd realized then that he wasn't the family dog, *her* dog; he was her father's puppet and a possible weapon.

"What's your name?" She tapped the glass to say hello, only to gasp and jerk back when the dog lunged at her with bared teeth.

"Holy shit! You're *definitely* not Scout," she mumbled and crossed to the other side of the porch so she could peer inside without having an angry German shepherd trying to intimidate her.

Had her father remarried? Did he have a live-in lover now that both children were out of the house?

Paige had said she didn't think so, but Sloane wasn't sure Paige would know. Once Clara "left," Ed had found solace in the arms of a woman named Katrina Yost, who'd worked for him as a receptionist at his car lot. Ed hadn't yet entered politics at that time; he was simply a businessman, so it didn't matter too much that Katrina wouldn't make a good politician's wife. She'd been quite a bit younger, didn't care for children and craved a great deal of money and attention. Ed had been too smart to let her squander his fortune, and too ambitious to spend all of his time catering to her or any other woman—Sloane's mother could've warned Katrina about that—so the relationship hadn't lasted more than two years. Katrina moved away after they broke up, and that was it. Sloane had never seen her again.

There had been others after Katrina, but Sloane could hardly remember their names. From that point on, her father had kept that part of his life very private. Rarely did he bring someone home to meet her and Randy, and, if he did, he introduced the woman as a friend.

Since he hadn't been elected mayor until Sloane was a junior in high school, she'd been around to observe him in that capacity for only a couple of years, but she guessed he'd become even more careful since going into public service. Her father had liked running the town, enjoyed having a position of power and authority, and romantic entanglements could all too easily go sour and threaten his image.

Her father's dog had figured out how to get inside the room she was now peering into, despite the fact that the door had initially been closed. Since he was once again growling at her, she moved on, around the house.

She hoped her father's pet couldn't get outside. That possibility gave her pause before she opened the gate into the backyard. They'd always had a doggy door. Chances were that hadn't changed. But if she could block it before the dog could come through, she'd be fine.

To throw the dog off her trail, she left the gate ajar, went back to the front and tapped the glass. That brought the German shepherd's nose to the window again, where he burst into an all-new barking frenzy, but as long as he was making so much noise, she'd be able to tell where he was.

After kicking off her shoes, she dashed around to the back, where she quickly shoved the antique steamer trunk, in which her mother had stored her and her brother's outside toys, in front of the back door just in time to stop the dog from bolting through it.

Scout's replacement wasn't happy about his inability to eat her alive. She could hear him jumping against the door and whining as if that might improve his situation.

Reasonably assured she was going to be okay, she turned to stare out at the yard. There were so many places to hide a body on this heavily wooded piece of land. As a child, she'd played here for hours and, as she grew older, she began to look, almost unconsciously at first, for anomalies in the soil. She'd also eyed any slab of concrete, outbuilding or tree and tried to remember if it'd been there before her mother went missing. In many instances, she couldn't rule out the possibility, but she never found anything definitive, never saw anything that stood out enough to warrant a deeper investigation.

She did see plenty of terrible things in her dreams, however. Her most common nightmare featured her sitting on the tire swing that dangled from the burr oak right off the back porch—and was there to this day, just like the toy box—happily laughing with her brother until she happened to glance down and see a hand sticking out of the ground.

She squeezed her eyes closed as the terrible feeling that nightmare gave her swept over her again. *Where are you, Mom? Am I about to ruin my relationship with Dad and Randy forever by insisting you could be here?*

She missed her brother so much, wished she could rely on him to support her in some small way, or at least be impartial. But she doubted that would happen. If he was anything like he'd been before, Randy wouldn't even give her an audience. Whenever she'd tried to bring up the sounds she'd heard the night their mother disappeared, he'd scowl and tell her that she'd been just a little girl when it happened and had no clue what she was talking about. If she insisted, he'd explode. "Dad would never hurt Mom! What are you talking about? That's nuts!"

She understood he was afraid they'd lose their father, too. But if their mother hadn't run away, if Ed was responsible for Clara's disappearance, didn't they all deserve justice? Wasn't it better to face the truth than let their father get away with such a terrible crime? If Ed had killed her, look what he'd cost them!

The dog had stopped making a racket. Sloane checked her watch. It was five thirty. Had her father come home? If so, had he seen her car parked down the street?

Didn't matter. He wouldn't recognize it as hers. That car could belong to anyone.

But she had left her shoes on the front lawn…

Her pulse notched up as she pressed her back to the wall of the house so that she couldn't be seen through any of the windows. Odds were he'd pulled into the garage, which meant he hadn't gone in through the front and might not have spotted her shoes.

But if he had, she didn't want to meet up with him alone in the yard where he might've buried her mother. The houses here were so spread out and the fences and trees so many and so tall, it was likely no one would even hear her scream.

She pulled out her phone while she waited, listening with baited breath, and sent a text to Paige, just so that someone would know where she was.

Stopped by to see the old house while my father was gone. Running a bit late. Be there shortly.

She wanted to add: If I don't show up, call the police, except Micah would probably respond, since it was Paige calling, and Sloane couldn't believe he'd be too upset if something happened to her. Not these days.

No problem, came Paige's response. Just got home myself.

Sloane let her breath seep slowly out as she edged around the house. She had to get out of there, couldn't hide in the backyard indefinitely.

Once she reached the front, she craned her neck to see the full length of the driveway.

If her father had come home, she couldn't tell. There was no car out in the open, and the garage door was down.

It was likely she'd panicked too soon. But she didn't care. She was leaving, and she was leaving *now*.

Hoping he was busy changing out of his work clothes even if he was home, she darted from the shadow of the house, scooped up the low heels she'd kicked off before and ran, barefoot, all the way back to her car. She thought she heard the dog barking again but her father didn't come out and call her name.

Her heart was still racing as she climbed into the Jag.

She'd just started the engine when someone knocked on the passenger-side window. Startled, she almost threw the transmission into Drive and took off without even looking to see who it was.

Fortunately, she didn't do that, because it wasn't her father. It was Mrs. Winters, the mother of a girl Sloane had known growing up named Sarah, who had cognitive disabilities. Sloane used to attend Sarah's birthday party each year, still remembered how impressed she'd been, even at a young age, by the constant, loving care her mother gave her. Watching the two of them had made Sloane miss her own mother.

Willing herself to calm down so she wouldn't seem too crazy, and cringing to think her father's neighbor had witnessed her mad dash to the car, she lowered the window. "Hello, Mrs. Winters. It—it's great to see you again. It's been a long time."

Like her house behind her, the older woman had once been attractive but had long since fallen victim to neglect. She glanced nervously up and down the street. "Come inside for a moment, dear," she murmured, her voice urgent, and hurried back up her own walk.

Micah remained at the station even though his shift had ended an hour ago. He'd been up since dawn, when he'd gone to the gym. It'd already been a long day, but he was staying late to catch up on some paperwork. He wasn't particularly behind, but what else did he have to do? He wasn't anxious to go home, didn't care to sit in his new rental house, staring at four empty walls. He hadn't yet hung a single painting, hadn't unpacked anything except the bare essentials, so the place felt foreign, unwelcoming.

He needed to settle in and make it a home, *his* home, but he was tempted to move back to the apartment above his parents' barn. He'd been living there for the past year, ever since the divorce, and helping with his father's chores when he had the opportunity and wasn't working himself. Keeping busy meant he didn't have to feel half the shit he felt when everything slowed down, but he needed to start living again, needed to establish some kind of social life, so he'd made the decision to move back to town. He had to face the void of no longer being a full-time parent at some point.

Problem was...he didn't seem to be adapting as well as he'd hoped.

And now Sloane was back.

Of course she'd return when he was still trying to climb out of the wreckage of his divorce.

He pulled his cell phone from his pocket and scrolled through his recent call history.

Ed McBride. 2:10 p.m.
Ed McBride. 3:40 p.m.
Ed McBride. 4:04 p.m.
Ed McBride. 5:31 p.m.

He'd ignored four calls from Sloane's father and one voice mail. Normally, Micah didn't have any trouble picking up for the mayor. These days, they played golf together on occasion. Back when he'd been dating Sloane, he hadn't cared for the man. He knew what Sloane suspected, even if she never talked about it. But no one else seemed to think Ed might be responsible for Clara McBride's disappearance, not even his son—especially not his son.

So five years or so after Sloane left, Micah had decided it was silly to carry a grudge when there was no evidence Ed was guilty of any wrongdoing. Sloane's father had been overbearing and overprotective—insufferable, at times—to Sloane, and that had made Micah defensive of her. But a lot of fathers with strong personalities fell into that trap. It wasn't proof Ed didn't mean well, that he didn't care about her. In fact, many would argue that it established the opposite, something Micah had come to understand now that he had a child of his own.

So why had he been avoiding Ed's calls? Why did he suddenly feel like a traitor maintaining a relationship with him? Micah didn't owe Sloane anything; he'd made that clear when he bumped into her earlier. And remaining friends with the mayor could be beneficial to his career.

He hit the button on his phone that would return Ed's calls.

"Micah, there you are!"

"Sorry, it's been a busy afternoon," Micah said, but that was a blatant lie. It'd been slow, which was why he'd been able to obsess over Sloane. It drove him crazy that she was all he'd been able to think about since their unexpected encounter, hated that the one person who'd hurt him worse than any other still held any power over him.

He was going to break her hold if it was the last thing he did.

"Can you hear me?" Ed asked. "I'm on my way home so I have to use my Bluetooth."

"You're coming through loud and clear," Micah said. "What can I do for you?"

"Just thought I should give you a heads-up." He lowered his voice. "Sloane's back in town."

Micah didn't let on that he already knew. He was too curious to hear what Ed had to say—why, after Micah had had no contact with Sloane for ten years, her father felt the need to make this call. "How do you know?"

"Paige stopped by my office earlier today."

"Paige..."

"Yeah. I helped her out with some parking issues she was having in front of her store, so she did me this favor."

Micah felt his muscles bunch. He wasn't cool with that. Regardless of how he felt about Sloane, Paige was pretending to be her friend. Going to her father didn't seem very friendly, very loyal, but he tried not to let his ex-wife's actions bother him. *It's not my problem.* "Then you haven't heard from Sloane yourself."

"Not since she left town ten years ago. You?"

Ed had stopped asking in recent years. "No. Never."

"So you have no idea why she's back?"

Micah rubbed a hand over his beard growth. "This is where she was born and raised. Isn't that enough?"

"After a decade of total silence?"

A decade was a long time. A child didn't usually cut off a parent without some reason, not unless that child was on drugs or acting out in other ways, and Sloane had never been a troublemaker. She was sensitive and sweet—but Micah couldn't allow himself to think anything that might soften his stance where she was concerned. He had to remain unsympathetic for his own protection. "Maybe she needs some time off. She's been working hard. We've all seen the magazines."

"Standing still while someone takes a photograph doesn't require a huge effort."

It could, Micah thought. He had no idea what was involved. He only knew that some of those photographs had been *stunning*, had literally stolen his breath. "Maybe she misses you."

The resulting silence led Micah to believe he'd surprised Ed with that suggestion.

"No, she would've been in touch if that was the case," he said when he rallied.

"She could miss Randy..."

"He hasn't heard from her, either."

"Then I'm out of guesses." It certainly wasn't because she missed *him*, as much as Micah wished otherwise. No one liked the idea that the person they'd loved more than any other could walk away so easily and not regret it in the end.

"She's staying with Paige for now," Ed said. "But Paige told me she's looking to rent a place, which means she plans to be in town for a while."

Micah wasn't feeling good about this call, and it went beyond Paige's actions, since Ed was bound to find out Sloane was in town sooner or later, anyway. "Is that a problem?"

"Not unless she tries to stir up a bunch of drama."

Micah leaned back in his chair. "And how would she do that?"

"She was so traumatized by her mother leaving that she's always blamed me, prefers to believe I did something to send her mother away rather than face the truth."

This was the closest Ed had ever come to referencing the reason for the rift between him and his daughter. "It *is* strange that no one has ever heard from Clara again, don't you think?"

Dead silence. "What are you saying?"

The temperature had dropped by fifty degrees. "I'm not accusing you of anything—"

"That's good," Ed broke in, "because I wouldn't take kindly to it."

It didn't take much to offend a proud man like Ed. The mayor felt he was above reproach. While that was something Micah could overlook when they were playing golf, Ed's arrogance bothered him now. "I'm just trying to understand where she might be coming from. I'm looking at the situation from her perspective." After all, Ed had been a grown man when everything went down; surely he had to have been in a better position to withstand the pain and psychological damage than his two children. Why couldn't he be a bit softer, have a little patience and understanding instead of seeing only how it affected *him*?

Because he was too selfish? Or was there something more going on, as Sloane suspected?

"Losing a mother is hard on a child," Micah said, "especially when you're talking complete and utter abandonment."

"I've never allowed Sloane or Randy to want for anything. They were fine without her."

Ed had brushed Micah's statement away as if it had no merit. But parenting wasn't as simple as making sure

Sloane and Randy had food to eat and clothes to wear. Ed couldn't replace their mother.

Micah wanted to say so, but he bit his tongue. This wasn't his fight. "I can't imagine Sloane has ever accused you of not taking care of her basic needs."

"I'm glad to hear she's given me a *little* credit."

"She isn't a mean person."

"Yeah, well, we'll see. If you hear anything from her, you'll let me know, won't you?"

Micah hesitated. He was getting the impression that Ed was preparing for a fight with his daughter by making sure everyone in Millcreek stood with him. Micah didn't have the best feelings toward his ex-girlfriend, but he couldn't bring himself to turn on her, even if there was some validity to the argument that she deserved it. He would always act to protect her, if he could. Love did that to a person. "She has no reason to contact me, so I'm sure I won't hear anything."

As soon as he disconnected, Micah almost called Paige. He wanted to ask what the hell she was doing going to Ed's office with the news that Sloane was back. He also wanted to know why she'd invited Sloane to stay with her in the first place. Sure, they'd once been close. But a lot had changed since then. Micah knew how terribly jealous his ex-wife could be, how many times Paige had thrown Sloane's name in his face and blamed her for their marriage not working. Sloane was trusting the one person who hated her most in the world.

"You'd better be careful," he murmured as if Sloane could hear him. He could imagine her assuming the best. She hadn't been around for the past decade, had no idea that Paige might be less than committed to her well-being. But he wound up shoving his phone in his pocket instead of confronting Paige. She'd make too much of it, take his involvement as proof that he still had feelings for Sloane. And that would only make matters worse.

He pushed away from the desk. He needed to worry about his own life; it was time to go home and unpack.

CHAPTER FIVE

Mrs. Winters—or Vickie, as she now insisted on being called—kept a close eye on the window as she gestured for Sloane to have a seat in her blue-and-gold 1970s living room. She was *so* preoccupied with what was or wasn't happening in the street that Sloane couldn't help glancing back over her shoulder.

"Is everything okay?" Sloane saw nothing noteworthy.

Vickie's dark hair showed significant gray at the roots, reinforcing the sense that she might be coming undone. "Fine."

Sloane didn't feel as though everything was *fine*, but, in an effort to be polite, she didn't press the issue. "How's Sarah?"

"She's…okay, I guess. I had to put her in a facility in June. As you know, I did my best to care for her here at home. I had her with me for thirty-seven years, but her health was beginning to deteriorate—she has a congenital heart condition, among many other things—and I didn't have the strength to continue lifting her and bathing her, that sort of thing."

"I'm sorry."

"It got very difficult there at the end. She started acting irrational, throwing fits, being temperamental. It wasn't like her."

Sarah's father had been a wealthy trial attorney, but he'd left Mrs. Winters—*Vickie*, Sloane reminded herself—shortly after Clara went missing. So Vickie had been on her own with Sarah for much of her daughter's life. "You've been an amazing mother, always so loving and kind."

"Thank you. You were kind to her, too. Don't think I didn't notice. So many of the other kids were—" her gaze fell to the dated and well-worn carpet "—well, cruel."

Sloane remembered the jibes and taunts chucked at Sarah like rocks. A few of her closest friends, even Paige, had been some of the worst offenders. *I can't believe you have to go to that retard's birthday*, she'd say. But Sloane had never felt that way. She'd always been grateful she didn't have the same challenges, could never understand such a lack of compassion. "She deserved better."

Vickie's forehead creased as though the memory pained her. "You always tried to stick up for her."

"I understood what it was like to be teased." For her height. She hadn't become attractive until she grew into her arms and legs and her braces had come off.

"Some people have to go through so much…" Vickie's words trailed off as her attention suddenly shifted. "Ah, *there* he is."

Sloane twisted around in time to see a silver Mercedes roll past the house. She couldn't make out the driver's face, but she didn't need to. "You've been watching for my father?"

"Yes. He's a little later than usual tonight. Something must've held him up."

That Ed was just returning meant he hadn't been home when Sloane fled his house. It was a relief to know that. But then…who'd quieted the dog?

Maybe no one. She found it a little hard to believe that her father's German shepherd had given up so easily. But if no one else was there, she had no other explanation. "I'm glad he's late. I was hoping to avoid him," she said so that Vickie wouldn't think she'd gone to visit him and would now wish to go back.

"When I saw you hurrying to your car, I thought that might be the case. Did Simone come out and chase you off, then?"

"Simone?"

"The woman he's seeing right now. I believe they met on some dating site."

That explained the dog. Someone *was* home; it just hadn't been her father. "They live together?"

"No. She has her own place in Dallas. Owns a PR company there, so they live mostly separate lives. Your father likes it that way. But she comes out every now and then to stay for a day or two."

Vickie sure seemed to be keeping a close eye on Sloane's father. Was there a reason? "I wondered if he was seeing someone."

"Simone doesn't always come to the door. She's not

from here, doesn't seem to feel as though she should have to deal with the 'locals.'"

"I didn't knock. I wanted to see the old place without risking a confrontation."

"Is that why you're back?"

The directness of the question made Sloane shift uncomfortably. "I don't know what you mean."

"Are you in Millcreek for a quick visit because you're homesick? Or are you planning to stay?"

Vickie seemed to be digging for something.

"I'll be here for several months, maybe longer." Sloane didn't address the reason for her return. Neither did she state that she was going to rent a house in the River Bottoms, which meant they'd soon be neighbors.

"That's what your father said."

Sloane gritted her teeth. Here was further proof that Ed had known she was coming before she arrived. "He mentioned I'd be visiting?"

"Yes. He also made a point of telling me that you may have some 'foolish ideas' in your head."

"Like…"

"He didn't explain, but I took it to mean he's concerned you might be returning to search for your mother. He asked me to let him know if I heard from you."

Sloane clasped her hands tightly together. It wasn't much of a surprise that her father had guessed her reason for coming home, but she was taken aback by the fact that he was already working to poison the people of Millcreek against her and anything she might say. How many others had he spoken to? "Is that why you invited me in? So you can report back?"

"Lord, no," Vickie said, but clearly she had *some*

purpose. What was it? She seemed to be feeling her way along, making sure it was safe. "I'm guessing Ed wasn't an easy man to live with…"

He hadn't been. He was particular, autocratic, always right, proud to a fault and, when he spoke to his children, he had no filter. But there were worse fathers. If it was true what he claimed about their mother—that Clara had run off and abandoned them—Sloane owed him a lot more than she did Clara. At least he'd stuck around, provided for them, raised them to adulthood. Her brother had made that argument many times while they were growing up: *What if* he *had left us, too?*

But what if their mother didn't return because she *couldn't* return? What if they could've had the love they'd been denied? And what if Ed was to blame?

Sloane struggled to come up with a response to Vickie's assertion that Ed hadn't been an easy man to live with that fell somewhere near the intersection of honesty and diplomacy. She had to be careful what she said, had no idea what might get back to him. "He can be a…*challenge*."

"A challenge…"

"Yes." Sloane cleared her throat. "Look, I don't mean to be rude, but what is it you want from me?"

Vickie seemed torn, but she soon scooted forward. "You were always a nice girl, so I'm going to take it on faith that you've turned into a nice adult and be up front with you. I'm not your father's biggest fan. I let him put a campaign sign in my yard when he was up for reelection. We live on the same street, after all. But I've never voted for him, and—" her chest lifted as she took a deep breath "—that's because I believe he had something to do with your mother's disappearance."

Sloane felt her eyes open wider. She'd only been back a day, and she'd already found someone else who doubted her father's story?

"I realize that might be shocking to hear," Vickie continued, "but I thought you might also suspect. I thought that might be at the root of the problems between you. Forgive me if...if I'm wrong. It's a difficult subject to broach."

She wasn't wrong. But Sloane still struggled to admit the suspicion she'd hidden for so long. She'd be accusing her father of *murder*, a man who had no criminal history—the *mayor*, for crying out loud.

She didn't want to ruin his reputation if she was wrong.

But she'd known she'd have to risk being wrong, and all the attendant damage it would cause, when she chose to return to Millcreek. There was no way she could take up for her mother without attacking her father's explanation of that night.

A bead of sweat rolled between her shoulder blades even though it was plenty cool in Vickie's house. "What makes you believe he might've been involved?"

Vickie got up and began to pace. "I saw something that night. But if I tell you about it, you'll have to keep it to yourself. It wouldn't be enough to bring him down, so there's nothing to be gained by letting him know I'm not the friend I pretend to be."

"If what you saw is something the police should know, I'll be duty-bound to speak up."

"No, you won't. Not yet. You'll have to gather a lot more than what I'm about to tell you for it to make a difference, especially around here. So there's no use getting him all riled up at me, making my life more difficult than it is already."

Sloane stood, too. "I'm not out to make life harder for *anyone*."

Vickie pivoted at the edge of the room and came back. "I believe that."

"I promise, even if I have to divulge what you tell me, I'll do all I can to protect you as the source."

"That might not help. The information alone might be enough that he can guess. But it's not as though I can remain silent any longer, anyway." She mumbled that last part mostly to herself. "It's getting to where I can scarcely live with myself. Someone needs to do something—at least look at the possibilities."

Sloane tilted her head to catch the older woman's gaze. "You're right about the rift between me and my father. That's why I'm back—to figure out exactly what happened to my mother."

Vickie hurried over and grasped her hands. "But instead of encouraging you to dig into the past, I should be trying to talk you out of it."

"Why?"

Her voice fell to a harsh whisper. "Surely, you realize it's not safe. He could kill us both. Make it look like an accident." She abruptly released Sloane. "Heck, given who he is, he might not even have to make it look like an accident. Look what he did to your mother! He simply said she disappeared. It didn't matter that it would be highly unlikely for a devoted wife and mother of two to leave her family—*on foot*, no less—in the middle of the night, never to be seen again. He's never had to account for that!"

Sloane's heart began to beat so loudly she could hear

it thudding in her ears. She still loved her father, hated to believe he might be dangerous, especially to her. But if some part of her didn't already believe that to be true, why was she still having nightmares? "I understand the risks."

There it was. The naked truth. She was afraid her father wasn't the man he pretended to be, that he was a calculated and cold-blooded killer—cold-blooded enough to come after *her* if he felt sufficiently threatened. Until this moment, she'd only ever admitted that to Clyde.

Vickie accepted her words with a solemn nod. "Okay, then, we might as well sit back down."

An ominous feeling crept over Sloane as she perched on the edge of the chair she'd been using a moment earlier. This was the point of no return. Her next question could very easily be the question to open Pandora's box…

"What'd you see the night my mother went missing?"

Ed McBride stood with one hand holding a glass of scotch and the other stroking the head of his dog while staring out the front window of his living room at the white Jaguar parked down the street. "She came *here*?"

Simone Gentry, who was curled up on the couch in her robe, took a sip of her own drink. Whenever she stayed over, and he had to work, she spent most of her time sleeping. She was one of those manic people who worked for days with little sleep and then crashed for an extended period, and when she crashed she often came to Millcreek because she didn't know anyone here, didn't feel any pressure to do anything. "She walked around in the yard. She didn't ring the bell—not that I could hear above the ruckus Ruger was making."

So she hadn't come to see him. That caused him to tighten his grip on his glass. Who did Sloane think she was? Not even Randy dared to treat him as if he didn't matter. And Sloane's unexpected professional success only made things worse, because it made her feel powerful enough to take him on.

He'd show her that was a mistake. He wouldn't allow anyone to get the best of him, even one of his kids—*especially* one of his kids. They owed him too much. "She went around back, you said?"

The ice in Simone's glass clinked as she set her drink on the coffee table. "Must have. Someone shoved that old toy box in front of the doggy door so that Ruger couldn't get out."

"How long was she here, snooping around?"

"Not very long."

"What was she doing, exactly?"

"I just told you all I know, Ed."

At the irritation in her voice, he bit back a sharp retort. Why was Simone so damn dysfunctional when she came to Millcreek? The woman she was in Dallas would've marched outside to confront Sloane instead of hiding away in the house, fresh from bed and still unproductive at dinnertime. "That's her car down the street, you said?"

"That's the car she got into, but then the neighbor came out and said something to her."

"You saw that?"

"Of course. I was standing right where you are, trying to figure out what was going on."

"And then what?"

She sighed audibly. “And then…*nothing.* They went inside.”

Pulling his gaze away from Sloane’s car—a much more expensive vehicle than most young women could afford—he turned to confront his girlfriend. “Are my questions bugging you?”

“A little,” she admitted. “It doesn’t matter how many times we go over it, there’s not much I can say. I can’t conjure up answers I don’t have.”

“Well, forgive me for pressing you, but if you hadn’t seen your daughter for ten years, you might be interested in hearing a few details.”

She crossed her legs and smoothed her robe. She had one headstrong daughter, a little monster who was with her ex-husband at the moment. The child was only eleven, but Simone told some shocking stories about how difficult she was to control.

Maybe one day Simone would have her own taste of what he was going through.

“Don’t take your bad mood out on me,” she grumbled.

He rolled his eyes and turned back to the window. “Don’t you have to be back in Dallas soon?”

“Tomorrow morning, actually. And with the way you’re acting now, I’m glad.”

He was glad, too. He was ready for her to leave. He liked the sex she provided. It gave him a nice outlet when he grew bored of the minutiae he had to sift through as mayor of a small town—whether residents thought the police were responding accurately to a case involving three children who’d been caught playing show-and-tell in a shed; whether there should be a stoplight at the corner of Western and Polk; whether

Hansen's Print Services, located behind a tiny subdivision, should be allowed a sign at the entrance to that subdivision. But he and Simone couldn't tolerate each other much longer than two or three days at a time, and it had been that long.

Behind him, he heard her get up. When she spoke again, she was standing right beside him, also staring out at Sloane's car. "Does your son know his sister is back?"

"Of course. I called him as soon as I heard she was coming."

"And? Is he as leery of her as you are?"

"I'm not *leery* of her," he said. But that wasn't entirely true. Sloane was the one wild card in his life, the only person he couldn't convince to see the past the way *he* saw it—and that could have all kinds of implications.

His cell phone vibrated in his pocket. He hated to look away from Sloane's car again, for fear he'd miss her when she came out, but whoever was trying to reach him only called back when he didn't answer, so he took a quick peek.

"Who is it?" Simone asked.

"Randy."

"Speak of the devil."

He didn't respond. She wasn't part of his "real" life, so he didn't feel she should have any input, sarcastic or otherwise.

He pushed the talk button. "Hello?"

"Dad? Have you seen her?"

He hadn't seen her, but it was possible he was looking at her car right now. "Not yet."

"Neither have I. Maybe she hasn't arrived."

"She's here."

"How do you know?"

The woman Simone had described to him sounded like Sloane, but he couldn't be positive, so he didn't mention that. "Paige stopped by my office."

"And?"

"She said Sloane is staying with her."

"For how long?"

"Until she finds another rental."

"So pressuring the Woodses to renege on the lease didn't help."

"I'm sure it sent a message."

"One she ignored!"

Randy had a point. Losing the house didn't seem to have deterred Sloane. "Maybe she took what they told her at face value. Maybe she believed they'd already leased it to someone else."

"And maybe she didn't but is just plain determined."

That wasn't a comforting thought…

"If she hasn't reached out to you, and she hasn't reached out to me, I doubt she's here to try to patch things up," Randy continued.

"I think that's safe to assume," Ed agreed.

"So what's she here for?"

That was the million-dollar question. Sloane had a successful career, had made something of herself. She didn't need him or Randy. It wasn't as if she was crawling back on her knees, like he'd always told himself she would. So why was she here? What did she hope to accomplish?

The possibilities raised the hair on the back of his neck.

Had she come back to bring him down, to ruin him?

If so, it didn't help that she was talking to Vickie

Winters. He could only imagine what Vickie had to say. She'd never forgiven him for breaking off the affair they'd been having in the weeks and months before everything went so wrong with Clara.

Was she telling Sloane that *she* was part of the reason Clara had attempted to stand up to him for a change? Or that she'd done everything possible in the twenty-three years since then to get back in his bed?

He doubted it. It was probably all lies. God, what had he ever seen in that drab, bitter, bitch of a woman? Clara had been twice the person Vickie was, and he'd been a fool.

Worse than a fool. But what was done was done. He'd put it behind him, and he wasn't going to allow anyone to dredge it up again.

"Wish I knew," he said. "We'll just have to keep an eye on her."

He froze as he saw Sloane come out of Vickie's house, watched with hungry eyes as she walked around the back of her car and slipped behind the wheel. Even from a distance, she was extraordinarily beautiful.

"Dad?"

Randy's voice made him realize that he'd quit listening to his son. "What?"

"Don't worry about anything. *I* know you didn't hurt Mom, okay?"

The memory of that night rose up but he quickly blocked it. "Thanks."

It wasn't until he'd disconnected with Randy and Sloane was long gone that he remembered Simone and turned to find himself alone in the room—except for Ruger.

"Simone?" he called, taking the stairs two at a time

until he reached the master bedroom, where he found her packing.

"What are you doing?" he asked from the doorway. "I thought you weren't leaving until morning."

"I figured I might as well head back early," she said.

He watched as she changed into a pair of tight-fitting jeans and a silky sleeveless tank. "Just like that?"

The zipper rasped as she closed her suitcase. "Yeah. Just like that. You've got some things to do, anyway. Am I right?"

He studied her dispassionately. His dog was more loyal than she was. But it didn't matter. Lucky for her, he didn't care if he ever saw her again. "Yeah, I do," he said. "Good riddance."

She glanced up at him, but she didn't argue, didn't express any surprise at his surly response. She just shrugged and kept packing, and he knew then that he'd never see her again.

CHAPTER SIX

It was a good thing Sloane hadn't needed Paige to call the police. When she returned, she found her friend so caught up in finishing dinner she didn't seem to be paying any attention to the clock, didn't even seem to notice that Sloane was late.

"Hey, you're back!" she shouted above the music that was blaring as Sloane walked into the kitchen with the items she'd purchased from the store.

"How are things going?" Sloane shouted. "Do you need any help?"

Paige was at the stove, frying strips of tortilla. "No. I'm almost done."

"I can barely hear you!"

She set her spatula aside long enough to turn down the music coming through her Bluetooth. "Sorry about that. Trevor's gone, so I was taking advantage of being able to play my music as loud as possible."

Sloane set the cake and wine on the counter. "Trevor's not home yet?"

"He came home, but he was bummed out about something that happened at school, so I let him call Micah. They left to hang out with each other for a while. You know—guys' night out. I thought it might be nice for us to have some time alone, anyway."

Sloane was glad that Trevor was getting to spend the evening with his father. The poor kid had seemed so bummed last night about the divorce, and it sounded as if whatever had happened today hadn't made him feel any better. "What went wrong at school? I hope it wasn't anything serious."

"His best friend, Spaulding, the one he walks home with after school, invited someone else to go with him and his family to Disneyland."

"Ouch! That's too bad."

"Yeah, it broke Trevor's heart. He never would've done that to Spaulding, but Spaulding has the right to invite whoever he wants, so there's not much I can do."

Sloane got out two glasses and uncorked the wine while Paige scooped the fried tortilla strips onto a plate lined with a paper towel. "Will Trevor stay the night with Micah, or will Micah bring him home?"

"Micah will bring him home."

"Even though it's a weekend?"

"It's *my* weekend."

Sloane poured herself a bit more wine than usual. She wasn't anxious to see her former boyfriend again and hoped he wouldn't come inside when he dropped Trevor off. She was having a hard enough time trying to forget their earlier encounter. And now that she'd spoken with Vickie Winters, she had what her father's neighbor had revealed swirling around in her head and causing her stomach to churn with acid. She was trying not to think about that until after dinner, though, when she could be alone. "Don't you have to work in the shop?"

"I have an employee who handles Saturdays and any other days I need, and I usually take Trevor with me on Sunday. I'm only open from noon to five on Sunday, anyway, and he likes to help out."

"So when it comes to Micah's visits, you adhere pretty strictly to the schedule set up by the court?"

"I bend now and then, but I'm cautious. I don't want Micah to get any ideas."

"Like..."

She started to grate a block of cheddar cheese. "Like trying to take Trevor away from me."

The cork squeaked as Sloane put it back in the wine bottle. "You think he'd do that?"

"I'm sure he'd like to. As far as he's concerned, the sun rises and sets on 'his boy.'" She paused to take a drink of the wine Sloane slid close to her. "He would've fought much harder for custody if he thought I'd give even an inch."

Paige sounded proud of herself but her words made Sloane sad for Micah. "He didn't fight?"

"Not at all. He didn't want it to get ugly, so he gave me everything I asked for."

Sloane hesitated before taking another sip of wine. "And you asked for the house?"

"I asked for everything—the house, the furniture, our savings, the car. Why not? *He* was the one who wanted the divorce. I didn't deserve it, hadn't done anything wrong. He had no reason to leave me."

So why had he? "He had to start completely over..."

"Yes, and he's still struggling to do that. He just barely moved back to town a few weeks ago after living above the barn on his parents' ranch for the past year."

Divorce was so difficult. Sloane had no right to pass judgment. She had to acknowledge that immediately, but the self-satisfaction she heard in Paige's voice bothered her. Paige had been out to punish Micah, to hit him as hard as she could and right where it counted, and he hadn't even put up his hands. "You're a good mom. I'm sure Trevor and Micah both realize that," she said, so she wouldn't have to comment directly on what Paige had just said. It made her cringe; she couldn't bring herself to act supportive.

"Yeah, well, I was a good wife, too—not that it made any difference in the end," Paige muttered and started setting the table.

"I'm going to wash my hands, okay?" Sloane set her glass down before crossing to the bathroom. She thought stepping out of the room for a moment might help put an end to the conversation. She'd come to Paige's house mostly because she'd missed her old friend and hoped to reestablish some of what they'd once had. But now she wasn't so sure she could salvage even that. It got awkward every time Micah's name came up.

He would probably always stand between them.

When Sloane returned, she again asked if there was anything she could do to help, but Paige insisted she had everything under control. To avoid picking up the same subject they'd been discussing before, Sloane lifted the lid to see what was bubbling in the Crock-Pot while Paige cut up an avocado. "Soup?"

"Yeah. Chicken tortilla. It's one of Micah's favorite recipes."

Micah again. Sloane replaced the lid. "Look, Paige, if you think I had anything to do with what happened between you and Micah, I didn't, okay? I haven't had any contact with him—not until we bumped into each other while he was trying to get that permission slip for Trevor this morning."

"I know that," she said.

"So am I just being self-conscious about the fact that Micah and I have a past? Because I'm getting the feeling you resent me, but I don't know why."

"Of course I don't resent you! I wouldn't have invited you here if I did."

"That's what I'd like to believe. Micah was with me first, after all. I've never tried to steal him from you."

"And I've never tried to steal him from you. You were gone before anything happened between us."

But they must've slept together very soon after she left in order to have had a child only a year later. And what Paige said about not trying to steal Micah wasn't true. Even before graduation, Paige had done everything she could to gain Micah's attention. One time she texted him in the middle of the night when Sloane was with him, watching a movie, to invite him over. Another time she got drunk at a party and gyrated all over him.

For the sake of the friendship, Sloane had ignored those instances and others, so Paige probably didn't realize just how aware Sloane had been. Sloane had only been able to pull that off because she'd been so sure of Micah, which was another reason she was surprised—and stung—by what happened so soon after she was gone.

Instead of holding Paige to the truth right now, however, she continued to act as if she hadn't noticed. She was trying to put the past behind them, not create a fresh rift. "I'm sad things didn't work out with your marriage. I can only imagine how painful a breakup like that must be." If it was any worse than the pain Sloane had felt having to leave Micah behind, she couldn't have withstood it. She'd almost called him *so* many times, would've done it if she hadn't been absolutely determined not to be that selfish. She'd loved him too much to ask him to choose between her and his family and the town they'd grown up in.

"The divorce was tough," Paige said. "But I'm not trying to make you feel as if it was your fault."

Then why had she told Trevor otherwise? "I appreciate that."

"How'd it go at your father's?"

Sloane wasn't sure they'd cleared up anything. What Paige felt seemed so different from what she said, but Sloane was eager to talk about something else, even if it was her father. "It was strange to see the place."

Paige scraped some sour cream into a small bowl. "Hasn't changed much, right?"

"You've been there lately?"

"I haven't been inside, but I've driven past it. My folks still live one street over."

"The old toy box is there in back," Sloane said. "So is the tire swing."

Paige got out a ladle for the soup. "We had such great times on that tire swing, didn't we?"

"We sure did." But Sloane's favorite memory included Micah and not Paige. He'd kissed her for the first time while pushing her on that swing.

Paige jerked her head toward the counter. "Can you grab the tortilla strips and the cheese?"

"Of course." Sloane carried both to the table while Paige brought the chopped avocado and sour cream—all garnishes for the soup.

"This looks delicious."

"I love making soup in the fall."

Sloane went back for her wine and carried Paige's over, too, since Paige had grabbed both bowls of soup. "I appreciate you taking me in. It's been nice to feel I still have a friend here."

"It's no problem. Really. I've told you that before." Paige chose the far place setting, so Sloane took the seat across from her.

"How do you think you'll like living so close to your father?"

"I don't expect to *like* it," Sloane said. "But I think it's smart."

Paige was sprinkling cheese in her soup when she glanced up. "In what way?"

Sloane took a deep breath. Maybe if she told Paige what she was doing in town, Paige would relax. Until she felt secure in the fact that Sloane hadn't returned for Micah, they wouldn't be able to connect with each other, to trust each other. "I'm here to find out what happened to my mother, Paige."

"You mean you're searching for her?"

"In a way. I don't think she's alive. I'm afraid… I'm afraid my father might've killed her."

"You *what*?" Paige cried.

Sloane was tempted to take back that statement. She'd always shied away from accusing her father outright. Even to her closest friends and Micah. Stating it meant she'd have to do something about it, and she'd known she was in no position. But things had changed. She *could* do something about it now. "Yes."

"I knew you sometimes wondered if things didn't go quite the way he said—that he chased her off instead of her leaving on her own and she was afraid to come back or something like that. But you're talking *murder*?"

"I was only five when I heard what I heard, but I don't know how else to interpret it."

"You're going to investigate your own father."

"Someone's got to do it."

Paige dropped her spoon in her soup, letting it clank against the edge of the bowl. "But you'll have to face down your brother, too. Heck, given who your father is, you'll have to face down the whole town!"

"No one has ever made a concerted effort to figure out what happened. It's time someone did."

"No matter what it might cost you."

"No matter what it might cost me."

"That has to have been a tough decision."

"It's been excruciating. But I would hope someone would do the same for me, if I went missing. Wouldn't you?"

Paige whistled as she let her breath go. "I guess I would."

Sloane hadn't been hungry in the first place, not after talking to Vickie Winters. So she didn't mind that her soup was getting cold. Paige didn't seem to mind, either. She seemed to have forgotten all about it. "Wow," she said.

"Yeah. So there you have it. I've waited long enough to know that no one else is going to step up to do the heavy lifting. In my mind, that gives me no choice."

Paige picked up her spoon. “But do you have anything to go on? Anything that might make a difference? What is it you remember?”

Sloane closed her eyes as she recalled the night she’d spent so long trying to forget. “I heard an argument.”

“Your parents were fighting.”

“Yes. That’d been happening a lot. It made me so upset.”

“But a lot of parents fight. *My* parents have fought over the years, too.”

“This wasn’t that kind of fight, although I tried to convince myself it was. I felt powerless to stop it, so I tried to go back to sleep. Then the anger in the voices I heard changed—grew almost…*malevolent*.”

“What were they saying?”

“It had something to do with cheating.”

“Your mom thought your dad was cheating?”

“I think so, but he seemed to be accusing her, too. They were talking about our kindergarten teacher.”

“Mr. Judd.”

Sloane nodded and dipped her spoon in her bowl to at least make an attempt to eat the soup Paige had been kind enough to prepare.

“He was young and good-looking, but so was your father.”

“Still, my dad must’ve been jealous. He said my mother was helping out in my class because she wanted to be around Brian Judd.”

“Did you ever see anything strange going on between Mr. Judd and your mother?”

“Never. She tried to tell my father that, but he wouldn’t listen. The yelling got louder. I remember covering my ears, wishing they'd stop." She stared at the soup in her spoon without really seeing it.

"And then?"

"And then I climbed out of bed and crept to the top of the stairs."

Paige held her drink around the rim, letting it dangle. "Did you see anything?"

"Not from that vantage point. But I could when I went down a few steps. My father had a hold of my mother and was shaking her. She noticed me first. When her eyes widened, he turned, jerked his head toward the stairs and shouted, 'Get back in bed. Now!' I desperately wanted to go to my mother instead, but I was so afraid of him I ran back to my room."

"Did you stay in your room or did you sneak out again?"

Sloane forced herself to swallow the bite of soup. She hadn't had anything to eat since the bagel and coffee she'd had for breakfast, but she could hardly taste it. "I was too frightened to do anything else. I lay in my bed, staring at the darkness, listening to the sound of my own breathing while they continued to argue."

"How'd it end?"

"With a crash and a thud. Silence after that. I held my breath and waited, but I heard nothing, no voices. Just someone moving around the house."

"Your father?"

Sloane brought up another bite of soup. "I can't be sure. The back door opened and closed several times. After a few minutes, I heard someone on the stairs."

"But you don't know who it was?"

"My father, I think. But I squeezed my eyes closed as

soon as those footsteps approached my room and pretended to be asleep as my door creaked open."

"Someone looked in at you?"

"Yes. Whoever it was paused in the opening for what seemed like a very long time, but I didn't dare move, didn't dare crack open my eyes until they went away."

"What happened after that?"

"Not much. More sounds, a lot of movement in the house, doors opening, that sort of thing."

Paige slid to the edge of her seat. "The movement of two people or one?"

"I couldn't tell. There was no more shouting, no more talking. Before long, a car engine started outside, and I got the feeling I was alone in the house."

"Your brother was spending the night with Staley Hicks, right?"

It didn't surprise Sloane that Paige would remember that detail. Several things about the night Clara went missing were common knowledge, and that was one of them. "Yes. I wished I could go to him in his room, but I remembered he wasn't home. The silence stretched and stretched. I can't say for how long because the next thing I knew, the sun was streaming through my window."

"You'd fallen asleep."

"Must have."

Paige added some more tortilla strips to her soup. "Who came to get you up for school?"

"No one. This happened on a Friday night. That's why Randy was allowed to sleep over."

"Of course. That makes sense."

"I waited, wondering if I'd hear my mother in the kitchen. When I didn't, I got up and went into my parents' bedroom, but it was empty. I found my father in the kitchen, sitting at the table drinking a cup of coffee. He had this far-off look on his face until he saw me, and when he realized I was there… It's hard to put into words." She nibbled at her bottom lip, staring past Paige, remembering. "His eyes narrowed as though I'd done something wrong. He asked me what I was doing up so early, and I told him I wanted to watch cartoons. I thought he was going to send me back to bed, thought he was still mad from the night before. But then he shoved himself to his feet, walked into the living room and turned on the TV."

"He didn't say anything about your mother?"

"Not a word. He sat on the couch behind me—I was on the floor—and fell asleep almost right away. It wasn't until I started getting hungry that I began to search more earnestly for my mother. He must've heard me calling for her, because he woke up, told me to be quiet, that she was gone, and lumbered into the kitchen to get me a bowl of cereal."

"'She's gone'? That's all he said?"

"I asked when she'd be back, and he said he didn't know."

"Are you sure you heard a car that night before you fell asleep? Because it's always been my understanding she didn't take the car. She left on foot. I don't know where I got that, because you would never talk about it, but it's the mental picture I've always carried around with me—of your mother, walking down a dark and lonely street at night."

"I have no idea where you heard it. Maybe from your parents. I'm sure people talked. No one double-checked my dad's story—not that I know of—but some of the details must've circulated through town. He claims she walked away, that when he calmed down he tried to go after her, but she was gone."

"Which suggests…what? Someone picked her up?"

"That's what he claims to believe."

"What do *you* believe?" She lowered her voice. "Don't tell me you think the car you heard was your father getting rid of her body…"

"I hate to even acknowledge that possibility, but I've always wondered." Sloane told herself not to divulge any more, but the words tumbled out in spite of that—maybe because she didn't want to seem like a terrible daughter for doubting her own father. "And I'm not the only one who suspects him."

Paige's eyebrows shot up.

Sloane had only ever opened up to Clyde. He wasn't connected to any of the primary players in this drama, which made it easier for her to voice her fears. Admitting what she suspected to Paige, who knew her father and brother and everyone else in town, felt like sacrilege. But the truth was the truth, and she had to come to terms with it. "Today someone told me they saw Dad drive past that night."

"Who?"

Sloane purposely chose the wrong pronoun to protect Vickie. "I can't say. I told him I wouldn't. And that's not the point. The point is that my father wasn't in his car, like we might imagine. He was in his truck—and he was towing the boat."

Paige's jaw dropped. "Holy shit! He wouldn't bother to hook up the boat unless…"

"Unless?" Somehow it was easier for Sloane to let Paige draw the obvious conclusion.

"He was going to the river. But why would he be

going there so late and right after your mother had stormed off?"

Sloane said nothing.

"Oh God! That's where he dumped her body—in the water somewhere!"

They stared at each other for several long seconds. Then Paige pushed her mostly untouched bowl off to the side. "Sloane, I'm scared for you," she said. "You realize it's been twenty-three years. Are you *sure* you want to dig all of this up?"

Sloane moved her bowl to the side, too, so she wouldn't spill it as she leaned forward. "What would you do if it was *your* mother?"

Paige pursed her lips in a "you got me" expression.

"I've tried to let it go," Sloane said. "Tried to come to terms with not knowing. But I can't. If he killed her, she deserves justice, and I'm the only one who can give it to her. I've sort of always known I'd have to deal with this eventually."

"Even though you'll be making an enemy of your entire family? You might need them one day!"

"When do you not need your family? I need them *now*, Paige. But I can't live a lie. Whatever happened wasn't as my father said, so I have to do something about it."

Paige seemed to mull that over as she took another drink of her wine. "What about your brother? Is there any chance you could get him to listen to you? To work with you to uncover the truth?"

"I haven't tried to speak to him in so long I can't be sure, but I doubt it. It's not as if he's ever reached out to me, even though he could've found me on social media as easily as you did."

After putting down her glass, Paige reached across the table to take Sloane's hand. "I can't imagine how terrible it would be to think you can't trust your own father, and that you can't lean on your only sibling, especially when you don't have a mother."

"That's why you meant so much to me growing up," Sloane said. "That's why it was hard for me to leave you. I was running away—from all of it, from everything associated with this place. But I couldn't keep running. I'm back to find out what happened to my mother, but also here to see if there's any way we can rebuild our relationship." Despite her professional success, and even though she did have Clyde, Sloane had felt so isolated and alone—without root or branch, as the saying went—in New York.

"Then I'm glad I reached out," Paige said. "Because I feel the same. I've missed you *so* much."

A noise at the door caused Sloane to turn and Paige to look up as Trevor came barreling into the house. "Look at this, Mom! Dad bought me a new baseball cap! Isn't it cool?"

"A new Rangers hat," she said drily. "How many of those do you have now?"

"Three. But none like this one."

"I see. That's awesome, then."

Sloane hoped he couldn't hear the sarcasm in his mother's voice. He seemed so much happier than she'd expected after hearing about his friend Spaulding.

"Are you two already done for the night?" Paige asked her son.

"Not yet. Dad promised he'd come in and check out my new video game before he went home."

Paige opened her mouth as though she would protest,

but Trevor was so excited he was already hurrying over to set up his gaming console. And the next thing Sloane knew, Micah was standing in the doorway.

CHAPTER SEVEN

Sloane felt Micah's presence in every fiber of her being. He didn't say much; he focused exclusively on Trevor, talked only about the game, how to work it, what the cheats were, how good Trevor was getting at playing. Even when Paige broke in to offer them both a bowl of soup—Micah's "favorite" soup—Trevor wasn't the only one to say he was full. Micah politely declined and immediately returned his attention to his son and the TV.

Sloane envied him his ability to function so capably and indifferently; she could barely breathe. It felt like he'd sucked all the air out of the room. She could tell Paige was keeping a close eye on her, so she was careful not to glance over at him, but she couldn't help straining to hear what he said, no matter how mundane the comment. His voice was so much deeper than it'd been in high school. If he ever decided that he didn't like being a cop, he could succeed in radio.

She and Paige made small talk while they finished eating. Sloane couldn't even taste her food. She managed to get most of it down, but the end of the meal came as a relief. Soon she'd be able to go to her room, where she could be alone, and she couldn't wait for the reprieve. Although she managed to answer correctly whenever Paige asked her a question, her mind drifted. Not only was she hanging on every word Micah said, she couldn't help thinking about the romantic relationships she'd had since leaving Millcreek.

More than a few men had come into her life over the past decade. Some, at least by most people's standards, would've been "great catches": fellow models, movie stars, musicians, producers, politicians, professional athletes and other wealthy, accomplished and interesting people. The most aggressive hadn't even met her before showing interest. They'd put out feelers, looking for her contact information after seeing her in an ad or on the cover of a magazine. Such inquiries typically came through Clyde, since he'd been her agent.

But all the men she'd dated in New York had one thing in common: they'd left Sloane feeling restless and ambivalent. No doubt that was partly where she'd gotten her reputation as an ice queen. Derrick Kelly, a professional hockey player and the last man to pursue her, had told her that nothing he did seemed capable of piercing her cool reserve, that he was looking for something a bit warmer when he came from the rink. He worked in a cold place; he didn't want to sleep in one, too.

Sadly, she'd had to tell him that probably wouldn't change. She hadn't heard from him since and had felt more relief than regret, indicating she shouldn't have been with him as long as she had been, anyway, which was about six months.

After ten years of shoving the past into a small corner of her brain, refusing to think about it or remember, the intense emotion bubbling up from someplace deep inside her wasn't only a sudden change, it was overwhelming.

"Should we take our dessert out back?" Paige asked as they finished up in the kitchen.

Sloane understood that her former best friend was weighing her every expression, every word, even the occasional hesitation, searching for meaning where there may or may not be any. Paige wanted to see if Sloane would rather stay in the house, where she'd be closer to Micah. She was transparent in that regard, so Sloane forced a smile and agreed to go outside. "Why not? The weather is perfect."

Paige poured them each another glass of wine while Sloane cut the cake. But before they could walk out of the house, a determined knock sounded at the door.

At almost ten o'clock, it was late for visitors, even on a weekend. Micah and Trevor must've heard the knock, too, but they didn't respond. They were too caught up in the game.

With a sigh, Paige put down the wineglasses she'd picked up from the counter. "Just when I thought we were safe from the outside world," she muttered and went to see who it was.

While she was gone, Sloane dropped her head back and tried to steady her nerves. She had another hour or so of chitchat to get through with Paige. She hoped Micah wouldn't stay that long, though. It was so much easier when he wasn't around. She needed more time to acclimate to Millcreek before coping with the residual feelings she had for him.

She'd just taken a big gulp of her wine, hoping that might help her unwind, when Paige called her name.

Sloane nearly broke the glass she set it down so abruptly. She'd expected to have a minute or two to pull herself together. Instead, she was being summoned to the door. "Yes?" she called, turning toward the sound.

Paige's voice came back to her. "It's your brother."

Pa-rump, pa-rump, pa-rump. Sloane heard three distinct heartbeats echo in her ears before she could bring herself to answer. *Randy.* She didn't know what to expect of him or their relationship. He hadn't done anything wrong, not to their mother, at any rate. He'd merely sided with their father, had somehow managed to maintain the kind of blind faith that'd proved so difficult for her.

But it was easier for him. He hadn't been there that night. He hadn't heard the same sounds or seen their father sitting so empty-eyed and haggard at the kitchen table the following morning, looking like some vagabond who'd wandered in. Neither had Randy experienced the coldness she'd sensed in Ed when he'd sent her back to bed during the night.

By the time Randy had returned, almost two days had passed since their father had asked Staley's parents if Randy could stay over another night. He'd also pawned Sloane off on the man's wife who managed his car dealership the Saturday their mother "left." Although Sloane had never stayed with Lee Martin's family before and had been miserable in such unfamiliar surroundings—somehow sensing, as she did, that her whole life had changed in one night, and not for the better—her father had insisted that he needed to try to find her mother so he could "talk some sense into her" and turned a deaf ear to her entreaties to go with him.

After what she'd learned from Vickie Winters, Sloane wondered if he'd merely been covering his tracks. Two days would give him plenty of time to get rid of any evidence that might contradict his story—like the hole in the wall that'd been there Saturday morning but was patched by the time Sloane returned Sunday night, and the broken lamp that'd been cleaned up and disposed of, a new, almost identical lamp put in its place.

"Sloane?" Paige appeared at the opening to the kitchen. "Did you hear me?"

She swallowed with some difficulty but nodded. "Yeah. I'm coming."

Paige stepped close enough to whisper, "Should I tell him you'd rather talk another day?"

Would that make it any easier? They didn't agree on their father. She doubted they ever would. If Randy had changed his mind, if he was any more open to having a relationship with her, he would've reached out while she was in New York, wouldn't he? So she'd be a fool to think more time would help.

"No." Straightening her spine, she smiled as best she could and moved past her former best friend, who encouraged her with a squeeze to the arm.

When she entered the living room, she thought she saw Micah glance back at her. But that impression registered only a split second before she came face-to-face with her brother and everything else fell away.

"Can I speak with you?" Randy asked tightly and indicated the door, asking her to join him outside.

He'd changed. He was five years older than she was,

so he'd been twenty-three, much more of a man than Micah, when she left. For the most part, he'd already filled out by then, but now he had a close-cropped beard she'd never seen him wear, a set of fine lines forming in the corners of his eyes and around his mouth and fifty or sixty pounds he could do without. He was also wearing a wedding band. Paige had told her he was married and had a three-year-old girl named Misty, but Sloane tried not to think of that. It was difficult enough not being part of *his* life. To know she was an aunt and had never even met her niece or her sister-in-law was almost unbearable.

He waited for her to go past him. Then he stepped into the puddle of the porch light with her. "So you're back," he said as he pulled the door and it clicked shut behind him.

"Yes." That simple word sounded strangled even to her ears. "Did Guy Prinley's wife tell you, too? Or did that come from our father?"

"Does it matter who told me? Did you think I wouldn't hear?"

"No." She pressed her back up to the porch railing, hoping to put what little space there was between them. "Not here in Millcreek."

He studied her closely. "What is it you want, Sloane?"

"Excuse me?"

"You heard me. *Why* are you here?"

Animosity rolled off him in waves, putting a knot in the pit of her stomach. He hadn't come because he wanted to see her, wanted to catch up with his baby sister. He was angry that she'd returned. "I can't come home?"

"You have no reason to. You must have made plenty

of money with as successful as you've been. You can live anywhere."

Struggling to stand strong despite the negative sentiment, she lifted her chin. "I got the message that I'm not welcome when Dad told the Prinleys not to rent me the house, Randy. You don't need to make it any clearer."

He stepped forward. "Then maybe I need to make something else clear. I will *not* stand by and let you ruin our father or his good name out of spite."

"That's what you think my motivation is? *Spite?* You're assuming this is an act of *vengeance*?"

"What else could it be? He wasn't a perfect father. I'll grant you that. He can be...aloof, at times. Strict, especially with you. But you were a girl."

"Which means he should've been harder on me than you?"

"He was just trying to protect you, for God's sake. He did the best he could."

Sloane braced herself by putting her hands on the railing behind her. "If he has nothing to hide, you have nothing to worry about."

"What does that mean?"

"You know what it means!"

"Then you *are* going to drag up the past." He raked his fingers through his hair, causing it to stand up in front. "God, don't you see what that will do?"

"Maybe it'll enable me to find peace, at last! The doubt and suspicion that has nearly eaten me alive has never been significant to you, but—"

"That's where you're wrong!" he broke in. "I've tried and tried to tell you to leave it alone, to put it behind you and carry on, because I know that things will only be worse if you don't!"

"I can't simply forget what I saw and heard that night, Randy!"

"What you saw and heard was almost nothing. Certainly not enough to destroy a man's life. You were only five years old. You were a young, frightened girl, and it's been more than two decades since Mom left. Memories become distorted with time, Sloane. That's a proven fact, and it means what you remember might not have happened the way you think it did!"

"Maybe I'm not remembering everything perfectly. I *hope* I'm not. I don't want to be right. But that doesn't mean I can continue to ignore the fact that we know little to nothing about our mother's disappearance."

"We have the word of our father. That should count for something."

"Don't you realize there are other men out there who have killed their wives, who come up with a plausible-sounding story to cover up such a terrible act? How can you be so convinced our father isn't one of them?"

"He has a track record of living a decent life, being a good parent—at least as good as he could be, given his own temperament and limitations. He isn't some drug abuser or…or ex-con!"

"That's why I've had such a hard time stepping forward! He isn't a likely culprit. I agree. And yet…"

"*And yet?* What else could matter in light of that?"

"There are too many unanswered questions—which you seem perfectly willing to ignore *indefinitely*."

"Because, unlike you, I love him!"

"I love him, too!" she cried. "That's what makes this whole thing so gut-wrenching."

"If it's so gut-wrenching, back away. Let it go."

"I can't. Don't you understand? I'm not the only one

who suspects he's not telling the truth. There are other people out there who…who have had the same question in their minds for all these years."

"Who?"

"I can't say right now."

"That's convenient!"

"It's not *convenient*, it's the way things are. I'm not lying. He's the mayor. Everyone's afraid to take him on."

He shook his head. "You do him such a great injustice."

"What, he's too fine a man to question?"

"On *this* level? Yes."

"I was *there* that night, Randy."

"So? Like I said, you were five. What if you're wrong? Do you think Dad will ever be able to forgive you for accusing him of murder? And not just any murder—of murdering the woman he married? The mother of his children? Do you think *I* will?"

"What if I'm right?" she countered. "Have you ever thought about that? What if he did kill her? What then? You don't care?"

"I don't see any reason to even consider the possibility. He told us what happened."

"When?"

He waved a dismissive hand. "We've heard bits and pieces over the years."

And yet their father had never been willing to speak about the incident openly and honestly. He'd always answered any questions they'd had with short, clipped sentences, which revealed almost nothing. "Sometimes we have to face harsh truths. You can't stick your head in the sand and assume everyone around you speaks only the truth."

His jaw hardened. "You're crazy! Our mother *abandoned* us! That's the harsh truth *you're* trying to avoid—and you're willing to risk sending our father to prison in order to achieve it. Why? How will tainting Dad's reputation or getting him embroiled in a police investigation help you or me or anyone else?"

"Our mother deserves justice!"

"And our father deserves more thanks than to have his daughter return to town only because she's bent on destroying him."

Sloane felt those words like a cup of cold water in the face. She gaped at her brother. "You don't know or care about me at all," she said. "And you don't care about the truth. You're only worried about yourself and how this might embarrass you or harm your status in this town." Tingling with hurt and anger, she tried to step around him so she could go back into the house, but he caught her by the arm.

"Don't you dare walk away from me. We're not finished yet."

"We're not finished because I won't agree to do what you want—which is essentially *nothing*."

She struggled to wriggle out of his grasp, but he wouldn't let go. He grabbed her other arm, too, his fingers biting so deeply into her flesh she was convinced he'd leave bruises. "You need to go back to New York or wherever else you live. *Tomorrow*. You have no reason to stay."

She winced beneath the lash of those words. As much as she'd been prepared for the worst, a part of her had still been hoping for the best. "You're hurting me," she ground out. "Let go."

"Tell me you're leaving town," he said, giving her a little shake.

"You have no right to lay a hand on me." She jerked back, hard, and managed to break his grasp.

He hadn't expected her to be that forceful, but her escape made him angrier. She understood just *how* angry when she turned to go and, with a muttered, "You stupid bitch!" he shoved her from behind, sending her headfirst into the front door.

Sloane struck the thick wooden panel so hard white streaks of light burst across her vision and she nearly fell. She hadn't quite righted herself when the door swung open and Micah filled the opening, wearing a dark glower.

"It's time for you to go," he said to Randy, his voice velvet over steel.

Slightly disoriented, Sloane touched the knot forming on her forehead. She staggered between the two men and tried to say something that didn't quite reach her lips, but dazed as she was, she could discern the expression of regret and then frustration that flitted across her brother's face. He hadn't meant to hurt her. He just didn't know his own strength.

At least, that was what she told herself.

"This isn't what it looks like, Micah," Randy said. "You have no business getting involved. Go back inside and let me finish talking to my sister. We'll work it out between us."

"Like you were working it out a moment ago?" Micah responded. "We could hear you shouting from inside the living room—and now this." He gestured to Sloane's injury, but Randy merely sneered.

"That was an accident. I didn't mean to push her so hard. She'll be fine."

Micah seemed tense. He was obviously reluctant to get involved, but the violence gave him little choice. He was a police officer, after all. "She doesn't look fine to me," he said.

"I'm okay." Sloane just wanted the conflict to be over, wanted to go inside and hide away in her room so she could sort out how this encounter had gone bad so quickly. She'd merely been holding her ground, trying to let her brother know that she wasn't going to back off simply because he didn't like what she was doing.

She hadn't expected him to be quite as adamant as he was.

She'd also hoped he'd missed her the way she'd missed him, and that love would soften his heart enough to make him listen to her and maybe commiserate a little even if he couldn't agree. She was his baby sister!

The men ignored her. They reminded her of two rams, locking horns. Nostrils flaring, muscles tense, they were hyperaware and particularly watchful of each other.

"We've always gotten along, Micah," Randy said, his statement coming off like a warning or threat of sorts. "I'd hate to see that change."

Sloane was tempted to reach out to her brother, to beg him to leave without causing any more trouble. She wasn't Micah's problem. He shouldn't have to do this. But she was slightly afraid of Randy, which was new to her and something she'd never expected. She'd known their relationship might be strained, but she'd never dreamed his disappointment and resentment would manifest itself like it had.

Micah's gaze never strayed from Randy's face. "Then you'd better leave."

"Fuck you," Randy snapped and stalked down the walkway to his truck.

Sloane was trembling by the time he peeled away from the curb. "I—I'm sorry," she mumbled to Micah and to Paige, who'd joined Micah at the door as Randy was walking away. "I didn't mean to bring trouble here, or to have something like this happen in front of Trevor. I signed the lease for my own place today." Paige already knew she'd found a place so Sloane stated it mostly for Micah's sake. "I should be able to take possession after the weekend."

Micah didn't say anything. He pivoted and went back inside. It was Paige who stepped out and pulled her into a hug. "I have a bad feeling about what you're doing," she whispered, as though stating it out loud would only make the situation worse.

Sloane did, too. But she'd made up her mind.

There was no turning back.

CHAPTER EIGHT

Micah couldn't forget the encounter he'd just had with Randy McBride. He'd never been a huge fan of Randy's. He was known around town to be a bit of a hothead, someone who felt he deserved more consideration than other people, probably because, thanks to who his father was, he usually got it. But Micah had never had any trouble with him personally.

Until now.

He played a few more video games with Trevor, trying to stay long enough to reestablish a sense of calm, but he was having trouble concentrating and had been ever since he arrived. After they'd gotten back from pizza, when Trevor had insisted he come in and check out the new game, Micah had known Sloane would be there. Her car was parked out front. But Trevor had been having such a rough time lately that Micah hadn't been willing to tell him no, which meant overlooking his own discomfort.

He'd planned to ignore Sloane, to do what he felt he should for his son and then get the hell out of there. But he couldn't turn a deaf ear to the raised voices he'd heard out on the porch or the sickening thud that'd caused the door to reverberate. Lord knew Micah wasn't excited to have Sloane in Millcreek, either. The sight of her yanked him back ten years, made him remember what it'd felt like to be so innocent that he'd fallen in love without the slightest comprehension of the devastation it could bring. She was a reminder of that devastation, of the hell he'd been through with his difficult marriage and subsequent divorce. He was *still* battling the guilt he felt over letting his son down because he couldn't love Paige enough to make her whole and happy. He didn't want anything to do with the memories Sloane evoked, especially now, when he was trying so hard to put it all behind him and get back on his feet.

But it was a free country. She had the right to move to town if she wanted and, as a police officer, he would defend that right.

He allowed himself another glance at the back window. Paige and Sloane were sitting outside. He could see Sloane rubbing the bump on her forehead. She'd hit the door hard. He couldn't believe Randy would be bold enough—or impulsive enough—to push her like that, especially when there were people nearby. What if her brother had waited to visit her until she'd moved into her rental house and was alone, with no one to intervene? How would that encounter have ended?

"Dad! You just *died*!" Trevor said with a groan. "Didn't you see that drone coming at you?"

Micah mumbled that he hadn't seen the drone and waited for his avatar to rejuvenate.

When he got killed again before he could even move the damn thing, Trevor laughed. "Man, you suck at this game."

"I'm tired tonight," Micah mumbled, but that wasn't true. He was bursting with adrenaline from his encounter with Randy, still wanted to punch the dude for acting like such a bully. Even worse, he was filled with an awareness he hadn't felt in a long while—sexual awareness. He couldn't help the hormones that flooded his body whenever Sloane was around, couldn't turn that off, which felt so defeating. After the past ten years, he'd assumed he'd beaten most of what he'd felt for her out of his heart and his brain.

His brain remembered. His heart was more stubborn.

He played for another fifteen minutes. When they couldn't get past the second level—a level Trevor insisted should be "easy"—because he couldn't keep up his end, Micah put down the controller. "That's enough for tonight. You'd better get in bed."

"What? No! Don't quit!" Trevor said. "I hardly ever get to play with you."

Micah checked his watch. "But it's getting late. We'll have to play another time. We don't want to wear out my welcome, do we?"

"You're not wearing out your welcome! Mom's busy."

"Which is why I should make you turn this off so she can relax with her friend and won't need to worry about you."

"*Her* friend? Isn't Sloane your friend, too?"

Micah cocked an eyebrow at him. "Do you mean Ms. McBride?"

"She told me I can call her Sloane."

"She did, did she?"

"Yeah. She's really nice. I can't believe her brother did that to her. You can't push people."

"That's true."

"So isn't he going to get in trouble?"

"He will if he does it again." Micah didn't care to explain that there wasn't a lot he could do for a shove like that, which could be construed as somewhat of an accident or unintended overreaction, especially given the fact that Randy was the mayor's son. There was no such thing as a lost recess for an adult.

And yet the next encounter could leave Sloane far more seriously injured.

"Just one more game!" Trevor pleaded.

"No more games," Micah clarified.

Trevor dragged his feet as he snapped off the console. "O-kay..." he said, drawing out the word as much as possible to reveal his disappointment.

It would've been easy to give in. Micah felt so bad for being the reason their family was no longer a complete unit that he tended to overindulge Trevor. But he knew that wasn't what was best for his son and was hoping to avoid such a common pitfall.

He tousled Trevor's hair. "You're okay now, right?"

"You mean about Spaulding? No. I can't believe he's taking Jeremy Schwimmer! Last week he told me he didn't even want Jeremy to come to his birthday party."

"Then it'll be a long weekend at Disneyland, and he might regret he didn't invite you, but in order to be a good friend you need to let him have other friends, too. You understand?"

Trevor hesitated. He wasn't quite ready to admit that.

Micah dipped his head to catch his son's gaze. "*Do* you understand?"

"I guess," he said grudgingly.

"So you'll let it go? You won't be mad at him on Monday?"

"Yeah, I'll let it go. But I'm not going to invite him to come along the next time *I* get to do something fun," he added in a sulky voice.

"That's okay," Micah said with a chuckle. "At that point, it'll be your choice, and it'll be his turn to respect it."

The slider opened and Paige and Sloane carried their empty dishes into the house.

"I'm taking off," he told his ex. "Thanks for letting me hang with Trevor tonight."

"Of course." Her lips curved into a warm smile, one that seemed engineered to cause Sloane to assume she'd been much friendlier during and after the divorce than she really had. She was putting on an act. He knew her well enough to understand that she was a master manipulator. But what was her game now?

He hoped to hell whatever it was had nothing to do with him.

Micah bent to hug Trevor. "Night, kid."

"Bye, Dad," he said and trailed Micah to the door, obviously reluctant to let him go.

Sloane didn't say anything to him, and he didn't say anything to her as he walked out. He nodded in Paige's general direction, which could've been interpreted as a nod to both of them.

But long after he returned home, forced himself to expend all his excess energy unpacking a portion of the boxes piled up in his living room and climbed into bed, he couldn't sleep. He kept thinking about the concern Paige had shown Sloane following the confrontation with Randy. Right after Sloane's brother had left, and both women had come into the house, he'd heard Sloane say, "I have no idea how he even knew where to find me! Guy Prinley or his wife must've alerted him to the fact that I was coming to town, but how'd he know I'm staying *here*?"

At which point Paige hadn't mentioned her own trip to city hall. She'd said, "I'm sure he just assumed. We were inseparable as kids. Where else would you stay?"

Once Sloane said good-night to Paige—Trevor was in bed by the time they retired—and went to her room, she closed the door, leaned against it and breathed a huge sigh of relief. Tonight had been difficult in so many ways. Having Micah in the house had brought back the devastation she'd felt after she left, had reopened a wound she'd hoped had healed.

And then there was seeing her brother for the first time since she'd graduated high school.

She fingered the bump on her head. It was tender, and she had a headache. But that was nothing compared to what was going on with her otherwise. Randy's unwavering faith in their father shook her confidence in what she was doing, caused the old self-doubt to spring up again; it was being unsure and unwilling to fully embrace what Ed might've done that had made her want to escape Millcreek in the first place.

She was tempted to drive out of town tomorrow and spend another ten years trying to ignore the past. Maybe her mother's remains would surface eventually and the police would be forced to open an investigation.

But after so long, what were the chances? If she left, she'd only be procrastinating the inevitable, would have to come back and deal with this at some point, because she *wasn't* wrong. What Vickie Winters had told her convinced her of that. And by then it would only be harder to find any evidence that remained. She already had twenty-three years working against her.

She peeled off her clothes and dropped onto the mattress. She didn't have the energy to bother with her nightgown. She wanted to pull up the blankets and pretend she was in her bungalow in the Hamptons, with Clyde still alive in the big house.

"I should've come here while I had you to talk to," she whispered to him.

Paige paced in her bedroom. The effects of the alcohol she'd consumed earlier had worn off, so the buzz was gone. She was glad Sloane was in bed, so she wouldn't have to continue to pretend that Micah's visit hadn't left her feeling empty—no, *desolate*—inside. She'd been like this since the divorce and had no idea how to recover, how to get over him.

He'd tried not to look at Sloane or speak to her tonight. Paige had witnessed the struggle. And although he'd largely maintained his indifference, that it required so much effort was revealing in its own right.

What was it about Sloane that made her so much better than Paige? Sure, Sloane was beautiful, more beautiful than most women. Paige knew she couldn't compete there, but that couldn't be all Micah cared about. Paige was willing to do *anything* for him. Besides, she was the mother of his son, whom he adored. Why couldn't he accept *her* love, crave being with her the way she craved being with him?

She'd asked herself that question so many times it had become a constant echo, not only in her head but in her soul.

Tonight's going to be another long night, she thought as she opened the drapes and peered out the window, into the backyard. Part of her hoped that Randy would come back and *really* punish Sloane—beat her to a pulp or at least permanently mar that gorgeous face so she'd be less of a temptation to Micah. Paige felt so much hatred at times. She couldn't believe she was capable of such negative emotion. But the other part of her, the part that loved Sloane, even admired her, felt instantly guilty. What kind of a woman was she becoming?

Whatever the answer to that question, she had Micah to blame. It made her crazy to think he might never come back to her. God, she missed him—missed cuddling up to him while he slept, missed seeing the beauty of his tall, muscular body as he stepped out of the shower, missed the envious glances she'd received from other women when they went to dinner or to a movie. But most of all, she missed making love. She hadn't been with anyone since, and twelve months was beginning to feel like an eternity.

She stepped away from the window, listening to the sounds in the house. Silence. Everyone was asleep. Still, she tiptoed when she moved to the door and attempted to turn the lock without making the characteristic click. Then she crossed to her nightstand and withdrew the vibrator she'd purchased several months ago. It wouldn't be as fulfilling, but if she turned off the lights and closed her eyes, she could pretend it was Micah.

As soon as she woke up the following morning, Sloane checked her phone for texts and voice mails. She was dying to hear back on the house, but Leigh Coleman hadn't sent her any type of confirmation.

Deflated, she dropped her phone on the bed beside her. "Shit." Her family was probably trying to block her from getting that house, too. She attempted to tell herself they had no idea which property she might be making a run at, but, with only a small amount of effort, they could figure it out. All they had to do was call on the houses that were available, exactly as she'd done.

Would Leigh tell Ed she'd applied for the River Bottoms mansion? Sloane hadn't mentioned it was a secret, hadn't wanted to alert Leigh that there might be a problem.

With a groan, she sat up. Her head hurt from when she'd plowed into the front door, and she was afraid the knot on her forehead was even bigger.

She'd find out when she went to the bathroom, but she wanted to make sure she didn't get in Trevor's way, if he was getting up, too. So she sat there, listening to see if anyone else was moving around while scrolling through some of her final texts with Clyde. He'd been in the main house and she'd been in her bungalow, trying to get a bit of cleaning done before she took him to yet another appointment when they'd had the exchange.

They're offering twice your normal rate.

I don't care. I'm on hiatus, remember?

You're not on hiatus. You're committing professional suicide by refusing to work while I'm sick. I don't expect you to take me to every doctor's appointment, especially now that I practically live at the hospital. It's too much. Call one of my kids. Have someone else stand in.

She'd already called his kids. She'd actually been interested in taking the job he was encouraging her to take. It was for Badgley Mischka. She admired many of their designs, but she'd turned down the offer because she felt Clyde needed her and another model could handle the shoot.

I want to be with you while I can.

I don't have long, Sloane.

That could be true. That's why I'm going to drive you today.

I'm saying you need to let go sooner or later. It might as well be now.

Let go? I will never let go of you.

I love you as much as my real daughters. I hope you know that.

Her eyes began to burn. Then her vision blurred as tears welled up. She'd saved that text because it was the only time Clyde had ever expressed his feelings toward her in words. He was the type who showed how he felt instead, which was what made him so trustworthy, dependable and safe. Her real father did the opposite: he might say the words, and even then very rarely, but there was no real depth of feeling there. So many times growing up she'd wondered if the man he pretended to be was only a facade.

Leaving Millcreek had been vital for her, the best thing she'd ever done. If she hadn't broken away, she never would've known what the love of a father felt like. But that meant she'd had to give up Micah. And now that Clyde was gone, she had to deal with the mess she'd left behind, not only with her former boyfriend but with her father and brother, too.

Since she hadn't heard anything indicating Trevor was up, she slipped into the bathroom. When she came out, Paige's door was still closed. Apparently, Paige and Trevor were sleeping in. Sloane considered going back to bed herself, but she figured she might as well get started on what she'd come to Millcreek to do. Why waste any time? The sooner she satisfied the questions she had about her mother, the sooner she could move on to friendlier climes.

She was about to grab her robe and her makeup bag so that she could go back into the bathroom and get showered for the day when she heard a *ping*. She'd received a text.

Hoping for good news, she grabbed her phone off the bed. *Hold out*, she silently admonished the leasing agent. *Don't let those bastards scare you away from letting me have the house.*

But the message wasn't from Leigh. It was from a number she didn't recognize.

It's Micah. Rich Coleman just called me. You might not remember him, but he went to high school with us, was a year younger. He's married to Leigh Coleman now. Said your father called the owner of the house and convinced him to reject your application.

"No!" she whispered as she read those words.

Why would Rich call you and not me? Leigh has my number.

Leigh gave your number to Rich, who gave your number to me. Neither one of them wanted to be the one to rat out your father.

They left that up to you? I guess they don't know how badly you hate me now. Or maybe they do and thought you'd enjoy delivering the bad news.

I'm not taking any pleasure in this, Sloane. Just passing along the word. Rich doesn't want any trouble with your father. He called me to see if they should tell you your application was refused without an explanation so you didn't have to know your own father is out there, working against you.

I already know he is.

Which is why I decided to be so transparent. This shows he's not going to back down. I think that's important for you to know.

Yeah, well, neither will I.

If her father made it impossible for her to get a house in Millcreek, she'd move into the only motel in town, The Wagon Wheel, and pay by the night. It wasn't the kind of place she cared to live in, but she wouldn't let her family—or Micah, for that matter—chase her away. Last night, Randy had hurt her feelings more than he'd hurt her head, but the more she thought about his behavior, the more indignant she became.

How dare he show up and act like such an ass? She had as much right to be in Millcreek as he did. He and Ed didn't own the whole town.

You need to think carefully about staying, Micah wrote.

I already have.

Your father is a powerful man here.

You want me to leave, too.

No response.

Thanks for that, old friend.

We were never friends, Sloane. But I am trying to do you a favor.

By telling me to beat it.

If that's how you want to put it.

Thanks, but I'm not going. Not yet.

Because...

Because I plan to find out what happened to my mother whether my father likes it or not.

Shit. I thought that must be what's going on. You're asking for trouble.

Oh well. Consider me warned. You don't have to look out for me anymore. I understand what I'm up against. I've got it from here.

I don't think you do, or...

What? she wrote when he ended with ellipses and didn't immediately add anything more.

Or you wouldn't be staying where you're staying, came his belated response.

What are you talking about? Paige was my best friend.

She was also my wife. Think about it.

She frowned as she considered his last text. He was trying to confirm what her gut had been telling her since she arrived. Paige wanted to be friends again, but jealousy made true friendship impossible—at least right now, while the divorce was still fresh. Got it. I'll make other arrangements.

She told herself to delete their exchange as well as his number. He obviously didn't want anything to do with her. *You really screwed up my life*, he'd said.

But she sat there for over fifteen minutes and couldn't

bring herself to hit the delete button. She actually did the opposite and added him to her contacts. Although she promised herself she'd never call him, somehow she found it comforting having him back in her phone.

CHAPTER NINE

When Sloane finished packing and came out of the bedroom, she found Paige sitting at the dining room table in her robe, sipping a cup of coffee while reading on her phone. Sloane had heard her get up, had heard Trevor turn on the TV, too. He glanced over as she moved past him with her bags, but he didn't say anything. He was too engrossed in his movie.

"You're leaving?" Paige said. "You got the house?"

Sloane set her luggage in the entryway. "Sadly, no."

The chair squeaked as Paige scooted away from the table. "So where are you going?"

"Since my father and brother are acting up, I figure I'd better get out of here. I wouldn't want there to be any more trouble, especially with Trevor around."

"You're expecting it to get *worse*?"

"Weren't you the one who was worried about that last night?"

"Yes, but somehow, now that he's gone and that bump on your head looks a little better, expecting the worst seems overly dramatic."

"Maybe it is, but I can promise it won't get any *better*. The battle lines have been drawn, you know?"

Paige got up and walked over. "But you didn't get the house, so what are your other options? You're not going back to New York..."

"No."

"Will you base out of Dallas or what?"

"I won't do that, either. I'm not leaving Millcreek. It'll be too hard to drive back and forth all the time." She needed to become part of the community again, to get people to open up to her. They wouldn't do that if they didn't feel they could trust her.

"So where are you going?"

"To the motel."

Her forehead crumpled. "What motel?"

"The Wagon Wheel."

"But that's a dump! Nothing like the places you're probably used to staying."

"It's not luxurious, but it's clean, and they offer free breakfast." She wiggled her eyebrows as though she considered that an appealing amenity.

"That might be okay for a day or two, but I can't see you staying there indefinitely."

"It's just a stopgap. Maybe I'll buy a house." She winked. "Bet my dad wouldn't see that coming—at least not in time to block me."

Paige bit her bottom lip. "You should stay here with me. It's got to be more comfortable than moving to The Wagon Wheel."

Sloane lifted a negating hand. "I'm not going to impose on you any longer. I'll be okay at the motel until I can make other arrangements."

"What about your furniture and all the other stuff you sent from New York?"

"I'll leave it in storage until I have somewhere to put it."

Compassion entered her eyes—compassion Sloane hoped was genuine. Micah's text had made her even more leery of Paige than she'd been before. It felt as though she didn't have a single friend left in this town, except Vickie Winters, who was more of an old acquaintance and no one she could lean on for comfort, encouragement or security. Vickie had made it clear she preferred Ed not know of her support.

"I'm sorry, Sloane. What your father and brother are doing completely sucks."

Sloane fought to maintain a determined expression. "They're trying to show me who's boss. But I'm no longer a young girl with no way to fight back. I can hold my own."

Paige didn't seem too encouraged by that statement. "You, against the two grown men who basically run this town?"

"My brother has some hand in running Millcreek? I thought he took over the dealership."

"He did. He took over and expanded. He has money, too, and he takes advantage of whatever perks the city gives him."

"And he gets a lot because of my father. Nepotism at its finest." Sloane imagined she was clinging to a not-so-stable tree limb hanging over a raging river. If she lost her grip, she'd fall and be swept away. "But don't worry, I'll manage."

"Okay." Paige pulled her into a quick embrace. "You'll let me know if you need to come back, though, won't you? Because you'll always be welcome here."

For a brief moment, Sloane wondered if *she* could be the one who was acting weird, jumping at shadows, distrusting *everyone*. Maybe Micah had *purposely* acted to undermine her trust of Paige. If, like her father and brother, he was anxious for her to be gone, that would be smart, because it didn't leave her with a lot of other options, not after being gone for so long. Some of her other friends must still live in town, but which ones? And how would she go about repairing those old relationships? She'd been so caught up in Micah her junior and senior years that she'd drifted away from most of her girlfriends even before she left. She'd tried to hang on to Paige, of course, though their relationship had also been affected.

"I appreciate all you've done. I want you to know that."

"So I let you stay here for a couple of nights, no big deal."

"I'm talking about the meals, too, and the friendship. Coming back to Millcreek hasn't been an easy thing for me."

"I wish it didn't have to be *this* difficult."

"I do, too." If only Micah hadn't married Paige, it would've been easier. At least then she'd still be able to trust her best friend.

"Mom, I'm hungry!" Trevor called out. "When are we going to have breakfast? Can we go out for donuts, or do we have to be at the store soon?"

"Megan Vance is working for me today, so we're free. But no donuts. They aren't healthy. I thought we'd have some eggs and then go over to the park and throw the ball."

He cheered up at that idea, and Paige turned back to Sloane. "Are you sure I can't convince you to stay—at least for the breakfast part of our Saturday plans?"

Sloane couldn't eat. She was too upset about losing the house. "No, I'm good. But thanks."

"Come tell your aunt Sloane goodbye," Paige called out to Trevor.

He turned off the TV and sauntered over. "Goodbye, Aunt Sloane."

Sloane smiled as she rested a hand on his shoulder. "Take good care of your mother, and I hope your father catches on to that game soon, so he'll be more fun to play with."

He grinned at her. "He's usually not *that* bad."

"Yeah, well, he was pretty distracted last night," Paige said.

At the sour note in Paige's voice, Sloane dropped her hand and gathered her bags. It was definitely time to go.

Micah didn't work until evening, when he had patrol duty. He'd probably spend his shift pulling over drunk drivers or answering disturbance complaints from the seedier side of town, since it was a weekend, but at least those duties would keep him occupied. This morning, he was trying to stay busy by fixing a leak under the kitchen sink. Although such repairs typically weren't the tenant's responsibility, Micah's landlord happened to be his mother's cousin and had given him a great deal on rent, so he was trying to help out in return. He didn't want to call up with a complaint before he'd lived in the house for a month, especially since it was such a simple fix.

He was almost finished when the doorbell sounded. Dropping his wrench, he wiped his hands and went to see who it was. He guessed it would be his mother, holding a sack of food she'd made. Yesterday, she'd left a message saying she was worried about him. She didn't think he was getting enough rest or taking the time to eat properly. But he'd told her, many times, that she had no reason to worry. After living at the ranch for the past year, where she'd had unbridled access to him, he was trying to put some space between them, to reclaim his privacy and autonomy. He was also putting off speaking to her because she liked to talk about "how he was recovering" and give him advice on finding another woman. He didn't like to acknowledge that he needed to recover. And he wasn't interested in dating—not even if it meant having sex again after almost a year.

He was so sure he'd find his mother on the stoop he didn't check the peephole before opening the door. He was thinking up an excuse he could give for why he still had so many boxes to unpack. She wouldn't be happy that he wasn't "settling in."

But it wasn't his mother. It was Sloane's father.

"Ed. What a surprise. Did we—did we have a tee time?"

Ed was dressed in a polo shirt and shorts, with the visor he generally wore when they went golfing shading his expensive sunglasses. "I thought we could swing by the course, see if they might be able to squeeze us in." His smile revealed a fortune in implants. Micah had never seen real teeth quite that big or that white. With all the time Ed spent at the gym, the tanning studio and getting his hair dyed, he was doing everything he could to battle the aging process.

Normally, Micah would've jumped at the chance to hit a few balls. He *loved* golf, and Ed was a fairly competitive partner, which made the game a hell of a lot more fun. But the aversion Micah had felt before, when he was in high school and dating Sloane, had reared up again, especially after what Randy had done last night and the call Micah had received from Rich Coleman this morning.

"Can't," Micah said, looking at a slightly distorted view of himself in the mirrored surface of Ed's aviators. "I have too much to do around here. I'm still not entirely moved in."

"Oh, come on. Whatever chores you've got will be waiting for you when we're done. What's a few hours of golf on such a gorgeous day?"

Ed wasn't used to being turned down. Most people jumped at the chance to be included in his inner circle, and Micah could tell he didn't expect today to be any different.

Tightening his grip on the door, so the tension he was feeling wouldn't manifest itself in a more obvious way, Micah cleared his throat. "Really, I can't. I have patrol tonight, so I have to make some progress here at the house. Maybe if I'd had more notice I could've planned around it."

Ed's smile faded. "Well, I wouldn't want to put you behind when you have such important stuff to get done," he said with a touch of sarcasm. "I'm sure Randy can pull away from whatever *he's* got going."

The mention of Randy provoked Micah into speaking up when he probably should've let Ed go. "Did you hear what happened last night?"

"Last night?" Ed blinked, a benign expression on his face. "No. What happened?"

Micah was certain Ed was playing dumb, but he answered, anyway. "I was at Paige's, playing video games with my son, and Randy showed up."

Ed's eyebrows slid above his sunglasses and he spread his hands. "So? He must've wanted a word with his sister. Sloane was there, too, am I right?"

"Yes, she was, but it wasn't just a word. He pushed her so hard she hit the front door, which left a big bump on her forehead."

The mayor's lip curled as if to say, *What's the big deal?* "I'm sure it wasn't *that* bad."

"It *was* that bad," Micah insisted, refusing to let him brush off the incident. "Any worse, and I would've had to arrest him for assault. You can't shove a woman like that, Ed. You can't shove anyone."

He ripped off his sunglasses. "You'd never arrest Randy, would you? You know he's not a bad guy. What happened last night wasn't his fault."

Micah caught his jaw before his mouth could fall open. "Whose fault was it?"

"Sloane's! Who else? She has no business here, not if she's only back to cause trouble."

"So far, she's not the one who's been acting out, Ed. And she has as much right to be in Millcreek as anyone else."

"You're standing up for her, given what she did to you? After she walked out on *all* of us?"

Micah didn't *want* to stand up for her, but he refused to pile on. She had enough going against her with the assholes who were related to her. "I'm not going to *punish* her for that."

"But she blindsided you! I've never seen a boy so brokenhearted. If she hadn't taken off, you never would've slept with Paige, never would've gotten Paige pregnant. Because of Sloane, you married a woman you didn't love!"

"Don't ever say that again!" Micah snapped.

"Why not? It's true."

Maybe it *was* true, but his personal life was none of Ed's business, and he didn't want anything like that to get back to Trevor. Trevor was struggling with the divorce. Micah could only imagine how the poor kid would feel if someone told him he was the only reason Micah had married Paige in the first place. "What's true is that I love my son, and Sloane had the right to leave."

Ed *tsk*ed as he shook his head. "I'm surprised by you, Micah."

A fresh jolt of adrenaline caused Micah to straighten. He was getting the impression if he didn't jump onto the "let's run Sloane out of town" bandwagon, Ed's disfavor would make it difficult for *him* to continue living in Millcreek. "Surprised that I'm trying to be fair?" he said. "To live and let live? To mind my own business and let Sloane mind hers?"

"She's not minding hers. That's the problem. She's back to make trouble for me—and I'm your mayor!"

Ed hadn't really come here to play golf. Maybe he was willing to hit the green, but he was using that as an excuse to get another shot at enlisting Micah's support where Sloane was concerned. Ed was trying to shore up his team where he guessed it would be the weakest, but Micah didn't like being manipulated. "Which means what, exactly? What am I supposed to do for you as *my mayor*?"

Ed's nostrils flared and a hard glitter entered his eyes. "You'd better not take her side or get involved in what she's doing, Micah. That's what I'm trying to tell you."

Micah didn't care for the threat in his voice. *"Or..."*

"You'll see how much better it is to be my friend than my enemy," he said and stalked off.

It took several minutes for Micah to overcome his outrage well enough to go back inside. Even then, he paced the length of his living room instead of returning to the repair on the sink. Who the hell did Ed think he was? And what did he mean by that parting salvo?

Unable to resist, Micah pulled his phone out of his pocket and sent a text to Sloane. Your father is a piece of work.

He waited several minutes but didn't get a response. He'd just decided she was going to ignore him when his phone pinged.

I grew up with him, remember?

He remembered. He just couldn't acknowledge how difficult it must've been for an innocent child to be subjected to such an egotistical bastard, because then he wouldn't be able to blame her for taking off the way she had, or for wanting to leave again regardless of what else Millcreek might hold.

"Damn you, don't soften—don't you *dare* soften," he muttered to himself and shoved his phone in his pocket so he wouldn't text her again.

* * *

The motel smelled of mildew. Sloane grimaced as she crammed her luggage on the woodgrain-laminated desk and a nearby dresser so she could check the mattress for bedbugs before allowing any of her belongings to come into contact with the shag carpeting.

She didn't find any black dots. The place looked worn but clean. Maybe she wouldn't get bitten or infested, but the walls were so thin she would be able to hear her neighbors as they came and went, not to mention the cars in the parking lot.

And she wouldn't have a refrigerator or a washer and dryer.

This was going to be pretty inconvenient. No way would she be able to stay here for long.

With a sigh, she pulled back the bedspread—she refused to touch more than a handful of the fabric, knowing it probably wasn't laundered for each new occupant—and sat on the sheets that, hopefully, *had* been changed. As much as she wasn't impressed with the room, she was relieved to have her own space. Catching up with Paige hadn't been quite as healing as she'd envisioned while she was in New York.

She tried not to think about Clyde and how much she missed him. As hard as it was, she had to move on without him. She had no choice. She also needed to make up her mind on whether she should give in and buy a house in Millcreek. She hated to make such a big commitment. She'd feel less mobile, unable to just pick up and leave when she wanted.

But maybe that would be a good thing. Maybe that would make her stay the course even in the dark moments, when her courage began to flag.

A knock at the door caused her to jump. The last thing she'd expected here at The Wagon Wheel was a visitor, especially because she'd barely checked in.

She wasn't prepared to deal with her brother again, so she checked the peephole first.

A beautiful blonde woman stood outside dressed in a pair of white ankle-length slacks, a sleeveless sweater with blue stripes, low heels and a pair of big-lens sunglasses. She had her hair pulled back so that Sloane could easily see her diamond stud earrings, and she was wearing other expensive jewelry, including a thick gold tennis bracelet on the wrist of the hand that held on to a small child, who was also wearing sunglasses and had her blond hair in pigtails.

Sloane removed the security chain and peered out. "Is there something I can do for you?" She couldn't imagine this woman would ever deign to stay at The Wagon Wheel, so who was she? She wasn't part of the staff. And Sloane didn't recognize her from when she'd lived here before.

Her visitor removed the Prada sunglasses she was wearing, and the child—a little girl dressed in denim shorts and a frilly top—gazed up at Sloane curiously. "I'm Hadley," the woman said. "Randy's wife."

Sloane pressed a hand to her chest. If this was her sister-in-law, the child had to be her niece. "How'd you know I was here?" she asked.

"I heard your father tell Randy you were staying with Paige, so I went by there a minute ago. I know her from her Little Bae Bae Boutique. I drop by there all the time. I even helped her have a garage sale in the parking lot last spring to get rid of her excess inventory. Anyway, she told me you'd left and were getting a room, and since this place is mostly empty midday, it wasn't hard to figure out which room you were in. I mean…your car has New York license plates, and it's parked right there, so…"

"Yes. That's my car." Sloane opened the door wider. She couldn't tell if this was a friendly visit, but she wasn't going to be unwelcoming, just in case. These people were part of her family. If she could connect with *any* member, she'd be grateful. Maybe then she'd feel less isolated, less adrift on the sea of life. "Would you like to come in?"

Hadley checked over her shoulder as if she was afraid someone might see her, but after a moment's hesitation, she guided Misty inside and stepped out of the way so Sloane could shut the door.

"I'm happy to have the chance to meet you," Sloane said. "This must be Misty."

The woman nodded but seemed nervous, poised for a rapid exit. "Yes. She'll be four in April."

Sloane crouched down so she could speak to Misty at eye level. "Look at you! Aren't you beautiful! I love your sunglasses."

Her niece gave her a shy smile before knocking her sunglasses off while trying to hide behind her mother.

"She's a good girl," Hadley said, bending to pick them up.

"I bet she is."

Hadley put the glasses in her purse. "What happened to your head?"

Sloane reached up to touch the injury. Apparently, Randy hadn't told his wife what he'd done. "Oh, um, nothing. I hit the door is all." She wasn't trying to hide what Randy had done. She just didn't think throwing his behavior up to Hadley would help their relationship. It would put his wife in the position of either defending or criticizing him, and forcing her to make that choice wouldn't start them off on the right foot.

"Looks like it must've hurt."

"At the time." Sloane smiled.

"I guess that'll keep you from being able to model for a while."

Was there a touch of envy in that question? Sloane got the feeling there was a deeper meaning to those words. "I'm taking a year off, anyway. And it's already feeling a bit better."

"Good. Well, I can't stay long. I just… I wanted to meet you."

"I'm glad you made the effort. I'm not sure I would've been brave enough to reach out to you, given how my brother feels about me. But I promise I'm not the heartless creature he's probably made me out to be." She wiped her sweaty palms on her jeans. "You must know he's not happy I'm in town. My father isn't, either. But I'm not here because I'm out to hurt anyone. I have certain memories I can't forget. That's all. And I feel like I owe it to my mother to make sure those memories are as wrong as Randy and my father insist they must be."

"Of course."

Sloane froze. "Excuse me?"

"It's what anyone would do for their mother. I'd do the same for mine. Randy told me you were there the night Clara went missing. I can only imagine how traumatic it must've been."

Just that much empathy felt like a warm hug. "Thank you for trying to put yourself in my shoes. I feel like every little sound from that night has been indelibly etched on my mind, which is why I have to do what I can to work through the issues it's caused. I hope you can understand, even if you don't agree with me being here."

"I *do* understand," she said. "That's why I stopped by, to tell you I think you're doing the right thing."

Sloane blinked several times. This was the last thing she'd expected her sister-in-law to say. But she didn't have a chance to ask the questions that rose up inside her—why, what did Hadley know?—before Hadley's phone went off.

Worry pinched Hadley's face as she gazed down at the caller ID. "It's Randy," she said. "I have to go." She pressed the talk button and rushed her daughter out of the room at the same time.

"What do you mean?" Sloane heard her say. "I didn't know you were trying to reach me. My phone was on silent for a while, but then I caught it and turned on the ringer… I'm not doing anything. I cleaned the house this morning, and now I'm about to get my nails done."

Sloane caught the door before it could close all the way. Hadley tossed her an apologetic glance before holding the cell to her ear with one shoulder so she could strap her daughter into the car seat in the back of her white Land Rover. But she didn't acknowledge Sloane as she closed the car door and jogged around to the driver's side.

Was she afraid of Randy or merely intimidated by him?

Sloane didn't have the answer to that question, but something was up.

CHAPTER TEN

"Micah's a good officer. You know that."

Ed sat at the bar with Bill Adler, the chief of police. Bill was supposed to take his wife to dinner at seven, which meant Ed didn't have long. He needed to make the most of this audience, needed to get out in front of whatever problems Sloane might cause. "Of course I know that," he said. "We've talked about him before. I've even said that he might make a good replacement for you, when you're ready to retire."

"That's a ways off." Bill sent him a sideways glance to confirm that Ed wasn't rushing the end of his career.

"Ten or fifteen years, at least."

Visibly relieved, he sucked the foam off his beer. "Having Sloane in town won't change anything, Ed."

Ed tossed a few peanuts in his mouth. "It could. Micah was madly in love with her at one time, and love does crazy things to a man. Who knows what he might do now that she's back?"

Bill's potbelly rolled over his belt as he leaned forward and glanced up at the TV, which was playing a TCU versus Texas A&M football game. "She's been gone for ten years. Micah's been married and divorced since then, and he has a kid. I doubt she has any power over him these days."

"He could still be in love with her. She's a beautiful woman. What man *wouldn't* want her? That clouds judgment. But there's nothing to be gained by opening an investigation of the night Clara walked out on me. Losing my wife that way, without a word since, has been painful enough."

Bill didn't respond immediately. He was too busy watching the Aggie's running back weave and cut through defenders to score a touchdown that put A&M on top. "Wouldn't *you* like to know what happened to her?" he asked when the play was over.

"No! There's no use wasting time and energy on someone who didn't love her family enough to stay and work things out. Clara walked out on me, pure and simple. I was there that night, remember? I know what happened."

"But it won't be *your* time and energy. Why not let Sloane do her damnedest to solve the mystery? Then maybe she'll be satisfied, and you'll have answers, too."

"Okay, and what if she *doesn't* find anything? What if all she does is cast a shitload of suspicion on me? I'm up for reelection next year, Bill. Why would I allow my own daughter to hand Chauncey Phillips, who's planning to run against me *again*, that kind of ammunition?"

Bill took another drink of his beer. "Yeah, I guess that wouldn't be good."

"No one will be a better friend to you than I've

been," Ed pointed out. "Definitely not Chauncey. He's a preacher, always spouting off about God and religion. He'd force all the bars to close, if he could, which would cost this city a fortune."

Bill frowned. "We can't have that."

"No, we can't."

"So what do you want me to say to Micah?"

"You don't have to say anything. Just don't give him a sympathetic ear if he shows up in your office, asking to open an investigation."

"Fine. If you don't see anything to be gained by it, I don't, either."

He said that now, but Ed had been in politics long enough to understand how easily a situation could turn on him, especially a situation as rife with unanswered questions as his wife's disappearance. Once Sloane made it apparent she believed he was guilty of killing Clara, that suspicion would spread and could grow until there was a whole faction in Millcreek determined to see he went to prison. That would give his political opponents and other detractors—Millcreek citizens who were mad he hadn't opposed a certain city ordinance, didn't stop a commercial building from being built next to a residential neighborhood or refused to help out with a zoning change—the power to ruin him. And if Bill felt his own job might be at risk if he *didn't* open an investigation, Ed had no doubt whose interests he'd put first. "It's easy for things to get twisted up, especially something that happened so long ago. That's all I'm saying."

"They won't get twisted up if we don't let them."

"Exactly my point. That's why I don't want an investigation."

Bill finished his beer and shoved the mug aside. "I

get it. Okay, have to go. My wife will be mad as a hornet if I'm late. But don't worry. I've got your back."

"And, as usual, I've got yours. That's the beauty of long-lasting friendships like ours, right?" Ed smacked him on the shoulder. "We've both worked for this city a long time. Sometimes you need a favor from me, and sometimes I need a favor from you."

"Like I told you before, it doesn't matter that Sloane's in town. Nothing's going to change."

That was her car...

Micah pressed the brake as he passed the motel. Still, he went by too fast to get a good look at the white Jag sitting in the lot, so he made a U-turn at the corner and drove past The Wagon Wheel again.

Sure enough, the car he'd spotted belonged to Sloane. There were plenty of nice vehicles in Texas, but he'd never seen a white Jaguar with New York license plates in Millcreek. He was surprised he'd spotted it—but maybe he shouldn't be. He was out on patrol, after all, taking a look at everything, and the motel was right on the main drag.

But what was she doing at The Wagon Wheel? When she'd said she'd make arrangements other than staying with Paige, he'd never dreamed she'd go *there*.

He eyed the drab brown building with its symmetrical line of red doors and the wagon wheel built around the sign in front as he pulled in. Other than the doors, which were newly painted, the place looked as dingy and decrepit as ever. She had to be beyond determined to stay here.

Her car was parked in front of No. 8, where light glowed around the edges of the drawn shade.

He told himself to get out of there, to go on about his business, but he didn't. He parked next to the Jag. He still felt no resolution for what'd happened between them before, had never received a satisfactory explanation for why she'd given him up along with everything and everyone else.

Besides, he felt he should warn her not to forgive or trust her brother. Here at the motel, she might think she was safe, that someone would come running if she ever needed help, but plenty of problems, even murders, occurred in motel rooms. The Wagon Wheel wasn't always busy, especially on weekdays, so the manager didn't remain on duty all night. The front office closed when it got late.

He doubted Randy would come over with the intention of hurting his sister, but he had such a bad temper there was no telling what he might resort to in a fit of rage—like what'd happened last night. And if he showed up at the right time, even a shouting match could go unnoticed, let alone something that wasn't quite so loud.

Micah glanced around before getting out. He half expected Paige, who had always been so paranoid he might try to contact Sloane, to jump out of the bushes and insist she'd been right all along. He didn't need the headache, but he went up and knocked, anyway. He hated feeling as though Paige was still so much a part of his life he had to avoid displeasing her. He wished he could be free of her once and for all, but because of Trevor, it'd be a long time before that would be possible.

Butterflies filled Micah's stomach when he heard the slide of the safety chain and saw Sloane crack open the door.

"You..." she said as if his visit had been fated.

Was she upset he'd come by? "Yeah, it's me," he said. "Do you have a minute?"

Her thick dark hair fell loose about her shoulders, she wasn't wearing any makeup, and she was dressed in a pair of sweats and a New York T-shirt with no bra. Most women wouldn't assume they looked particularly good dressed down like this, but to him she couldn't look any better. She seemed real, approachable, like the old Sloane—not the famous model who'd become so intimidating in her fame and beauty. It was in that moment he realized just how much he'd missed her as a friend and not only as a lover. "Of course."

She stood back so he could come in, but that only made the jittery feeling inside him worse. He could smell her perfume, couldn't help remembering how she'd pulled off her own shirt the night they'd made love. He'd been too afraid to take it that far, since she'd stopped him every other time.

It required some effort, but he managed not to let his gaze fall to her chest.

"I'd offer you something to drink but, of course, I don't have anything," she said.

"I'm on duty."

"Right. The uniform. It looks great on you, by the way."

He wished that compliment didn't make him feel as good as it did. To cover for his weakness where she was concerned, he gestured at the cheap print of a Texas prairie hanging above the bed and the other shabby furnishings. "This is your best alternative to Paige's house?"

"Until my father finds out where I am and manages to talk the motel owner out of renting me a room, yes."

"Not *everyone* is going to kowtow to his demands."

"We'll see about that. He's two for two so far. But this motel seems to need the business, so I'm hoping I've got a decent shot."

When her lips curved into an appealing smile, it was so hard not to forgive her. "What if he does? What will you do then?"

Her smile vanished. "I'll have to figure out something else, I guess."

"As stubborn as you are, you'll probably live in your car before you'll let your family chase you out of town."

Fresh concern entered her eyes. Micah noticed because he couldn't seem to look away from them. He'd always loved their golden, amber color and the thick fringe of long, dark eyelashes that contrasted with the lighter color. "I'm staying until I'm satisfied I have the answers I need."

"And then you'll be leaving. *Again*," he added, to remind himself as much as gain any kind of confirmation.

She stared down at her feet. "Yes."

He noticed the small desk in the corner. The lamp was on, and her laptop was open. From the looks of it, he'd interrupted her while she was working. "I stopped by to tell you something."

When he saw her tense, he guessed she was bracing for an unkind comment. "What is it?"

He hated that she expected him to be no different than her father and brother, who were being so cruel. "You need to be careful. If your father *did* kill your mother, he won't sit back and let that information come out. You understand what I'm saying…"

"Do you believe there's any chance, even a remote one, that he did it?"

Micah debated whether he should tell her about her father's visit. Ed's behavior was beginning to make Micah wary of what he'd begun to take for granted since she left—that whatever problems she'd had with Ed were her own, that Ed would never really hurt anyone. Now that Micah was beginning to question Ed's character, he felt Sloane needed to understand that whatever vestiges of love and familial tenderness she might have for her father, it didn't change the fact that he was out trying to get everyone to shun her.

The only thing that stopped him was the possibility that hearing it would hurt her—yet again. "Less likely things have happened," he said. "That's why I'm here. If you're right about that night, I can't overexaggerate the danger you could be in."

Impulsively, he lifted her chin to examine the bump that was turning into a nasty bruise on her forehead but dropped his hand when a wave of longing crashed over him. It'd been ten years since he'd touched her, and he'd missed her so much. As if that hunger wasn't bad enough, he'd also gone a year without even kissing anyone, so he was especially vulnerable to the desire that was slamming into him. "Your brother could be dangerous, too."

"No. Randy didn't mean to hurt me last night—"

"Don't stick up for him," he broke in. "He hurt you and then he minimized it, which is a warning sign."

She gave him a grudging nod. "Okay, I'll do what I can to protect myself."

"And what will that entail?"

"I'll be careful?" she said lamely.

"Buy some pepper spray, be aware of your surroundings at all times and never go into an alley, an empty building or a deserted area alone. Try not to come and go late at night, either. This place may feel safe because there are usually other people within a close distance, but that doesn't mean they will hear you cry out if you need them."

She rubbed her arms as though his words caused goose bumps. "Thanks for the visual."

"If I'm scaring you, that's what I'm trying to do. Scared people are more cautious."

"I'm hoping to find that my father *didn't* hurt my mother. You understand that, right? I want to believe in him. I want a father, even if it's an imperfect one. I just… I have to remove the doubt in my heart before I can fully embrace him or…or try to improve our relationship."

Micah couldn't imagine what it'd be like to feel as though he couldn't trust his own father. Or to grow up wondering if his mother had abandoned him—or been murdered. His mom had always been his biggest champion, had tried to shield him from every pain or discomfort, so much so that he'd been taking all she offered for granted, especially lately. He'd even been irritated by her constant concern and advice.

He needed to call her and check in. "How will you find out what happened to your mother?"

"I'll talk to everyone who knew her, see what she was like in those last days, what frame of mind she was in, if she ever mentioned leaving my father, or if she might've been seeing another man, and hope to dig up enough information that…that I can believe she ran away."

He hooked his thumbs in his heavy gear belt and

leaned against the wall, mostly to put a little more space between them. "When we were in high school, you told me that on the night your mother left, she was fighting with your father about your kindergarten teacher."

"That's what I remember."

"You should start with him."

"If he's still in town. If not, I'll have to track him down. I also want to contact Katrina Yost."

"Who?"

"The woman my father started seeing almost immediately after my mother…left." She finished her sentence on an uncertain note, since she didn't really know what happened. Even that testified to how difficult this whole thing was for her. "Maybe he said something to her at one point that seemed odd or raised questions. You never know. I have to talk to everyone."

Micah let his breath go in a deep sigh.

"What?" she said.

"You need help."

"No, I don't."

He pushed off the wall. "Yes, you do. You're taking on Goliath, and you're doing it all alone."

"And how do you propose I get this help? At some point, I may hire a private detective. But it's too soon for that. I need to gather what information I can first, or he'll get nowhere. I mean, who in this town would talk to him, especially about my father?"

"I agree. It's better not to involve a stranger quite yet. There might come a time for that, but I'll be able to help you much more."

"No, you can't help me, Micah. If you get involved, my father will turn on you, too. He might even go after your job. I don't want to be responsible for that. I feel bad enough about...about letting you down before."

He felt bad about that, too. He'd been honest with her when he told her it had screwed up his life. But he couldn't blame her *entirely*. He wouldn't have succumbed to the temptation Paige had put in front of him if he hadn't been so hurt and angry, but he was still the one who'd let Paige climb into his bed and gotten her pregnant. Besides, he was a cop, and he knew Clara McBride's disappearance should've received more police attention than it had. Sloane deserved to know that *every* effort had been made to find her mother. "I don't see anyone else who's both capable and willing."

"Micah, no..."

"There's a convenience store down one block," he said. "Do you remember it?"

"The Circle 7? Of course."

"Meet me in the alley behind it tomorrow afternoon—at one."

"For what?"

"I'm going to pick you up there. I'd rather not be seen together. If Paige finds out we've had any contact, she'll make life miserable for me where Trevor's concerned—and I want to protect him above all else."

"It's not worth the risk. And it's sad that she'd make your life difficult just because you're helping me."

"She won't see it as help. She'll see it as the ultimate betrayal."

"Where will we go after we meet?"

"To my house. We'll make a list of everyone you should talk to, and I'll do what I can to track down anyone you might not be able to find on your own. I have access to databases you don't."

"Wait. You just told me not to go into any alleys, but you want me to meet you in one?"

He was fairly certain she was joking, but he didn't laugh, didn't want to let his guard down to that degree. He was going to do what he could to help her because no one else would. Anyone would want the answers she craved, so he felt some empathy there, but he wasn't going to get his hopes up about anything else. "That's different. I'll be there waiting for you."

When she hesitated, he added, "You trust me, don't you?"

"Of course I trust you," she replied. "Why wouldn't I? Only my family hates me worse."

He raised his eyebrows at her apparent sarcasm. "I don't *hate* you. I hate what you did to me."

"You're obviously holding a grudge. So why are you offering to help me?"

"Because your father's an asshole, and you're so convinced he's lying you have *me* wondering."

He walked out of her motel room before he could say more. He figured it was best to leave the subject there, but he wanted to believe that helping her would mean she'd not only get her answers, she'd leave that much sooner. Then he, too, could put the past behind him and get on with rebuilding his life.

Sloane couldn't concentrate after Micah left. She turned on the TV to create a distraction, hoping she'd at least be able to nod off and get a good night's rest. She'd been under so much stress since she'd arrived in Millcreek. She needed a break, would start fresh tomorrow. But she couldn't relax any more than she could concentrate. She kept thinking about meeting Micah in the alley behind the Circle 7 and going to his house. It was *so* nice of him to help her; it couldn't hurt to have a cop on her side, but it wouldn't be easy to spend time with him, either. There were too many memories. Given her situation, she felt she'd done the right thing by leaving, but regretted what it'd cost her.

Her phone began to ring. She grabbed it, assuming it was Micah telling her to forget about his offer to help. He'd be smart to stay away. She would only complicate his professional life if her father found out, his family life if Paige found out, and his love life if she wound up in his bed even though she would be leaving again, which she feared was a distinct possibility. The attraction she'd felt when she was only seventeen and eighteen hadn't disappeared despite all the effort she'd put into subverting those feelings.

He had so many reasons to avoid her.

But it wasn't her former boyfriend who was trying to reach her. It was her father. The number that showed up on her screen didn't have a name attached; she'd deleted him from her contacts. But she recognized it. It was the same number he'd had before she left.

Her number was different, however. So the question was—who'd given it to him?

She shook her head in discouragement. Nothing in this town seemed beyond him. Did she fully understand what she was up against?

No wonder Micah was worried.

Tempted to let the call go to voice mail, she bit her bottom lip. She wasn't ready to speak with her father. But she couldn't let him know he intimidated her. He'd only grow bolder if he thought he had her cowed.

So she forced herself to hit Talk. "Hello?"

"Heard you were in town," he said without preamble.

He sounded the same, as confident and in control as ever. "Who told you?"

"Everyone. You don't have any friends in this town who are more loyal to you than they are to me, Sloane."

Immediately, she thought of Micah and began to worry about what could happen if her father perceived him as taking the wrong side. "Is that what you were trying to prove when you convinced the Prinleys and whoever owns the River Bottoms house to turn me down?"

"I was merely trying to save you a lot of time and trouble. Not to mention grief."

"And I should interpret that how, exactly?"

"I've told you what happened the night your mother went missing. At this point, I'm not sure why there's any question."

Filled with nervous energy, she climbed off the bed and began to pace in the short amount of space available to her. "Just because you said it doesn't make it true."

Her words were met with stony silence. She squeezed her eyes closed, wishing she'd held back a little. Her father had never taken kindly to being challenged. Yet he felt free to say whatever *he* thought, no matter how critical or autocratic, and he expected others to tolerate it. She'd always wondered why he felt he could play by a different set of rules than the rest of the world, so she supposed she was reacting to that unfairness.

"Are you trying to start a fight between us, Sloane?" he asked at length. If there'd been any warmth in his voice at the beginning of the call, it was gone now.

No. She didn't want to fight with him. She'd seen him smash more worthy opponents. Whatever he did, he made sure he came out on top. But that was just it. *Someone* had to oppose him, keep him honest, make him more sensitive to the needs and wants of others. "I don't have any choice," she admitted.

"That's not true," he said. "You have all kinds of choices. You had a nice life in New York, have made something of yourself with that pretty face."

She had no doubt that was an intentional slight. "As opposed to you, since you've built your fortune with your mind and talents?"

"Something like that. You should be happy with what you have and not press your luck."

Her stomach knotted as she struggled to decide how to respond. "That sounds like a threat, Dad."

"Do you think I'll let you ruin my reputation? Smear my name? Get people whispering about me and saying the most terrible things possible—that I might've killed my own wife? If you expect me to sit back and take that just because you're my daughter, you're going to have a rude awakening."

How dare you ever question me! That was what he was really saying. He hadn't changed. If anything, he'd grown *more* egotistical. "I'm not out to hurt you, Dad," she said. "I just need to know more about Mom and the night she went missing. You've never really said what happened."

"She *left*, Sloane. What more do you need me to say? She walked out on all of us!"

"On *foot*."

"Yes."

"And you went looking for her."

"Once I calmed down."

"But you found no trace of her."

"None whatsoever, and I've never heard from her since."

She dug at the cuticles of her left hand as she pivoted to head back across the room. "That doesn't strike you as odd?"

"Of course it does! Like you, I think she's probably dead. Otherwise, she would've been after me for money at some point. But *I* didn't kill her! I don't know how much clearer I can state that."

Sloane wanted so desperately to believe him, but her memories of that night and what Vickie had told her forced her to continue pressing him. "What were you driving when you went out looking for her?"

The line went quiet; she assumed he was taken aback by this question.

"Dad? Did you hear me?" Sloane asked.

He didn't like that she wasn't accepting him at his word. She could tell. When the answer finally came, he spoke more tentatively. "My truck. Why?"

"Is there any reason you were pulling the boat?"

This time he didn't respond. He hung up.

CHAPTER ELEVEN

After her call with her father last night, Sloane had tried to cancel with Micah. She'd texted him to say that he needed to stay out of it, that he should ignore her presence in town and go on about his business as if he'd never known her, but he'd refused. He'd said he'd pick her up at the motel if she wouldn't meet him in the alley, and she couldn't let him do that for fear someone would see them together and report it to her father, Paige or both.

"You're too stubborn for your own good," she grumbled above the country music he had playing on the radio as she climbed into his truck behind the Circle 7. A fairly new Ford F-350 with a double axle, it was obviously an expensive vehicle, and yet it had already seen some use. She imagined he'd carried hay, equipment and other things with it while working for his parents at their farm and liked that it was a practical car for him and not something to show off, like so many of the rich men she'd dated in New York who cared more about their flashy Ferraris or Lamborghinis than they did the people in their lives. Granted, Micah's truck wasn't quite *that* costly, but his attitude—that possessions were meant to be used and not worshipped—appealed to her.

He turned down the music. "The sooner you figure out what happened, the sooner you can get out of Dodge."

She shot him a glance. "So you're doing this to get rid of me?"

"If you're leaving, anyway, sooner is probably better for both of us, right?"

"Yeah, I guess." She kept her gaze on the buildings they passed—the bank, the post office, the gas station and the thrift store—while he drove so she couldn't admire him. She'd seen a lot of good-looking men in her line of work. Some were downright beautiful. But none were as ruggedly handsome as Micah.

"Where do you live?" she asked.

"I have a rental a few blocks from here."

Because he'd given the house to Paige, who'd demanded it. "How many bedrooms does it have?"

When he came to the stoplight, he turned his full attention on her. "Why do you want to know?"

She'd just been making small talk, trying to ease the awkwardness, but belatedly realized that sounded as though she was looking for a place to stay. "Just wondering," she muttered and rummaged through her purse to get her phone, which had dinged.

Paige had texted her: Hey, come by the store today. I'd love to get your opinion on my new display.

She hesitated, trying to decide what to text back. She didn't know how long she'd be with Micah, didn't want a commitment to Paige looming over her right when she was about to start working on the details surrounding her mother's disappearance.

"What is it?" The light turned green, so Micah gave the truck some gas.

"Paige is asking me to come by the store."

He scowled. "When?"

"Later today, I guess."

"Are you going to go?"

"No, I'm going to put her off until tomorrow. I'd like to make as much progress as possible while you're off and have the time."

He didn't say anything, so she told Paige she'd stop by if she could but it would most likely be in the morning.

"My father called me last night," she announced as she put her phone away.

Micah turned the radio even lower. "What'd he say?"

"He thinks my mom is dead."

"He told you that?"

"He told me she must be, or she would've come back to him for money at some point."

"He believes money is everything."

"True."

"Did he mention whether he killed her?" he asked wryly.

"He's suggesting she met with foul play *after* she left the house. But he doesn't seem to be too concerned with what happened."

"He's not even *a little* curious?"

"If he was, he would've looked into it long before now. He wants me to let it go. He made that clear."

There was a slight pause before Micah asked, "How'd it feel to talk to him?"

A sudden upwelling of emotion took Sloane off guard. Her father had cut her deeply when he showed no concern for her or her welfare—only for how her return might affect *him*. But that wasn't what brought tears to her eyes. This was the type of question the old Micah would've asked—the Micah who'd cared about how she was doing and what she was feeling.

Averting her face, she cleared her throat to give herself a split second to overcome her reaction. "It was fine." There was no point in telling him the truth. What good would it do to admit that hearing her father's voice had been brutal? That she'd thought she was prepared for that moment, but his anger and indifference had felt like a sledgehammer to her heart?

Micah was already doing more than he should to help her. She had no right to cry on his shoulder. If she didn't want him to be targeted by her father, she couldn't elicit or depend on his sympathy. That would only tempt him to get more involved, which wasn't safe. "I can handle my father."

He gave her a skeptical look as they pulled into the drive of a one-story beige stucco house with a small patch of grass in the front and an empty dog run on the side. "Do *not* underestimate him," he said, tilting his head for emphasis.

The warning made her uneasy. Not for the first time, she wondered if she should have kept running from the past instead of returning.

No, she might've procrastinated too long already.

After so many years, how would she find anything definitive, anything that proved her father was or wasn't complicit in her mother's disappearance?

"Do you have a dog?" she asked.

He seemed surprised by the question. "No. *I* barely live here."

She climbed out of the truck as he came around front, swinging his keys on his index finger. "What's that supposed to mean?" she asked. "You don't stay here?"

"I stay here. I just haven't had time to unpack."

After following him to the door, she stood in the entryway, gaping at the sparse furnishings and cardboard boxes. Micah had only bothered with the absolute necessities. All the rest of what he owned sat in boxes along the periphery. He was even using a box as a coffee table. She could see a plate and a cup on it, between the TV and a worn leather couch. "I think you could use a dog."

"Why?"

"It'd give you a good reason to come home at night."

"Like I said, I've only been here a month."

"It wouldn't take more than a day or two to get rid of all these boxes."

"I'll get around to it," he said and stacked the dishes he'd left on the kitchen table in the sink so they'd have some room to work. "At least *I've* got a place to stay. You're the one at the motel."

"Ouch!" she said.

He smiled as though he enjoyed needling her, so she rolled her eyes. "This might be a place to stay, but you can't really *live* like this."

"Obviously you've never been through a divorce, or you'd know you can live through a lot worse. I'm lucky

I had the money to get a couch and a TV." He scratched his neck. "I was careful to make sure they weren't too appealing, though. Otherwise, Paige would've asked for those, too."

"Yeah. I'd like to say something about the way you divided up your property, but it's none of my business, so..."

He shot her a glance. "So you won't, and that's a good thing. You have no idea how much you will sacrifice to get out of something until you're in that position."

"I understand that, to a point. Still, there's fair and then there's getting taken to the cleaners."

"I don't care about the money or the property. Trevor is the only thing that matters to me."

But Trevor wasn't the only thing that mattered to Paige. She was obviously looking out for herself. So who was looking out for Micah?

Sloane opened her mouth to say that—only to close it again. She'd been right in the first place. What'd happened in his divorce wasn't any of her concern.

She took her laptop out of her leather bag and put it on one corner of the table. His computer was open at the other end, as if he'd worked through breakfast.

"Can I get you something to drink?" he asked.

She arched her eyebrows. "Do you have a clean glass? God forbid you might have to unpack another box."

"I could wash the one I've been using," he said, as if unpacking really would be too much effort.

When she laughed, she realized it'd been a long time since she'd experienced any type of levity, what with Clyde's sickness and death, the way his children had started treating her the second they didn't have to answer to him and the daunting prospect of returning to Millcreek. "I wouldn't want to put you to any trouble."

He responded to her sarcasm by making a show of washing the glass that'd been on the table. Then he opened the fridge, which was empty except for a cube of butter, a six-pack of beer, some ketchup and a pitcher of water with a filter on top.

"You must not eat here very often, either," she said, standing on her tiptoes to peer in over his shoulder as he grabbed the water.

He closed the door. "I don't. Other than toast and coffee in the mornings, I eat out. But since it's your fault I'm in this situation, I don't think I'd criticize."

He was joking. She could tell by the half smile on his face. But the desire to laugh disappeared as soon as Sloane heard those words. "I'm sorry, Micah. Truly. I never meant to hurt you. You were…you were the best thing to ever happen to me."

After filling the glass, he put the pitcher back in the fridge, but when his eyes met hers, something powerful passed between them. The attraction was still there, hadn't changed at all, which made her nervous.

They were playing with fire…

"Don't worry about it," he said. "Life is life, I guess. You can't script it."

Sloane changed the subject. "What about Trevor?"

He handed her the water. "What about him?"

"Surely you've got *his* room all set up. Because if you haven't, we should do that right away, before we start in on my investigation." She put the glass on the table. "Come on, I'll help you."

He caught her by the elbow. "He's got a bed and a dresser for the odd night he comes here, but I was living in the apartment above my parents' barn before this, so I usually take him back there. I believe consistency and stability are important, that it'll help him get through this rough time, and he likes being around the animals and spending time with my folks."

Sloane remembered her conversation with Trevor in the middle of the night but chose not to mention it. Why make Micah feel any worse for demanding the divorce? If he could've stayed, he would have. It was obvious Trevor meant that much to him. "How'd you like living on the farm again?"

"Better than I like living here."

"Then why'd you move back to town?"

He grimaced. "My mother doesn't know when to stop treating me like a kid. I was afraid I was getting *too* comfortable."

The admission made her laugh again. "At least you recognized it."

"I'm trying to rebuild my life."

"Are you seeing someone? Is that part of rebuilding? Part of the motivation to move here?"

"Does it look like I'm seeing someone?" He gestured at the boxes as if they told the entire tale.

"No, but it's been a year since your divorce, so that should be happening soon, right?"

"I'm not interested in dating at the moment. That would only complicate life for Trevor. He's so hurt over the divorce. I don't want him to feel as though my love life was more important to me than staying in the family for his sake. And I don't want to make him feel as though he has to accept some other woman as a mother figure."

"*Your* happiness is important, too," she said softly.

"That's why I left."

She crossed her legs and braved the question that burned uppermost in her mind. "You were *that* miserable?"

"Paige and I weren't…compatible."

"Why?"

He took a seat in front of his computer. "You wouldn't think so, but being loved too much can be worse than not being loved at all."

She wished he'd elaborate on that statement, give her some idea of what their marriage had been like. But he started typing as if he was ready to get down to business, which indicated she'd pushed about as far as he was comfortable with.

"I did a little research when I got home last night," he said.

"And?"

"And I found your kindergarten teacher. He no longer lives in Millcreek but he's not far."

"Where is he these days?"

"Fort Worth."

She stood. "Should we drive over and talk to him?"

"I've got his number. I suggest you call first, see if he gives you the impression there's anything worth exploring."

He read out the number and she put it into her phone, but didn't call it right away. "There's something I should probably tell you before we get started on this whole thing," she said.

He shifted his gaze from his computer screen. "What's that?"

"I think my father might've dumped my mother's body in the river."

"It's close to the house, would be an easy thing for him to do. But nothing has ever turned up. Usually a body will wash ashore. Why do you think that?"

She'd promised to protect Vickie as much as possible, but she also felt that in order to make the most of Micah's help, she should be completely open and honest with him, tell him everything she knew, especially because she trusted him not to disclose what she shared. "Do you know Vickie Winters?"

"No."

"She's a neighbor who's lived down the street from my father for years. She told me that she saw my father the night my mother went missing, pulling the boat."

She'd expected him to gasp and believe she had good reason to doubt her father. Instead, he pursed his lips.

"No reaction?" she prodded.

"I'm thinking," he replied.

"About?"

"Motivation. How reliable is Vickie Winters?"

"What do you mean? What reason would she have to lie?"

"That's what I'd like to find out. Does she dislike your father? Have a vendetta against him? Is she opposed to his politics? Does she prefer someone else take over as mayor?"

"You think *she* might be lying?"

"Anyone can lie, Sloane. Or maybe she's simply mistaken. Could be what she's remembering happened on a totally different night."

She let her breath go in a long sigh. "Will I ever be able to figure out what happened to my mother, Micah? With any certainty, I mean?"

His blue eyes once again met hers, and this time she thought she saw a hint of compassion there. "We'll see," he said.

The bell rang over the door while Paige was in the back room, organizing her stock of children's shoes. She'd just finished creating a display in the window featuring the new pink rain boots she'd received on Friday, and she planned to bring out a few more winter styles.

"Mom?" Trevor called.

She'd left her son to watch the front. Otherwise, even with the bell on the door, she wouldn't have felt safe leaving the cash register unattended. She'd never had any trouble in Millcreek; it was a pretty safe town. But there were getting to be more and more homeless people milling around outside, eating from the trash cans on the boardwalk or hanging out in the alley behind the store, hoping the sandwich shop down the block would throw away any day-old bread.

She parted the drapes that hid the back end of her store and saw Sloane's father in the shop.

Growing up, she hadn't cared for Ed. He'd been so strict with Sloane and totally uninterested in her. Even as Sloane's best friend, she'd felt invisible to him. But now that she was an adult, he was taking notice, and she found him to be quite attractive, especially for his age. Most women in Millcreek did. He took care of himself, had plenty of money and more than his share of power. Being recently single and feeling so inadequate after suffering the rejection of the only man she'd ever loved, she couldn't help flirting with Ed, especially because she could tell he liked being able to draw the attention of a woman his daughter's age.

Flattering him had its rewards, too. He'd already done her a few favors—like making sure the three parking spaces in front of her store were designated "Little Bae Bae" so that the patrons from the sandwich shop didn't take up the whole lot, recommending her to the banker who'd given her the small business loan she'd needed to expand her shop and inviting her to various mixers, which had raised her status in town. She got the impression he was considering asking her out, but since Sloane was back, Paige was glad he hadn't. No doubt Sloane would find that distasteful, even if there wasn't any question about him killing her mother. As much as Sloane was concerned that might be the case, Paige wasn't convinced he'd gone that far. Ed was such a pillar of the community. And it didn't help that Paige couldn't even remember Clara.

"What a nice surprise," she said. "I wasn't expecting you."

"I was driving by and saw the shop open, thought I'd drop in to see if Sloane is still staying with you."

Paige felt disloyal revealing *anything* about Sloane. But how could she withhold such simple information and still retain Ed's friendship? After all, he was the one who was staying in Millcreek. Paige guessed Sloane wouldn't be there long.

Besides, she'd already told Hadley, his daughter-in-law, where to find Sloane, so word would get back to him eventually. "Not anymore."

"Where'd she go?"

Randy's wife hadn't already notified him? Hadley had to know that was information Ed would want. "She's over at the motel."

"The Wagon Wheel?"

"Someone almost as tall as my father pushed her into the door while she was at our house," Trevor piped up. "I can't remember his name, but he hurt her head."

Ed scarcely glanced at Trevor. "No one *pushed* her, son—she fell. It was an accident."

Someone *had* pushed her and they both knew who. If Micah hadn't stopped what was happening, Randy might've done more damage. Ed was attempting to rewrite history, proving he had no problem covering up the past when it suited him. But Paige let it go. A lot of people did that sort of thing. Minimizing a confrontation didn't make someone a murderer. "Yes, The Wagon Wheel."

"That can't be comfortable." He seemed to take pleasure in the fact.

"I'm sure it isn't."

"Why'd she leave your place?"

"*Someone* I know wasn't too happy she was there, so… I worked it out," she said with a wink. She hadn't had anything to do with Sloane's decision. Sloane had moved to the motel on her own, but Paige figured she might as well score a few points with the mayor by taking credit for the relocation.

She could tell she'd made him happy when he beamed at her. "Thanks. I owe you one."

"Good." She leaned close and lowered her voice. "I'll make a note of that."

His gaze lingered ever so slightly on her breasts. "Let me know when you want to collect."

As Ed walked out, Paige caught her son watching her with a confused expression. Trevor had figured out that something was going on under the surface of that exchange, and it made her feel terrible for being so two-faced. She wasn't the kind of person to wrong a friend. So what was going on inside her head? Why had she just flirted so brazenly with Sloane's *dad*? She'd been nice to him in the past, but she'd never gone that far.

"Do you like the mayor?" Trevor wrinkled his nose to suggest he couldn't see why.

She ruffled his hair. "Of course not. He's just a friend."

"He's *old*."

Paige forced herself to laugh, but this wasn't about age or attraction. Sloane had so easily won the man Paige wanted that there was some appeal in returning the favor—in capturing the heart of the man whose love had eluded even the beautiful girl no one could get over or forget.

"Come get me if anyone else comes in," she said and went back to finish organizing her stock. As she worked, she told herself she was only interested in Ed as a friend.

But only a few minutes later, she got a text from him.

I've got two steaks for the grill and a 150-year-old bottle of wine. Would you like to come over for dinner?

CHAPTER TWELVE

"What are you waiting for?" Micah asked.

Sloane had Mr. Judd's number in her phone but still hadn't initiated the call. "I'm putting my thoughts together."

He nudged her. "You're *stalling.*"

She glared at him. "No, I'm trying to decide what to say."

"You know what to say! We've gone over it two or three times."

"But it could be awkward—*will* be awkward, especially if he doesn't remember me. And why would he? How many hundreds of kids must he have taught over the years?"

"He hasn't been teaching for the past decade. He's a principal these days."

"That means he's dealt with an even greater number!"

"None, I'm sure, who turned out to be famous. Besides, if he had a thing for your mother, he'll remember you, especially since she went missing that same year."

He had a point. But Sloane was afraid to learn whether her mother had been having an affair. She wasn't sure how she'd feel about it if the answer was yes. She had such great memories of Clara, who'd spent hours reading to her and her brother, playing with them out in the yard or cuddling with her to help her fall asleep. Adultery didn't fit the picture she had of her kind, loving mother. And since Sloane was already disillusioned by her father, she didn't want to face further disappointment, didn't want to ruin her mother's image, too. Then she wouldn't be able to respect either parent.

"Sloane?" Micah prompted. "We've spent all day listing everyone who knew your mother and researching their contact information. It's time to start talking to those people."

Micah didn't understand what was at stake. But it didn't matter. She couldn't let her reservations stop her. People were human. They made mistakes. She had to be willing to see Clara for who she really was in order to find out what'd happened to her.

After a calming breath, she made the call.

Part of her prayed it would go to voice mail. She'd never confronted Mr. Judd about what she'd overheard the night her mother went missing. Other than her brother, Paige and Micah, she'd never told anyone here in Millcreek. Before she left, she'd been too loyal to her father, despite her suspicions. She'd also been afraid of how he might react if word ever got back to him. After all, if he *was* responsible for her mother's disappearance, there was no telling what he might do to her, especially while she was living under his roof. He could make her disappear just as easily.

It didn't go to voice mail; a man answered after the first ring.

"Is Mr. Judd there?" she asked, but she knew she was talking to him, and he confirmed it with, "This is Mr. Judd."

"This is Sloane McBride."

Silence.

"I was in your kindergarten class over twenty years ago," she added, digging at the cuticle on the thumb of her left hand.

"Yes. I remember. Congratulations on all the success you've had in modeling."

Micah was right. Not only did he remember her, he'd been following her career. "Thank you. I'm sorry to bother you after so long, but—"

"How'd you find me?" he broke in.

She decided not to drag Micah's name into it. She was hoping to keep him out of what she was doing wherever possible, so there'd be less chance of a backlash from her father or anyone her father could manipulate into punishing him for taking the wrong side. "I, uh, had a private investigator track you down."

Micah made a snorting sound, but she waved him off.

"A private investigator," Judd repeated.

She squeezed her eyes closed, hoping he'd believe her. "Yes."

"Then this *is* about your mother."

What else would she be calling him about? Gripping the phone tighter, she looked up at Micah to find him watching her closely. "Yes, it's about my mother."

"Can you give me a minute?" Judd asked. "I need to…to go into another room."

"Of course."

Sloane muted her phone. "He's trying to find a private place where he can talk."

"That's a sign he's got something important to say," Micah told her.

But what kind of important? A lot hung in the balance, either way.

After several minutes, Judd returned.

"Sorry for the wait," he said. "My daughter and her kids are here and…well, it's not the best time to go into this. But I've been anticipating your call—or someone else's—for so long I feel the need to take it, to at least hear what you have to say."

Micah grabbed her hand so she couldn't draw blood on the cuticle of that thumb. "It's not what I have to say. It's what I have to ask," she said into the phone.

"Which is…"

She glanced at Micah one last time for encouragement. "Did you have an affair with my mother?"

"No," he said, but he hesitated just enough that Sloane couldn't take him at his word.

"I'm afraid that wasn't very convincing."

She heard him sigh. "I guess the answer depends on your definition of *affair*."

"You don't know what an affair is?"

Micah moved closer and tilted the phone so he could hear.

"I never had sex with your mother," Judd said. "Things between us didn't…didn't go that far. But I cared about her, and I'd be lying if I said our relationship wasn't drifting in that direction."

Sloane felt weak in the knees, but she couldn't sit down because Micah was standing there, listening in. She tried to overcome the sensation. "So my father was right. Something was up."

"He's mentioned me to you?"

"No. You were what my parents were fighting about the night she disappeared. I heard them."

He muttered something that sounded like a curse. Then he said, "That makes me feel terrible. I never wanted to make her life any harder. You have to understand, she was *so* lonely, so miserable. She and your father had drifted apart. They couldn't get along, fought all the time. She wanted to leave him, but he wouldn't let her go. She told me if she left without his agreement, he'd make sure she did it with nothing—including you and your brother—but she refused to give up her kids."

"She stayed with him because she didn't want to leave *us*." A flash of happiness zipped through her. That confirmed what she'd always felt in her heart, that her mother wouldn't simply abandon her.

"She felt trapped, as though there was no way out," he explained. "And the worst part? She claimed he didn't love her. That he was only trying to save face. She said he had so much pride he'd be 'embarrassed' for people to know his wife had walked out on him. When I met her, she was trying to make things work but was hoping he'd realize that they'd *both* be happier in a different situation."

"Was she expecting to…to be with you at some point?"

"That might've been a secret wish. When you get involved in something like…like what happened between us, you aren't thinking logically. I merely offered your mother my friendship, a shoulder to cry on, that sort of thing. There was no ill intent. The sexual interest came later, after I began to care about her in a…a different way."

Sloane could smell Micah's cologne. She could also feel the heat of his body. As sick as she felt, it was hard not to lean into him. "And you believe she had feelings for you, too."

"I do."

"But it never turned into a full-blown affair."

"She disappeared before that could happen."

"Does your wife know?"

"I told her after Clara went missing. I was wondering what'd happened to her, was worried about her, couldn't let it go. It really tore me up. She could tell I wasn't myself."

Micah covered the phone with his hand, pushing it away from her mouth while he whispered in her ear. "Ask him if he ever went to the police."

"Did you go to the police?" she asked when Micah let go.

Judd seemed taken aback. "About what?"

"About the fact that you knew my parents were having marital problems. That they were fighting. That my mother wanted out."

"No. Why would I?"

"Because she disappeared, and that means… Well, it could mean…"

"That your father was responsible?"

She swallowed. "Yes."

"A lot of couples have problems, Sloane. Leaving is getting out, too."

"You believe she ran off, even though she told you she would never leave me and my brother."

"People can be pushed only so far. She was sort of fatalistic about her situation, if that makes sense. I assumed... I assumed that aspect caused her to give up and go somewhere else to start over."

"And when the days and months passed and you didn't hear from her?"

"I *did* hear from her. Or so I thought."

Sloane felt her jaw drop. *"What?"*

"I received several calls late at night from an unknown number. I thought it was her, trying to work up the nerve to talk to me, or that she was at least letting me know she was okay."

"How long did that go on?"

"For several months."

"But you never actually spoke to her, never received any proof she was alive."

"No."

"And you never wondered if my father could've harmed her?"

"It crossed my mind," he admitted. "But I had no real reason to suspect him. I couldn't tell the police anything that might shed any light on the situation—other than that they were unhappy as a couple, and she would be unlikely to leave her children. And if I did that, if I caused a fuss and demanded an investigation, my own wife and family would be embarrassed at a time when I was fighting to save my marriage. After I confessed my feelings for your mother to my wife, I couldn't keep going back to that relationship. I just... tried to move on."

So, in the end, he hadn't stood by Clara, either. He'd let her go like everyone else.

"Ask him how your father knew about the two of them," Micah whispered and, once again, Sloane repeated what he said to Judd. She probably would've gotten around to asking that question herself. She was curious about the answer. But Micah was thinking rationally, objectively, while she was trying to cope with what she was hearing. The more she learned, the more she couldn't believe that the police had never taken a serious look at her mother's case.

"He caught her talking to me once, on the phone."

"And that gave you both away? She couldn't have pretended it was about me?"

"It was too late for a call from a teacher. Besides, who can say how much he overheard?"

Sloane started digging at her cuticle again, but this time Micah stopped her immediately. "So you'd talked on the phone before. That's why you thought it was her calling after she disappeared."

"Yes. Cell phones weren't as common back then, so I'd given her my home number in case she ever needed help. Your father made her so...upset, uneasy, worried."

"Would you say she was also *frightened*?"

"I don't know if I'd go that far."

Because he'd feel responsible for not doing more to help her?

"I was merely trying to assure her that someone cared, I guess," he said. "That she had someone she could reach out to, if it came to that."

Sloane hated the thought of her mother, desperate and crying, pinning her hopes on a man who was married to someone else and couldn't do much. "Did she call you the night she went missing?"

"She might have. The phone rang that night, late. But before I could get to it, whoever it was had hung up."

"You don't know who it was."

"Caller ID said unknown number and the person left no message. But she wouldn't call me without blocking her number, and she sure as heck wouldn't leave a message. That's why I believed those other calls—the ones that came after—were her, too."

Sloane switched the phone to her other ear and turned so that Micah could still hear. "Did you try to call her back?"

"I didn't. I was afraid I'd only get her in trouble. Even if I blocked my number, your father would've known it was me because...because of the previous time, when he caught us talking."

"So what do you think happened to her?"

There was another long pause.

"Mr. Judd?"

"I have no idea. I'd hate to even venture a guess."

He seemed to avoid all the truly difficult questions.

"Do you believe she left?" Sloane pressed. "Moved away? If so, you should know that she's never reached out to me, *ever*. Not even after I graduated and left Millcreek. And not after all the success I had in my career. Wouldn't you expect that seeing me on the cover of a major magazine would draw her out even if nothing else could? If she was alive, I mean."

"I believe she would've reached out long before you appeared on the cover of any magazine. *If* she could. She loved you a great deal."

Sloane didn't realize she had tears streaming down

her cheeks until Micah went to the bathroom and returned with some toilet paper. There was an emptiness inside her she'd carried around ever since her mother went missing. She looked and sounded normal, but she felt like the walking wounded. She was now an adult, had accomplished a great deal in a difficult industry, but none of that could make her whole. She craved Clara's smile, her smell, her touch, almost as if she were still a child, and it was that craving, more than justice, that had drawn her back to Millcreek. With Clyde gone, she simply couldn't continue to ignore that a piece of her was missing.

"Sorry, I don't have any tissues," Micah mumbled.

That didn't surprise her with so much of his stuff still in boxes.

Embarrassed by her emotional reaction, she turned away to wipe her face.

"Are you okay?" Judd asked.

He'd been talking, but she'd quit responding, hadn't even been listening. She'd been caught up in the memory of her mother's gentle touch, the sound of her laughter and the warmth of her loving embrace—and how jarring and traumatic the night Clara went missing had been. How many nights since then had she lain awake going over and over everything that'd happened? Sometimes her father would be in another room, talking on the phone or moving about the house doing whatever, and she'd wonder if he was really the man he pretended to be.

"I'm fine." She walked several steps away from Micah, keeping her back to him so that she could pull herself together without having to do so under his watchful eye.

"So…what's going on?" Mr. Judd asked. "Why are you calling me now, after so long? Is there some sort of official investigation or—"

"Nothing official. So far, it's just me, trying to find my mother. I'm not sure why it took me so long to begin this search, except that my father is a formidable enemy and looking for my mother means completely alienating him."

"You're in a very difficult situation. I'm sorry for that, but I hope you're able to find her."

"If she's alive…"

"It must be terrible to consider all the possibilities."

She grappled with tears again but managed to swallow the lump in her throat. "It's time *someone* did."

There was another long pause, which made her believe he was wrestling with his own emotions. "You're right."

"Let me know if you remember anything else—anything my mother said or did—that might be significant."

"I will."

She disconnected and turned to see Micah leaning against the wall with his arms folded. "So? What do you think?" she asked, but he didn't seem to be analyzing what he'd heard. His expression wasn't thoughtful or absorbed—it was more of a dark scowl. Why? Was he angry he'd had her come over, brought this shit back into his life?

He seemed to be searching for what he wanted to say, for the right words to express *something*, and that made her uneasy. After dredging up so much pain from her past, she felt raw, couldn't tolerate hearing him accuse her of leaning on him when she'd let him down so badly before—if that was where this was going.

"I'm sorry," she said, jumping in before that conversation could even get started. "It was never my intent to draw you into this mess. And don't worry. I won't bother you again. You've done enough. Getting me the contact information for so many people, and coaching me on how to approach them, has been a huge help." She hurried over to the table and started shutting down her computer. "That's all I needed."

"You're packing up?"

"Of course. I didn't mean to stay this long. I'm ready to go back to the motel and let you get on with…with whatever you have planned for this evening."

He shoved off the wall and jammed his large hands in the front pockets of his jeans as he walked slowly, almost reluctantly, toward her. "Sloane, I'm the one who owes *you* an apology."

She froze as he stopped a few feet from the table. "For *what*?"

"For being so angry with you. For how I've treated you since you've been back."

"You haven't done anything." She put her laptop into her big leather bag. "I know it's difficult to have me in town after what I did."

"That's just it. You have as much right to be here as any of the rest of us. I was just being immature and selfish, looking at the situation only from my own perspective."

She slid her purse into her leather bag, too. "It's okay. You've always had parents you could love, admire and trust. It would be difficult to imagine growing up without that."

He moved a step closer. "Don't be so easy on me."

"Because…" For a second he seemed like the old Micah, the boy she'd loved. "Micah?"

"Never mind." He pulled out his keys. "We shouldn't be having this conversation. I'll take you back to the motel."

She wanted to tell him how much she'd missed him. That she would've stayed in touch if she could've handled that along with everything else she was going through. But she couldn't. That first year away from home had been the most difficult of her life—had encompassed so many big decisions and changes—but she didn't have a better excuse than the one she'd already offered him.

Time seemed to stand still as they stared at each other. She thought she saw a flicker of some softer emotion in his eyes. Was it regret? She felt something, too, but she refused to categorize it. She didn't dare even acknowledge it for fear she'd wind up going against her better judgment.

"I shouldn't have made love with you before I left," she finally said. "That had to have been confusing. But I didn't do it to…to take something from you I shouldn't have. I wanted you to be my first—to at least be able to keep, and treasure, the memory."

"God, Sloane," he said, but she didn't get to hear what he was about to say next. The door opened and Trevor came running in, yelling, "Dad!"

CHAPTER THIRTEEN

Trevor skidded to a stop at the edge of the dining room the minute he saw Sloane. “Oh. I didn’t know *you* were here,” he said.

Micah’s heart jumped into his throat. “Trevor, did you try to call me?” He hadn’t had any plans to see his son tonight. Paige was usually more protective of her time with Trevor than she’d been this week. She had something Micah wanted and she loved being the gatekeeper, the one in charge. It made her feel powerful to deny him, to make him comply with her wishes. But Micah tried not to focus on the way she used their son as a weapon against him. If he allowed himself to resent her too much, they wouldn’t be able to get along, and they *had* to get along. He was determined to keep life pleasant for Trevor.

Trevor yanked his gaze away from Sloane. This was the first time he’d ever seen another woman in Micah’s house, and, of course, it would have to be Sloane. Trevor had to be thinking that all the bullshit he'd heard his mother spout off about Sloane—about *them*—had to be true. "Yeah. Mom called from the car," he said. "You didn't pick up."

Sloane seemed nervous as she licked her lips. Obviously, she understood what this would mean. "Could your phone be dead?"

"It's possible." Micah didn't have time to look for it right now. Hoping to avoid a scene in which Paige went off about how she'd known all along that he still had a thing for Sloane, he started for the door. "Where's your mom?" he asked his son over his shoulder.

He was hoping to hear that Paige had already driven off, but Trevor didn't have a chance to answer before Micah saw his ex coming up the walkway. Of course she hadn't left. She would never forego an opportunity to see him. Especially right after he moved out, he'd "bumped" into her almost everywhere. She drove by his house, frequented the places he liked to go, that sort of thing.

"What's going on?" he asked her.

When Trevor came to the door, too, Micah put a hand on his shoulder so he'd stay put and couldn't go back to the kitchen where Sloane was. Paige couldn't see Sloane from where she stood, so if Trevor would only hold his silence, Micah felt he might be able to get out of this.

"I have a dinner date," Paige said. "Can you take Trevor for a few hours? I tried to call but…"

"I don't know where my phone is."

"I figured I could just swing by. You're always asking for more time with him, so I felt it was safe to assume you wouldn't mind."

"I *don't* mind." He squeezed Trevor's shoulder to make it less obvious that he was trying to keep him in place. "I'll take him whenever."

"He hasn't had dinner yet," she said. "Sorry about that. I was in a hurry to get ready and didn't have time to stop anywhere."

Micah could tell she was hoping the news that she had a date would evoke enough curiosity that he'd ask who she was seeing. But he didn't care. As long as the guy was a decent human being and would be good to Trevor, he'd been hoping she'd meet someone else. Maybe then she'd forget about *him*, let him move on without punishing him every time he said or did something that proved he wasn't coming back.

It was also possible she was lying about having a date. She'd done that sort of thing before—pretended she had other male interest in order to make him jealous. She'd even done it while they were married. Once, she almost got him into a fight with Blake, another guy on the force, at a picnic in the park because she insisted Blake had made a pass at her. It turned out others had seen Blake's "pass" and it was simply a smile and a wink after telling a joke.

"I can throw some chicken on the grill and steam some broccoli." Since he'd moved his grill without putting it into any sort of box, it was sitting on the patio, ready to go. He just needed to get the groceries. "What time will you be back?"

"I have no clue. Would it be a problem if it's late?"

"No. But he has school tomorrow. Maybe he should just stay here rather than wait up."

"Yeah!" Trevor was excited by the idea, probably

because she'd never allowed it before. "Dad can drive me to school in the morning."

"But what would you wear?" she asked.

"We could stop by your house, with your permission, of course," Micah quickly added, "and get whatever he needs."

Her hesitation led Micah to believe she might really have a date. Otherwise, Trevor's enthusiasm would've been enough to prompt her to say no. She was too afraid Trevor would love his father more than his mother, that she'd "lose" her son, too. That was part of the reason she rarely let them spend extra time together. "He has his field trip tomorrow, so he'd need to pack a lunch."

"We can manage that, too, Paige."

She glanced between them. "Okay, well…can I call you in a couple of hours? Let you know?"

He wasn't going to argue when he wanted her gone as soon as possible. "Sure."

Relieved that she remained unaware of Sloane's presence, and that she might leave without finding out, he started to shut the door the second she stepped away, but she stopped it.

"How do I look?" she asked and twirled around.

She'd put some effort into getting ready. She had on a purple blouse with sleeves that widened below the elbow and tight-fitting black jeans with heels. And she was wearing more makeup than usual. "You look great," he said, but only to be nice. He couldn't be a fair judge. They'd been through too much together. How many times had she said he didn't love her because she wasn't as pretty as Sloane? Sloane was gorgeous. There was no doubt about that. But it wasn't her looks that made the difference. He was always tempted to explain that to Paige, except he knew it would only make her *more* insecure. Then she'd feel she didn't measure up in other ways. Whenever she launched that argument, he'd simply shut down, refuse to talk about it. There was no reason to engage her on the subject. She was right about the underlying problem: he preferred Sloane and always had.

"Have a great night," he said.

She seemed to come a little undone by the authenticity in his voice. "You don't care?"

"Paige, let's not go into that right now, okay? You're the mother of my child. You're doing a great job raising Trevor, and I will support whatever makes you happy."

"That's the part that drives me the craziest," she muttered. "You say such nice things but feel absolutely *nothing*. Nothing gets below your skin. Nothing reaches your heart."

"Paige, *please*."

"Don't worry. I'm leaving," she snapped, and he shut the door as soon as she stomped off.

"You didn't want me to tell Mom Sloane is here, did you?" Trevor said, looking up at him.

Micah pinched the bridge of his nose as he considered how to answer this question. It didn't feel right to ask his son to keep a secret from his mother, and yet who Micah had over was none of Paige's business. Not anymore. "Since your mom and I are no longer married, she doesn't have to know about everything I do, everyone I see. That's called respecting my privacy."

"So you don't want me to tell her?" he clarified.

Micah sighed as he realized that Trevor wasn't going to understand such a careful skirting of the truth. "No, I don't want you to tell her."

"Does that mean Sloane *is* the reason you left?"

Sloane was the reason he should never have married Paige in the first place. But then there was Trevor. "She's not, no." Not in the way Trevor intended, anyway. "I had no idea she'd be returning to town. Sloane and I are just friends, and we should have the right to be friends, don't you think?"

He scuffed one tennis shoe against the other, obviously torn between logic and what he'd been told by his mother. "I guess."

"I'm trying to help Sloane. That's why she's over."

"With what?" he asked.

"Her mother went missing when she was a little girl. We're trying to find her."

"Because you're a policeman."

"That's right. But what we're doing is nobody else's business. That's why you aren't to say anything to your mother or anyone else."

Trevor pulled his bottom lip between his teeth as he considered what he'd been told. "And Mom will cry if I tell her..."

She'd yell a lot, too, but Micah held his tongue. "Probably."

"I don't like it when she cries."

"Neither do I."

"Then I say we don't tell her."

"That would be best," Micah agreed.

"Okay. Can we eat?"

Micah laughed at how quickly Trevor was ready to move on. "Yeah. I'll get right on it."

Sloane appeared at the end of the hallway with her leather bag on her shoulder. No doubt she'd held off so she wouldn't interrupt his talk with Trevor, but now that the discussion had ended… "Sorry to put you in a difficult position," she said. "Is there Uber or some other car service here in Millcreek?"

"Apparently, you think this town has grown a lot more than it has," he said with a chuckle and rested his hand on Trevor's shoulder as they walked back toward her.

"I was doubtful. I just hate to trouble you to take me back to the motel when your son is here, and he's hungry."

"Then maybe you'll agree to stay and eat with us, let me take you back later," Micah said.

She obviously hadn't expected the invitation. "I'd rather not impose. I have my car at the motel, so I'll be able to get dinner on my own."

"There's no need. We can all run over to get the groceries. It won't take long."

"It's okay with me if you eat with us," Trevor volunteered.

Sloane's gaze shifted to Trevor and came back again.

"My cooking will be as good as any restaurant," Micah added, and she finally offered him a hesitant smile.

"Okay."

Throughout dinner with Ed, Paige had a difficult time forgetting about her encounter with Micah. She almost wished she'd mentioned that her date tonight was with Sloane's father. At least that would've elicited a reaction.

But Micah hadn't asked. That alone made the encounter upsetting. Unlike so many other divorcées, she couldn't complain about her ex being stingy or abusive or jealous. Micah had been insufferably nice throughout the divorce, had given her everything she asked for and was always there for Trevor. Even when she claimed she needed extra money, just to make him see how much more expensive it was for them to live apart, he'd write her another check. He gave her much more than what was stipulated by the court.

He did so out of guilt, of course. He felt bad that he didn't love her and couldn't stay with her even for Trevor. So she used that to her advantage. Why shouldn't he suffer when he'd made *her* suffer so terribly?

"Are you okay?" Ed stepped onto the back patio, where they'd eaten, with another bottle of wine.

Her expression was far too pensive, she realized, and forced a smile. "I'm great."

"You liked your meal?"

"It was magnificent." Sloane's father had treated her like a princess ever since she arrived. He'd made corn on the cob, asparagus, baked potatoes, filet mignon and Alaskan King crab legs, which she'd only ever eaten twice before in her life. Together they'd also polished off a rare and expensive bottle of wine while he told her interesting stories about his job, city gossip and how he wanted to go to Paris and Rome one day, as though he might take her with him.

Dating a wealthy guy had its benefits, even if he was older, she decided as she stared out over the backyard. In the past, Paige had made entirely different kinds of memories at this house. She used to play in the tire swing, hide in the garage and roll down the hill that was off to one side. It was a bit jarring when she thought about it, but Ed didn't seem to be bothered by the fact that he'd first met her as a little girl. He also didn't seem to be nearly as bad as she'd envisioned, given what Sloane believed about him. Despite her fears and worries after Randy's visit, Paige was now thinking that maybe Randy had a right to be upset. What if Ed was innocent? Accusing someone of such a heinous crime would not be fair. If anything, Clara must've done something to piss Ed off so badly he reacted in a rage and caused a terrible accident. He was an impassioned person. She could see him erupting and then covering up anything that eruption had caused. But now that she was sitting here having dinner with him, she couldn't imagine him intentionally harming anyone.

He popped the cork and refilled her glass. "I want you to know something."

She looked up to meet his gaze. There were a few wrinkles at the edges of his eyes, which were more amber than brown, like Sloane's. And the smile lines around his mouth were more exaggerated than those of the men her age. But he still had classic good looks, had always reminded her of George Clooney. "What's that?"

He bent down so his mouth was close to her ear. "You've been driving me crazy in those jeans."

That comment was totally inappropriate to say to a friend of his daughter's and yet Paige couldn't get angry. She'd come here knowing his offer was of a romantic nature, and she'd been flirting with him ever since she arrived, testing her power. "You're no longer seeing that woman from Dallas?" she asked. "The one I've spotted you with around town?"

He put the bottle down and sat in his own seat. "Simone? No. That was never serious. I won't move away from Millcreek, and she won't leave Dallas, so we were doomed from the start."

Wasn't that what he liked? Then he never had to make a commitment. She'd heard enough gossip about his love life to understand he was a ladies' man who preferred to keep his options open. "I've never known you to date anyone from town. They *all* come from outside, don't they?"

He gave her an endearing, almost boyish "you got me" grin. "There hasn't been anyone here I've been particularly interested in. Until now."

Paige couldn't help being flattered. Out of all the women in Millcreek—and he could have his pick—he'd chosen *her*. It'd been so long since she'd felt desired. She wasn't sure Micah had *ever* really been turned on by her. It was possible she'd only imagined he was, at times, because that was what she longed to see.

Although she'd trade anything to hear Micah say what Ed had just said and mean it, that wasn't going to happen, at least not where they were in their relationship right now. So why not take what she could get? A rich older man to spoil her wouldn't be terrible, even if it didn't last. With Ed she didn't have to be the aggressor. That was a powerful aphrodisiac. She hated feeling as though she was constantly fighting for the smallest crumb of Micah's attention. The fact that Ed would be the last person in the world Sloane or Micah would feel good about her dating also made him appealing. She'd never seen herself as the type of person who would go after revenge for *any* reason, and yet the resentment and hurt she carried around with her had turned her into someone she didn't even know, someone she never dreamed she'd become.

"You're not worried that this could get complicated?" She regarded him from beneath her eyelashes as she sipped her wine.

He leaned back to study her. "I don't see any reason we have to look too far down the road. Why don't we simply enjoy the here and now? I'm having fun, aren't you?"

Ruger sat at his feet. The dog didn't dare beg for food; Ed made sure he knew better. But the animal was, no doubt, hoping someone would drop a morsel. She could tell by the level of attention he paid her hands, how he watched as she lifted every bite to her mouth.

"Can I feed him this last piece of meat?" Paige indicated what she had left on her plate.

"No, that wouldn't be smart."

"Because he might take off my hand?" she said with a chuckle.

Ruger's behavior when she first arrived had frightened her. He'd seemed determined to tear her to pieces, until Ed opened the door. Then he'd calmed down and behaved impeccably.

"Don't let him fool you. He's not a vicious animal."

"He sounded downright dangerous when I rang the doorbell."

He stroked his dog's head. "Naw, he'll put his tail between his legs if he's ever really challenged. He's nothing like some of the other dogs I've had over the years."

She put her fork on her plate, couldn't eat another bite. "You sound disappointed."

"I am, a little. I respect strength. Don't you?"

She felt herself flush. He was characterizing himself as strong, powerful, and she understood why. "But does your *dog* need to be mean? What is it you'd like him to do? If he was prone to bite, and he got loose, he could go after one of your neighbors."

"I wouldn't mind him going after one certain neighbor." He winked at her. "I'm kidding. It's not that I'd like him to do anything in particular. I guess it's like owning a fast car. You'll probably never go screaming down the freeway at 150 miles per hour, but it's nice to know you've got what it takes under the hood. I don't have a security system. I don't need one with a dog like this."

"You don't need one, anyway. We don't have a lot of crime in Millcreek, especially in this area. I doubt anyone would dare break into *your* house, anyway."

He reached over and took her hand. "Paige?"

She watched him adjust her rings so they were all straight. "What?"

"Why are we talking about my dog?"

Her mouth went dry. "I don't know. I'm nervous?"

"Because..."

"I haven't been with anyone except Micah and...this seems to be drifting in that direction."

"Are you concerned about how he might react if we get...involved?"

Not in the way he thought. She *wanted* to rattle Micah, to wake him up and make him realize that he was walking away from the best thing to ever happen to him. "We're divorced. What I do is no longer any of his concern."

"Good. Because I don't give a shit what he thinks about it." Ed's chair scraped the concrete as he pushed it back and stood. "I bought you a gift today, one you're going to like."

Paige's heart started to thump against her chest. What was she doing? She had the sudden feeling she'd gotten herself into something she might later regret, but she also felt she was in too deep at this point. "What is it?"

"It's in my bedroom," he said. "I'll show you."

CHAPTER FOURTEEN

Sloane couldn't remember when she'd had a better time. Things were sometimes awkward between her and Micah—when there was a lull in the conversation and their eyes inexplicably locked for no particular reason, or they happened to brush against one another as they were moving around the cramped kitchen, cooking or cleaning up, but Trevor provided a nice distraction. Sloane enjoyed getting to see how he behaved with his father.

She liked the happier, more relaxed kid he was with Micah better than the worried, sad kid he was with Paige. She could only attribute the difference to each parent's attitude. Micah acted as if all was well, so Trevor responded in a similar manner. Paige acted as though she was miserable, and that meant Trevor had to worry about her and carry a lot of angst. The impact Paige had was sad and yet Sloane couldn't fully blame her. She understood that Paige was struggling emotionally and probably couldn't help what she was doing to her kid.

"Can we watch a movie?" Trevor asked when the dishes were done. Micah had insisted he help clean up. It would've been easier to do the work without a third person in the kitchen, but Sloane respected that Micah was trying to teach his son to do his part.

"Not tonight, bud," Micah said. "You've got school in the morning."

Trevor's scowl looked a lot like Micah's when he was displeased. "A movie doesn't take long."

"It takes two hours, and that's two hours you need to be sleeping."

Trevor went to the window to part the blinds and peer outside. "We haven't heard from Mom. Maybe she's still planning to pick me up."

Micah checked his watch. "I doubt she's coming tonight. It's almost ten. She must've forgotten to call, is probably assuming I'll put you to bed—which is exactly what I'm going to do."

He looked back over his shoulder at them. "Is Sloane staying over, too?"

Sloane chose that moment to break in. "No. I've got to get back to the motel. You wouldn't mind riding along while your father drives me, would you?"

"No."

"Good. Thanks for letting me have dinner with you." She grabbed her bag. "Ready?" she said to Micah.

He scooped his keys off the counter and followed them out.

Sloane felt better leaving his house under cover of darkness; there was less risk of being seen together.

On the ride, they talked about the changes that'd taken place in Millcreek while she was gone. "Have you seen the new arts center at the high school?" Micah asked.

"They have a new arts center?" she said.

"They requested a new gym but they couldn't get the money appropriated until they upgraded the computer lab and arts department."

"So when do they get the new gym?" she asked drily.

"Soon." He grinned. "Thanks to your father. He fought for it."

"I'm not surprised. He was always a big sports buff."

"How come you're staying here?" Trevor asked as they pulled into The Wagon Wheel.

Apparently, he hadn't been paying attention when she'd said she was going to the motel this morning—or he hadn't clued in to what or where the motel was. "There aren't a lot of other options in this town," she said as she climbed out.

Micah rolled down the passenger window, so she shut the door before saying goodbye. "You won't be calling anyone else on the list we put together tonight, will you?"

"No. It's too late. People here are already leery of me. The last thing I need to do is give them reason."

"Have you been thinking about what Mr. Judd had to say? Do you believe him—about the unknown caller?"

She remembered how remorseful and sincere her kindergarten teacher had seemed. "Yeah, I do."

"Who do you think made those calls?"

She hiked her bag up higher on her shoulder. "Who do *you* suppose?"

"It would be a smart move for your father to make,"

he conceded. "Since Mr. Judd knew the extent of your parents' marriage problems, it would be one way to make it seem as though your mother was still..." he glanced back at his son and, she knew, tempered his words for that reason "...capable of making calls."

"Right."

"Your father's an expert at playing people, is all about neutralizing possible threats."

"How do *you* know?" she asked in surprise.

"He's been trying to neutralize me ever since you got back."

"This is the first you've mentioned it."

"I didn't see any reason to upset you, but maybe you should be aware of how he works."

She already was. She'd grown up with him, after all. The way he'd withhold his love if she ever said or did anything to displease him was just one of his manipulative tactics. He'd trained her and Randy like he trained his dogs—to believe the only thing that mattered in life was his approval.

It made her sad to think Randy was still an emotional slave to their father. So what if he'd inherited the dealership while she'd had to make her own money? The trade-off—the freedom—was worth it.

"What did he do?" she asked.

"We'll talk about that later. Get some sleep, okay?"

She nodded, thanked him for dinner and stepped away from the vehicle so he could leave.

He cast her a final glance before putting the transmission into Reverse. Then she was looking at his taillights as he pulled out of the lot.

Who would've thought Micah would be the one to help her?

She shouldn't be relying on him, she told herself. She'd promised herself she wouldn't, even if she had the chance. But his profession made him invaluable to her investigation. What he'd done for her today had saved so much time and energy.

As she crossed the walkway to her room, she shook her head at how narrowly they'd missed being discovered by Paige. "That was close," she muttered as she used her key card to unlock the door.

Although she was tired, she was filled with a strange sort of nervous energy, was planning on taking a hot shower to help her calm down and quit thinking about Micah. So many things kept swirling through her head, sending odd impulses to her body. The way he smelled. The amount of muscle he'd put on. The thickness of his hair and the dark beard growth on his face. She still had a thing for him, which was something she *had* to get over, especially because she could never stay in Millcreek, not with her father here, and he'd never leave Trevor.

The memory of his kiss, from when they were in high school, rose in her mind, making her wonder if he'd kiss the same way as a man, or if that had changed.

Stop thinking about him, she chastened herself. Shower and bed. That was what she needed to focus on. But as she went inside, she stepped on something, heard it crinkle.

Was it a bill? Did the front office think she was checking out?

When she snapped on the light, she discovered that someone had slipped an envelope with her name on it under the door, and it wasn't on the motel stationery. It said McBride New & Used Autos in the upper-left corner.

* * *

After stopping by Paige's house to get some overnight clothes for Trevor and settling him into bed at his place, Micah milled around the boxes in the living room. He was trying not to think about how great it had been to have Sloane in his house all day. He'd wanted her to stay the night, was glad that Trevor was over so he couldn't ask her. It was crazy how quickly the past ten years could fade away when she was around. All the anger and resentment seemed to melt and disappear, and he just wanted her back, which was so insanely masochistic.

Quit obsessing about her! He should be thinking about his ex-wife instead. He still hadn't heard from Paige, which was unusual. She'd never dropped Trevor off without making clearly defined plans, had never just left him, especially all night when he had school in the morning. Was this another attempt to manipulate him—one where she was intentionally trying to make him believe she might be in trouble to get him to show some concern?

If so, he didn't want to reward that kind of behavior. He cared about her as a human being, as Trevor's mother, but he wasn't in love with her, and he knew if he caved in and *did* show that he was getting worried, she'd assume too much and would once again start to hope for more.

He decided to wait it out. Maybe she was having such a wonderful time that, for once, she'd forgotten about him. That would be a good thing. If she could get over him, maybe they'd have the chance to establish a healthier relationship, one in which he'd be given more time and freedom when it came to their son.

His phone rang. Assuming he was hearing from Paige at last, he checked the caller ID.

It wasn't her; it was his mother. Surprised that she'd be up so late, since she and his father were both early risers, he hit the talk button. "Mom, what are you doing up this time of night?"

"It's only eleven."

"That's late for you."

"True. I've been on the phone."

"Talking to..."

"My sister. Who else?"

He chuckled. She and his aunt June, who together with her husband and oldest son owned the breakfast café in town, were identical twins, and they talked to each other every day. "What was so important that you didn't head to bed as soon as you hung up with her?"

"She said there was a lot of talk at the restaurant this morning."

"About..."

"Sloane McBride."

He stopped moving. He'd been wondering when his parents would learn of Sloane's return. He'd decided he wouldn't be the one to tell them. He was too transparent where Sloane was concerned, didn't want his mother to start offering advice on his love life. "What about her?"

"She's here. In Millcreek."

When he didn't respond, she added, "Hello?"

"I haven't gone anywhere."

"Well? Are you surprised? Excited? What?"

He couldn't lie to her and say he didn't know Sloane was back. She'd see through that instantly. And Trevor could accidentally say something about having dinner with Sloane that would give him away. Then the fact that he'd lied would be more telling than the truth. "I know. I bumped into her at Paige's last Friday."

"She's staying with your *ex-wife*?"

"They used to be friends, remember? *Best* friends."

"Until Paige fell in love with you."

He scratched his neck. "Yeah. That definitely complicated things." Paige's behavior had to have been hard on Sloane, in addition to everything else she was going through, but he hadn't thought much about it at the time. He'd been young, self-absorbed and so confident he'd have Sloane forever he'd simply ignored Paige's overtures, didn't let them bother him.

"So was it good to see her? Are you glad she's back?"

He dropped his hand. "Mom, don't start playing matchmaker. She's not a viable option for me."

"Why not?" she asked. "You've been in love with her since you were sixteen. *She* was the girl you should've married."

"Are you forgetting that she ran out on me?"

"What did you expect her to do? Marry you at eighteen?"

It didn't escape his notice that Sloane had said something similar. "She's the reason I got involved with Paige."

"You're the one who slept with Paige. You have no one to blame but yourself for that."

"You're suggesting I should've known she'd be back eventually, should've waited ten years? Do you understand how long ten years is to an eighteen-year-old?"

"Maybe she would've come back sooner if…if things had gone differently."

"She wouldn't have. That's what I'm telling you."

"Well, she must regret leaving. She's here now, isn't she?"

"She's only back to look for her mother."

"She told you that?"

"Yes. I helped her today, found some people she needed to talk to."

"How nice of you!"

"Thank you," he said in exasperation. "Are you finally back on my side?"

"I've always been on your side, Micah. You know that. But what are the chances she'll find her mother after so long?"

"Not good, which was why I was trying to help."

"Will her father get behind this search? Really make something happen?"

"Are you kidding? He's up for reelection next year. He doesn't want people starting to speculate on whether he killed her. Think of what his enemies could do with that."

"*Killed her!* Don't tell me Sloane believes that's a possibility."

"I'm afraid so. Her parents were the only two people there that night—except her."

"What does *she* remember?"

"Nothing definitive," he said, because he didn't want his mother telling her sister, who might tell God-only-knew-who-else that Sloane remembered her father getting physical with her mother. Ed was leery of Sloane's return as it was. If rumors like that started to circulate, he'd be livid, even more determined to silence her.

"I bet she looks good…"

Micah bit back a sigh. "She's a model. Of course she looks good."

"You didn't feel anything when you were with her? You're over her?"

God, he wished he could say that. Instead, he'd spent most of the day trying to stop himself from imagining what it would be like to take her back to bed. He felt he could provide her with a much better experience now that he wasn't a virgin himself.

But he couldn't sleep with her, even if she was willing. He'd be asking for more of the same kind of hurt she'd dished out before. He wasn't going to be stupid enough to walk off another emotional cliff. "Mom, stop."

"I'm just asking!"

"I won't talk about it."

"Because you'd like to get her back."

He dropped onto the couch and stared at the ceiling above him. "I'm about to hang up..."

"Just give me a little hint! Then I'll know what to do."

"*You* shouldn't do anything. This isn't any of your business."

"But I can't stand seeing you so unhappy."

"I'm *not* unhappy. I'm a big boy, coping well with being a single dad until I'm ready to start dating again."

"Which will be when?"

He heard the challenge in her voice. "Soon."

"You're just trying to mollify me."

"Desperately," he admitted.

He heard her make a sound of irritation. "If you won't let *me* get involved, you'll have to fight for her yourself. Do you hear? This is your chance. If you want her, make sure you give it all you've got."

Micah hated how those words made his heart pound. Part of him wanted nothing more than to fight for

Sloane. But besides all the crap he'd have to deal with when it came to Paige, and some legitimate concerns for what another woman entering the picture at this juncture would do to his son, especially *this* woman, they'd been apart for ten years. Did he even really know her?

It was possible the woman he remembered, the woman he wanted, didn't even exist anymore…

Except…he'd spent the day with her, and she didn't seem to have changed a great deal, despite all of her success. That was the weird thing. Being with her had been exciting, easy, natural. But it was possible he just wanted to believe she was the same because of some testosterone-driven compulsion to conquer her at last.

"Good night, Mom. I'll call you later," he said and went to charge his phone so he could go to bed. He had to be careful or he'd screw up his life again—and the stakes were a lot higher nowadays.

CHAPTER FIFTEEN

Sloane sat on the bed, staring at the envelope she'd found. She hoped it was from her brother. She wanted it to contain an apology for how he'd treated her on Friday or at least an honest admission that he had his own suspicions and uncertainties about what had gone on twenty-three years ago. Being the only defector in the family made her feel terrible. Even if Randy refused to delve into the past under any circumstances, she wished they could at least have a heart-to-heart, that she could gain a little understanding for why she had to handle the situation differently. She missed him, missed their father, too, in a weird, crazy way.

Or maybe she didn't miss her father *exactly*. She just wished for things to be different between them. The bond that tied a child to his or her parent, even if that parent was difficult, wasn't easily broken. So as much as she'd tried, at times, to forget him and move on, there seemed to be no escape from the feelings of guilt and inadequacy, the desire to please him despite her misgivings and the temptation to give him what he wanted and remain silent, pretend that night had been no different than what he said so she could return to the family.

But she couldn't give in, not without feeling even worse for ignoring her intuition and abandoning her mother, who hadn't had a champion in all the years she'd been gone. Clara deserved more.

"You're just destined to be conflicted," she said to herself and braced for whatever she was about to find as she ripped open the envelope. It wasn't that Randy believed in their father's innocence. That was what bothered her most. It was that he was determined not to believe anything that could threaten his own well-being. There was a difference between not believing and *refusing* to believe.

Sloane unfolded the letter and checked the signature at the bottom. It wasn't from Randy; it was from Hadley, his wife, or so she thought. There was no official signature, just an *H*, but with the letterhead, that assumption stood to reason. Hadley had had something to say when she stopped by earlier, something she hadn't had the chance to put into words before Randy had called and sent her scrambling to get Misty back in the Land Rover.

Sloane propped the pillows behind her and leaned back while she read.

Sloane,

Sorry I had to rush off. That wasn't the first meeting I'd hoped it would be. But I came to tell you that I think you're doing the right thing. I can't say why, but keep looking. You'll find what you want eventually.

—H

Sloane read the letter again, more carefully. Hadley knew something, something she didn't want to say. But...what? And how might that impact the investigation?

Carefully folding the sheet of paper, she put it back in the envelope and then into her purse. While encouragement was good, she needed details, which meant she'd have to approach her sister-in-law, gain her trust and get her to talk.

She picked up her phone to text Micah, only to put it down before she could. She'd tell him tomorrow or the next day, whenever she had the chance. She couldn't turn to him every few minutes.

But her resolve lasted all of eight minutes.

You still awake?

When he didn't answer right away, she assumed he was asleep and went to wash her face and brush her teeth. But his response was waiting for her when she was done.

Yeah. I'm here. What's up?

She nibbled at her bottom lip. Apparently she hadn't stayed away from Millcreek long enough because he still held the same power over her he had before. Hadley left a note under my door.

Your brother's wife? What kind of note?

One that tells me I'm on the right track, to keep looking.

You're kidding.

No.

Her phone rang.

Sloane pulled her knees into her chest as she answered Micah's call. "Did I wake you?"

"Not really. I was just starting to doze off." His voice had a slight rasp, as if he was half-asleep. She liked the sound of it, liked that the harshness that'd been there before, when she first returned, was gone. "What did she say exactly?"

"You *were* sleeping. We can talk about this tomorrow."

"No, read it to me."

"Okay." She reached for her purse and did as he asked.

"Wow. I'm shocked," he said when she was done.

"Me, too."

"I can't believe she'd put her name on that, knowing she'd probably get into a lot of trouble if Randy found out."

"*Trouble?* You make it sound like she's a child."

"Hadley is completely cowed, Sloane. She lets your brother make *every* decision."

"How do you know?"

"I've seen them together at various functions. He treats her like a doormat."

"So you know her?"

"Only peripherally."

"Is there any chance you have her cell number or some other way to get hold of her?"

"I can get her cell phone and address. Just make sure you don't go to the house when Randy might be there."

"The more you talk about him the more I realize he's turned out a lot like our father."

"He's definitely a chip off the old block."

That wasn't something Sloane was pleased to hear, but the way Hadley had scrambled off the second Randy had called lent the claim some credibility.

She skimmed the note again. "So what do you suppose she's talking about? 'I can't say why.'"

"She has something specific in mind. She's seen or heard something over the years, or she wouldn't leave you a note like that."

"But if it's anything *too* damning, why hasn't she come forward before?"

"I told you—he's in charge. I get the impression she's even a little scared of Randy. It could be she's trying to get it off her chest without having to be the one to instigate an investigation."

"That makes sense."

"She doesn't want Randy and your father to blame her. She's not as brave as you are."

"I'm not sure you can call it brave. Maybe reckless."

"This way, she can clear her conscience without having to do the dirty work. But you need more. You'll have to get her to open up. Or... I don't know if it's smart for *you* to be the face of this thing. Maybe with what you've told me so far—your memories and Vickie saying she saw your father take the boat out that night—I can talk to my chief, see if he'd be willing to let me start an official investigation."

"No, don't go to him yet. I think we'll get more doing things the way we are at the moment."

"How do you figure?"

"I get the feeling people are willing to talk because it's just me. They don't believe I have the power to do anything to my father, that nothing will come of it, so they feel comfortable expressing their own worries and concerns about that night. It's more like gossiping this way, seems fairly innocuous. But if we make it official, put what they say on the record, they could get spooked, clam up."

"Depending on what Hadley knows, and if she's willing to talk, that could change things."

"I'm guessing she won't open up easily. She might feel as though she's gone as far as she can." And Sloane knew what kind of shit would rain down on Micah if he stepped up to fight for her. "At least she's given me hope that I'm not destroying any chance I may ever have to reconnect with my family for nothing."

"At some point, we're going to have to make the investigation official."

"If I can get enough to take it in that direction. Anyway, we can talk about this later. I'm sorry to have bothered you so late."

"Not a problem."

"Micah?" she said, stopping him before he could hang up.

"What?"

"Did you ever hear from Paige?"

"No."

"What's going on with her?"

"I have no idea."

"She *couldn't* have known I was there..."

"She wouldn't have walked away if she did. She would've raised hell."

"In front of Trevor?"

"It's happened plenty of times before—and for far less reason."

She slid lower in the bed and pulled up the covers. "Does it bother you to think she's seeing someone else?"

"Not at all."

"What if...what if she's not just hanging out with this guy? What if she's *sleeping* with him?"

"I don't care about that, either."

He answered so quickly and was so resolute she couldn't help but believe him. "You're over her."

"Sloane..."

"What?"

"You're the only woman I've ever wanted—in my bed or out of it," he said and hung up.

Paige felt sick, dirty. She'd known she was making a mistake the second Sloane's father started taking off her clothes, so she wasn't sure why she'd let the whole thing continue. He'd been saying what she needed to hear, she supposed. How sexy she was. How he'd wanted her for a long time. How he was going to treat her better than any man she'd ever been with. He'd hit her up at a time when she had almost zero self-esteem. That Micah hadn't been able to love her, and couldn't even fake it, ate her up inside, made her feel she was destined to be overlooked by those who meant the most to her.

But that wasn't all of it. If she was being honest, she'd

done it to punish Sloane. She couldn't compete with Sloane, had never been able to compete, and that made her hate her best friend almost as much as she loved her.

God, what kind of a person was she?

Paige held her shoes with one hand while scrubbing the other over her mouth in an effort to get Ed's saliva off her face.

She glanced back at the house, which was dark now, from the front walkway and saw Ruger in the moonlight, watching her from the window with knowing eyes, and purposefully turned away. Ed had asked her to stay overnight. He'd said it was too late for her to go out, that he'd make her breakfast in the morning, but she could tell he didn't really care if she stayed, wasn't all that invested in her well-being. He'd gotten what he wanted. He was merely putting on a show with the nice talk—just as he'd been putting on a show while they were having sex, trying to act as though it was somehow more than him using her.

She was just another one of his conquests. Nothing more. But she couldn't blame him entirely. She'd been using him, too—as a way to strike back at Sloane, which was crazy. What she'd done had only made her feel worse.

The act itself had seemed *interminable*. Finally, he'd climaxed, and then he'd dragged out all kinds of sex toys to use on her, and she hadn't even wanted to be with him enough to enjoy taking her turn. She'd just played along so he wouldn't know how repulsed she was, how badly she regretted the whole thing.

She wondered how many other women he'd used those toys on and nearly gagged.

How could she have stooped so low as to sleep with her friend's *father*?

"Just hold yourself together. You can't fall apart here," she whispered, over and over, as she unlocked her car and tossed her shoes inside. She planned to stand in a hot shower and scrub until she felt clean again. But she didn't drive home as she intended. By the time she turned out of the River Bottoms and reached town, she was shaking and crying so hard she could barely see to drive.

Banging on the door woke Sloane. At first, she was so disoriented she thought she'd slept in and the maid was hoping to clean the room. She was about to yell for her to come back later when she realized she'd only closed her eyes an hour ago. According to the alarm clock on the nightstand, it wasn't yet midnight.

Was it Hadley? Had Randy found out she'd been by the motel?

"Coming!" she called so that whoever it was wouldn't wake up the motel's other patrons. She was afraid there'd been a fight between her brother and his wife or something else terrible, so she didn't even bother to pull a robe or sweatshirt over her tank top and panties before rushing to the door and gazing through the peephole.

The lighting was poor outside, making it difficult to determine the identity of her visitor, but it looked like Paige.

She left the chain on but went ahead and cracked open the door.

Sure enough, it *was* Paige, just not the Paige Sloane was used to seeing. This Paige had mascara streaking down both sides of her face, her hair was mussed as if she'd just climbed out of bed, her clothes were wrinkled and she wasn't wearing any shoes. "What happened to you?" Sloane cried and quickly removed the chain so that she could let her friend inside. *"Are you okay?"*

Paige was sobbing uncontrollably. Sloane had never seen her so upset. "What's going on?" she asked. "Don't tell me something's happened to Trevor or Micah..."

"No, it isn't that. It's...it's the guy I went out with tonight."

"He didn't attack you!"

Paige wiped her face with the back of her hand. "Worse."

"What could be worse?"

"I slept with him."

"And it was *that* terrible?"

"Yes, but it was also my own fault."

"Who was he?"

She opened her mouth, closed it again, then shook her head. "I don't want to say. Never mind. I shouldn't have come here. I can't tell *you*."

She turned to go, but Sloane caught her. "Of course you can tell me. You can tell me anything."

"I wish I hadn't let him touch me." Covering her face, she broke down sobbing again. "I can't believe I did. I'm *such* a terrible person."

"Anyone can make a mistake, Paige. It's been a hard year, which is why we have to be kind to each other and to ourselves."

"You don't understand."

"I understand that you did something you regret."

"Yes..."

"But if it's over, done, you can't take it back. So put

it behind you and forget about it, because you're *not* a terrible person."

She looked up. "I am! I was glad when you left, Sloane. I wanted Micah more than anything. I took him even though I knew he loved you, and now…and now I've done this, too."

Although stung by the admission that Paige was glad she'd left when she'd had such a hard time, especially that first year, Sloane couldn't help feeling some compassion at the same time. "Calm down, okay?"

After pulling her to the bed, Sloane dragged the blankets up around her shoulders. It wasn't cold, but Paige was trembling like a soaked kitten.

"I've screwed up my life," she said. "Micah hates me. *You* hate me."

"I'm sure Micah doesn't hate you. And I don't hate you, either." Sloane was conflicted when it came to Paige, but *hate* was far too strong a word for someone she still wanted to love. "You were like a sister to me growing up. That type of thing goes deep and can't be easily destroyed."

Paige sniffed and wiped her face. "That's why I reached out to you on Facebook last year. I wanted to reclaim what we once had. I thought it was a tragedy for us to let go of each other."

"It *would* be a tragedy." Sloane put an arm around her. "I can't pretend I'm not hurt that you were glad when I left, but that was a long time ago."

"And I'm sorry. I'm *so* sorry!"

Sloane rubbed her arm. "It's okay. I forgive you."

"You shouldn't. You have no idea…"

"I know we're friends, and that's what friends do.

Anyway, I already have. So about that guy you were with tonight…"

Paige blanched. "It was terrible."

"Who was it?"

She stared at her feet without answering.

"Paige?"

She couldn't seem to look Sloane in the eye. "Just someone I met," she mumbled. "You don't know him. I don't even know why I slept with him. No, actually, I do. I needed someone to appreciate me for me and not want you instead, and I felt like he could give me that."

Any residual anger Sloane felt immediately melted into pity. "Oh, Paige…"

A fresh tear rolled down her cheek. "Pathetic, isn't it?"

"It's not pathetic. It's sad. Obviously, you don't know how special you are."

"If I was special, Micah would never have left me."

"That's not true. Maybe you weren't right for him, but that doesn't mean you won't be perfect for someone else."

"You mean someone *I* don't love?"

Sloane went into the bathroom to get some tissues. "Someone you *do* love," she said when she returned. "You'll find the right man, the right time, the right situation. You'll see."

Paige accepted the Kleenex. "Now I feel even worse."

"What are you talking about?"

"You're too generous. I came here so you could scream at me, tell me what a bad friend I've been. Instead you try to comfort me."

"We can't always pick who we love." Sloane sat beside her again. "I've never been your enemy, Paige."

"I don't need you to be," she said, her voice nasal from her crying jag. "I'm my own worst enemy. Wanting someone you can't have does something to you, Sloane, especially when you've given that person the very best you've got."

Sloane held her hair back so she could see her face. "You're going to get through this. You'll find what you need. You'll see."

"That's just it. I need Micah. I feel like I'll *die* if I don't get him back."

That was the last thing Sloane wanted to hear. It shoved *her* into the interloper's position, made her feel guilty for her own feelings for Micah. "He's a good guy."

"You're a famous model. You can have anyone. But he's all I've ever wanted."

Sloane said nothing but the comfort she was offering suddenly became awkward, mechanical, fake. Just when she was beginning to feel some closeness with Paige, they approached the same old barrier.

"So I should forget about tonight?" Paige asked, thankfully changing the subject.

"Yes. It's over. Don't think of it again."

"I doubt I can let it go that easily."

"Because you're upset and you're exhausted. Things will look a lot better in the morning."

"Okay." She leaned over to rest her head on Sloane's shoulder. "I'll be a better friend to you from here on out. I promise."

"I know you will." Sloane couldn't change how she felt about Micah, so as off-putting and upsetting as it may be, it could be the same for Paige, and that made it wrong to hold her feelings against her.

"Can I stay here with you for a few more minutes?" Paige asked. "I can't face going home to my empty house. I'll just relive what happened tonight, over and over, if I do."

"You don't have to go home at all. You can stay with me."

"Are you sure?"

"Positive."

Paige managed a wobbly smile as Sloane rearranged the bedding so she could cover her up. "It's not the end of the world, okay? Somehow you'll get through this difficult time." She hoped they *all* would… "You used protection tonight, though, right?"

"You mean condoms?"

"Or something else."

"I'm not on the pill. I haven't had sex with anyone in ages. But he told me he's had a vasectomy."

For Paige's sake, Sloane hoped that was true. She almost said she should've made him use a condom, anyway, but she didn't. It was too late now, and Paige felt bad enough as it was. "Good."

Paige closed her eyes only to open them again. "Sloane?"

"What?"

"I'll get everything figured out."

"Of course you will." She had to. Trevor was depending on her.

Sloane turned off the light. Then she silenced her phone, in case Micah called in the morning—she didn't want that to happen when Paige was around—and crawled in on the other side of the bed. She assumed Paige was asleep. That was how exhausted her friend had seemed. But a few minutes later, she heard Paige's voice.

"Remember how often we stayed with each other when we were kids?"

"Almost every weekend."

"I'm so glad you're back in town. This is like old times, isn't it?"

"Yeah." Sloane adjusted her pillow. "The good old days," she said, but it made her sad to think that, because of their feelings for Micah, their relationship would probably never be the same.

CHAPTER SIXTEEN

In the morning, after Sloane hugged Paige goodbye, she spent the day avoiding Micah. As she'd known ten years ago, she couldn't see him, couldn't be around him, or she'd want him. There was no getting past that. He had been a huge amount of help, and she was grateful, so she *had* returned several text messages from him. But she'd given only minimal responses, especially when he texted that he'd stopped by Paige's after taking Trevor to school to make sure she was safe and found her coming home in the same clothes she'd had on the night before.

Sloane wasn't about to tell him what Paige had done. She didn't want to give him any reason not to get back together with her, if there was even a chance of that. Then she'd be to blame if Trevor couldn't have his father in the house. Why would she create an obstacle for their family when she wasn't going to be in town for more than a few months?

Since she cared for everyone involved, especially Micah, she was trying not to make a mess of everything while she was in Millcreek. And she had plenty to keep her busy and distracted.

She'd been trying to reach Hadley, to ask about the letter she'd found under her door. Micah had given her Hadley's cell phone, but it was disconnected. When she told him that, he said she must just recently have gotten a new one. That meant Sloane had only her address. She'd gone by Randy's house a couple of times in the middle of the day, when Randy should be at the car dealership, but no one had answered her knock either time. Only when Sloane had asked the neighbor, who was out getting his mail on her last visit, did she learn that her sister-in-law had taken Misty to Arkansas to visit her parents.

No wonder Hadley had felt brave enough to leave that note; she'd been heading out of town for ten days.

After returning to her motel for the second time, Sloane tried to track down Katrina. As the woman who dated her father after her mother disappeared, Katrina might know something. Micah had been able to provide Katrina's last known address and a work number but neither of those turned out to be current. Katrina had worked for a series of car dealerships over the years, been married and divorced twice and had lived all over the state, so she wasn't easy to track down.

It was a relief when Sloane called a dealership in Dallas, and the woman who answered the phone explained that although Katrina no longer worked there, her stepbrother, Toby Squires, was a salesman. She put him on the line right away and as soon as Sloane told Toby who she was, he gave her Katrina's phone number. She didn't even have to explain why she wanted it. He didn't seem to care; he only wanted to be helpful.

After that, she managed to reach Katrina and set up a lunch date in Fort Worth, where Katrina was once again living. Her father's former girlfriend had been surprisingly friendly, but Sloane suspected her celebrity was part of the reason. Katrina had been quite taken with the fact that Sloane had modeled for some of the biggest luxury brands in the business. On the phone, she kept saying things like, "I've told *all* my friends that I knew you when you were just a little girl." Maybe that was why Toby had readily provided her number; he'd heard of Sloane. Or he was trying to curry favor. He'd texted her afterward to see if she'd go out with him, but she'd politely declined, saying she wasn't going to be in the state long enough.

By the time night fell, she was exhausted. She went to bed early, grateful that she'd managed to avoid Randy, her father and Micah today.

She expected to toss and turn. She'd had trouble sleeping since she moved back to town. But she nodded off right away.

In the morning, she found a text from Micah waiting for her.

Any luck getting hold of Hadley?

No. She's out of town and, without her cell phone number, I'm afraid we'll have to wait until she gets back.

Someone has to have it.

Someone we can get it from?

Possibly. I'll text my mother. She's pretty well connected here in town. If she doesn't have it, she might know someone who does.

Thanks for trying to come up with it.

What about Katrina? Have you talked to her?

Briefly. I'm meeting her for lunch today.

Where?

Fort Worth. She works at another car dealership there.

That should prove interesting. I'm on duty or I'd go with you, came his response.

She frowned when she read that. You've done enough. Really. If you can come up with Hadley's cell phone number, that'd be great. Other than that, I can handle it. She didn't want to leave him any worse off than she'd found him.

Fortunately, he didn't respond.

Because she had an hour's drive, Sloane didn't have long to wait. Almost as soon as she got ready and had breakfast, she left for Fort Worth.

Katrina had chosen the restaurant, which turned out to be a small, trendy place downtown called Monty's. It was crowded, but Sloane didn't have any trouble finding Katrina. She was standing by the hostess station. Sloane would've recognized her anywhere; she hadn't changed much.

"Look at you!" Katrina said as Sloane approached in a brown jumpsuit with a wide belt, ankle boots and some chunky jewelry. "You're all grown up, and you're just *gorgeous*!"

Sloane could tell Katrina now dyed her hair. It was so much darker than before. Her acrylic nails were painted a bright red, which matched her lipstick, and the way she kept smoothing her ankle-length shirt and white boho top suggested she was proud of the ensemble. "You look great yourself."

"I can't believe you bothered to look me up. You were only…what…five, six when I was seeing your father? I wasn't sure you'd remember me."

"I definitely remember you." Sloane didn't add that it wasn't fondly, as Katrina seemed to assume.

"How is your father, by the way?"

"I wouldn't know," Sloane said. "We don't talk."

"I'm sorry to hear that." Did Katrina's response indicate they didn't talk, either? If so, that would be good news as far as Sloane was concerned. She wanted to learn what Katrina remembered of that time without those memories being muddied or influenced by more current impressions and information—and without Katrina feeling as though she was stabbing Ed in the back by being honest about what she may have heard or seen.

"It was my choice, for the most part." Sloane added the qualifier at the end because it was probably too late to undo what she'd done. Maybe these days it was her father's choice, too.

The hostess approached with their menus. "Right this way, ladies."

They were taken to a small table near the window where they could see hordes of business people on the street outside hurrying to and fro.

They made small talk as a young man brought them

water and they perused the menu. Sloane learned that Katrina had a little boy who was eight and being raised by her first husband in San Antonio, that her mother had passed away two years ago and her father lived in Wyoming, that she was hoping to like her current job at Russ Green Truck & Auto much more than her previous one, where she claimed to have been sexually harassed by her boss. She was currently living with her stepbrother—the one who'd given Sloane her number.

"I appreciate you taking the time to meet with me," Sloane said after they placed their order and the waitress left the table.

"I was excited to get your call. But I admit I'm a little bewildered as to why we're here."

"This has to do with my mother."

Katrina's eyebrows knitted but Sloane couldn't decide if it was manufactured confusion. "Your *mother*?"

"I'm trying to find her, and I hope you won't mind helping me."

"Of course not. I remember how badly you missed her. You were like a lost puppy back then. And your father...well, he didn't know how to relate to you, so I could tell it wasn't easy."

Sloane felt her smile grow ever more brittle. "You mean he was too busy running his own life to care about mine."

Katrina stiffened. "He was...busy."

With *her*. Perhaps that was why the comment made her uncomfortable, but Sloane didn't add that. She was disheartened to see that Katrina still seemed loyal to her father. "I remember."

"Anyway, your mother was gone by the time Ed and

I started dating so I'm afraid I won't be able to tell you anything."

"You didn't know her?"

Katrina took a quick sip of water. "Not *really.*"

"You worked at the dealership, didn't you? I'm assuming she came in occasionally, that the two of you talked."

She straightened her napkin as well as her silverware. "She came in, but not for any length of time. I was half her age and just an employee. It's not as if she was interested in being my friend."

Sloane took a drink of her water as she tried to read Katrina's body language. She seemed uptight, apprehensive—completely different than when they'd first met up. "Is it true that you were having an affair with my father at the time?"

Her tongue darted out to wet her lips. "No! Of course not."

When Sloane lifted her eyebrows to show her skepticism, Katrina scowled. "We weren't having an affair!"

"Is that what I'd hear if I contacted everyone who worked at the dealership when you were there?" Sloane asked.

Katrina lowered her voice. "Look, you're not going to blame me for what happened."

"I'm not trying to blame *anybody,*" Sloane said. "I just want the truth. I want to know what happened to my mother. Wouldn't you want the same if you were me?"

She didn't seem to have a ready answer. At length, Katrina said, "Of course. Anyone would. But I had nothing to do with it. Ed said she left. That's all I know."

The waitress brought their drinks, so Sloane waited before continuing the conversation. "You believed him?

You never doubted, never saw anything that made you wonder?"

She pulled her purse into her lap and scooted her chair back. "I'm not sure I'm willing to continue with this."

"Because..."

"Because I don't like being put on the spot."

"So you *were* sleeping with my father."

With a sigh, she suddenly gave up the charade and scooted her chair back under the table. "If I was the only one, maybe I'd feel guilty about that. But I wasn't. Your father slept with most of the girls who worked for him. Once your mother had children, he wasn't as attracted to her. At least, that was the excuse he gave me."

Sloane was afraid she might break her glass she clutched it so tightly. *What a bastard...* Even if her father wasn't guilty of murder, he wasn't exactly admirable.

"*I* wasn't the aggressor," Katrina was saying, still trying to absolve herself of any guilt. "I wasn't out to break up your family."

Sloane forced herself to let go of her glass so she could stir another packet of sugar into her iced tea. "So why'd you do it?"

"I don't know. I was nineteen. Nineteen-year-olds do a lot of stupid things. I suppose I was flattered by the attention of my rich boss."

At least that part seemed genuine. The rest? Sloane wasn't so sure. "I appreciate your honesty."

Katrina blinked at Sloane's sudden reversal. "You're not upset?"

"It's more that I'm not surprised."

"About..."

Sloane chose not to elaborate. "Did my father ever say anything about my mother that gave you a funny feeling?"

Katrina screwed up her face, apparently considering her response. "No. Never."

"Was he sad she was gone?"

"Absolutely."

"But you just told me he wasn't attracted to her."

"Sexually, he wasn't. It doesn't mean he didn't love her."

"It sort of does," Sloane argued. "He started openly dating you, a woman half his age, within two months of her disappearance. That says something, too, doesn't it?"

She shrugged. "People react to grief differently."

"You don't suspect he might've had any culpability in her disappearance?"

She shook her head, but the fear in her eyes contradicted her denial. "Believe me, the man I knew would never hurt anyone," she said, "least of all the mother of his children."

"He hurt her by sleeping around."

"I mean he wouldn't *physically* hurt her. Your father was a devoted family man."

Again, Sloane felt a certain disconnect, as if Katrina was rehearsing words that had no meaning for her. "How could he be a serial cheater *and* a devoted family man? A man who was broken up about the loss of his wife *and* someone who was ready to move on within weeks?"

"Men are men. They may chase a few skirts. It doesn't have to mean anything. Maybe having sex with me was how he dealt with his grief."

This wasn't making any sense, and Sloane was beginning to suspect she knew the reason. "Thanks for being so transparent with me."

Katrina didn't seem to know how to interpret her comment. "You're welcome," she said at length.

Sloane made a show of picking up her purse and digging through it. "Do you happen to have the time? I'm supposed to take some medication at twelve thirty..."

Katrina found her phone. "Twelve twenty."

"Oh good. I've got ten minutes. Would you mind setting a timer?"

"Not at all." She tapped in her password so she could utilize her clock app. "Why are you on medication? Is there something wrong with you?" She set her phone by her plate.

"I'm on an antibiotic to clear up a bronchial thing, that's all." Sloane put her glass down and pretended it was an accident when she tipped it over.

Katrina shrieked and jumped to her feet but not fast enough to avoid a lapful of cold liquid. Fortunately, the tea had run straight across the table and not doused the phone. "Damn it!" she cursed as she tried to brush off what she could.

"I'm so sorry!" Sloane offered those around them who'd turned at the disruption a sheepish smile so they'd go back to their meals.

"This is a new skirt!" Katrina complained and hurried off to the bathroom so she could clean up.

As soon as she was gone, Sloane rescued the phone so it wouldn't get wet—and scanned through Katrina's recent call history.

Sure enough, immediately after Sloane had spoken to Katrina to set up this lunch yesterday, Katrina had called Millcreek's city hall. There were several calls and texts between her and Ed's cell phone since then, too.

Sloane clenched her jaw as she read through them.

Are you sure I should have lunch with her?

Yes, of course.

I don't know. I'd love to meet her now that she's a famous model and everything—my brother would flip his shit if I was able to hook him up with her—but I'm a little nervous about everything that happened.

As far as you know, nothing happened. Why not take the opportunity to disarm her for me? Convince her I was destroyed by Clara's disappearance.

I doubt she'll believe me.

I don't remember you being a bad liar.

I'm not as good as you! And she doesn't trust me to begin with, so that's not an easy place to work from.

Come on. I'll make it worth your while. Tell her that we didn't get involved until after Clara left, that you were merely trying to comfort me and things got a little out of control.

Maybe we should rehearse it, then? Do some role-playing? And you can tell me what you'll give me for helping out. ;)

I remember you like jewelry.

I do. I'll call you in a minute.

The texts ended there. Sloane had no idea what had been discussed on the subsequent call, but she was checking to see if there'd been any email exchanges between them when Katrina came back.

"What are you doing?" she cried as she rushed forward.

Sloane cursed silently. She'd been hoping to forward those texts and any emails to herself or take pictures of them with her own phone, but she hadn't had enough time. "Just making sure you're as full of shit as I thought." She slid the phone back over by Katrina's plate before tossing a twenty on the table for the meal she wasn't going to eat. "You can send the rest of the bill to my father or take it out of whatever he promised you to lie to me," she said.

"What do you mean, *no*?" Micah said.

His police chief continued clipping his nails into the trash can he'd pulled out from under the desk. "I have to explain that answer?" He didn't bother to glance up.

"I'd appreciate a reason, sir. I said I'd look into it on my own time, that it doesn't have to be anything official, which shouldn't be a problem. I'm only asking for the file, so I can see what's been done so far, who's been interviewed and what they said. It's been a while, might be time to go back and interview everyone again."

"I looked at the file myself day before yesterday. There's nothing of any merit in there."

Micah stepped forward. "*You* have the file? That's why I haven't been able to find it here at the station?"

Adler shoved his trash can back under the desk and scooted forward. "I took it home with me right after I heard that Sloane was back in town."

"And?"

"Like I said, there's nothing in it that warrants a closer look."

Micah threw up his hands. "So who's been interviewed?"

"Everyone who should've been."

Micah had a hard time believing that. "And? What did they say? Where's Clara McBride?"

"They didn't know, and neither do I. But I have no reason to believe this is a police matter."

"No one has seen or heard from Sloane's mother since the night she disappeared. How often does a woman go missing without any further word and still be alive?"

"It happens."

"Not as often as she turns up dead."

"That's the thing. There've been no reports of a body, no notable amount of blood or sign of a struggle, and no witnesses have come forward with any accusations."

Because there was no one other than Sloane in her parents' house that night! "A devoted mother like Clara wouldn't walk off and leave her kids."

"Depends on how badly she might want to get away from her domineering husband, right? Clara knew Ed would never allow her to take the children. Leaving alone would be her only escape."

"So you're admitting he was domineering."

"Anyone who's been around Ed for five minutes could tell you that."

"You're also acknowledging that she was unhappy in the marriage."

"Ed'll tell you himself that they were struggling. He thinks she was having an affair and that she ran off to be with the other guy."

"She wasn't having an affair, but she was falling in love with Brian Judd, who taught kindergarten right here at Millcreek Elementary."

Adler's eyes narrowed. "Who told you that?"

"You mean to say Ed never mentioned the name of the guy she was supposedly cheating with? That's pretty pertinent information, a detail most people would want to know. But I can see why he might leave it out—since it also happens to contradict the whole 'she ran away to be with her lover' excuse, seeing as her lover never went anywhere. She walked away from the man she was getting involved with here in Millcreek along with everyone else, which is even more unusual."

Adler scowled, clearly not pleased by Micah's rebuttal. "It's not all that unusual if she was planning to start over brand-new. Judd was married, too. It wasn't as if she could have him."

So he *did* know about Judd. "He might've left his wife, if given the chance."

"And he might've told Clara he never would. We don't know. We weren't privy to their secret conversations."

"Still, if Ed believed his wife was having an affair, he couldn't have been happy about it. No matter how unemotional he might seem about that news today, in his mind, she was cheating on him. That creates motive."

“Watch your mouth,” Adler snapped.

Micah reared back, shocked by the sudden flash of temper as Adler got up, came around and closed his door. “You’re talking about the *mayor*,” he said in a harsh whisper. “We don’t go around accusing people, especially people like him, not without hard evidence.”

“We might not have *hard* evidence, but we certainly have circumstantial evidence.”

Adler lumbered back to his seat. “Which may or may not mean anything. We can’t ruin a man’s career off of a ‘we should’ve heard from her by now.’”

“Have you ever talked to Sloane about her mother’s disappearance, sir?”

“Look, I know you love this woman—or think you do.”

Micah opened his mouth to argue but Adler didn’t give him the chance.

“But she was five years old when her mother left. Do you really think I should open a police investigation *of the mayor* due to memories that are more than twenty years old and are from the perspective of a young child?”

“You don’t know that she’s remembering wrong. She claims her parents were fighting about Judd that night.”

“So what if they were? Maybe Clara was tired of all the fighting. Maybe that’s why she took off!”

“Sloane has spoken to someone who saw Ed tow his boat out of the neighborhood that night.”

“The boat?”

“Yes, in the middle of the night. Why would he need to take the boat out if he’d just had a fight with his wife, and she’d left him?”

“You need to stop,” Adler said. “I don’t want you

going after this. I'm telling you, it'll only ruin your career."

"I'll be discreet. I swear it. I just want to learn more."

Adler's double chins wagged as he *tsk*ed. "Micah, even if we dive into this, what're the chances we'll be able to prove anything beyond a reasonable doubt? We'll make enemies for nothing."

Micah felt his muscles bunch. "For *nothing*?"

"Yes! Because you're thinking with the wrong head!"

Micah was tempted to say, *At least I'm thinking with one of them*, but he knew that would be foolish. If he wanted to keep his job, he'd already pushed this as far as he could.

"Ed likes you," Adler said in a more conciliatory tone. "He has big plans for you. Don't let Sloane derail all of that." He was trying to come off as paternal, was pretending he cared about what might happen to Micah's livelihood, but Micah guessed he was far more worried about what might happen to his own.

"Clara didn't even come back for her mother's funeral," Micah said, ignoring the more personal stuff Adler had dredged up.

"Maybe she didn't want to see Ed again, didn't want to face her broken-hearted children and all the other people she'd let down."

That was a lame response, and he had to know it. This conversation was driving Micah crazy. He thought it should be going in a completely different direction. "I don't believe that," he said. "I don't believe *anything* could've kept her away."

"I'll tell you what," his chief said. "If you're still interested in finding out what happened to Clara McBride, we can look into it next year, after the election is over and Sloane is gone. Then at least I'll know you're doing it for the right reasons."

"The right reasons?" Micah echoed. "A woman has gone missing and might be dead. Isn't that the right reason?"

"She went missing twenty-three years ago, so quit acting like it's some kind of emergency. It isn't fair to sink Ed McBride's chance at another term by bringing this up right now. Timing can be everything in an election. For all we know, that's what Sloane is *trying* to do—get back at her father for some slight, either real or imagined. Why, after ten years, has she shown up now? We can't let an embittered daughter cause us to lose our jobs just because you're dying to get back in her pants."

Micah clenched his jaw. "That is *so* messed up, I don't even know how to respond," he said and walked out.

"Micah!"

He didn't turn back. That exchange was bullshit, so anything else Adler had to say on the subject would be bullshit, too.

The bottom line was this: Ed had stacked the deck in his favor. He even had the police department in his pocket. Which meant Sloane wasn't going to be able to bring her father down even if he deserved it.

CHAPTER SEVENTEEN

"Well, aren't you the cat who swallowed the canary."

Ed pulled his attention away from the text he was composing on his phone to see Edith Wegman, his sixty-something-year-old receptionist, filling the doorway of his office at city hall. He should've closed his door when he returned from lunch. He'd been so preoccupied he hadn't heard her coming and hated feeling as though she'd been watching him unawares.

"What are you talking about?" He put his phone in his pocket as she came over.

"The look on your face." She handed him the mail when she reached the edge of his desk.

"What look?" he asked as he glanced through the stack.

She wiped the sweat beading on her upper lip. She was always complaining about hot flashes, which he found distasteful. He'd never liked old women. "Mayor

McBride, I've worked for you long enough to know when you're pretty darn proud of something. Did you just make a million dollars? Secure a key benefactor for the campaign? Hear that your opponent is dying of cancer?"

"Aren't *you* funny," he said.

She adjusted the necklace that had all of her grandkids' birthstones on it. "Just trying to share your excitement."

"There's nothing special going on." He'd merely been trying to decide what to say to Paige to make her think last night had meant something to him. He'd never dreamed he'd be able to get Sloane's best friend into bed, but it had been surprisingly easy. He'd neutralized Micah by meeting with the chief of police, and now he was sleeping with Sloane's childhood friend, who'd already kicked her out of the house. She wouldn't have the support of either of them while she was in Millcreek, and if *they* wouldn't support her, who else was there for her to turn to?

Edith smoothed her too-tight dress. "Come on. You weren't smiling like the Cheshire cat for nothing."

The old battle-ax never let anything go. She reminded him of the nuns who'd been in charge of the private school he'd attended as a child. He'd hated one so much he'd put a bunch of earwigs in her desk before school one morning. When she reached into her drawer, she'd screamed, jumped to her feet and fallen, twisting an ankle, which had taken her out of school for three days. The memory of that moment—his revenge for calling his parents to tell them he'd been picking on another student—made him chuckle. Although she'd suspected it was him, she couldn't prove it, so she'd had to give him the benefit of the doubt.

Still, as much as Edith behaved like Sister Kathryn, she had her place in his life. Her reputation as an upstanding, God-fearing, no-nonsense woman was part of the reason he kept her around. Her presence in his office helped to create an honest image, which was important in this day and age, when almost all politicians were assumed to be corrupt.

"If you must know, I was trying to text the woman I had over for dinner last night," he said. He'd actually sent her a brief message when he got up, but she hadn't responded yet, and he wanted to engage her again.

"Miss Gentry?" Edith guessed.

"No, Simone and I are no longer seeing each other."

"I thought you liked her. I mean…you've been seeing her for months. Isn't that some kind of record?"

Simone had been convenient; that was all. "Record or no, it's over. I like this woman better."

He handed several of the letters he'd glanced through back to her while stacking the rest neatly on his desk. "Send out our standard response on the park issue. The city doesn't have the money to do what these people are asking right now."

"If we waited to repave Brazos Boulevard, we could fund the park and do the repaving later," she pointed out.

"Keeping the main drag looking top-notch is more important," he said, but what she didn't know was that the contractor rebuilding the road could always be counted on for a nice kickback.

She sighed. "Okay. If you say so."

"I say so," he said but stopped her as she was leaving. "Actually, before you do anything else, could you send a dozen roses to the Little Bae Bae Boutique here in town? Have the card read, 'I had a nice time last night. Hope to see you again soon.' Then I won't have to decide what to text."

She gaped at him. "You're kidding me."

He stood. She had such a strict sense of right and wrong, he didn't like her looking down that narrow nose at him. "About…"

"You're sending flowers to Paige Evans? That's who you had dinner with last night?"

"That's right. Is there a problem?"

"Isn't she a friend of your daughter's?"

"Sloane left everyone behind without a backward glance ten years ago. I don't think she has any friends left. Do you?"

"But what about the age difference? What is she… *twenty-seven*?"

"She's at least twenty-eight, old enough to know if she wants to have dinner with me. And she's divorced, which makes us both available. That's all that matters. Age is just a number."

Her lip curled in disapproval. "People are going to talk about this."

"People will talk about anything." Besides, he *wanted* the news to get out. The fact that Paige was nearly half his age wouldn't be the best thing to carry into the next election. His opponent would definitely have something to say about it. But it'd been years since he'd dated anyone else in Millcreek, so he was fairly confident his reputation could withstand the blow. It wasn't as if he could be painted as a womanizer. With the possible exception of Edith, most people had no idea how many women he'd been with over the years.

Sloane was the real enemy, the only one who could possibly destroy him, and linking his name with Paige's would help to discredit Sloane. After all, Paige wouldn't be dating him if she believed he was dangerous, and if Sloane's best friend didn't believe he was dangerous, why should anyone else?

"Why are you still standing there?" he asked Edith. "The boutique closes at five."

With a huff, she lumbered out of his office and slammed the door.

Sloane rolled down her window, hoping the air would blow the steam off the anger boiling up inside her. For most of her life, she'd been reluctant to contest her father's version of the past. She didn't want to falsely accuse an innocent man. But those texts she'd read proved how readily he lied. And it wasn't just the untruths that enraged her. He didn't care about all the pain and angst he'd caused her.

Tell her that we didn't get involved until after Clara left, that you were merely trying to comfort me and things got a little out of control.

She wished she'd taken him on sooner. He deserved for *someone* to stand up to him! Poor Clara. Her life could've been so different if she'd married someone else.

Sloane glanced over at her phone, which she'd put in the holder on her console before leaving the restaurant parking lot. She wanted to call Micah and tell him everything she was thinking and feeling. Without Clyde she had no one to turn to, no one with whom she could share her worries and fears. But the memory of Paige crying in her motel room last night made her hesitate. *Not him.* And not just for Paige's sake. If Sloane really cared about Micah, she'd let him live his life. What Ed did—whether he killed Clara or not—didn't have to affect Micah, not if she made sure it didn't.

She just hoped she was strong enough. She kept imagining him leaning forward to kiss her, what it would feel like to have him slide his hands up under her blouse or take her to bed again. It didn't help that she was so damn starved for love. She felt as though she'd been in hibernation for the past ten years and was only now coming out of it, hungrier for a man—for him—than she'd ever been before.

She pulled off the freeway to get gas, but once she filled up, she found herself once again fighting the impulse to call Micah. She sat there, arguing with herself for over fifteen minutes. Paige and Micah were divorced. She could call him if she wanted. He was with her long before he was with Paige. But she wasn't planning to stay in Millcreek, and there was no way she'd ever drag him away from his son even if he'd be willing to leave, which he wouldn't. So why start anything?

Soon, she was just frustrated and mad enough to call the dealership that now belonged to her brother instead.

"McBride Auto."

Sloane slid her seat back, so she wouldn't feel confined by the steering column. "Is Randy McBride there?"

"Can I tell him who's calling?"

"His sister, Sloane."

Elevator music came on as the operator put her on hold. She closed her eyes and rested her head on the back of the seat as she listened, wondering if he'd take her call, and what he'd say if he did.

Finally, the girl she'd spoken to before came back on the line. "He's with someone. Can I have him get back to you?"

"No, I'd rather wait."

"It might be a few minutes."

Would he *ever* answer? Sloane decided to find out. "I don't mind."

"Okay," the woman said in a "suit yourself" voice and the elevator music began to play again.

Sloane watched the clock for ten minutes. She'd just decided that he wasn't going to speak to her and was about to hang up when she heard him say hello.

"Randy?"

"Sloane?"

"Yeah, it's me."

"What do you want?"

He didn't sound the least repentant for having shoved her into the door. Suddenly, that made her as mad as her encounter with the lying Katrina. She'd always tried to see the situation from Randy's perspective, to feel some empathy for what he might be going through—his fear of losing his beloved father—but he never seemed to cut her any slack in return. "I wanted to tell you that I finally understand where you're coming from."

She could tell he wasn't quite certain how to respond. "You do?"

"Yes. It isn't that you don't believe me about Dad. It's that you *do*."

"You need to stop all this bullshit, Sloane," he responded, his voice almost a growl. "I don't know how many more ways I can tell you. Nothing good can come from digging up the past."

"Not for Dad—and maybe not for you. But I don't give a shit. Not anymore. I've had it, Randy. I won't stop until I have the truth, no matter who it destroys."

"You think you can take us both on?" he asked.

"I guess we'll see, won't we?" She was shaking when she hung up. She shouldn't have provoked him. She guessed Micah would freak out if he knew. But she was tired of letting Randy push her around—literally and figuratively. She'd needed to speak up for herself, needed to take charge.

The phone rang before she could fully recover. Assuming it was Randy, calling back to let her have it, she checked the caller ID. But it wasn't the dealership; it was Micah.

She battled with the desire to hear his voice, to tell him everything that'd happened, to drive straight to his house and walk into his arms. The song "Bring It on Home to Me" by Little Big Town had been playing on the radio before she stopped for gas, and that was exactly what she wanted to do. Unburden herself. Melt into his strength.

But she didn't. She turned off the ringer and slipped her phone in her purse so she wouldn't be tempted to answer if he called back. Then she adjusted her seat so she could drive and headed to Millcreek.

Micah got Sloane's voice mail yet again. Why wouldn't she pick up? He had something important to tell her, something that changed *everything*.

He texted her: Call me. I need to talk to you. And still she didn't respond.

He was really beginning to worry when he went to the motel at nine, a time when he thought she'd be back and getting ready for bed, and she wasn't there. *What the hell?* She'd been gone all day. He knew because he'd been down Brazos Boulevard several times earlier while he was on duty and couldn't help checking the lot with every pass.

"Damn it, where are you?" he muttered and flipped his truck around so he could drive by Paige's. That was the only other place he figured she could be, but her car wasn't out front, so he didn't bother to go in. He didn't want Paige to know he was looking for Sloane. As far as he was concerned, it wasn't any of his ex-wife's business.

Could Sloane have gone to her father's? Or Randy's?

He hoped not, but he was on his way to check both houses when he spotted a white Jaguar at the Royal Flush, a fairly new bar popular with the younger crowd, and immediately turned in.

Sure enough, he recognized the New York license plate on the Jag. Thank God he'd found her.

Tuesday night was ladies' night, where well drinks for women were only a dollar, so it was crowded. He parked as close as he could, pocketed his keys and strode to the entrance.

BJ, the owner, waved as soon as Micah passed the bar. Micah had provided security for BJ last summer, whenever he featured a popular band. Since his divorce, Micah had been taking on almost any side job he could line up. He needed the money, and staying busy helped keep him from dwelling on the guilt and worry he felt for what his divorce might do to his son.

He scanned the crowd for Sloane and found her dancing with some guy he didn't recognize. They were dancing too close, which bothered him, but not as much as the fact that she was drunk. He could tell by the way she was moving, the way her head lolled as she stared up at the lights.

After weaving through the tables to reach the dance floor on the far side, he tapped her partner on the shoulder. "Excuse me. Sorry to interrupt, but I need a moment with this woman."

The guy tried to shrug him off. "Not now," he responded and pulled Sloane even closer.

Sloane had her eyes closed and was resting her head on the guy's shoulder as if she was too dizzy to do anything else, but she looked up at the sound of his voice and squinted to bring him into focus. "Micah?"

She was drunk all right. "Yeah, it's me."

"I'm dancing."

"I can see that."

"And I don't feel anything."

Was that what this was all about? Getting numb? Avoiding the pain?

Part of him couldn't blame her. He empathized with what she was going through. But it was a damn dangerous thing to do, especially in a bar where there were so many men dying to get such a beautiful woman on her back.

"Do you mind?" her partner said. "She's with me. Find someone else."

The guy thought he had a good thing going—a chance of getting lucky—which caused Micah's hands to curl into fists. "She's in no condition to give consent, so she isn't leaving with you, regardless. You might as well let go and walk away, find someone else yourself."

Her partner lifted his hands and backed up. "Dude, I'm not trying to take advantage of her."

"Good. I'm happy to hear that," he said, because just thinking about what might've happened made him see red.

"Let's get out of here," he told Sloane, but as soon as he took her hand and started leading her out, the guy she'd been dancing with cut him off.

"Wait a second. If she's not leaving with me, she's not leaving with *you*."

"Wanna bet?" Micah said.

The guy got right up in Micah's face. "I don't like you."

Micah glared back at him. "I don't give a shit whether you like me or not. I'm taking her home. Now. So step aside, or you and I are going to have a serious problem."

The guy must've heard the resolve beneath his words, must've understood that Micah was willing to take it to a whole other level, because he stepped out of the way, allowing Micah to get past him.

Micah pulled Sloane along until they got outside and reached his truck. "Why haven't you been answering my calls?" he asked as he lifted her into the passenger's seat.

She closed her eyes again and let her head fall back. She was completely out of it. Given her condition, he wasn't expecting a coherent answer. So she surprised him when she looked up at him and said, "Because I knew I'd just want to rip your clothes off. That's all I've been able to think about since I came home."

Micah felt an immediate tightening in his groin but

took a deep breath to offset the sudden deluge of testosterone. “You have a very unusual way of showing interest,” he said and secured her seat belt before closing the door.

CHAPTER EIGHTEEN

It was pitch-black when Sloane woke up. Where was she? Her head hurt, and her hair reeked of smoke and alcohol.

With a groan, she patted her surroundings. Then she smelled something subtler, a hint of cologne and some pine-scented soap on the pillows and sheets.

That scent connected with a memory, and suddenly she realized where she had to be. She sat up so fast her head began to pound. “Micah?” she called into the darkness.

He wasn’t in bed with her. She was wearing a large, soft cotton T-shirt—presumably one of his—and she was alone. But she heard movement almost right away, coming from the living room: footsteps in the hallway before her door swung open.

“Are you okay?” he asked, his large body filling the opening.

The concern in his voice felt as good as a soft hand to the face—reassuring, calming. Her disorientation eased instantly. “No. I feel sick.”

“Do you need to throw up?”

“Maybe. I don’t remember ever drinking so much before in my life. But it didn’t matter how many shots I took. Nothing seemed strong enough to make me forget.”

He leaned against the doorjamb instead of coming all the way into the room. “You seemed completely out of it when I found you, so I think those shots were working better than you imagine.”

“Unfortunately, I’m already able to think clearly.”

“You don’t sound excited about that.”

“I’m not.”

He chuckled. “There’s a bowl beside the bed, and I put a glass of water and some painkillers on the nightstand.”

“Thanks. I’ll take the painkillers now.” She fumbled around, trying to turn on the lamp but couldn’t find the switch, so he came over, wearing nothing but a pair of worn jeans, and turned it on for her.

She blinked until she could tolerate the light, at which point he handed her the pills and held the water steady so she could drink.

“What happened?” he asked as he put the glass back on the nightstand. “Why’d you get so wasted? Or is that normal behavior for you these days?”

She rolled her eyes. “It’s not normal behavior for me. Alcohol ages you, and it’s not good for your skin. As a model, I never touched it. Last night was a desperate attempt to check out for a while. That’s all.”

“What pushed you to that point?”

"I went to Fort Worth to meet with Katrina for lunch."

"How'd that go?" he asked, shoving his hands in his pockets.

"Not good. She did nothing but lie to me. Told me my father was destroyed when my mother left. He was such a good family man. He would never hurt anybody. Yada yada. But the proof that they'd colluded on what she should say was right there, in her phone."

"You saw her phone?"

"I had to spill my drink to get her to leave the table so I could grab it, but then I read several text messages between her and my father."

"So you were upset when you left there."

"Not from that so much. I mean…it wasn't *good* news, but it wasn't entirely unexpected. My decision to go to the bar had more to do with Randy," she said as her memory of the day snapped into sharper focus.

"Don't tell me he came to the motel…"

When she heard the harsh note in Micah's voice, she knew the thought of Randy bullying her made him defensive and found that comforting, too. Clyde had been her anchor since she'd left, the one thing that had held her steady. Now he was gone, she'd been cast adrift, and it was so much harder not to go back to Micah. She wished he'd pull her into his arms and hold her. Losing her mother and then Clyde had left such a void, one she had no idea how to fill.

But it wouldn't be fair to expect Micah to be there for her. "No. I called him at the dealership while I was on my way back to Millcreek."

"*You* called *him*."

Too weak to continue sitting in a fully upright position, she slumped against the wall. The bed had no headboard, but it had a far better mattress than the one at the motel. “Yeah, I called him.”

“Because…”

“I was *dying* to tell him to go fuck himself.”

Seeming even more concerned, Micah sat on the bed beside her. “Please tell me you didn’t do that.”

“Actually, I did—more or less.”

“How’d he take it?”

She battled back the nausea that threatened. “Not very well.”

“Shit.”

She peered through the dark to see him wearing a scowl. “Sorry. I was so angry I felt like I was going to explode. I had to do something.”

“I understand. It’s just…”

The muscles in his arm bulged as he ran a hand through his hair. He’d been so skinny in high school. Now he was a man in his prime. “What?”

“Never mind. I’ll tell you later, when you’re feeling better.”

She struggled to get her mind—and her eyes—off his bare chest. “Tell me now.”

“It’s nothing. Just don’t say anything else to your father or your brother, okay? I mean *nothing.* Stay completely away from them.”

“I can’t promise anything,” she grumbled. “What I said to Randy is nothing compared to what I’d like to say.”

“You left town ten years ago without telling anyone you were going. And you haven’t contacted anyone since, not until now. They know how you feel.”

She pulled her legs in to her chest. “I’m sorry you were caught up in…in all of that when you had nothing to do with the problem. Collateral damage," she murmured. "Will you ever forgive me?"

"Not if I can help it."

She blinked at his words. "Why hold on to a grudge?"

Her skin prickled as his gaze ranged over her. She recognized the sexual hunger in his eyes. "Surely you can guess the answer to that question."

"Then you can guess why I didn't accept your calls today," she told him.

"You knew I was trying to reach you and purposely didn't pick up?"

"More or less. I went to the bar instead." Suddenly, she became self-conscious about the fact that she didn't remember changing into his T-shirt. "Anyway, did *I* take off my clothes or…?"

He lifted his hands to show his innocence. "You did. Absolutely."

"In front of you?"

"Yep. Whipped your shirt right off." A smile curved his lips as if he liked the memory. "I had a hard time stopping you from taking off my clothes, too."

"I was trying to *undress* you?"

"You were grabbing me, pulling me up against you, trying to kiss me."

She cringed. She remembered some of it—the need, the frustration and then the disappointment when he kept setting her away from him. No wonder she'd woken up feeling so terrible. "Sorry about that."

"Saying no was probably the hardest thing I've ever had to do," he admitted. "But you weren't capable of giving consent, so I had no choice. And I didn't want it to happen like that, anyway. If I ever take you back to bed, it's going to be because you want me for a lot more than a quick ride when you're inebriated."

She wanted him when she wasn't inebriated, too. The alcohol just made the desire more difficult to deny, which was why she'd behaved so badly.

"What if it was two or three rides? Or… I don't know, maybe as many as we want while I'm here?" A few moments ago, she'd barely been awake. Now she was fully alert and her heart was banging against her breastbone. She knew she was going back on everything she'd told herself she'd do—letting all her good intentions unravel. But if she hoped to make it through the next few weeks, she couldn't be fighting two separate battles. She needed to be able to focus on what she'd come here to accomplish.

He studied her closely. "Are you making me an offer?"

"I am." She lowered her voice. "I want to feel something good, Micah. Something fulfilling like it was before. After ten years, I'm tired. I'm looking for shelter from the storm."

"We'll see," he said and stood up. "For tonight, you'd better get some rest."

She'd just bared her heart to him, and he was leaving? "We'll *see*?" she repeated as he walked out.

She heard him laugh, but he didn't answer.

"I'm going to rescind my offer in the morning!" she called after him.

"Then you're not sure of what you want in the first place," he called back.

"You want to make love to me, too, or you wouldn't have brought me here!"

"I brought you here to keep you safe!"

"Was I so drunk you didn't think I'd be safe alone at the motel?"

"We'll talk about it in the morning."

"Talk about what? Is there something else? What aren't you telling me?"

"Go to sleep!"

"I can't believe you're staying on the couch! I *know* you want to get naked with me."

When he spoke again, all hint of humor was gone. "I'm not going to lie about that," he said. "Good night."

The following morning, Micah threw an arm over his eyes as he heard the shower go on. It'd been a rough night, and it wasn't getting any easier with daybreak—not while he was lying there, remembering the sight of Sloane after she'd taken off her blouse last night. He wanted to give up and join her, take what he could get, even if it was only temporary. But he told himself he'd be a fool to accept so little when he wanted so much more.

To distract himself from the desire pumping through his veins, he got up, made some coffee and checked his phone. He'd missed a call from the detective in Keller he'd spoken to yesterday, Detective Ramos. He needed to get back to him. Ramos wanted to talk to Sloane, but first Micah had to break the news—news that had him far more worried for her than he'd been before.

"That smells good."

He glanced up to see Sloane coming toward him. She had her hair up in a towel and was wearing nothing except his T-shirt.

He scowled when he felt his body react to the sight of her long, bare legs. Only by sheer dint of will did he keep from scooping her into his arms and carrying her to bed.

"What?" she said.

"You're not going to make this easy on me, are you?"

She smiled when she realized what he was talking about. "You're the one who wasn't interested," she said and let her breasts brush his arm as she went around him to put a piece of bread in the toaster.

He knew she was teasing even before she laughed, but whether she was joking didn't matter to his body. He grew hard instantly. "I didn't say that."

She pushed the lever down, turned to lean against the counter and arched her eyebrows. "Then it's too bad you missed your chance."

He set down his mug and walked over, locking her between his arms, his body and the cupboards. "You might be more of a temptation now that you don't smell like a pool hall," he said and started to slide his lips up the soft skin of her neck.

He wasn't sure what he was going to do when he reached her mouth. He wanted to kiss her so badly, but he knew how fast that small spark would burn through his restraint.

She dropped her head back to give him better access, which only made him harder. But then the doorbell rang and he heard his ex-wife calling his name.

"Damn it," he muttered as he dragged himself away.

Sloane was biting her bottom lip and watching him intently when he looked up. "Are you going to tell her I'm here?"

"Hell no," he said and tried to regulate his breathing in hopes of slowing his racing pulse.

"Micah?" Paige yelled again.

"Just a sec!" After casting Sloane a final, silencing glance, he went to the door. "What's up?" he asked as soon as he saw Paige on his stoop, showered and ready for the day. She was obviously on her way to work, which meant Trevor had to be at school already.

"Sloane's car is at the Royal Flush, but she's nowhere to be found."

He pretended as though she'd dragged him out of bed and he wasn't quite with it yet. "So what are you saying?"

"I'm saying her car's at a bar that isn't even open at this time of day, but she's not at the motel, either. I've been trying to call her since dinnertime last night and have gotten no response. All my calls go straight to voice mail."

"Where do you think she is?"

She kept trying to look around him. Whether she suspected the truth or was just being nosy in general, he couldn't say. She was always trying to learn as much as possible about where he'd been, who he'd been with and how he was living.

He stood in the center of the doorway so she couldn't see anything other than what she could glimpse on the right or left and hoped to hell Sloane's clothes weren't lying on the floor within eyesight. Sloane had started peeling them off as soon as he'd gotten her home, but he was fairly certain they'd at least reached the living room.

"You haven't seen her?" she said. "I'm starting to get worried."

"No, but let me get showered and I'll go see what I can find." He wasn't going to tell on himself. If there was a chance Paige might not find out he'd been at the bar, too, and left with Sloane, he had to take it. For Trevor's sake, he had to keep her as happy as possible—and anything to do with Sloane sent her crazy.

"You don't have to work today?"

"Not until three."

"Well, you don't have to be the one to look for her. I'll call her father. He might be able to tell me something."

Micah didn't insist that he'd go out searching, because he already knew where Sloane was.

Paige hesitated as though she wasn't quite ready to leave. "Trevor enjoyed the field trip on Monday."

"I'm glad he was able to go."

"Thanks for getting that permission slip and turning it in. I'm sorry I was a bitch about the key."

She'd been a bitch about so many things, but he was willing to forget it all if she'd just back off and leave him be. "No problem."

Still, she stood there, gazing up at him with such longing he could barely look back at her. "Do you know what it does to me to see you like this?"

He wasn't sure what she meant. He hadn't even showered. But the expression on her face and the tone of her voice were making him uncomfortable. He was trying to decide what to say, how he could head off what might be coming next, but she didn't give him the chance to interject.

"I'd do anything to get you back, Micah. *Anything.* Just tell me what it is you need."

He cleared his throat as he searched for the magic words to make it all better, but those words had eluded him their entire marriage, so he doubted he'd be able to come up with them now. "Paige—"

When she heard the tone of his voice, she put up a hand. "Never mind. I know what you're going to say. It's just that none of it ever makes any sense to me. We could be the happiest family on earth, if only you'd let us. I know how much you love Trevor."

She hadn't approached him like this in several months. Shortly after he'd filed for divorce, she'd switched from pleading to exacting revenge. Occasionally, however, she went back to pleading.

A vengeful Paige was difficult to deal with, but a pleading Paige was somehow worse. "I'm sorry. It has never been my intention to hurt you."

"That's it?" she said. "I bare my heart and soul to you, and you say you're sorry?"

"You need to stop," he replied. "We can't keep going through this. It's over between us. For good." Maybe if he said it enough, she'd give up. He'd never met anyone as tenacious as she was.

"Sometimes I hate you as much as I love you," she snapped and started to march back to her car. But before he could close the door, her steps slowed and she turned. "Will you do me one favor?" she asked. "After all we've been through?"

What was coming now? "If I can," he replied.

"Don't get back together with Sloane."

He raked his fingers through his hair. "Paige—"

"Please?" she broke in. "I couldn't bear to watch. I'm not asking this to deny you anything. It's that I love her, too. Don't you see? She was my best friend, and I now have a chance at rebuilding that relationship. So if *you* can't love me, at least let me have her love."

He hesitated. What in God's name was he supposed

to say to this? Did she understand how much *he* loved Sloane? How much he'd always loved her?

Did it matter?

Not if Sloane was leaving. It wasn't as if he could ever talk her into staying. She'd made that clear, so he figured he might as well give Paige the reassurance she craved. "You don't have anything to worry about."

"Couldn't you put a little conviction behind that?"

"She's leaving, Paige." He could tell she expected a promise of some sort. But he also knew that wasn't a promise he could give, because if he could change Sloane's mind, he would. "You need to move on. You don't believe me, but I want you to be happy. I always have."

"Right. That's why you've made me so miserable," she grumbled.

"That was never my intention."

She shook her head as she walked away, and he remained at the door, watching to be sure she drove off.

A few seconds after he went back inside, Sloane came around the corner. "I'm sorry for putting you in such a bad situation. I'll get dressed so you can take me to the motel. I'll call her from there so she won't worry."

He caught her by the arm. "You'll have to call her later."

Her eyes widened. "Why?"

"Because I can't take you back to the motel. It's not safe there. That's why I didn't take you last night."

A confused expression claimed her face. "I don't understand…"

Letting go, he rubbed a hand over his beard growth. "This won't be an easy conversation. So let me shower and shave before I explain, okay?"

Her normally smooth forehead creased. "This is what you wanted to tell me last night."

"Yes."

"It's about my father."

He nodded. "There's been a new development."

"Okay. So are we not going to talk about what just happened with Paige?"

He let his breath seep out in a long sigh. "I don't know what to say."

"She's still hoping to get you back."

"I'm not going back," he said. "Believe me, if I could've made it work, I would have."

CHAPTER NINETEEN

Sloane dressed in what she'd worn the night before; it was all she had. Then she made Micah's bed. The water went off while she was folding the T-shirt he'd loaned her, so she knew he'd be getting out of the shower soon. What was he about to tell her?

She was afraid to find out, but she was also filled with hope that she might finally get some answers. Had Micah uncovered something that proved her father either guilty or innocent?

She was cleaning up in the kitchen when Micah came out wearing a clean pair of jeans and a T-shirt with no shoes, his hair still wet. He poured himself a fresh cup of coffee but when he offered her one, she refused. She was jittery enough, didn't need the caffeine.

"Have a seat." He gestured at the kitchen table before taking the opposite chair.

"This feels serious," she said. "What's going on?"

He took a moment, as if it *was* serious, and he was trying to decide where to start. "Growing up, what did you hear about your grandparents on your father's side?"

"Not a lot. My dad didn't talk much about his parents."

He looked into his coffee cup, obviously tempted to take a sip, but there was still a curl of steam coming off it. "He didn't say *anything*?"

She searched her memory for various tidbits she'd picked up over the years. Her grandparents had never been part of her life, so she hadn't thought a great deal about them, had never asked questions, especially once she learned the story of how they'd died. She'd feared those questions would be too painful for her father to hear, hadn't wanted to make him relive such a terrible ordeal. "They bought my dad a brand-new Corvette on his sixteenth birthday, so I guess that says they were rich and he was privileged, to a degree."

"Somehow that doesn't surprise me. He's still privileged. But he's liked Corvettes for that long?"

"From the beginning. He wrecked that first one after only a few days, though. That was the reason he refused to give me and Randy a car even though he could easily have done it, what with the dealership and all. Instead, he made us share an old Volvo he picked up at an auto auction."

Micah took a careful sip of his coffee. "That's it? That's all you know?"

She turned the saltshaker in a circle. "Not all but close. His father worked hard and was gone a lot. His mother was a stay-at-home mom who volunteered at the school. That's why my father was so adamant my mother do the same—stay home and take care of us, help out in our classrooms, that sort of thing. Which is ironic, since she fell in love with one of my teachers."

"Did you get the impression your father was close to his parents? That they were nurturing, loving?"

She continued to turn the saltshaker. "Tough to say. He didn't complain about them, but neither did he speak fondly of them. It was more like they never existed in the first place. Unless my father recalled something from his past that changed how he was going to handle the same sort of issue in the present, he never brought up his childhood."

"Give me an example. You mean like the car thing?"

"Yeah. His parents bought him a car when he was only sixteen, but that didn't work out. In his mind he was too young. So he wasn't going to make the same mistake. We would get a car but only after we were older and had graduated from high school—not that I stuck around long enough for that."

"You were only days away from getting it. I remember going with you to pick it out. So why didn't you wait? You could've taken it with you. At least you would've had an asset you could use or sell, something with which to go out into the world. You didn't *have* to leave on a bus with next to nothing."

"Didn't seem right to take it. That wasn't the kind of person I wanted to be. Anyway, Randy and I were another example of my father bringing up his past but only because it related to the present."

"You and Randy?"

"He often mentioned he was glad we weren't the same sex. He said that way we wouldn't compete with each other."

"Was there a lot of sibling rivalry between him and his brother?"

"He claimed Sterling tried to outdo him in everything." She pushed the saltshaker against the wall, where she'd found it, and clasped her hands in her lap to hold them still. "But who knows if it was all Sterling's fault. My father is so competitive. He has to win at *everything*. I remember how hard he would play against Randy on the basketball court when Randy was only sixteen. He had to prove he was superior, couldn't ever let Randy feel as though he stood a chance against him." She grimaced as she remembered the disgust she'd felt watching. "It was annoying to see a full-grown man do that to a boy, made me defensive of my brother. I was even younger than Randy and yet I knew there was something ungenerous about his behavior, even unkind. But Randy didn't seem to notice. He's always worshipped the ground our father walks on."

Micah made a clicking sound with his mouth. "Your father has such a big ego."

"The biggest," she agreed. "The man I knew could never allow anyone else to be in the limelight."

"And you believe that extended to his brother."

"I'm almost positive of it. He was jealous of Sterling. When Randy asked to play water polo in high school, my father instantly refused. He said Sterling used to play, that he never wanted to see another water polo match as long as he lived. I thought it was because the game reminded him of his brother, but the longer he talked, the more I realized it had nothing to do with Sterling. He hated going to the matches because they weren't all about him. He wasn't on the team, wasn't the focus of the event. He said something like, 'My father didn't understand that I had better things to do than sit there, worshipping the baby of the family like they did.'"

Micah stretched out his legs and crossed them at the ankle. "He said 'worshipping'?"

"He did. It struck me as odd, too, which is why it has stuck with me for so long."

"Sterling must've been a good player."

"He was better than good. When we were watching the Olympics one day, my dad mentioned that, had Sterling lived, he probably would've made the team."

Micah stared into his cup for several long seconds before he spoke again. "That's interesting."

"Why?"

He didn't answer. Instead, he posed another question. "Did your father seem particularly upset whenever he talked about the deaths in his family?"

"Not especially. But he'd lost them years before, when he was only twenty-two. By the time Randy and I came along and were able to have that type of discussion, I supposed he'd already dealt with his grief, grown accustomed to the reality. It wasn't as if the man who'd shot them wasn't caught, wasn't as though he couldn't close the door on that chapter of his life because he had to worry about the guy who killed his family being out on the streets."

Micah put his elbows on the table and leaned forward again. "The guy was caught but never tried, right?"

She racked her brain but couldn't recall ever hearing that. "I don't know."

"He hung himself in his cell before the case could even go to trial."

She hated the mental image those words created even

though she couldn't sympathize, given what he'd done to her grandparents and uncle. "Randy once asked if the guy was in prison and my dad said he was dead. He didn't elaborate, probably because we were just children. But how does whether he went to trial change anything?"

"The police never really had the chance to press him, to see if anyone else was involved."

She scratched her neck. "They thought there might be someone else?"

"Yes. The house wasn't tossed. And the man who killed them knew right where the valuables were, didn't waste any time searching."

"Maybe my grandma or grandpa told him where to find everything in an effort to save their own lives—or Sterling's. That wouldn't be unusual, would it?"

"No, but they were shot the second they walked through the door, didn't have time to say or do anything. And the alarm? It had been disarmed twenty minutes before they arrived."

"You're saying the perpetrator had the code?"

"He must have."

"How?"

"That's one of the things the police were planning to ask. Sam—that was the guy's name, if I remember right: Sam Something—claimed it was never on to begin with, but it was. They proved that via the monitoring service. The alarm actually sounded before the code could be entered, so it called the monitoring service, but then someone disarmed it immediately after, so they didn't send the police. And only the family or someone close to them would know the code, so..."

She pressed a hand to her chest. This conversation

was drifting into far darker territory than she'd expected. "Wait… You don't think… I mean… You're not suggesting…"

"*I'm* not suggesting it, no," Micah said. "But there is a detective in the Keller Police Department—"

"Keller?" She didn't recognize the name, didn't think she'd ever heard it before.

"It's a suburb of Fort Worth. The police department there is contracted to cover Westlake, where your father's parents lived when they were killed. So they were the ones to investigate."

She came to her feet. "How'd you learn all of this?"

"Mostly by chance. I went in to ask Chief Adler for the file on your mother's disappearance—"

"You did?" She couldn't help being sidetracked by this latest revelation. "But I told you not to let anyone know you were remotely involved. You realize you'll have to live in this town after I'm gone. You need to remain friends with my father, if possible, because even if I've found *some* evidence to suggest he might've killed my mother—like Vickie's sighting of him pulling our boat that night—and could find more, it might never be enough. What if I can't prove anything? Can't hold him accountable? He'll remain in charge, do all he can to make your life miserable! He always gets even with his enemies. I may not know a lot about his early life or his relationship with his family, but I can promise you that much. He can be very vindictive."

"Which is why I can't let you oppose him on your own."

"Yes, you can! I don't want anyone else to be hurt, especially you."

He came to his feet, too. “But you don’t know anything about investigating a murder.”

“Then I’ll hire another private investigator.”

That took him back; she could tell. “You’ve hired one before?”

“While I was in New York, as soon as I had the money.”

“And he couldn’t find anything?”

“He was trying to locate my mother and came up with nothing. I didn’t ask him to investigate my father.”

“Why not?”

“Because I wasn’t willing to commit to the idea that my father might really have murdered my mother. I was hoping to come back and be reassured, not shaken to the core. But it hasn’t gone that way, so I have to toughen up and do whatever is necessary. Especially now, considering what you just told me.”

He held out a beseeching hand. “Sloane, you’re going to need more help than some private detective who doesn’t know anyone. If it’s about your father, people here will only talk to someone they trust. Someone like me.” He pressed a thumb into his chest. “I’m a police officer they’ve seen and know, and I haven’t been gone for a decade.”

“No! I don’t want you to take that risk.”

“It’s not up to you.”

“Then I’m leaving.”

He caught her arm when she tried to get around him and forced her to turn and look at him. “You should know that Chief Adler is siding with your father. When I asked for your mother’s file, he gave me some crap about having it with him, that he was looking into the case and I shouldn’t worry about it. But I could tell he wasn't going to do anything with it. So I was pretty pissed off when I walked out. Colt Green, who happened to be sitting outside the chief's office, overheard part of the conversation. He called me after I left the station to tell me that someone from the Keller Police Department had been in touch a few days ago, asking about the mayor. So I made a few calls and spent some time on the phone with a Detective Ramos. That's how I found out your father might also be responsible for the slayings of his parents and brother."

Sloane had always wondered if jealousy might've led her father to harm her mother, but she'd never even considered the possibility that he could be responsible for multiple murders—that he could be a complete psychopath, as he'd almost have to be in order to orchestrate the deaths of his father, mother and brother. Especially at twenty-two! What kind of a young man did that? She had to find out who he really was, but she felt as though she was trying to move a mountain. "He believes my father might've...what? Paid the man who shot them?"

"Yes. For their money. He inherited millions."

"He would've inherited that money when they died, regardless. He didn't need to kill them."

"True, but he most likely would've had to wait years. And he would've had to split what he inherited with his brother. There's also the fact that he was flunking out of school, which surprised me."

"Whoa, wait. He was *flunking*? That can't be true."

"His parents would've been shocked, too, had they lived long enough to find out. They thought he was about to graduate. Keeping that information from them could've been a secondary motive."

"Oh God." She shook her head. "He claims to have a degree!"

"That's a lie. Ramos can tell you that for sure."

Sloane sank back in her seat. "I can't believe this. It's so much worse than I thought. He's a pathological liar and a psychopath."

Micah knelt in front of her. "There is some circumstantial evidence and a lot of nagging questions about his family's deaths. But let's try to keep an open mind. Ramos just took over the case from an older detective who's retiring. He's going to take a fresh look. He doesn't have any solid proof yet."

"You have to admit that it's highly unlikely two such tragic events would happen to the same man. I don't know why I never considered it before."

"It could be a coincidence. Perhaps losing his father, mother and brother in such a horrific way damaged him, made him capable of what he might've done to your mother. Don't take it too hard, not yet. There're enough red flags that Detective Ramos would like to speak with you. That's all. If they could've connected him with the shooter, things would've gone much differently—trust me."

She covered her face as she tried to absorb the implications of what she'd been told, which were even worse than what she'd expected. Who was her father? Did she even know him? She'd inherited his genetic material, which made her feel as though she might be tainted.

"I'm sorry." Micah took her hands. "This can't be easy to hear, no matter how estranged you are from your father."

Tears welled up. "Can he be the same person who took me and my brother to Disneyland that time? Who took us to the cabin in the summer? Who drove us to the doctor when we were sick, bought my dress for prom, attended my high school graduation? Granted, if he took us anywhere, he didn't seem particularly interested. He spent most of the time on the phone or brought a woman along to watch us and entertain him. But everyone has faults. At least he did *some* nice things. Do murderers take their kids to a cabin during the summer? Or Disneyland?"

"Some murderers are very good at compartmentalizing, Sloane. They honestly believe the victim is at fault for provoking them, or whatever. Anyway, no one is all bad."

The warmth of his touch acted like an inoculation. She could feel his strength traveling up her arms, bolstering her spirits. "But I don't understand why this is such a surprise. Why didn't I know my father was under suspicion for a triple homicide that occurred even before my mother went missing?"

His thumb moved soothingly over her fingers. "The answer would be timing and location. It's been thirty-five years since that event, so the case has been cold since forever. And your father was never the primary suspect. He was at university, miles away with plenty of people to corroborate his location, when the shooting occurred. His youth, close connection to the family and airtight alibi made him an unlikely suspect, so no one ever pointed a finger in his direction. Can you imagine accusing someone of such a horrendous crime when they have just lost their family? You couldn't do that, not without irrefutable evidence. Because of the delicacy of the situation, the detective who had the case was very careful about broadcasting his suspicions. He couldn't afford to be wrong. It would cause the whole department to look bad. Plus, you didn't know your father was a suspect because the killings occurred outside our area. No one could prove your father was involved. They've found no forensic evidence in all the years since."

Her mind was busy playing back various snippets of the night her mother went missing, the morning after, the things she heard her father say about her mother over the years, the many times he talked as though he'd been the perfect husband and Clara had been the one to let him down. He twisted everything, always. "My father is so cunning."

"That's true whether he's innocent or guilty. Just the way he's reacted to having you back in town has proven that. But given the circumstances of those old murders, it's no surprise you didn't know your father might not have been everything he pretended to be—the grieving survivor of a family that was brutally murdered."

She stared into Micah's blue eyes, felt the familiarity of what they'd had before and realized just how much she'd missed him. She'd used Clyde's friendship to build a dam between them, to try to compensate for having to leave him, but that hadn't really changed anything. "I feel like the daughter of Ted Bundy or… or John Wayne Gacy!"

He brought her hands to his lips and kissed her knuckles. "Even if he's as bad as those serial killers, it doesn't mean *you're* anything less than you've ever been. You're nothing like him."

She reached out to smooth a piece of hair off his forehead. That action came so naturally to her she couldn't resist, and she needed him in this moment—felt like she'd needed him all along. "But that's why you don't want me to go back to the motel. You think I might be murdered by my own father."

He winced at her words but didn't back away from them. "If he can kill his mother, father and brother—and his wife—he wouldn't hesitate to do whatever was necessary to silence you."

Of course he wouldn't. What was she to him if he couldn't love his own parents? "What should I do? Should I go stay with Paige?"

He held her chin as his gaze lowered to her lips. "No. I won't let you go there, either."

"Because..."

"Because you're going to be staying here with me." When he leaned forward, she knew he was going to kiss her. She felt the inevitability, the same overwhelming attraction that had brought them together before and didn't even consider stopping him. She wanted him too much and had wanted him for too long.

"What about Paige?" she asked before their lips could meet.

"Don't even mention her," he replied and then they couldn't say anything.

CHAPTER TWENTY

"So how do you feel about having Sloane back in town?"

Paige paused from arranging the merchandise she'd received the day before to frown at her older sister, who'd stopped by the store to bring her an iced mocha. Yolanda was wonderful, but she was so much older she'd always felt more like an aunt than a sister. And because she'd lived out of state until three months ago, Paige hadn't had the chance to be close to her two nieces, either, who were only a year apart and both in college these days. "I'm torn. I love her. I will always love her. We were so close growing up."

"But..."

She returned to folding the cute pink-and-white sweaters with matching hats on the tabletop she'd cleared off in order to display her new winter items. "It's complicated." So complicated that she'd slept with Sloane's *father*, a man in his late fifties, whom she'd thought was handsome for a man his age but wasn't nearly as attracted to as she should've been in order to do what she did. Now just the thought of him made her slightly nauseous.

She glanced over at the flowers Ed had sent. She hadn't even thanked him for those, didn't know what to say, especially since he'd been texting her as though he'd like to see her again.

Morning beautiful. Thanks for a fantastic night. She'd gotten that shortly after she'd opened the shop on Monday. The flowers had arrived later, probably because she hadn't responded to the text.

She'd hoped that would be the end of it until she could figure out some way to let him know they weren't in a relationship. But this morning she'd received:

Is everything okay? I haven't heard back from you. If something is wrong, let's talk about it. Why don't we have dinner again tonight?

She shuddered as she remembered the intimacy that'd followed their first meal together. What she'd done made her feel foolish—and now that she had a bit of distance from it, more mortified than anything else. She hoped no one would ever find out, especially Sloane.

"It's Micah, isn't it," her sister was saying. "He makes all your other relationships complicated, because you're not over him."

In general, Paige tried not to talk about her ex-husband. It was bad enough that Micah had left her. She preferred her friends and family not know how truly lopsided their relationship had been. But she couldn't seem to let go of him, couldn't bounce back and move on. The desire to be with him was simply too great. Some days it completely consumed her. "I'm afraid I'll never be over him," she admitted.

Sympathy registered on her sister's face. "Oh, Paige. Time will help. I thought the same when Doug and I first started having trouble. It tore me up inside to think about divorce or being alone. I forgave him for his first affair—and his second—because I loved him. I didn't want to break up our family. But he wouldn't quit cheating. So once Alice and Ashley graduated from high school, I pulled myself together and got out."

But their situations weren't the same. Couldn't she see that? "Micah never cheated on me, Yo. He treated me great, and he was an excellent father."

"If that's true, why were you so unhappy when you were married to him?" she asked.

"I wasn't unhappy *exactly*."

"Really? Because you seemed miserable, at least in ways. Maybe we didn't spend a lot of time together. I was going through my own shit at the time. But I'll never forget how swollen your eyes were at Christmas a few years ago."

Something had been missing, something Paige needed and wanted. It had felt imperative at the time. She loved Micah so much she wanted him to feel the same about her. But now she wished she hadn't pushed him so hard. If she could've been happy with what he already offered her, they'd still be married. Maybe that was the worst of it. He probably would've stayed if only she'd backed off a little.

She kicked herself over that all the time, wished he'd give her another chance. She'd be less critical and more grateful to have him in her home and in her bed if he would.

"I was stupid," she said. "I should've realized what I had, that asking for more would mean I'd get nothing."

Her sister came over to put an arm around her shoulders. "You deserve his whole heart."

"Part is better than none!"

"No, you were right not to settle. You'll realize that one day. But given how you feel about Micah, why would you encourage Sloane to return to Millcreek?"

"I didn't encourage her! After Micah moved out, I contacted her on social media, thinking we could be friends from afar. Suffering the rejection I felt from her—that she would leave and never contact me again—was almost as hard as having Micah leave me. I haven't mattered to either of the two people I've loved most in the world, aside from my family and Trevor. I needed answers, needed to understand why she could walk away from me so easily."

"And did you get those answers?"

"More or less."

"But they haven't changed anything."

"She says her leaving had nothing to do with me, but that doesn't help the sense of rejection it gave me."

"And now she's back."

"She's the one who started talking about coming home! What was I supposed to say? *Don't?* I'm afraid to have you here? Stay away from Micah?"

"No, but you didn't have to welcome her with open arms. You made it easy for her, let her stay at your house!"

"Aren't you listening? I don't want to lose her *and* Micah. You were gone from the time I was four years old. I was basically raised as an only child, and that gets lonely. Mom was so involved in her church stuff, before she got mad at the pastor and quit going altogether, and Dad was working at the brewery all the time. Sloane filled a big hole in my life. She became a second sister to me, someone I could trust, confide in and laugh with. There were times, plenty of them, when it felt like we had only each other. She meant the world to me. You shouldn't cast those people aside easily. Why should I let Micah rob me of Sloane, too?"

Her phone began to ring. She was hoping to hear from Sloane, to find out where she'd been and why she hadn't been responding, so she checked to see who was calling and quickly hit the silence button. It was Ed, and she wasn't ready to have *that* conversation.

She took a sip of her drink, but before she could jump back into the discussion, Ed texted her—and what she read made her heart sink.

BJ Engle just called me. You know him, right? He owns the Royal Flush. Sloane left the bar with Micah last night. Are they getting back together or what?

"What is it?" Yolanda sounded concerned. "You suddenly look pale."

Paige could barely breathe but she lowered her phone so that her sister couldn't read Ed's text. It hadn't been twenty minutes since Micah had told her he didn't know where Sloane was, that he hadn't seen her. But if they'd met up at the bar last night, he had to be lying. Sloane had gone home with him, which meant she was probably there this morning, too. It made sense, since Sloane wasn't responding.

Paige couldn't believe it—except she really could, which was the problem. She felt sucker punched. This meant Sloane couldn't have been sincere when she'd been consoling her over Micah. She was merely playing along. And Micah had lied to her face at his front door.

Damn them both! How dare they make a fool of her!

Obviously, neither one of them cared about her at all. And to think Sloane had very likely overheard everything she'd said to Micah this morning. They'd probably both been secretly laughing at her!

"Paige? What's going on?" Yolanda asked.

"Nothing," she replied. "I just… I have to get something over to the school for Trevor. Can you watch the store?"

"Sure, but I'm not very good at working the cash register."

"You did fine when you helped me last week."

"I made it through but that was only for a few minutes. Can you take a second to go over it again?"

No. She couldn't. She had to get over to Micah's. She wanted to see if Sloane was still there, wanted to catch them together so they couldn't lie out of it. "I don't have time, but it's slow this morning, so you should be fine," she mumbled and hurried through the back storeroom to where she'd parked her car in the alley.

Micah's heart was pounding like the pistons of an engine. He'd dreamed of Sloane even while he was married. Maybe that was why he'd been riddled with guilt the whole time he'd been with Paige, why he could never properly defend himself when she accused him of cheating. He *had* visited Sloane's Facebook page. He rarely went on social media for any other reason.

And he'd bought every magazine he'd known she was in—all of which he'd had to hide. But he'd never tried to contact her, not after those first few days and weeks when he'd spent the money he'd received for graduation driving all over Texas, hoping and praying he'd find her, and his parents had finally convinced him that he was wasting his time and money. She'd left him. That was her choice, and he had to respect it, even though he wanted her back much worse than he'd ever wanted to come home to Paige, before or after they were married.

Now he had her in his arms again, after ten long years. Once he kissed her, they melted into each other and began making out so frenetically and intensely they could barely breathe. He had his hands up her blouse almost immediately—and she was yanking on his T-shirt, trying to take it off without pulling away long enough to do it effectively.

"I hope you won't regret this," she murmured when he removed his own shirt. They both understood they should think about what they were doing, but they were too far gone to change course. Even if it meant taking Paige back to court to make her respect his parental rights, Micah was seizing this moment, the opportunity to feel Sloane beneath him again. He wanted to experience what it was like to make love to her as an adult instead of a boy.

"I'm not going to back out. Are you?" He held his breath as he lifted his head so he could look at her. He knew how difficult it would be if she shut him down. He'd already committed himself. But she didn't bail out.

"I'm not going to change my mind, either," she said and lifted her arms so that he could drag off her shirt. He unsnapped her bra and tossed that on the floor, too, and he wanted to remove her jeans, but he didn't have the chance before she drew his mouth back to hers.

"I thought I'd never taste you again," she whispered against his lips.

He was enjoying the feel of her tongue moving with and against his. But he was hungry for more than a kiss, even a good one, and he couldn't seem to get to it quickly enough to satisfy the raging desire that threatened to burn him up.

He managed to slide her jeans down over her hips by moving his mouth to her breast so he could reach. He peeled them down low enough she could step out of them without disengaging entirely. But when she moaned and dropped her head back, his knees nearly buckled, and he feared he wouldn't have the strength or the stamina he'd always dreamed of having should he ever get this opportunity.

"I've never felt the way you make me feel," she said.

He pulled away from her breast so he could see her face. "What do you mean? Surely you've been with other men."

"Three, to be exact. But with each one, I just pretended it was you."

Could this be true? He'd convinced himself that she couldn't have cared about him, not like he'd cared about her. "You've never fallen in love?"

"Not since I fell in love with you."

He wasn't sure what to say. This was opposite to everything he'd been telling himself for the past ten years—and made the fact that he'd lost her so much more tragic. "You are the most beautiful woman I've ever seen," he said, "and I thought that long before you were famous."

She was wearing nothing but her panties—a lacy white scrap of fabric that covered only a small triangle in front. He had on his jeans and nothing more when she stood on tiptoe to kiss him again. The moment her breasts came back into contact with his bare chest, he felt such a powerful surge of testosterone that his strength returned in a rush. He wanted to sweep her into his arms and carry her into the bedroom so he could drive into her in a feverish act that had more to do with claiming what he'd wanted for so long than intimacy or pleasure.

When she lifted his hand to her breast, he cupped the soft mound while kissing her again. Then he *did* sweep her into his arms, couldn't help acting on the impulse.

"Do you have any birth control?" she asked as he carried her into the bedroom.

"In the nightstand." Fortunately, that was one thing he'd decided to buy when he moved to town. Paige had been on the pill while they were married, so he hadn't had any reason to buy birth control, not for a long, long time. Doing so was more of a statement, a promise to himself, than anything else, but he was glad he'd done it.

"Are you sure you want to do this, Micah?"

"You're kidding, right?"

"I'm worried about Paige."

"Don't be. I was faithful to her when we were married, but I don't have to be faithful to her anymore."

"I doubt she'll look at it that way. And if she finds out, there will be problems..."

He was so sick of Paige and how she tried to control him. It went all the way back to when she got pregnant. Although he'd never actually accused her, he was convinced she'd meant to trap him. "I'll fight her in court if I have to." Until this moment, he'd never wanted anything badly enough to oppose her to such a degree. That was why he'd given her the house, the car, the alimony she'd requested. He hadn't been trying to hurt her with the divorce, and he wasn't trying to hurt her now. He simply wanted the next few minutes with Sloane so badly he wasn't going to walk away just because Paige felt he should.

"It'll be okay," he said and hoped to God that was true as he peeled off his jeans.

Micah had always been athletic. His body hadn't changed in that regard. He was just more powerfully built these days, especially through the arms, shoulders and chest. His thighs were thicker, too, and he had beard stubble he hadn't possessed back then.

When he noticed her studying him, he hesitated, his smile a bit unsure. "What?"

"You look incredible," she told him. He'd tossed her onto the bed but hadn't yet climbed onto it himself, so she had a great vantage point from which to admire the improvements.

His smile broadened as he joined her. "You're acting as though this is the first time you've seen me."

"It's the first time in ten years."

"Am I different?"

"About twenty pounds different."

"You, on the other hand, haven't changed at all."

"If anything, I've lost weight. I haven't been careful with my diet, not like I was when I was modeling, but..."

He ran his fingers down between her breasts, which weren't particularly large but they were perfectly formed. "But..."

"My friend was…sick."

"Clyde, right? The one who died of cancer?"

She nodded as he smoothed the hair out of her face. "You miss him," he said.

She nodded again. "He was like the father I always wanted and never had, Micah. Unlike my own father, I believe he really loved me, and I can't explain how good that felt."

A thoughtful expression claimed his face as he moved his thumb over her lower lip. "How could he not?"

Sloane had been about to say she was having second thoughts, after all. She didn't want to hurt Paige. She couldn't stick around to be with Micah long-term. But the sweetness of that statement and the look on his face… She couldn't stop what was happening; it was bigger and stronger than she was.

"I want to take this slow," he said as he touched his lips to hers. "But I doubt I'll be able to hold back. Not this time. I'm dying to touch you and taste you everywhere all at once. What you do to me… I'm helpless against it."

She slid her arms around his neck and licked the edge of his mouth. "Then where will you start?"

His smile slanted to one side. "Maybe I'll start here…" He kissed her lips. "Or here." He nipped her neck before moving down to her breast. "Or maybe…" he slid off her panties "…I'll start right *here*."

He spread her legs in a possessive movement that made her gasp. *"There?"* she said.

Holding her so she couldn't push him away, he ran his tongue lightly over her. "Why not?"

Her stomach muscles tensed with anticipation. "Because that…that makes me too self-conscious."

"You don't have to be self-conscious with me. I was the first man to ever see you, to ever touch you."

That was true. She wanted what he was offering, but she also wanted to talk him out of it so that he'd move on to something that made her feel less open and exposed. "You never did *this*."

"Because you didn't let me take off your clothes until graduation night. And by then I was so eager to make love to you I never thought of it. I just wanted to get inside you as soon as possible."

She laughed at the memory, but she'd been just as eager, every bit as in love and anxious to see what having sex with him would be like. "I'm not complaining. It's just that I've never let *anyone* do that."

"Really?"

"That surprises you?"

"Sort of. You must've had plenty of opportunities."

"Not as many as you think. I'm an introvert, remember?"

"I remember. I love your quiet, your reserve. I find it soothing. But the fact that you've never had this experience only makes me want to give it to you more. So don't tell me no."

She dragged in a deep breath to compensate for the excitement building in her body.

"Sloane?" He slid his hands up under her, tilting her at the perfect angle to make what he wanted more accessible. "Say yes. You told me you trust me."

She *did* trust him. It made no difference that they'd been apart for so long. This was Micah, the only boy she'd ever loved. If anyone was going to know her in this way, she wanted it to be him. As he'd just said, he'd been her first in every other way, so this seemed natural. "I do trust you."

"That's a yes."

"That's a yes," she repeated.

The satisfaction on his face nearly made her laugh. "I'm glad, because I can almost guarantee you're going to like it."

"I like it so far," she said and told herself to let go and embrace the moment. She'd been fighting her feelings—as well as her desire for him—for so long. Why not allow what they both wanted to happen while she was in Millcreek? Be happy and fulfilled for a change and worry about everything else later?

"I'm just getting started," he said and, a moment later, she felt the warm wetness of his mouth.

"Wow, that's good," she said on a shaky exhale.

"How good?" he asked, his breath warm against her flesh.

"It might be the best thing I've ever felt."

He lifted his head. "I told you you were going to like it."

Trying not to writhe beneath him, she clutched the bedding on both sides of her as he went back to work. "You were right. But I want you inside me, and since I've been waiting for ten years, it doesn't feel like I can wait another second."

"You can wait," he assured her. "Let it build."

"How long?" she asked.

"We're getting there."

Unable to resist the pleasure he was giving her, she closed her eyes and arched her back and was soon so lost in sensation that nothing else could intrude—no worries or regrets or hesitation. His name was the only thing on her mind when her hands found their way into his hair and she cried out as he brought her to climax.

Sloane and Micah had to be in Micah's house. Where else could they be? Sloane's car was still at the bar. Paige had driven past on her way from the store and saw it sitting there, alone in the empty parking lot. And Sloane wasn't answering the door when Paige knocked at the motel. She'd stopped there on the way, too.

So she had to be here with Micah, Paige decided when she saw that his truck hadn't moved.

She pulled out her phone to text Sloane again:

I'm getting really worried about you. Please respond so that I know you're okay.

Micah had said he had to work at three, at which point he'd promised to "look" for Sloane. Paige grimaced as she, once again, went over their interaction at the door.

"Bastard," she muttered, smacking the steering wheel. "You knew exactly where she was."

When her phone signaled an incoming text, she glanced down to see who it was. She'd also texted Micah to say she still hadn't heard from Sloane. She wanted to see how he'd respond, hoped he'd compound his lie so that she could throw his words back in his face when she caught them together.

But this wasn't Micah or Sloane; it was Ed. As soon as she left the store, she'd replied to Sloane's father that she was going to drive by Micah's house to see if he and Sloane were together.

Do you see anything?

Not yet.

Should I try calling Micah?

No. He won't answer. If I'm right, he's too busy. The kind of busy she imagined made her seethe. She couldn't watch him get back with Sloane, couldn't see them around town, holding hands, smiling lovingly at each other. Not after everything she'd been through. Just imagining it made her sick. She'd loved both of these people with all her heart. She'd admired them, catered to them, tried to be whatever they needed in return. But nothing she did seemed to make a difference. They didn't care about her sacrifices; they didn't care about her at all.

She wished they were just…gone, so that she wouldn't have to think about them anymore. Then she wouldn't have to see Micah every time he came to pick up Trevor, wouldn't have to notice how he glanced away whenever she searched his face for some hint of concern or care for her.

You said he works at three, right? Ed wrote. He'll have to come out then. If Sloane is there, do you think she'll stay at his house while he's gone or that he'll drop her back at the motel?

It was likely she'd come out. She had to answer her calls and texts at some point, and she wouldn't want to do that at Micah's. What if Paige said she was going to stop by?

As Ed said, Micah would have to come out to go to work, but Paige couldn't wait to prove her suspicions.

Her sister was already in a panic. Almost as soon as Paige had left, a customer had come in and tried to pay for a baby dress with a credit card. Because Yolanda couldn't figure out how to process it, she wanted Paige to return to the store as soon as possible, before the woman came back. So Paige couldn't stay here watching Micah's house much longer. And yet she couldn't miss this opportunity, either, couldn't give up her position on Micah's street until she confirmed that both Sloane *and* Micah were untrustworthy assholes who'd never been any sort of friend to her.

I can get him out of the house earlier than that, she wrote back to Ed.

How? What are you going to do?

I'm going to tell him Trevor forgot his lunch money, and I'm too busy at the store to run it over. He'll do anything for Trevor, even pull away from Sloane.

And if he didn't, she'd really have reason to hate him. That he'd put his love for Sloane above her was one thing. That he'd put Sloane above Trevor moved into completely new, unforgivable territory.

And when he finds out Trevor has lunch money? Ed asked.

I'll tell him I forgot giving it to him, that I had a moment of panic, thinking our child would go without.

Okay. Do it. But I hope you'll confront Micah if he walks out with Sloane, let him know what a fool he is for allowing her to drag him into her baseless suspicions.

Make sure he knows he's just screwed himself where you and Trevor are concerned.

That was what she wanted to do—to let him have it. She'd been so nice since the divorce, so hopeful that he'd come back if only she was appealing instead of hurt and angry. It had been such a struggle to subvert her true feelings. Now all the effort she'd put toward that made her feel stupid, as though she was letting him take advantage of her kindness and love—which was why another idea, a *better* idea, was taking shape in her mind.

Again, she glanced down at Ed's many texts. Sloane wasn't going to end up with Micah. Not if she could help it.

I'm pretty sure they're together, she told Ed. And if that's the case, Sloane will definitely get Micah to help her. He'll open a police investigation, which will, at the very least, sink your reelection. They might even manage to drum up enough "evidence" to see that you're charged with Clara's murder.

When he didn't respond for several minutes, she knew he had to be fuming and felt a measure of satisfaction for striking back at Sloane so quickly.

She'd just texted Micah about Trevor needing lunch money when Ed's response finally came in:

That will never happen, he wrote.

CHAPTER TWENTY-ONE

Sloane locked her legs around Micah's hips the moment he pressed inside her. After having just brought her to climax, he was so aroused that action alone nearly sent him over the edge, and he hadn't even started to move.

He'd been so sure he'd never have the chance to make love to her again. This seemed like a dream, like one of the many he'd had since she left, except that it was so raw and real and totally unscripted it was completely different from everything he'd imagined before.

The scent of her perfume, something he hadn't associated with her in the past, mingled with the headier smell of sex to create a new memory, one he responded to in a very primitive way. The fact that they were doing something that felt so forbidden added a whole other dimension. There would be a cost for this—with Paige, with Sloane's father, maybe even with Trevor.

That last possibility terrified Micah. He was willing

to face any repercussion except the loss of his son, but he refused to think about that right now. He wouldn't lose Trevor. He'd fight for his visitation, do whatever he had to in order to remain part of his son's life. He wasn't doing anything wrong. It was only fair that Paige respect his right to move on, even if that meant he spent the day in bed with Sloane.

He hated to think it might all be over too soon, so he sought to savor it while he could. Putting most of his weight on his elbows, so he wouldn't crush her, he stared down at her while trying to regain control. He was feeling so much from a physical standpoint he was amazed by the tenderness that swept through him on a much deeper level when she gazed back at him as if she was just as lost in the moment.

"It's so good to be with you again," she murmured, pushing a lock of hair off his forehead.

He couldn't hold a grudge against her, he realized. As hard as he'd tried not to, he'd already forgiven her for leaving him and everything he'd been through in the past ten years because of it. Which was crazy. She hadn't even been back a full week. This approach was going to lead him right back to where he'd been.

"God, what would it take for me to hate you?" he asked.

Her eyebrows came together even though it was obvious she understood, at least a little, the way he meant those words. "You *want* to hate me?"

"It would make my life easier."

"I think you did hate me, didn't you? It felt like it when I first saw you at Paige's house."

He shook his head. "I didn't even come close."

The sweetest smile he'd ever seen curved her lips. "If it helps, I could never hate you, either."

So what did that mean? Where would they go from here? Micah had no idea since nothing had really changed. She wouldn't stay in Millcreek, could never survive here with her father and brother running the town and the suspicion she harbored about her mother. And he couldn't leave. Not with Trevor still so young.

"Don't," she whispered and caught his face between her hands.

"Don't what?" he asked.

"Think." She guided his lips back to hers, kissing him so thoroughly he couldn't resist moving inside her—and soon he *couldn't* think. He had the only woman he'd ever truly loved beneath him. Nothing could erode the pleasure that brought him.

What a day. What a week! Ed had never dreamed his waif-thin daughter would ever have the guts to oppose him, but she didn't seem to be backing off and running away. Even Randy was surprised by her determination and commitment.

Ed had been pacing all morning, wondering what he should do next. He'd just pivoted at the window when Edith walked into his office.

"You haven't sat down once this morning," she said, frowning to find him away from his desk yet again. "What's wrong with you? You're acting like a caged panther."

"It's nothing," he snapped to get her to back off. "What is it you want?"

She handed him a file. "You need to sign these letters so they can go out in today's mail. And Chief Adler is on line one."

Chief Adler—that didn't bode well. They'd already discussed what needed to happen. Was the chief of police calling with bad news?

Ed hurried over to pick up the phone but hesitated when he realized that Edith hadn't left the room. She was standing just inside the door, watching him with a skeptical expression. "What is it?" he asked.

"You haven't been yourself lately."

For good reason. Everything he was, everything he'd established, could come tumbling down in a heartbeat—and all because of his own daughter, who was only twenty-eight and had somehow gone off and made something of herself without his help. Randy had stayed and relied exclusively on him, but not Sloane. He had to respect her for that, but he certainly didn't have to like her. "Stop making something out of nothing."

She continued to appraise him. "Don't tell me things have already soured with Paige Evans…"

The blinking light on his phone acted like a homing beacon. He wanted to answer so he could talk to Bill, but he didn't want to do it while Edith was in the room. "Since when have I ever let a woman upset me? My personal life is none of your business, anyway."

She harrumphed. "It's none of my business until you want me to send flowers."

"That takes you five minutes!"

"So? If she's pregnant or something like that, it would affect *my* job as much as yours. People around here won't take kindly to their mayor sleeping with a woman half his age and getting her pregnant. Especially a local woman they have to face every day. Not if he isn't going to marry her. And I'm guessing that would be the furthest thing from your mind."

"Stop it. I haven't even slept with her," he lied.

"Maybe it was the message you had me put on the roses, but I find that hard to believe."

He rolled his eyes. "Will you quit it? It doesn't matter who I sleep with. What I do with my off hours doesn't interfere with my ability to do my job."

"Said every politician who crossed that line."

"Do you mind? The chief of police is waiting! She's not pregnant, okay?"

"Good. Because I think you're crazy to trust her. She's already trapped one man. Do you want to be next?"

"You don't know anything about her."

"I know she got pregnant with Micah Evans's child on purpose. No one wants to say that out loud, but it's true. His mother used to be a good friend of mine. She told me that one day, while we were sitting in church."

"The gossip in this town is unbelievable."

"True, but making it in politics means you have to take that into account. Isn't that what you always tell me?"

"I've done pretty good on my own so far."

"But you're not yourself right now."

"Let it go, Edith. We're both going to be fine." He was using Paige, not the other way around. "But I appreciate your concern," he added facetiously. "Now, will you get out of my office so I can do my work?"

With a final, dubious glance, she trudged out.

"And close the door behind you," he called after her.

Only after the door slammed did he pick up the phone. "What's going on?" he asked Bill.

"You're not going to like it," came the reply.

He'd had a feeling. Perching on the edge of his seat, he began kneading his forehead. "Please tell me you're keeping up your end of the bargain."

"I'm doing what I can, but you need to be aware that this could get away from me."

"Get away from you how? You're the chief of police, for God's sake!"

"It's not that simple. Keller PD has been back in touch."

Ed's stomach cramped as soon as he heard the word *Keller.* He didn't want to think of the past. "Detective Polanski's bothering you again? Don't tell me that old bag of bones is still trying to pin my family's murders on me."

"Not him. Polanski has retired. There's a new detective on the case by the name of Ramos—a young guy, familiar with all the latest forensics. He's going through the case, checking every statement, looking at every detail."

"Shit..."

"See what I mean?"

Ed's mind raced through the possible implications. Bill needed to stand his ground. That was all there was to it. "You can handle Keller PD. Your predecessor did, didn't he? And I wasn't even mayor back then."

"But I've got Micah, a member of my own force, trying to stick his nose into everything. So that's different, right? If Ramos and Micah get together on this... Well, that could change a lot of things."

"Whether they team up or not, there's no way they'll ever tie me to the deaths of my mother, father and brother. I wasn't even in the area."

"But like you said, the investigation itself could be enough to sink your reelection. And innocent men are charged with crimes all the time. Having Sloane in town, claiming you're responsible for Clara's disappearance, is bad enough. If people start hearing that the police in Keller believe you might've had something to do with the deaths of your parents and brother, well...you'd be surprised how quickly things could turn around on you."

Ed came back to his feet. This was getting bad. He had to do something before it got any worse. "Don't worry. Sloane won't be sticking around. And once she's gone, Micah will back off, that new detective won't get any farther than Polanski did and everything will return to normal."

"You sure about that?"

There was no way to be sure—unless he saw to it. "Positive," he said and got off the phone.

Micah wanted to stay in bed with Sloane, to drift off to sleep with her bare body cradled in his. The real world would come crashing in soon enough. He had to work at three, and it was already noon. He wanted to preserve these few seconds.

But regular life drew him back even sooner than expected. A few minutes after he rolled off her, he could hear his phone ringing in the other room. Although he'd heard it a few times while they were making love, he hadn't been paying attention, not enough to consider answering. Now, however, he was beginning to wonder if something was wrong.

After placing a kiss on the bruise Randy had made

on Sloane's forehead, he crawled out of bed and went in search of his cell.

It wasn't hard to find, since it was ringing again.

Paige was trying to get hold of him. Because he didn't care to talk to her, he silenced the sound but checked to see what he'd missed in the past hour.

"Jesus," he muttered when he saw that she'd tried to reach him at least fifteen times, including both calls and texts.

Where are you?
Why aren't you picking up?
Trevor isn't going to get lunch. He doesn't have any money...
Can you answer your damn phone?

All of her texts followed the same theme, so he didn't bother listening to her voice mails. That she had a legitimate reason to contact him made him feel like a jerk for being irritated with her. He'd invited her to reach out whenever Trevor needed something.

He glanced at the clock that was resting against the wall since he hadn't yet gone to the trouble of hanging it. His son's lunch period had already started, but he was close enough to the school that he could still make it in time to buy Trevor a meal. "Sloane?"

"What?" she called back.

I got it. On my way, he typed into his phone and a swoosh told him the text was sent.

"Why don't you take a nap while I run over to the school?" he asked as he hurried back to the bedroom to get dressed. "Trevor needs lunch money."

"No." She dragged the sheet with her as she sat up.

"I can't sleep. I need to pick up my car and go to the motel so I can get cleaned up for the day."

"Okay, I'll take you with me and drop you at your car. But once you're packed at the motel, bring your stuff over here. There's a key under the mat. Let yourself in if I'm at work and keep the key in your purse."

She wrapped the sheet around her as she climbed off the bed. Other than her panties—Micah had no idea where those had gone; he certainly hadn't been keeping track—all her clothes were in the living room. "Micah, I don't think I should stay here with you."

He pulled on his boxers and his jeans. "Where else would you go? Where else would you be safe?"

"I'll stay at the motel."

"No. Definitely not." After talking to Detective Ramos, he felt adamant about that.

She shoved a hand through her tousled hair. "You really want me to stay here?"

"I do."

"But I don't want to cause you any trouble..."

"I appreciate that, but I can take you in if I want. Paige will try to twist it into some kind of betrayal of Trevor, but I rarely bring Trevor here, so it won't affect him. I mostly take him to my folks' place when I have him, remember?"

"Doesn't matter. If Paige decides to make an issue of it, it'll affect Trevor whether you want it to or not."

"She's acting concerned that she can't get a hold of you, so hopefully she understands the threat you're facing. You'll be safest here with me, and I think we'll make good roommates," he added with a wink.

"Roommates?" she echoed. "If what just happened is any indication, we won't be sleeping in separate rooms."

"I see that as a good thing."

"After a year of celibacy, I bet."

He shot her a grin but she sobered. "Micah, becoming accustomed to that kind of intimacy will only make it harder when I have to leave..."

He found a clean shirt and yanked it on over his head. He wanted her to stay in Millcreek. He'd always wanted her to stay. But he hadn't been with her for ten years, had no idea how she'd changed, how he might've changed, if they were as compatible in reality as it seemed in his head—and in his bed. Maybe the past hour had been more about leftover desire and pent-up frustration than anything else. Why overthink it or try to decide too much too soon? "Staying here isn't any kind of promise."

"Then you're okay with our relationship remaining casual."

He shoved his wallet in his back pocket and scooped his keys off the dresser. "I've been married and divorced since you lived here before, and I have a son to think about. I'm not asking for a commitment. I'm not even sure I could give *you* one. We just came back into contact. Let's take it one day at a time."

She seemed relieved. "Okay. I'll think about it."

"What's to think about?"

"I'm hoping I might be able to make a smarter decision when I'm not looking at you in those jeans and that T-shirt and wanting to take them off again."

Spotting her panties on the floor partway under the bed, he walked over to retrieve them. "I'm glad I'm not the only one who thinks this ended too soon."

He tugged on the sheet as he handed them off, but

she accepted the panties while holding fast to her only covering. "Hey! You're fully dressed!"

"So? You're a model. Surely, you've got to be comfortable with a little nudity," he teased. "I expect to be the lucky beneficiary of that."

She scowled at him. "It can't be *that* casual."

"Because..."

"It's different when you care about the man who's looking at you." The way she spoke, without even a hint of a smile, told him she was sincere, which caused his chest to tighten so much it scared him. Perhaps he'd been too cavalier about his relationship with her. Perhaps he wouldn't be able to maintain the emotional distance he needed.

"Those are the kind of statements that will get us into trouble," he said.

She lifted her chin. "So no statements like that."

"None."

"And no expectations, either."

When he kissed her, she allowed him to lower the sheet a bit. "I say we start there," he said and cupped her bare breast before going out to get her clothes so she could dress.

"You've got to come back. You've been gone for over an hour!" her sister complained. "I've had at least four customers, and I can't even open the till! Don't you care about your business?"

Paige didn't care about anything right now. As far as she was concerned, the rest of the world could burn to the ground, including her business, if it meant she had to leave before she was ready. Micah had texted her five minutes ago to say that he'd take care of getting Trevor some money, which meant he should be coming out of the house any second.

Would Sloane be with him?

Paige pulled herself up higher, so she could get a better look. Where the hell was he?

"Hang on for a few more minutes," she said to Yolanda. "I told you, Trevor forgot his lunch money."

"So call Micah! Can't he help? Even if he's on duty, he should be able to swing by the school."

Her palms were beginning to sweat and her heart was knocking against her ribs. She didn't want to see what she thought she'd see, was still praying it wasn't so. "I haven't been able to reach them."

"Them?" her sister echoed.

"Him. I meant him!"

"But it can't take this long to drive over to the school!"

Paige pressed a hand to her head so that she didn't start screaming. "Yo, please. I need a few more minutes."

"Fine. Then I'm going to turn the sign to Closed. I might as well. I can't actually sell anything. I can't figure out how to work this damn register. You were only gone twenty minutes last time!"

"Don't close. At least people can come in and look. If they want to buy, they can come back."

"But will they? That's the question. I can't believe you'd risk losing customers like this."

Paige thought she saw movement at Micah's door, but she was parked down the part of his street that curved to the right before coming to a dead end. It wasn't all that easy for her to see, but unless he was going to visit someone who lived in one of the ten houses deeper in this small neighborhood, he'd never travel in her direction, which gave her a degree of confidence he wouldn't notice her.

"Quit worrying," she told Yolanda. "Micah's giving me most of his check each month. So much that I'm not even sure what he's living on. Financially, I'm fine."

Her sister fell silent. At the same time, Paige caught her breath. She saw movement. But was it two people or just one?

"You're starting to scare me, you know that?" her sister said at length.

"What are you talking about?" She was barely listening, but she knew Yolanda wasn't happy.

"Are you doing something to get Micah's attention?" Yolanda demanded. "Does this have to do with him and not Trevor? Because you need to leave that man alone. I'm sorry you can't get over him. I feel bad about that, because I want you to be happy. But if he wants out, you have to let him go."

"This has nothing to do with Micah," she lied.

"Then where could you be?"

"At the school. I have to go in now. I'll be back soon," she said and disconnected.

Yolanda didn't understand. Sure, she'd had her difficulties. Infidelity could be heartbreaking. But her husband had had one fling after another. He hadn't loved, passionately and enduringly, another woman the entire time they'd been together. Paige had spent her whole adult life living in the shadow of Sloane's memory—a woman who'd turned out to be a famous cover model! How could a regular girl living in a small Texas town ever compete with that?

Maybe she'd wanted Sloane to come back to prove the real person couldn't be as perfect as the one in those glossy images. But this wasn't going in the direction she'd hoped.

Forget about him, her sister had once said. As if it was that easy.

She caught her breath as two distinct people came into her vision. Micah was with Sloane, all right. As tall and thin as Sloane was, there could be no mistaking her. She must've been with him the whole time, just as Paige had suspected.

Paige covered her mouth as tears sprang to her eyes. Deep down, she'd been hoping to be proven wrong, had been hoping she wouldn't drive away from the neighborhood hating both of the people who'd always meant so much to her.

Letting go of the steering wheel, she fell back against the seat but could still see Micah open the door for Sloane. She could also see him duck his head for a quick kiss and felt as though someone had just punched her in the stomach.

"You son of a bitch," she whispered and dialed Ed's cell phone.

"What's happening?" Sloane's father asked.

"They're back together, all right. I'm watching them now. You'd better do something, because I promise you, if Micah thinks Sloane might be right, he'll leave no stone unturned trying to help her."

CHAPTER TWENTY-TWO

Sloane couldn't help feeling conspicuous as Micah ran into the school. She was wearing the same clothes she'd had on yesterday—the same makeup, too—and her hair was mussed from being in his bed. She was afraid someone would see her in his truck before she could talk to Paige. She had missed so many calls and texts from her former best friend that she had to respond soon. It had already gone too long. It was just difficult to decide what to say. While she wanted to be honest with Paige, she didn't want to hurt her.

She took out her phone. I'm fine, she wrote. But I need to talk to you. Do you have a few minutes that I could come over tonight? Maybe after Trevor goes to bed so we can talk in private?

She was just about to send that message when Micah came hurrying back.

"Did you make it in time?" she asked as he climbed behind the wheel.

"He'd already eaten. Paige had given him money, so this was all for nothing, a wasted trip. I don't know what she was thinking, going into a panic like that."

"I guess the good news is that Trevor was able to eat." She smiled, hoping to ease his irritation. Paige had dragged them out of bed during the afterglow of their first time together in ten years, but considering what Paige had expressed at the motel, Sloane couldn't help wondering if she had simply been testing Micah to see if he would take care of the problem for her as quickly as he did. Sloane believed that was entirely possible, but she knew Paige was reeling, so she kept her mouth shut. She felt sorry for Paige. Plus, she didn't want to build animosity between Micah and Paige when they had to get along for Trevor's sake.

"Yeah, I guess so," he said as he started the truck.

"I'm thinking about sending this to Paige. If I'm going to move in with you, I feel like I have to be totally up front with her."

He paused before putting the transmission in Reverse so he could read what was on her phone. "Should I be there for this? Maybe we should tell her together."

"No. Showing up unified would make it even harder for her. It would feel like we're teaming up. I'm sad because I know she's struggled a great deal with the divorce."

"I tried to make it as easy on her as I could," he said as he backed out of the parking space. "She just won't let go."

"I know. She expects us to do what she needs in spite of what we may want or feel."

"I'm not going to get back with her, regardless, so what does it matter if I'm seeing you or someone else?"

"That's the logical way to look at it, but emotion isn't logical."

"She needs to let go. I've had it."

"I understand why you're getting impatient. I hope *she'll* understand that it's not fair for her to ask me to stay away from you, not when you and I were together first. After all, I've overlooked the way she flirted with you way back then, pretended I didn't see it. I did that to preserve the relationship, but now she's acting as though she wasn't the one who crossed the friendship line for the sake of a guy."

"Nothing you say will change her mind. She just wants what she wants, and I can't deliver it."

"Still, I need to try to explain, try to get her to understand, for the sake of the friendship."

"Good luck. I hope she treats you okay—and doesn't do anything to make things harder for me where Trevor's concerned."

"She would never do that," Sloane said and sent the text. "She loves Trevor."

He shot her a glance as he turned out of the school. "Question is...does she love him more than she's about to hate me?"

There was a man Sloane didn't recognize sitting in a nondescript sedan at the motel when she pulled in. He was off in the far corner of the lot and didn't seem to have a room. He kept looking down as though he was writing or reading while waiting for someone, and she quickly figured out who he was looking for. As soon as he saw her park in front of her unit, he got out and hurried toward her.

"Sloane McBride?"

She felt her eyebrows shoot up. "Yes?"

He showed her a badge. "I'm Detective Ramos from the Keller Police Department over in Fort Worth. I was hoping to have a word with you."

She should've guessed he was a detective. He had the average barber-type buzz, a small paunch that suggested he ate too many greasy burgers while working long hours, was wearing a dated tie with a sports coat that didn't quite match—and Micah had mentioned that there was someone on the Keller force who wanted to speak with her. She'd figured Ramos would call, hadn't expected him to drive all the way to Millcreek, not without speaking to her first.

"Sure, I…" She glanced uncertainly at her door. It felt weird to meet with a stranger, especially a male stranger, in a motel room, but she figured she should be safe with a cop. She didn't want to discuss her father out in the parking lot, where they could easily be overheard by a maid, the manager or another patron. "Let's go inside."

He stood at a respectful distance while she dug around in her purse for her room key and let him in.

Fortunately, the maid had tidied the bed, since she hadn't bothered. "This is about my father and what happened to his family, right? Micah Evans, an officer on our own force here in town, told me you wanted to talk to me."

"Yes. I spoke with Officer Evans. He felt you wouldn't be opposed to giving me a few minutes of your time."

She put her room key back in her purse. "I assumed you might call, but…"

"Sorry if I've surprised you by just showing up. I find face-to-face interviews far more effective."

He didn't seem sorry at all. She thought he'd appeared out of the blue on purpose, so she couldn't compose her thoughts beforehand. "This could be a wasted trip. I know nothing about...about what happened before I was born."

"Your father never talked about the loss of his parents and brother?"

"I knew they were gone, but he never went over the specifics."

"And you didn't ask?"

"He must've mentioned the most basic details at some point, because I knew my grandparents and uncle had been murdered when they came home to find it being burgled. But I can't remember a specific conversation where he talked about where he was that night, how he found out, what the next few days were like or how he felt about the man who killed them. I would like to have heard the story from his perspective but have always hesitated to bring it up for fear it would be too painful for him."

"Did he grieve for his lost family, then? Act as though he missed them?"

"If he did, he did so silently. Like I said, he never talked about them. It's been a long time since that terrible crime, and the man who shot them is dead. Do you really think there should still be an investigation? Or that you'll be able to find anything new even if my father had a hand in it?"

"Maybe, with your help."

She motioned to the chair near the small desk in the corner. "Then have a seat. I'll sit here on the bed."

He did as she suggested. "I'll apologize to you right off the bat, Ms. McBride," he said.

This approach took her by surprise. "Because..."

"The questions I have to ask might not be easy to answer. No one wants to believe their father could be capable of murder, especially this kind of murder."

She drew a shaky breath. It was one thing for *her* to doubt her father; it was quite another to have an outsider—a police officer, no less—suggest Ed might be guilty of such heinous crimes. "I'll answer as honestly as I can. I'm not trying to hide anything. I want the truth, probably worse than you do. It's terrible not knowing if I can trust my own father."

"Then you have your doubts."

Basic loyalty caused her to hesitate, but she reminded herself why she was in town and answered truthfully. "I do."

"Is there a particular reason?"

"The disappearance of my mother. No one knows what happened to her, and I believe he could be responsible."

"I find that alarming myself." He took out a pad and pen. "Your mother went missing twenty-three years ago, correct?"

"Yes."

"Why don't you walk me through what you remember about that night?"

Sloane told him everything—about the sounds she heard, the fact that someone had come to look in on her but she'd been too afraid to open her eyes, the way the house had gone silent, giving her the impression she'd been left alone, and her father's haggard appearance the following morning, which suggested he'd been up all night. But she didn't mention the information Vickie had provided about the boat, or Hadley's statement that Sloane should keep pressing. Sloane knew Ramos was only interested in the case as it pertained to his own, that he wasn't going to investigate it for her—it wasn't in his jurisdiction—so she saw no reason to put Vickie or Hadley on his radar.

"It's my understanding the police here haven't done a lot to look into what happened," he said.

"That's true."

He frowned as he read over the notes he'd taken while she talked. "I'd offer to run your mother's name through some databases, see if I get a hit, but I've already done that, and I came up empty-handed."

"You're not the only one. When I was in New York, as soon as I'd made enough money, I hired a private investigator to look for her. I was twenty-four. He, too, tried every database available."

"Which makes me believe she's no longer alive."

She frowned. "It makes me believe that, too. So does the fact that she never would've left me and my brother."

"Could you see your father…harming her?"

She curved her nails into her palms. "I hate to say yes to that question, but she hasn't come back, so I'm afraid whatever he did went well beyond 'harming.'"

"What about his parents and brother? Could you see him being involved in their deaths?"

"No. I can't imagine he could orchestrate the deaths of his whole family, especially at such a young age. Who would do that?"

"A young man who didn't want to disappoint his folks by telling them he was flunking out of college despite all the financial support he'd received. A young man who wanted to be sure he inherited their money. Patricide isn't a new thing," he said. "The Menendez brothers are a notable example. And there have been others."

She lifted her hands. "Then I guess I can believe it. I believe he might've murdered my mother, right? But who knows what the truth is? People are complex. They're not all good or all bad. My father isn't an obvious monster."

"Believe me, murderers rarely are, or they'd be a heck of a lot easier to catch." He smiled in an effort to put her at ease, but she couldn't relax. She was too torn. Was she doing the right thing opening up to him, or was she getting her father into a lot of trouble for nothing?

No matter what she did, she kept coming back to the same question: Was she the hero or the villain of the story currently unfolding in Millcreek?

"What we need is proof, real evidence, not my opinion," she said. "Other than the fact that my father inherited his parents' assets, which gave him a motive, and he probably didn't want them to know he wasn't graduating, what makes you suspect he was behind the whole thing? Micah—Officer Evans—said you don't have any evidence that places him at the scene of the crime, and you can't find a connection to the guy who actually pulled the trigger."

"Part of that's true. Your father has an airtight alibi, wasn't in the area that night. But I found a connection to the shooter. Just yesterday," he added with a touch of self-satisfaction.

Her face began to tingle as a surge of adrenaline caused her to sit taller. "What's the connection?"

"I have a picture that proves they were both at the Whiskey River Bar & Tavern a couple of months before the robbery and shooting took place."

"A picture?" After all the intervening years, finding something like that seemed so random it was almost unbelievable.

"Yes. I spoke to Sammy Smoot's family the day before yesterday, asked them about his activities, if he'd ever gone to Texas A&M and so forth. They told me he didn't have the money to attend school but he was living and working in the area as a bartender. Larry Polanski—the detective who had this case before me—had been told the same thing, so it wasn't new information, but I was making the rounds, seeing if anyone changed their story. Larry believed your father very likely met Sammy at the bar or at a party. He was certain they knew each other and yet they both denied it. In your father's statement, he said flat out that he'd never been to Whiskey River, and Larry couldn't prove otherwise, couldn't find anyone who remembered seeing him there. This was before cell phones, of course, so it was much harder to track someone's movements."

"So how'd you do it?"

"I went to the bar."

"Don't tell me it's still open after thirty-five years!"

"Believe it or not. Same guy owns it. His son runs it these days, but the son wouldn't know anything. He's too young. Anyway, I drove the three hours to College Station to talk to the owner—"

"And he had a picture of my dad at the bar?"

"Not exactly. He didn't recall ever seeing your father's face and didn't know he had the picture. After we sat in a corner booth and talked, I had to walk down a long hall to get to the bathroom where I saw dozens and dozens of photographs taken through the years."

Sloane was hanging on every word, her heart racing. "What kind of photographs?"

"I'm getting there. For a while after the bar opened, when it was still new and exciting and not the ho-hum average bar it is now, whenever a new band came to play, the owner would snap a picture of them at closing and hang it in the hall. He thought it would be fun to have if any of them ever became famous. He liked helping musicians get a start, so that hall filled up quickly, mostly with pictures coming from the early years."

"Don't tell me my father was in one of *those* pictures! He's never been involved with a band!"

"He didn't have to be. Whoever was left in the bar when the band took this pic often jumped in to do rabbit ears, stick out their tongues, act crazy. It often turned into a drunk, boisterous end-of-night kind of thing. After the owner got each picture developed, he'd put the name of the band and the date at the bottom—"

"And hang it up," she finished.

"Yes. I saw two dozen pictures from that year and the year before, and I studied them all. Larry, the detective before me, might've seen them, too, but he must not have thought to look any closer. What were the chances, you know? I had to get a magnifying glass to be able to see some of the faces clearly. There were thirty, forty people in some shots. But I'm glad I made the effort, because there it was—a picture of your father and Sammy Smoot standing with a bunch of other patrons and a band named Nightshifter."

Goose bumps broke out on Sloane's arms. "Can I see that picture?"

"Sort of. I took a snapshot with my smartphone so I could send it to Larry. It'll be clearer once I scan the original, which I'll do when I get back to Keller, but this should work for now." He found what he wanted on his phone and got up to cross the short distance between them.

Sloane held her breath as he enlarged the photograph and pointed to a small, blurry face. "That's your father right there, isn't it?"

She could hardly breathe. "It looks like him. Where's Sammy Smoot?"

He only had to move his finger an inch. "Right there."

"Micah, I'm talking to you."

Micah blinked and looked up from the desk he'd been using to finish some paperwork before heading out on patrol. Colt Green, the officer who'd told him about the Keller Department's interest in Mayor McBride, was standing over him, but he'd been so deep in thought, so consumed with reliving what'd happened with Sloane only a few hours earlier—both enjoying the memory and wondering if he'd live to regret taking things so far—that he hadn't heard a word. "What's up, man?"

Cole glanced at the chief's office—the door was closed—and lowered his voice. "Did you get hold of that detective from the Fort Worth area? John Something?"

"Ramos? I did. Thanks for letting me know about him."

"No problem. Just don't tell anyone I'm the one who mentioned him to you, okay?"

"I won't say anything."

"I appreciate that." He seemed relieved as he started off, so relieved it made Micah slightly uncomfortable.

"Colt!" he said, coming to his feet.

Colt turned around and, when Micah waved him back, somewhat reluctantly retraced his steps. "Yeah?"

"Would it be a big deal if I *did* mention it?"

"It could be."

Micah gave him a searching look. "Why?"

Colt gripped his own shoulder as if trying to ease some tension. "The mayor's pissed off about it. I heard him shouting earlier, when Chief Adler was talking to him on speakerphone. Something about Keller PD and that son-of-a-bitch detective who's trying to cause trouble for him. Adler said there was nothing he could do about that, and McBride told him he'd better make sure he didn't run into similar bullshit from *this* department—"

"But *he* doesn't run this department," Micah broke in.

Colt lowered his voice even further. "Wanna bet?"

Micah felt the hair on the back of his neck stand up. "He'd better not go after my job..."

Colt sent another worried glance at the chief's door before leaning in. "That's the thing, bro. I heard your name. I'm pretty sure the mayor's trying to get you kicked off the force."

Micah clenched his jaw. "*For what?* He has to have a reason!"

Colt motioned for Micah to keep his voice down. "Just know they're looking for one and be careful, okay?" he whispered. "Stay away from Sloane. Don't get involved with her."

"Okay," he said, but that was just lip service, something to calm Colt's fears. Micah *couldn't* stay away. He was still in love with her.

CHAPTER TWENTY-THREE

When he saw Sloane's name come up on his caller ID, Micah was just heading out on patrol. He was still angry over what Colt had told him but he wasn't quite sure how to handle it. He was tempted to confront Ed, ask him who the hell he thought he was, mayor or not. But he was beginning to view Ed a bit differently, could see what it might be like to get on his bad side and didn't want to provoke him for fear any reaction would include some repercussion to Sloane.

And to think she'd lived with that bully, had been *raised* by him.

It was becoming easier and easier to understand why she left—and to admire her courage for returning.

"Hey," he said when he answered. "Have you talked to Paige?"

"Not yet. I sent her that text, but she hasn't responded, and I haven't had a chance to follow up. Detective Ramos is in town. He caught me just as I reached the motel and asked to talk, so I haven't even showered."

"How'd it go?"

"It was disturbing. All I've ever wanted is to know what happened to my mother. I never intended to destroy my father in the process."

"If he's committed murder, he has only himself to blame."

"I know. It's just that familial loyalty can be such a strange thing. I'm afraid I'll feel responsible for any negative ramifications he might face, even though I shouldn't. And thinking about him going to prison, the person who raised me and has always acted as if he'd be in charge until the end of time, makes me feel as though the ground is giving way beneath my feet."

"Parent-child relationships are complicated, Sloane. Especially when they involve shit like this."

"Apparently so. Anyway, I didn't call to complain. I wanted to tell you that Detective Ramos has found a connection between my father and Sammy Smoot, the man who shot my grandparents and uncle."

Although Micah had barely left the station, he pulled to the side of the road. "Are you kidding me?"

"Definitely not. In my father's original statement to police, he said he'd never been to the Whiskey River Bar & Tavern, and no one claimed otherwise."

"That's what Ramos told me when I talked to him, too."

"Well, he's found a picture showing both my father and Sam standing in the bar with the band that was playing that night."

Micah smacked the steering wheel. "Holy shit! Your father's a psychopath and yet he wields all kinds of power here in Millcreek. He's essentially running this town."

"He's formidable. He must be guilty of killing his parents *and* my mother. There are too many unanswered questions, too many coincidences, and he's the one common element. Don't you think?"

As suspicious as Micah was, he hated to agree too readily. In this case, there wasn't any DNA evidence, fingerprints, a documented trail showing Sam received money from her father or anything like that. There wasn't any forensic evidence at all. Even the picture wasn't exactly a smoking gun. Ed and Sam were both about the same age, they were both hanging out in a college town and that had been a popular bar. It wasn't entirely out of the realm of possibility that their paths had crossed and they didn't know it. It could be that Ed had stopped by that place so briefly he hadn't really catalogued it in his brain, that he'd been too drunk to remember or he was too scared—or too smart—to admit he'd been there for fear he'd go to prison for a crime he *didn't* commit.

"That's a great start, a step in the right direction. But I wish Ramos had something solid, something that proved your father's involvement without a doubt."

"I do, too, but at least we have more now than we did before."

"That's true," he said. "Have you packed up?"

"Not yet."

"Why don't you do that now? I'll be right over to take you to my house. You can shower there. I don't like you being anywhere your father or brother can find you."

"My father or brother could easily find me at your place."

"Neither of them would expect you to be there, not if you're still registered at the motel and your car is in the lot. Word that we're seeing each other again hasn't gotten out yet. So maybe you *shouldn't* tell Paige. We might be better off keeping it to ourselves for a while."

"I *have* to tell her, Micah. Secretly staying with you when she's crying on my shoulder over how badly she wants you back would destroy our friendship for good. I might already have crossed that line with what happened today."

He couldn't regret today. He'd wanted to be with Sloane ever since he'd been with her the last time, and it had been a long, long wait. "You can't trust her. She'll tell your father where you are. She's no friend to you, or she'd care more about your happiness and less about her own."

"Maybe with all the modeling success, she feels I've had enough sunshine in life, and she should be allowed the one thing she needs to be happy."

"Problem is, even if you weren't in the picture, I wouldn't go back to her. I left her before I ever knew you were coming back."

"I know. It's just… God, this is so hard. It's been a long time since she and I were close, but the bonds we forged when we were young are hard to break. In order to be the kind of friend *I* want to be, I have to be honest with her."

He dropped his head into his hand and rubbed his forehead. "I wish I could convince you not to do it."

"Trevor might already have told her."

"I doubt he's said anything. He wouldn't do it on purpose, and it's far too soon for him to slip up."

"Still. This is a small town. If I'm staying with you, we won't be able to keep it a secret for long."

"If Ramos has found the connection between your father and the shooter, we may not need long," he said. "Is he going to arrest him?"

"Not yet. The DA has advised him to keep working on the case, to try to strengthen it. You said yourself that what he has isn't as incriminating as we need it to be."

"Some detectives are more bullish than others. I thought maybe he'd give it a shot, since he isn't likely to get a lot more. If your father wasn't at the crime scene, it's not as though he can go back and test any evidence that was saved for DNA, which is how so many cold cases get solved these days."

"He said there are a couple of loose threads that might yield something."

"Like..."

"Someone paid for Sam's sister to have a liver transplant not long after Smoot hung himself in jail. They've never been able to trace that money. The family claims it came from anonymous 'donations.' But now that Ramos has proof my father and Smoot likely knew each other, he's planning to press the family, to see if he can't get one of them to talk about how they got the money."

Micah adjusted his bulletproof vest. Not only was it heavy, it could be so damn uncomfortable, especially when it was warm outside. "That's why Smoot did it? To save his sister?"

"That's what Ramos believes. But why would he kill himself *before* the transplant?"

"Maybe he hated himself for having to do what he did. Maybe he feared he wouldn't be able to take the pressure, was afraid he'd give up your father and his sister would never get the transplant he was trying to give her. Maybe he couldn't tolerate the abuse he was getting in prison or had psychological problems to begin with. Who can say? But if that's what he did, it's sort of beautiful—in a very dark and twisted way. He sacrificed himself for her."

"He also sacrificed three others who didn't have a choice!" she said.

"His family might view it differently. It's possible they won't dishonor his memory by talking to the police."

"Then there will be nothing more Ramos can do. He said he has to be careful. He can't arrest someone like my father—a high profile figure with the money and temperament to sue—unless he's fairly certain the DA can make the charges stick."

Micah swore under his breath. "If Ramos can't get the family to talk, or find something else, that picture won't make a damn bit of difference in the end. The case will go cold again."

"And I'll only be *more* afraid of my own father than I was before. We have to do something, Micah."

"What?" Chief Adler had told him, in no uncertain terms, to leave it alone.

"We have to prove he killed my mother."

"I'm not sure that's possible. He's had twenty-three years to hide his connection to the crime, and he has the police chief in his back pocket. Adler won't let me investigate."

"That would have to change if we brought him proof."

"It would take a body."

"Then that's what we'll look for. I've been thinking..."

"About..."

"When Vickie told me my dad took the boat out that night, I automatically assumed he'd gone to the river. It's close. It would be so easy to back up, dump a corpse and then get out of there. But you said a corpse would likely have washed ashore."

"With that fast-moving water, yes."

"And my mother never did. So what if he didn't dump her in the river? What if he took her up to Lake Granbury, where he'd have more privacy and could weight the body so it would stay submerged?"

"You had a cabin up there," he said, remembering. "We drove up once, during our senior year."

"And my dad pitched a fit about it when he found out."

"Because we went without asking. He said we wouldn't be allowed to see each other again if we ever went back."

"Which I found odd even at the time. As long as he was free to live his life, he didn't care much about what Randy and I did. He liked you, and the fact that we were always together meant he didn't have to spend time with me himself. So I was super surprised that he had a problem with us visiting the cabin for a day to lay out by the water."

"You're saying he didn't want us there for a different reason than the lack of parental supervision."

"Could be. I have no way of knowing for sure, but if he hasn't sold the property, it might be worth going up to look around. It's not as if the police ever searched our house here in Millcreek, let alone the cabin at the lake."

"But the lake's an hour away. And you were only five years old at the time. Would he have left you alone for that long? You could've gotten up, wandered around in the street looking for him or your mother and been hit by a car. Or been grabbed by a stranger. Or wound up in the river, which is only a short distance away."

"If he'd just committed murder, I doubt he'd hesitate to leave me for several hours, especially if it was in the middle of the night. Someone came in and checked on me to make sure I was sleeping. So there's that. And he looked as though he'd been up all night when I saw him in the morning."

Micah watched as various cars, trucks and vans rolled past him on the street. The drivers probably assumed he was trying to catch speeders. They invariably slowed the moment they noticed him. But he wasn't interested in writing any tickets. He didn't enjoy that part of his job even when he had to do it. "I can't imagine we'll find anything. After so long, there wouldn't be much of her left." He winced as he said those words, hoping they weren't too graphic. They were talking about her *mother*, after all. But Sloane was too focused on the goal to notice his choice of words.

She was strong and determined, he realized. In those areas, she reminded him of her father more now than she ever did ten years ago.

"There'd be bones," she insisted. "Maybe even clothes, bindings or the weights he used. We could dive down and take a look."

"Except I don't know how to scuba dive."

"Then I'll go alone. I'm certified. I say we get my suit and tank from my storage unit in Dallas and go up there tomorrow. If he dumped her in the lake, I'm guessing he would've gone to an area he's familiar with. That's what most killers do."

Micah was taken aback by the authority in her voice. "How do *you* know?"

"I've been watching true crime shows for years, marveling at the cases that get solved, watching how they do it and hoping mine will someday be solved, too. Sometimes, it's the smallest thing that brings the truth to light. That's what I've learned."

"Sloane, I'm afraid for you to get your hopes up too high."

"I know that we're searching for a needle in a haystack, Micah. But I have to look, for my own peace of mind. I have to do all I can. You understand, don't you?"

"I do," he admitted.

"So… I bet he would've used the boat launch next to the cabin. He'd feel most comfortable there. And if he was in a hurry, was afraid he'd be seen, he may not have gone that far out on the water, especially in the dark, where he'd have to use a light and could be easily spotted from the vantage point of the other cabins. Plus, he'd want to make the drive home before it started to get light."

"In case you woke up early?"

"Again, so that he wouldn't be seen."

He found it sad that she didn't believe she figured into her father's thinking at all, that she didn't matter. "Do you remember how to get to the cabin?"

"Of course."

"Good, because I was there only that one time. I doubt I could find it on my own. We should search the inside, too, while we're there."

"We will."

"Can you get the key? Will it be under that rock where we found it the last time?"

"It's a possibility. People are creatures of habit and routine. If we can't find it, we'll have to break in."

To the mayor's cabin…

Micah considered what Colt had just told him at the station. If he got caught, he'd be kicked off the force.

"Micah?" she said. "Are you okay with that?"

He had to be, because he wasn't going to let her do it alone. "Yeah, I'm okay with that."

"So don't come get me. I'll head over to my storage unit in Dallas for my scuba stuff."

"Stay in touch."

"I will."

He caught her before she could hang up. "What about Paige?"

"I'll keep trying to get hold of her."

He wished she didn't feel the need to do that. She had no idea how vengeful Paige could be. But maybe she was right, and not telling her would only make matters worse when she found out. "Okay. See you later."

Paige was closing up her shop at five when the bell jingled over the door and Ed came in. "Hey." She managed a smile but was too upset about Sloane and Micah for that smile to be genuine. She'd thought she was striking back at Sloane by sleeping with Ed, had felt so repentant and apologetic afterward, and *why*? Sloane had had the last laugh. She always got the last laugh.

"How are you?" he asked.

She tucked her hair behind her ears. "It's been a rough day. What about you?"

"I'm fine. Just a little upset that my only daughter

would malign my name and try to mess up my reelection bid—and that she'd get Micah to help her. I thought Micah and I were friends. How many times have we been golfing together?"

"That's what you're worried about?" she said. "Your reelection?"

He stiffened. "What else would I be worried about? Her mother left in the middle of the night, and I've never seen her again. I haven't harmed anyone, Paige."

Then what'd happened to Clara? Paige wanted to ask but bit her tongue. She was in a bad mood, but she wasn't going to offend Ed. She had enough problems. "I heard Edith talking to her sister at the drugstore when I went in to get some painkillers for my headache an hour or so ago," she told him as she put the money from the till in her cash bag so she could make a deposit at the bank on her way home.

He hesitated. "And?"

"She was saying something about a detective from Keller coming to town and asking a bunch of questions about you."

His scowl deepened. "Edith doesn't know when to keep her mouth shut. All she does is talk."

"I hope you're not in any trouble, that everything is okay."

"It's fine."

"But why would a detective from an outside police department come to Millcreek to investigate Clara's disappearance? Has something turned up?"

"No, nothing. Nothing will turn up, either, not after twenty-three years."

"That detective must've wanted *something*."

"Don't worry about it," he said, a hint of irritation in his voice. "I'm telling you it was nothing."

The fact that he didn't explain indicated the opposite, but she couldn't push him any further. "I'm glad, because Micah and Sloane are already trying to make trouble for you."

"That's why I'm here," he said. "You were Micah's wife. I'm thinking you would know if he's ever misused his power as a police officer."

She looked up after slipping her moneybag in her purse. "In what way?"

"Did he ever let a friend off the hook for speeding or other traffic violations, even though that friend had clearly broken the law? Did he park illegally or use his siren to circumvent traffic lights? Did he do any racial profiling when making traffic stops? Did he ever use his cruiser as his personal vehicle, or wave his gun around?"

"No, none of that."

He frowned as though he wasn't pleased with her answer. "Officers have access to all kinds of state and national databases—the National Crime Information Center, the DMV, et cetera. They can even get banking, telephone and credit information. Has he ever accessed a database that's supposed to be used for official investigations only?"

"Why would he do that?"

"Lots of reasons. Maybe he was curious about a friend or neighbor, wanted to see where they used to live or work or if they were in debt, or he wanted to check out a business associate he was interested in investing with. Maybe he even used those databases to try to find Sloane."

Or Clara. She could see where he was going and shook her head. “I don’t think so, Ed.”

“Surely, he’s done one of those things.”

“Not that I remember.”

He pulled out a piece of paper that had *Complaint* written across the top. “Paige, he would have to access one or more of those databases to look for Clara, so we both know he’s done at least that much. If you’ll just sign this, I’ll take it over to Chief Adler, and we can teach Micah a lesson once and for all.”

“You’re trying to get him fired?” She was appalled by his swift and ruthless revenge even though she’d helped instigate it.

“I’m not *trying*. He’s stabbed me in the back, which means he’s no friend of mine. He won’t be on the force much longer, let alone ever make chief.”

Paige was angry with Micah, too, but she couldn’t bring herself to lie about him when it would mean the loss of his job. She wanted him to love her. That was all.

She should never have gotten involved with Ed. He was willing to go *much* further than she was. “No. I don’t feel good about that.”

Sloane’s father seemed taken aback by her refusal. “He’s never wanted you. He’s made you feel inadequate ever since you got involved with him, made you look like a besotted fool. Signing this will be hitting back, which is what he deserves. Show him he should’ve had more respect.”

“No,” she said. “He’s my son’s father. If I get him fired, how will he pay his child support?” She laughed weakly, as if that was her real motivation. She thought

Ed might understand that reason before any other, but she couldn't have signed it, regardless.

"Sloane can take care of that for him. She has lots of money. And everything that's happening is her fault."

He held the document out and pulled a pen from the cup that held several at her register. "Come on."

"This isn't right," she said. "I can't do it."

He heaved a dramatic sigh. "I promise you'll be sorry if you don't."

She scowled at him. "I don't care. I want you to get out of my store. I have to pick up my son."

He shook his head, feigning disappointment. "I hoped it wouldn't come to this, but you're forcing my hand," he said and pulled out several photographs from inside his jacket, which he spread on the counter for her to see.

Paige gasped. He had photographs of her at his house, when they were in the bedroom, only they were taken from a vantage point that made it seem as though the camera was outside the bedroom, as though someone was spying on them while they had sex and was snapping those shots.

"How'd you get these?" she cried.

"Obviously, I had a camera set up, although I've since removed it. That's the downside to this, why I would rather not have had to go this far. I'm going to miss that camera."

She scarcely heard him. Her ears were ringing too loudly. If these photos were to get out, Trevor's teachers would see them, his friends' parents, his baseball coaches. And the religious sector of Millcreek would never shop at Little Bae Bae again. It would ruin her business, her self-respect, her whole *life*.

Staggering back, she bumped into the wall. "You're in these shots, too," she managed to choke out. "Surely, you can't want anyone to see them. What about your reelection?"

He took his time glancing through them, a wistful expression on his face. It was all she could do not to snatch them away and destroy them, but she knew he could easily print more. He wouldn't have made it *that* easy for her. "I doubt it'll hurt my reelection," he said. "Because I'm in the pictures, too, no one will suspect I took them in the first place, or leaked them. And since I got to choose which pictures to use, I've made sure none of them show me in an unflattering light. You look like you're enjoying that dildo, though."

He'd chosen the most humiliating photos he could for her. "Oh my God. You set me up!"

"Come on, don't take it too hard. A lot of the guys in town will be turned on by this. That's *something*, isn't it?"

Hot tears gathered in her eyes. No one would *ever* forget it.

He pulled out a monogrammed handkerchief—the pretentious bastard, as if anyone carried one of those these days—but she refused to take it. "Suit yourself," he said and shoved it back in his pocket before handing her the pen and sliding that complaint in front of her again.

She couldn't even read it for her tears, but after she wiped her eyes and the words came into focus, she realized that she'd be accusing Micah of something far worse than using his cruiser as his personal vehicle. "It says here he held his service revolver to my head!"

"You know how some couples fight," he said with a chuckle.

"Micah will hate me," she murmured as she stared down at it.

"Oh brother," he said. "Don't let that upset you. I'm pretty sure he already does."

CHAPTER TWENTY-FOUR

Sloane hadn't been able to get hold of Paige. She'd tried half a dozen times—both calling and texting—and received no response. Once she returned from Dallas, she even went by Paige's house.

It was dark inside and no one came to the door. She went to the boutique after, but it was closed and empty; Paige wasn't working late. Although Sloane considered driving by Paige's parents' house, she didn't feel comfortable going over there, in case Trevor had told his mother about finding her in Micah's kitchen on Sunday.

Since Paige wasn't responding after being so eager to find out if Sloane was okay, Sloane could only assume she was angry, and there was nothing she could to do change what'd happened earlier.

If she was being honest, she wouldn't change it even if she had the choice. Being with Micah had been beyond anything she'd ever experienced, especially after missing him for so long. Maybe he was different in some ways she had yet to discover, and she'd been crazy to sleep with him so soon after coming back into his life. She told herself she couldn't really know him after a decade of having no contact. But he felt like home, as if she knew him better than anyone else on earth, and that made it all too easy to fall back into his arms, especially because he'd made it clear that he'd never wanted to lose her.

She tried dialing Micah to tell him that she was fairly certain Paige was onto them, but she couldn't reach him, either, which was odd. He was the one who'd told her to stay in touch—and now he wouldn't pick up? She grew uneasy when he didn't return her call for more than an hour, but, assuming he was busy with work and would get back to her as soon as he could, she used the time to move from the motel to his house. She didn't bother trying to keep her room at The Wagon Wheel, didn't leave her car in their lot as a decoy. Since she planned to tell Paige that she was staying with Micah, there was no need to pretend.

As soon as she put her suitcase in Micah's bedroom—she didn't know how long she'd be staying so she didn't unpack—she pulled on some sweats and walked out to the kitchen, where she set up her computer and went online to see if she could find out anything about scuba diving in Lake Granbury.

It wasn't a popular destination for divers, so there wasn't much information, but she found a website where one guy had posted about it. According to him, it was thirty-six to forty feet deep with a clay-muck bottom and visibility under five feet. That wasn't ideal. And with a lot of submerged trees and trotlines, which were used to catch catfish and had as many as fifty hooks along several feet of fishing line, it could be difficult to navigate, maybe even dangerous if she were to get caught up in it. She wasn't going to mention that to Micah, however. She was too determined to make the dive.

After she knew what to expect, and couldn't find any more information, anyway, she closed her computer and glanced at the clock. Why hadn't Micah called?

She was about to get her phone so that she could try to reach him again when she heard keys at the door and stood in anticipation. He'd said his shift didn't end until midnight, so what was he doing home?

"Micah?" she yelled, to be sure the person she heard was him.

"Yeah, it's me," he called back before the lock clicked and he swung open the door.

She hurried toward him. Now that she'd given in to the desire she'd felt for so long, she was eager to touch him again, to hold him.

But she could tell by the look on his face that something was wrong, so she stopped before she reached him. "What is it?"

"I've been suspended from the force," he said as he stalked into the kitchen and threw his keys on the counter.

He was livid. She'd never seen him like this.

A cold fear swept through her. "What do you mean?"

"I'm talking about my job." He opened the fridge and pulled out a beer. "I'm suspended pending an investigation."

She came to stand at the opening of the kitchen,

watching as he pulled the tab and took a long drink. "For what?"

He wiped his mouth. "Paige is accusing me of holding my gun to her head while we were having an argument."

"Are you kidding? You would *never* do anything like that!"

"Well, I wish they'd take your word for it, because you're right. Nothing like that ever happened. Paige and I certainly argued. It seemed like we were fighting almost every day there at the end, which is why I finally left. She was so possessive, absolutely obsessed with the idea that I was going to cheat on her. But my service weapon never came into it."

"So why would she say it did?"

He tipped his beer at her. "Why do you think?"

"But I didn't tell her about us, Micah," Sloane said, and now she was glad. "I was going to. But I haven't been able to reach her, and I've tried several times. She hasn't responded. For that matter, I couldn't reach *you*, either."

"I couldn't answer. I was too busy fighting for my job. Chief Adler called me back to the station to inform me of Paige's accusations and to tell me he will be personally investigating my 'behavior.'"

"Chief Adler should be investigating my father's behavior, not yours!"

"This is the result of Paige's jealousy. I can't escape it, even after the divorce."

"But why would she go after your job? She depends on you to pay child support."

A muscle moved in his cheek. "It's your father. He's behind this somehow, too."

"You think they're in on it together?"

"That's all I can figure. Colt, a friend of mine on the force, told me your father was trying to get me fired. He overheard him on the phone with our chief. Ed must've realized it would make Paige mad if we were to get back together, so he convinced her to exact a little revenge by signing that complaint."

Sloane raked her fingers through her hair. "I feel so terrible. I knew better than to let you get involved, but I did it anyway."

He set his beer on the counter. "Don't talk like that. Come here." Stepping forward, he pulled her into his arms, resting his chin on top of her head. "We'll fight them," he said. "We'll fight them both."

"But what can we do? What if Chief Adler believes her—or pretends to in order to give my father what he wants?"

"I'm hoping they'll question Trevor, and that they'll believe what he says."

Trevor was nine, only four years older than she was when her mother went missing. No one had thought to ask her if she'd heard or seen anything unusual—or what she thought happened that night. They assumed she'd have no input, or that the input she did have couldn't be trusted because she was only a child.

She feared they'd ignore what Trevor had to say, too, or claim that Micah must've done it when Trevor wasn't around. If that happened, it would come down to Paige's word against Micah's, and with Sloane's father—the mayor, no less—putting pressure on Chief Adler to kick Micah off the force…

Sloane knew which direction this would go.

Slipping out of Micah's arms, she marched across

the living room toward the bedroom so she could get dressed.

"Where are you going?" he asked, following her.

"To my father's. I won't let this happen."

"Arguing with him won't help. So why put yourself in a position to be hurt?" He tried to catch her shoulder, but she dodged his grasp.

"Because I have to do something! I won't let him hurt me through you."

"Don't worry. We'll figure out a way to hold him accountable."

She didn't bother to turn back. "How? I've always felt so powerless with him—since I was just a girl," she said as they reached the bedroom. "All I ever wanted was to feel he was a good man, to be able to admire him and believe in him." She peeled off her sweats and began rifling through her suitcase. "But some people are simply *not* good people. You'd like to see the best in them, but it's not there. That's a tough realization when talking about your only parent, but it's high time I accepted that as fact. I've been treading softly, hoping I'm wrong, trying to give him the benefit of the doubt, and he's used even that to his advantage."

She snatched up a bra and started to put it on, but Micah closed the distance between them, took it from her grasp and tossed it aside. "I don't want you anywhere near him," he said.

"I have to let him know how I feel. I have to tell him that I will never forgive him for going after you, and I won't rest until I find my mother. If he's responsible for her death, I'm going to make sure he rots in prison for the rest of his life!"

"Let's not *tell* him what we're going to do, Sloane. Let's show him."

"We'll do that, too. But I no longer have any reason to hold back. God, I've been acting like the little girl I used to be who tried so hard to please him, to finally meet his expectations and receive his approval. I've been fighting with one hand tied behind my back. And why? He doesn't love me. He never has."

"*He* may not love you." He gripped her shoulders to get her to stop moving and look him in the eye. "But *I* do."

She gaped at him. "How can you say that?"

"How can I *not* say it? It's obvious!"

"But look what I've put you through! And now there's this!"

"Sloane, if anyone asked me which means the most to me—you or my job—there'd be no question. I'll get by somehow, because what I really want is standing here in front of me. Nothing has changed for me. I've loved you since we were in high school. If I haven't been able to get over you in ten years, I'm pretty sure I never will."

His words frightened her at the same time she felt a flicker of hope. "I don't want to hurt you," she said. "And I'm afraid that's what I'll do. Again. If I can't hold my father responsible, if he continues on the way he's been, I'll begin to feel I have to escape this place, escape him and my brother and the memories of my mother, and I'll leave, Micah. I don't see *any* love as being strong enough to block all that."

His hand slid up her bare stomach. "You're selling love short. Your dad didn't know how to love. But I'm not your dad, and I'm not eighteen anymore." He held her chin with his other hand so she couldn't look away from him. "You can rely on me."

"Why would you ever *let* me rely on you? That's the question! I've only been back a week, and I'm already destroying your life!"

"No, you're not. We'll get through this. We deserve the chance to be together, if that's what you want, too."

"I would like nothing better, but…"

"But what? There's nothing standing between us. Not anymore. Paige already knows. She must, or she wouldn't have lodged that complaint. Don't give her or your father even more power by allowing them to come between us. That's one way we can beat him, beat them both, even if we can't do anything else—by living our lives and finding happiness in spite of the roadblocks they've thrown in our path."

"Happiness? That's just it! He'll make us both miserable if I stay."

"It doesn't have to go that way. Let's fight for what we have, Sloane, for what we *feel*," he said, and she closed her eyes as he lowered his head to kiss her.

Nothing had happened. Why? What was taking so long?

It was almost ten, well past dark with a stout breeze adding a chill to the air and moving the dried leaves on the ground, when Vickie Winters stood at her mailbox, frowning at the much bigger house down the street while pretending to sift through the letters in her hand. Ed was home. She'd heard him come past her place in his newest Corvette—the cherry red one; she'd seen it after hurrying over to part the drapes. He'd been going way too fast, as usual. He didn't have to worry about getting in trouble. Laws didn't apply to him.

But that was going to change. He'd cast her aside so long ago, had quit taking any notice of her at all, which was fine. She didn't care about that. It was the damage he'd done before she resented, how he'd wrecked her life without a second thought and now seemed to find her so beneath him he didn't even deign to acknowledge her if they crossed paths.

He had zero remorse. He'd willfully done as much damage as he could and walked away without a backward glance.

She watched a light come on in the second story of his house while remembering the first time he'd ever taken notice of her. Although they'd briefly met here and there as neighbors before, the day she'd bumped into him on the sidewalk as he was coming out of his garage and she was pushing Sarah in her wheelchair down at that end of the cul de sac had been different. She'd been trying to get her daughter some sun, something she herself had needed to lift her spirits, and he'd stopped to smile and joke with her—so handsome and self-assured.

Ed being Ed, he probably could've charmed *any* woman. She'd watched it happen over and over with others since. That was her only consolation. She wasn't the last fool to fall for his act. But she'd been especially vulnerable in those days, which was why she still held it against him. After she'd had Sarah, she'd become almost invisible to her husband—and everyone else, it seemed. She didn't live near family, and all Dean did was work, often out of state, leaving her to struggle through each day caring for their special needs daughter alone and without respite, gratitude or love.

Dean had been a selfish bastard. She didn't miss him. But no one was worse than Ed. Ed fell into a whole other category. She believed he was a true sociopath, and she wasn't going to let him continue to escape the consequences for his misdeeds.

She'd told him that once, and he'd laughed in her face. But he'd see that she was no one to be trifled with, that she was more than the weak, powerless woman he'd used down the street.

Shoving her mail into one pocket of her jacket, she pulled her cell phone from the other. She and Sloane had exchanged contact information, so Vickie had her number. She'd expected to hear from Ed's daughter by now. What she'd told Sloane should've launched a police investigation, but there'd been no word.

At the risk of seeming *overly* interested, she looked Sloane up in her contacts and sent the call as she went back into the house. It was late to be bothering people, but Vickie had waited twenty-three years for the right moment to give Ed what was coming to him, and she was running out of patience.

Besides, there was one other thing she could tell Sloane…

"Hello?"

The voice on the other end of the line was filled with sleep. Vickie would've hung up, except she knew the caller ID had already identified her. "Sloane? It's Vickie."

"Yeah. I…uh… I saw your name."

"Sorry, have I bothered you too late?"

"No, I dozed off a little early tonight, that's all. Can you give me a second?"

After putting her mail on the table, Vickie locked the front door and made the rounds to be sure the other doors were locked, too. She'd just returned to the kitchen when Sloane came back on the line.

"What's up?" Sloane asked, her voice more strident.

"Nothing much, which is why I feel bad that I woke you. I was just wondering how things are going."

"You mean with my father..."

"Yeah. Have you heard from him?"

"Of course. Nothing goes on in Millcreek that escapes his notice, especially when it threatens him."

Fortunately, that wasn't *entirely* true. Vickie knew he didn't see her as having any power, that he'd be surprised at what she was doing—and how far she was willing to go in order to make him accountable, at last. "Have you learned anything more about what happened to your mother?"

"Not a lot. My father is doing all he can to encourage me to give up and leave. But I won't."

Vickie had hoped to let Sloane lead the charge. She hated for Ed to realize she wasn't as broken and cowed as he believed, didn't want him to turn his sights on her. That was why she'd asked Sloane not to use her name unless absolutely necessary. But maybe she should step forward. She had to support Sloane. This was the chance she'd been waiting for, and it could be her only chance. "If it'll help to tell the police what I said about him taking the boat out that night—"

"I've already told Micah Evans. I'm not sure if you've met him—"

"That was the boy you used to date in high school."

"Yes. He's a police officer these days, and he's been helping me. But only unofficially. The rest of the force—they won't get involved."

"How can they *not* get involved?"

"They keep saying there's no evidence, that this is a witch hunt designed to malign the mayor for political reasons. Bottom line, they're too afraid it'll cost them their jobs to oppose him. If they try and fail, they're screwed, so they won't get involved. But I think he might've dumped my mother's body at Lake Granbury. I'm taking my scuba gear up there to the cabin my father owns tomorrow to search."

"You're going *into* the lake?"

"If he was towing the boat that night, I believe he'd go to the lake before the river."

"Even though the river is so much closer?"

"He wouldn't want her body to be found floating in a river that's almost in his own backyard. The lake makes more sense."

Vickie had been to the cabin, too. She remembered every detail of that place as if it was yesterday. It had been one of her few weekends away from Millcreek during her marriage. Dean had been traveling on business to meet one big client or another—he worked in corporate law and represented some of the big Fortune 500 companies—and Ed had hired an in-home hospice worker to care for Sarah while they were gone. That he would do such a thing for another man's wife and daughter had been bold, daring. If her husband had called the house, he could so easily have realized something was up. But he rarely called when he was away. By then he'd gotten tired of hearing about how lonely she was.

So she'd gone.

At first, that weekend had been magical, but after the first two days, Ed had lost interest in her and wound up bringing her back early. She'd never been more confused or hurt, kept wondering what she'd done to cause him to back away. But he had no reasons he could express. In the end, she'd decided she was simply too nice, too easy and too desperate. He was a man who liked a challenge, and she'd been in no position to give him one.

"I hope you find something," she told Sloane, closing her eyes as she recalled the smell of the grass and low-lying shrubs that surrounded the cabin and the feel of the expensive linens on the bed where she'd made love with Ed.

"So do I," Sloane said.

Vickie almost let her hang up. She had to be careful, let this develop naturally or Sloane wouldn't trust her. But at the last second, she spoke up. "There's something else you should know, something I haven't wanted to tell you because, well, it's not the type of thing you're going to want to hear."

"What's that?"

Vickie could sense the tension in those words. "Your mother was pregnant."

There was a brief silence before Sloane said, "How do you know?"

"She told me. She was so worried, so afraid for when your father found out."

"Because he didn't want any more children?"

"Because it wasn't his."

CHAPTER TWENTY-FIVE

Micah could hear the low murmur of Sloane's voice in the other room. He'd felt her get out of bed so she could talk without waking him, but as tired as he was after an exhausting day—and then making love twice in the space of an hour—he hadn't been able to drift off again. Not only was he wondering who would call her so late, now that he was completely sated, he was worried about his job and how he'd pay his child support if that job went away. He figured he could work for his parents, at least in the short-term. They'd try to help. But he didn't want to be a burden on them. And he'd left the farm because he'd always wanted to be a cop.

He reached over to get his phone so he could see if Paige had returned any of his calls or text messages. He was hoping to reach her, to talk her into withdrawing her complaint. What she'd said was such a terrible lie. He'd never dreamed she'd go that far, had always believed she was a fairly decent person despite the way she'd nearly suffocated him with her love.

"Shit," he muttered when he saw that she still hadn't responded. That concerned him more than anything else. She'd never behaved quite like this. If she persisted in telling people he'd held a gun to her head, she'd not only cost him his job, she'd cost him his reputation and the ability to work for law enforcement in the future. And worse than anything, she could possibly use that to make it impossible for him to see his son again. Maybe that was what this was all about.

With a sigh, he returned his phone to the nightstand and fell back on the pillows, rubbing his eyes with his thumb and index finger. Making love with Sloane had been passionate and intense. He felt completely consumed when he was with her, which was the most satisfying experience he could imagine. But he wasn't sure how he was going to deliver on some of the reassurances he'd given her. He'd told her everything would be okay, that they just needed to stick together and work as a team, which sounded good in theory, especially because he didn't want to lose her again, but he wasn't sure how, exactly, they were going to prevail—especially when they had so many things to consider. He'd promised himself when he left Paige that he wouldn't bring another woman into Trevor's life right away, that he'd give the poor kid some time to adjust.

But this wasn't just any woman. This was *the* woman, the one he should've been with all along.

That made a difference, didn't it?

He hoped so. He hated the thought that it might be too selfish of him to even ask.

The hum of Sloane's voice in the other room stopped.

He propped himself up on his elbows, waiting for her to come back to bed, but she didn't.

Something was wrong.

He got up, pulled on his boxer briefs and went to find her.

She was sitting on the couch in nothing but his T-shirt, which she must've scooped off the floor as she hurried out of the room.

"What is it?"

She startled. Apparently, she'd been so deep in thought she hadn't heard his footsteps. "I'm sorry. I was trying not to wake you."

"Don't worry about it." He sat beside her and took her hand. "Who was on the phone?"

"Vickie Winters."

"Your father's neighbor?"

She nodded.

"She said something to upset you?"

"I don't know if *upset* is the right word, but she definitely dropped a bombshell. She said my mother was pregnant when she went missing."

"Whoa!" He took a moment to think that over. "Did your father know?"

"I'm guessing he did. That might be what sparked the argument they had that night—why it got so bad."

"Was she supposed to be on the pill or something?"

"Vickie claims my mother told her he had a vasectomy after I was born."

Micah felt his eyes widen. "Yikes!"

"Exactly."

"So whose baby was it? Brian Judd told you they never had sex, that the relationship didn't progress that far."

"He had to be lying. She couldn't have been seeing anyone else. She was always with us kids."

"Maybe he loved your mother enough to try to preserve her reputation. If she is no longer with us why would anyone have to know about the baby? I could see myself trying to protect you in that way."

She rested her head on his shoulder. "That's what you think he was doing?"

"It's a possibility."

"I guess. But it was a shock to hear something like that, makes me feel even worse for my mother and the situation she was in. She was so miserable."

"I didn't know Vickie Winters and your mother were friends."

"They must've been, to a degree. I'm getting the impression my mother didn't have a lot of people she could count on back then, so it's conceivable she'd tell Vickie. Vickie said my mom was terrified for when my father would find out."

"I can imagine." He smoothed her hair back—a strand was tickling his face—but she sat up almost immediately, took her phone, which she'd dropped in her lap, and began scrolling through her contacts.

"What are you doing?" he asked.

"I'm calling my brother," she replied.

Claiming she had the opportunity to go to a trade show in Las Vegas, Paige had taken Trevor to her parents' house as soon as Ed left her store and asked them to watch him for the next few days. She'd also lined up Megan Vance, her only employee, to take over at Little Bae Bae.

It hadn't been easy to talk Megan into working the

extra days—that was more than they'd agreed when Megan was hired, and Megan had had to rearrange her schedule in order to be available—but Paige had pleaded with her. She'd *had* to leave, *had* to get out of town. She couldn't stand the idea of seeing or speaking to Micah or Sloane—especially Micah—after what she'd done. And yet, if she retracted her accusation, she'd face something much worse. So there was nothing she could do to stop what was about to happen.

"It's his own fault," she kept muttering to herself. "None of this would've happened if he hadn't left me. I didn't deserve to lose my husband. I was a loving, devoted wife and mother." But all the excuses she'd dredged up since leaving Millcreek gave her little comfort. A lie was a lie. She'd ruined Micah's career to save herself from the humiliation she'd have to face otherwise.

She'd been driving for four hours when she saw the lights of Houston ahead, but she wasn't ready to stop. She had no idea where she was going or where she'd end up. Maybe she'd turn around and go to Austin or back past Millcreek to Dallas. As long as she didn't have to see anyone she knew until the worst of it was over, she didn't care where she stayed.

She glanced over at her purse, which was sitting in the passenger seat. She'd turned off her phone and hadn't powered it up since she'd loaded her suitcase into the trunk. She knew she had to be receiving a barrage of calls and texts. Micah freaking out. Sloane, too. Even her parents would be shocked when they heard the news. Shocked and saddened. They'd always liked Micah, which was why she hadn't mentioned the document she'd signed when she dropped Trevor off. She'd simply hugged her son, told him she loved him and would be home soon and jumped in her car to get the hell out of town.

As much as she hated herself for running away, every time her conscience started to get the best of her and she began to slow down with the intention of turning around, she'd picture the graphic photographs Ed had in his possession. She'd rather *die* than have the whole town see him using a dildo on her. So then she'd give the car some more gas and put even more miles between her and Millcreek.

She didn't even power up her phone when, distraught and exhausted, she finally rented a room in San Antonio and dropped, sobbing, onto the bed.

Randy didn't answer on the first try. Sloane was tempted to get dressed and go over there. She would have if Micah hadn't stopped her. Instead, she kept calling—again and again and again—and, finally, he answered.

"What the hell, Sloane?" he snarled in lieu of hello.

Sloane steeled herself for a difficult conversation. "Did you know that Mom was pregnant when she disappeared?"

Silence.

"Randy?"

"It doesn't matter."

Too agitated to remain sitting, Sloane sprang to her feet and began to pace. "How can you say that?"

"I don't see how it changes anything! It doesn't tell us what happened to her."

"The baby wasn't Dad's, which tells us she was in

a precarious situation. How do you think Dad would react to learning *that* news?"

More silence. Sloane glanced at Micah, who was still on the couch, watching her closely. He was on edge, thought Randy might get ugly with her.

"He'd be angry, right?" she said. "Maybe even *enraged*?"

"You're heading down the wrong road." Now her brother sounded more weary than he did angry.

"I don't think so. I still don't know a lot about the situation back then, but I've learned a few things. Mom was unhappy in her marriage. She was unfulfilled. She was lonely. And she had a serial cheater for a husband. She was ripe for falling in love with someone else, and that's exactly what she did. I've even talked to the man she was involved with—my kindergarten teacher, Mr. Judd! You've heard that name before, haven't you?"

"You know I have," he said.

"He's what they were fighting about the night she went missing."

"So? You've told me that before!"

"It's relevant because the pregnancy was probably why it got so explosive between them."

"You're driving me nuts," he said. "Why can't you leave this alone?"

She pivoted at the boxes that were stacked around the perimeter of the room. "Because I'm finally getting somewhere."

"You believe Dad killed Mom because she was pregnant with another man's baby."

"Yes!"

"How do you know Brian Judd isn't the one who killed her, Sloane? Maybe Judd was afraid she'd tell Dad and didn't want him to find out. Maybe he was afraid his wife would leave him. Maybe both!"

"No. Brian Judd loved Mom."

"Enough to divorce his wife? Because the way I understand it, they're still together."

Sloane had no good comeback. "He's admitted to me that he cared about Mom," she insisted. But he'd also lied and claimed they'd never slept together—not that she was going to tell Randy that.

"Listen to me. One night when we were both a little drunk, Dad told me he pushed Mom into the wall the night she went missing and made a big hole in the sheetrock. He even showed me where."

"See? I heard that happen, saw the hole in the wall. I was telling the truth, and my memory is sound!"

"Just listen to me. He said he was as shocked as she was by what he'd done, so he let her go, at which point she ran out of the house, crying. Feeling bad, he followed her, hoping to bring her back—until he saw her go into the neighbor's house."

Listening intently, Sloane stared at her bare feet as she moved. "Most likely to call the cops," she said as she pictured her mother hurrying next door. "So why didn't they come?"

"If she called them, they would have. The fact that they *didn't* means she called someone else. Dad said a car came a few minutes later. He believes it was Brian Judd."

"Did Dad ever ask the neighbor to confirm?"

"No, because he'd recently had an affair with her. He'd broken it off by then, but she was hurt and angry. He didn't want to knock on her door and make a bad situation even worse."

Sloane felt nauseous. How many women had her dad slept with? "He'd recently had an affair with *the neighbor*? My God! He was already sleeping with Katrina from the dealership."

"Which is why Mom and Dad were so unhappy."

"And this is the man you remain so loyal to?"

"I've never said he wasn't a cheater, Sloane. I've only said he wasn't a murderer."

She shook her head. "Poor Mom. Which neighbor was this? The Bancrofts or the Dooleys?"

"Neither. It was Vickie Something. She lived a few houses down, remember? Took care of a mentally impaired daughter."

Sloane nearly dropped her phone. "Vickie *Winters*?"

"Yes."

"You're sure?"

"That's the name Dad told me."

So why hadn't Vickie told *her* about Clara coming to the house that night?

"Sloane?" he said when she didn't respond.

"I'll have to call you later," she said and hung up.

"What is it?" Micah asked when she sank onto the couch next to him, her mind reeling as she tried to remember every detail of her two conversations with Vickie Winters. Vickie had seemed so honest, so nice. Who wouldn't trust a woman who'd done all she could for a disabled child?

"I don't know what to think," she replied.

"About what?"

"Vickie Winters is up to something."

"Like..."

"That's what I'm trying to figure out. Revenge?"

"For..."

"According to Randy, she and my father had an affair shortly before my mother went missing. And my mother ran to her house that night, likely to use the phone."

"Wait…she didn't tell you either of those things?"

"No."

Sloane couldn't sleep after her talk with Randy. She listened to Micah's steady breathing in the bed beside her while wondering if she'd misjudged her father after all. Brian Judd could've been driving the car her father claimed to have seen that night. Brian could also have murdered Clara so that his wife wouldn't learn of the pregnancy—or to get her and the baby out of his life in order to save his marriage. He'd lied about having slept with Clara, hadn't said a word about the baby, which proved he was capable of deception.

What else was he hiding?

Or maybe it was Vickie Winters who'd murdered Clara. She could've done it in a jealous rage. Or she could've done it to punish Ed for rejecting her, hoping he'd get the blame and go to prison for the rest of his life.

But if that were the case, why hadn't Ed ever pointed a finger at either of them? And how did that explain the murders of her grandparents and uncle possibly being tied to her father? Was that photograph from the bar meaningless? A fluke?

"Are you okay?" Micah mumbled, still half asleep as he pulled her against him.

He must've been able to tell that she was tense. "I can't sleep," she said. "Brian Judd lied to me—"

"He might've had good reason—"

"And he might not have. Vickie hasn't been honest,

either. She's told me a few things but left out other important facts. If she was trying to help, why wouldn't she be completely up front?"

"Because you might use what she told you to build a case for your father's innocence instead of his guilt?"

"That's just it. We have no way of knowing. Katrina could've had something to do with my mother's disappearance, too. But that conversation I read between her and my father could've been referring to a lot of things."

"Like…"

"Their affair, for one. His womanizing. What he's said about his wife. It doesn't *have* to mean they murdered her."

"Or it could mean they did it together. The thought of replacing Clara, of being the next Mrs. McBride might've been irresistible, and Katrina's youth might've exaggerated the allure, made it more difficult to realize the permanence of death."

She shifted in the bed. "She didn't seem to be suffering from too much regret."

"She's a shallow person. Killers are often shallow people. They want what they want, and they act to get it, regardless of the consequences to others."

"We *have* to find my mother's body, *have* to prove there's been a murder and work from there." She propped her head up with one arm. "We need forensic proof if we're going to get anywhere. Otherwise, I'll be left wondering, and doubting my own father, for the rest of my life."

He slid his hand up to her waist. "We'll give it our best shot. Tomorrow. Try to get some sleep so that you're sharp while you're looking."

She fell back and managed to drift off after that but

was awakened before seven, when Micah's cell phone began to rattle on the nightstand.

Sloane, her eyes feeling puffy from lack of sleep, held still while she listened to Micah's side of the conversation.

"What happened?… But why is Trevor with you in the first place?… She never told me about it, and she hasn't been answering her phone… You can't reach her, either? I can't understand why she won't pick up for you… Right. Yeah, I guess she could've lost her charger… Of course. I'll be right there."

He rolled out of bed and started yanking on his clothes. "I'm sorry," he said when she rose up on her elbows. "We'll have to put off going to the cabin until later, maybe even tomorrow."

"Why? What's going on?"

"That was Paige's parents. She left Trevor with them yesterday at dinnertime. Said she had an opportunity come up at the last minute to attend a trade show in Vegas, and she couldn't miss it. She told them she needed them to step in because I couldn't take him."

"Why would she say that?"

"I have no idea why she's saying and doing *anything* right now, and, apparently, neither do they. They must not have heard about the complaint Paige filed against me, because they didn't mention it, and they're treating me the same as always."

"So…where are you going?"

"Trevor was trying to slice an apple for his lunch and cut his finger. Tracy thinks he needs stitches. They can't get the bleeding to stop, and neither one of them can drive him to the med center. Burt has already left for a meeting with some investors who are interested in his brewery, and she has a school board meeting at eight."

She climbed out of bed. "Do you want me to go with you?"

"I do, but considering what's happening right now, it's better if you don't."

She could understand. She felt terrible for all the chaos and upset her involvement in his life was causing. "Then I'm going to head up to the cabin," she said, reaching for her panties.

He paused before pulling his T-shirt over his head. "Don't go without me. I want to be there."

"To do what? Watch me dive under the water?"

"Yes. Exactly. Otherwise, you'll have to dive from an unmanned boat."

"I wouldn't do that under normal circumstances, especially in the ocean. But I'll be in the lake, where I wouldn't have to swim for long even if I *did* happen to lose the anchor line, which is something I'm cautious never to do. I'll only go out far enough that I can dive where it's a bit deeper and come back toward the cabin, fairly close to shore."

"How will you notify those boats that might come by that you're underwater so you don't get hit? Is there a flag or something like what you hold up for a skier?"

"There won't be many other boaters out this time of year. The water's too cold. But, yes, I have a diver-down flag."

"I don't like the idea of you up there all alone."

"I do. It's *better* if you stay away. If you were to get caught breaking into the cabin, you'd be in even worse trouble than you are now."

"Paige has already ruined my career."

"But we're not going to let this end where it is. We're going to fix it."

"So you're really going up there without me."

"I know what I'm doing, Micah. I've done a lot of diving the past ten years." She loved the peace of swimming under the water. Nothing from the world above, even light, could penetrate if she went deep enough. She'd never dived in a freshwater lake, but she figured it had to be far less dangerous than the ocean. At least she wasn't going to run into a Moray eel, a shark or a jellyfish. "I'll be fine."

He seemed tempted to argue, but with Trevor hurt, he didn't have time. She watched him pull on his shoes without bothering to tie the laces, heard his keys rattle as he grabbed them from his dresser. "Call me as soon as you can. I'll be worried."

"I will. I hope Trevor's okay."

"Tracy didn't seem overly concerned, so that's good. He just needs a few stitches, she said. I'm more worried about what'll happen when he hears that his mother is claiming I put a gun to her head. The divorce has been hard enough on him. He doesn't need this."

"What do you think Paige is up to? She wouldn't suddenly rush off to a trade show like that, would she?"

"No. Leaving was all about signing that complaint. But even her parents can't get hold of her, so we're not the only ones."

He brushed his teeth, paused to kiss her goodbye and jogged for the door. "Please be careful," he called back.

As soon as he left, Sloane tried to reach Paige herself. When her call transferred to voice mail, she disconnected and sent a text message.

What you're doing to Micah isn't right. You need to tell the truth. Think about the damage you're causing his career, how long this will stay with him. And consider what you're doing to your son when you lie about his father.

She shoved her tangled hair out of her face while waiting to see if she'd get a response. Nothing came, so she typed a second text.

I'm sorry that you're angry with us. But Micah and I love each other. We can't change that—not even for you.

She stared at those words for several seconds before sending them. Was she ready to state it that strongly? Would she stay in Millcreek just to be with Micah even if she couldn't solve her mother's disappearance? Could she face bumping into her dad and brother around town? Survive them doing all they could to make her life miserable? Could she honestly see that as her future?

How could she do anything else? What she'd just written was the truth—it was time she made a stand where Micah was concerned.

Assuming she'd finally get some sort of response from Paige, no doubt a negative one, she held her breath and pushed Send.

But, again, she received nothing in reply.

"What the heck?" Sloane sat there, willing Paige to say *something*. Sloane wanted to help Micah, make that complaint go away.

After ten minutes, however, she began to feel the pressure of everything else she was facing. Giving up for the moment, she shoved her phone in her purse and went into the bathroom to pull her hair into a ponytail and brush her teeth.

When she was finished, she put her toothbrush in the holder Micah used. She'd already started to turn away when the sight of their toothbrushes standing side by side made her pause. Her toothbrush belonged in that holder next to his, just like she belonged with him.

She should never have tried to give him up. They had the right to be together, to be happy, she decided, and felt Clyde would agree. Clyde had tried to tell her that before. She just hadn't been ready to listen.

She smiled as she remembered her late friend. "I won't let anyone make me leave Micah again," she whispered to Clyde as if he were there to hear. Then she hurried out of the bathroom.

It was time to head to the lake.

CHAPTER TWENTY-SIX

The key wasn't under the rock where it used to be kept when she was growing up. Sloane was going to have to figure out how to break in, but at least, after she got off the highway, she hadn't passed anyone on the road who seemed to pay any attention to her. Although there were other lake houses in the area, her father owned a large lot, and he didn't have any close neighbors. He liked his privacy, so he'd gone one step further and chosen a home hidden by trees even though they obstructed the view. In order to see the water, she had to walk down a narrow path to the slip where he docked his boat under a roof to protect it from the sun.

The cabin itself was made of brick and natural, treated wood with a steep green metal roof and lots of windows. Sloane had always liked it here. She'd spent many weekends over the summer at Granbury, had been kissed for the first time, at fourteen, by the grandson of the woman who'd once owned the cabin closest to them. But then she'd met Micah and no other boy had mattered after that.

She walked around the cabin, looking for the best way to get in. She would park her car in the garage to keep it hidden in case someone did happen to come by, carry her scuba gear down to the boat and take it out so she could dive in deeper water. She could always paddle back toward the shore. Given the currents of the lake, she'd have a better chance of finding something in the submerged vegetation and trotlines. Items like clothes—and bones—could easily get caught up there, so she planned to focus her search wherever she saw that sort of natural net.

Unfortunately, she couldn't find an easy way inside the cabin. All the doors and windows were secure. Either she'd have to break the door leading into the garage, which was only slightly more flimsy than the heavy wooden doors that led into the house itself and could possibly lead to another locked door going into the house, or she'd have to break a window.

She decided to go with the window.

Bracing for the noise, she averted her face in case the glass went flying, and struck the main pane of the window in the downstairs bedroom. That room was the most isolated in the house, as far as layout, and faced away from the lake, so she was hoping no one would hear or see her.

Although she was prepared for the crash, the sound of shattering glass seemed to echo across the lake. Heart thumping, she used a blanket she'd taken from Micah's house to knock out the remaining shards so she wouldn't cut herself getting in and managed to climb through in spite of being nervous and scared.

Once she was inside, she didn't feel a sense of accomplishment or safety; she felt shaky and emotional. The nostalgia that swamped her was overwhelming. The woodsy scent brought her back to those summers she'd spent in this place, back to a time before she and her father were estranged and she was still hoping, like Randy, to corral her doubts and shove them into the back of her brain, where she wouldn't have to think about them.

Drawing a deep breath to galvanize herself, she left the back bedroom, which had always been Randy's, and walked through the rest of the cabin to see if anything had changed. Over the years, her father had taken down most of the pictures her mother had put up, including all the family photographs that contained Clara. Sloane remembered them disappearing. She'd been offended he'd put them out of sight but she'd been unable to challenge him, since she was so young and this was his house.

To her relief, she found that they were still stacked against the wall in the walk-in, attic-like closet on the second story. At least he hadn't thrown them away.

A lump formed in her throat as she looked at each one. Her favorite was a picture of her mother posing with both her and Randy. Randy was nearly six; she just a baby.

She touched her mother's face through the glass, thinking how pretty and kind she'd been, how subdued but thoughtful. Sloane remembered one time, after her father had spanked her and sent her to her room, Clara had come up to make sure she was okay and simply sat and held her until she felt better. That was her favorite memory of her mother. That moment of feeling loved in spite of everything. But it worried her that so many of her other memories of Clara were beginning to fade. It'd been so long, and she'd been so young. Sadly, the memory that remained the clearest was the night her mother had gone missing. Sloane doubted that would *ever* fade. She'd relived it too many times.

Feeling the pressure of time—she needed to be sure she got out on the lake while the sun was high in the sky and the weather good—she put that picture back, only to pick it up again. Why couldn't she take it with her? Her father didn't care about it. He'd probably never even notice it was gone.

She put it in her car when she got her scuba gear. Then, just before she took the keys to the boat from the drawer where her father had always kept them and went down to the dock, she took out her phone to see if Micah had texted her. She was worried about Trevor and the situation with Paige.

Sure enough, she'd heard from him: You there yet? You okay?

I'm fine. I managed to get inside the cabin but not without some damage to one window. I'm about to head down to the water. How's Trevor?

Happy to be missing school in spite of his finger. The doctor should be seeing him soon. We've been in the waiting room this whole time.

But his finger is going to be okay?

I think so. It's barely deep enough for stitches.

Any word from Paige?

None.

She hadn't received anything either. I'm going to the boat now. Wish me luck.

You know I do, he wrote back, and she slid her phone into her purse and left it on the counter. She didn't want it in the boat with her; didn't want it anywhere near the water, since she hadn't been able to find her waterproof case, what with all of her things packed in storage.

The water was calm and the weather cool, so she considered herself lucky. Wind and/or a lot of boating activity could stir up the sediment on the bottom, making visibility even worse than recorded by the diver who'd detailed his experience online.

As she gazed back toward the cabin, past the bulrush and water stargrass, she suddenly wished she'd waited for Micah to come with her. Being with someone would be safer; there was no arguing that. But the lake wasn't deep enough for her to go down very far. At one atmosphere, or about thirty-three feet, her bloodstream could still get saturated with nitrogen—which, in this situation, was more a function of how long she'd be down than depth—but the shallower the dive, the longer the air in her tanks would last. She figured she should have a good solid stretch of time to search, maybe as much as three and a half hours.

After she dropped anchor, she finished getting suited up, raised her diver-down flag and took a moment to gauge the distance she was from shore, in case something *did* go wrong and she had to swim back. She knew where she was. This was the lake she'd played in so often as a kid. And, like usual, she'd be careful to keep her eye on the anchor line so she didn't get disoriented.

After settling her mask on her face and making sure she had a good seal, she sat on the side of the boat, put the regulator in her mouth and fell back, letting the weight of her tank pull her over the edge and into the water.

Micah scrubbed a hand over his face as he waited for the doctor to finish bandaging Trevor's finger so they could go. The kid had four stitches but was in fine spirits. The young were so resilient.

"Can we go to lunch?" Trevor asked after they'd been released and Micah guided him out of the med center.

"Sure." He pressed the button on his key fob that would unlock the truck. "What would you like to eat?"

They climbed in before Trevor answered. "How about a burger?" he said as he put on his seat belt.

Micah chuckled. "Why'd I even ask?"

As soon as Micah found a place Trevor liked, he pulled in, but he was a bit too uneasy to eat a full meal. Not only was Sloane at the cabin, scuba diving in the lake alone, no one had heard from Paige. He kept asking himself what could be going on with his ex-wife. How could a mother leave town and then turn off her phone when she had a young son?

He checked for messages again, as he'd been doing all morning, while they went into the burger joint. He wanted to hear that Sloane was okay and receive some word from Paige.

But there was nothing.

"Dad? What do you want?"

He glanced up to see the person behind the cash

register waiting for his order. "What'd you get?" he asked Trevor.

"A burger, fries and a vanilla shake."

"A shake?"

"You won't let me have soda."

"Because soda has too much sugar—and that isn't much different from a shake, right?"

Trevor lifted his bandaged hand. "But I have a hurt finger, and you feel sorry for me, *right*?"

Micah rolled his eyes. One shake wasn't going to kill the kid. And Paige wasn't around to find out, so it couldn't cause an argument. "Fine," he said and ordered a bacon burger for himself.

He'd finished paying and they were finding a table where they could sit and wait for their food, when he received a call from his mother. He assumed she'd heard about his suspension, or she'd heard about Trevor and his finger. Either way, he needed to reassure her, so he answered right away.

"I have Hadley McBride's cell phone number for you," she announced.

"You what?" It took him a moment to switch gears. She didn't know about his suspension or Trevor, or she would've started the conversation differently.

"The other night you asked me if I knew anyone who could reach Hadley. You said you needed to talk to her."

"I do, but you told me you didn't have any mutual contacts."

"I asked around. Turns out your aunt June has the same hairdresser, Sally Redfern, and Sally had Hadley's number right there in her appointment book when June went in to have her hair done this morning."

"Sally was willing to give out that information?"

"Not exactly."

"What's that supposed to mean?"

"It means June didn't ask. While she was waiting for her color to process, and Sally was off shampooing someone else, she saw the book sitting there, open for all to see, and turned through it until she found Hadley's last appointment. Her number was right by her name."

"Aunt June didn't get caught?"

"She did but she said she was just looking back to see how many weeks it'd been since her last color."

"That's pretty resourceful." He created a contact and put the number in his phone as his mother rattled off the digits. Then he thanked her, kept word of his suspension to himself—he was still hoping to work that out before the news broke—and told her about Trevor cutting himself, at which point she had to talk to her grandson.

He allowed them a couple of minutes to chat, but once the food was ready, he took the phone back, sent Trevor to the counter to get the burgers, told his mother he had to go and called Hadley.

The lake was exactly as the diver who'd posted on the internet described. Dull, with only the occasional largemouth or striped bass swimming around for company. Less than five feet visibility. Muddy at the bottom. Lots of submerged vegetation, rocks, fishing lines and junk.

Sloane listened to the sound of her own breathing as she swam in slow-moving laps stabbing a pole into the lake bed to see if there was something buried underneath in the section she'd designated as the area her father would most likely have dumped her mother. Given the conditions he had to have been facing that night—the need to act quickly, the darkness and the location of the cabin with the privacy it afforded him, she felt she'd chosen well. If she were him, this was where *she'd* come.

She found an old tire, lots of beer bottles and cans, several lost shoes and eyeglasses, swimsuit tops and bottoms, even a shiny necklace, which she kept in case it had belonged to her mother. But she knew in her heart it didn't. It was too cheap, more like a teenager's necklace than something the wife of a wealthy man like her father might own.

Careful to avoid the fishing hooks attached to the trotlines that'd become entangled with the submerged trees, Sloane stayed down as long as she could, searching for anything that might be suspect—a black plastic bag, bones, the nightgown her mother had been wearing that night, which she remembered clearly despite her young age, even a hank of her mother's thick, dark hair—but after exhausting all her oxygen, she hadn't found anything to lead her to believe this was where her father had dumped her mother's body.

Just before she rose to the surface—slowly to give the nitrogen in her blood time to dissipate through her lungs—she turned in a full circle to gaze in every direction. Searching the lake had seemed like such a great idea, such a finite and doable task, but after spending one whole afternoon underwater, she realized just how big the lake was and how difficult it would be to find something that'd been dropped in there only yesterday, let alone over two decades ago.

Exhausted after swimming for so long and filled with a sense of futility and disappointment, she grabbed hold of the anchor line and let it guide her to the top. She could spend every day for the rest of her life out here and never find anything. That was the truth of it. Her father had won. She didn't have a chance of holding him accountable for what he'd done, and she never had.

After spitting out her regulator and removing her mask, she used the rope ladder she'd put out before diving to get back on the boat. The wind had kicked up enough to give her a chill, and it looked like rain on the horizon. She frowned at the sky before removing her flippers, raising the anchor and motoring to the cabin.

What a difference three hours had made in the weather, but now that she was finished diving, she wasn't too worried about it. She'd be inside for the next couple of hours. She planned to look around a bit more before she left. After all, she'd broken a window. She should make the most of it even though her hopes of finding any evidence had fallen to almost zero. She'd been through the cabin once already, understood how quickly current years could erase all traces of previous years.

She peeled off her wetsuit before getting out of the boat and carried it, along with her equipment, up to the cabin. As sad as she was that she wouldn't be able to bring her mother the justice she deserved, she was relieved to be out of the water. The lake was getting choppy as the wind increased.

She set her gear near the door, so she could put it in her trunk when she left, and stood at the living room window to watch the storm gather. She could remember her mother looking out this same window, just as she was doing now.

"Where are you?" she whispered. "What more can I do?" She'd believed she could handle the investigation alone, that sheer determination would change everything. But the past week had taught her that an entire army of detectives probably couldn't figure out what happened that night.

Lightning zigzagged through the sky. She guessed thunder wasn't far off. With a sigh, she walked over and turned on the heater to combat the cold air whistling through that broken window. She couldn't seem to get warm. She knew some of it had to be the encroaching despair she was feeling, but she couldn't shake it.

Before searching the cabin more thoroughly, she decided to let Micah know she was okay, but when she went to get her purse, it wasn't there.

Micah plugged his left ear while pressing his phone to his right. It wasn't easy to hear above the dust storm that'd come up while they were eating, but he didn't want to go back into the restaurant, didn't want anyone to overhear him, and he didn't get in the truck with Trevor for the same reason.

"Hadley, listen to me," he said. "I understand you're in a difficult position, but I need you to tell me what you were referring to in that note you left Sloane." He'd already said as much, had been going around and around with her since she'd picked up, but he was hoping his persistence would pay off. She seemed to be torn, so he kept working on her. "You know what she's been through, how sad it is that she has no idea where her mother went. If Ed had something to do with it, we need to hold him accountable."

"I want to help, Micah, I really do," she said. "But I can't get involved."

"Why not?"

"You know why. Ed doesn't like anyone to get in

his business. And I'm his daughter-in-law. I have to get along with him."

"We'll figure out a way, if we can, to claim the information came from someone else. But please help. You could hold the piece of the puzzle that makes all the rest come together. Have some compassion for Sloane—and for Clara. She was a good woman. She deserves for someone to stand up and tell the truth."

"But the truth isn't what you think! Ed didn't kill her!"

He ducked his head a little more since he was having trouble hearing. "Then who did?"

She sighed into the phone—at least he thought he heard that above the wind. "I can only tell you what Edith once told me, in confidence."

"Edith?"

"Ed's secretary at city hall. We were working together on his last campaign and..."

He could tell she was reluctant to continue. *"And?"*

"And somehow the subject of who he was dating came up. She mentioned that none of the women he'd been with over the years could hold a candle to the woman he'd married. I said it was sad that Clara was gone, that I hoped she'd come back one day so I could meet her and she could get to know her grandchild. Then Edith gave me this funny look, like I should know better. I asked her why she was looking at me like that, and she said, 'She's not coming back, Hadley.' So I asked her how she knew that, and she told me Clara was pregnant when she went missing."

"How'd Edith know she was pregnant?"

"She said Ed broke down in his office only days after Clara disappeared and said he thought she was dead, that she'd been pregnant with someone else's child and the father had been furious about it because he didn't want his wife to find out, take his children and leave him."

"So why didn't Ed go to the police?"

"This is the part I'm afraid to talk about," she admitted. "I don't want to cause problems for my father-in-law. He's not an easy person to like in some ways. He can be arrogant and egotistical and all that, but he's been good to Randy and I. We wouldn't have the dealership or most the other stuff we have without him."

"I need to know," Micah said. "I'll protect you as much as I can, but there are other people involved. They deserve some consideration, too."

"I agree. That's why I feel I should speak up. But..."

"Hadley, you've come this far..."

"Fine. I guess there was a time when the police were trying to pin the murder of Ed's parents and brother on him. The detective investigating their deaths tried to say he hired the man who shot them so he could inherit their money, which is crazy. Anyway, he was afraid to go to the police about Clara, thought it would bring all of that back and destroy his political career. Not only that but he and Clara *were* having marital problems. They *had* had an argument the night she went missing, and he *had* been seeing other women. Edith said he knew he'd look like the bad guy."

"So he just ignored the fact that his wife went missing?"

"He believed she was already dead and going to the police wasn't going to bring her back."

Micah squinted to keep the dust out of his eyes. "Did

he mention the father of the baby? The man he thought killed her?"

"No. Edith said he wouldn't tell her who it was, but her niece is a teacher at Millcreek Elementary School, and *she* said Clara was always helping out in Brian Judd's class."

There was the name Micah had expected. "Because he was Sloane's kindergarten teacher," he said, just to see if she'd offer more to substantiate what she was telling him.

"She was going beyond helping out, Micah. Edith's niece saw them kissing in his class one day when she stopped in after school to say goodbye."

Trevor banged on the window to see what was taking Micah so long, but Micah waved him off. "So Edith believes Brian Judd killed Clara McBride because she was pregnant and news of their affair was bound to come out?"

"That's not the only reason she thinks he did it. Edith said her niece also told her he didn't show up for school the day after Clara went missing. And when he did show up a day later, he had four scratches on his cheek. Looked like someone had gouged him with their nails."

"Did she ask where he got those scratches?"

"He said he was play-fighting with his kids."

"And Edith's niece didn't buy that?"

"No, because he was acting funny, too. But don't let Ed know I'm the one who told you all this. He doesn't want an investigation, especially now, with another election coming up."

"I won't tell him."

"I hope it doesn't come back on Edith, either. That's the thing. But… I don't know. I *have* felt as though I needed to say something. It sort of feels good to have it off my chest, to be honest. I've thought a lot about Sloane over the years, felt bad for her."

"I appreciate your help," Micah said.

"What did you say?"

The wind was growing stronger and louder. She couldn't hear him. "Thank you!" he shouted and climbed into his truck to call Brian Judd.

"What's going on?" Trevor asked. "What took you so long?"

"I'm working on something," he said. "I need another minute."

Trevor gave him a tortured look, as if he was so bored he couldn't wait any longer, but Micah didn't have time to encourage him before a woman answered at Brian's house.

Micah glanced over to see his son messing with the bandage on his finger and reached over to stop him. "Is Brian there?"

"I'm afraid not. Who's this?"

"An old friend of his from college." Micah wasn't sure it was necessary to lie, but he couldn't risk putting Judd's wife on the defensive by explaining who he really was. "Can you tell me when he might be back?"

"Oh, not for a while."

"What time does he normally get home? Is he still at the school?"

"No, he took a vacation day and went fishing up at Lake Granbury."

Micah couldn't believe his ears. "Did you say Lake *Granbury*?"

"Yeah. With the weather turning, I can't imagine

he's still on the water, but it'll take him an hour or so to drive back."

"Has he been planning this trip for a while?"

"It was sort of last minute. Can I have him call you?"

Micah told her he'd call back and disconnected. He had to get to Sloane right away. He tried calling her to warn her that Brian Judd was in the area. After what he'd heard from Hadley, he was worried Brian might not be happy they were digging up the past. If he'd killed Clara, as Edith believed, he'd no doubt risk a lot to keep that hidden.

But Sloane's phone didn't even ring, indicating she'd turned it off.

Why? Micah wondered. She knew he was worried about her.

The most probable answer to that question made his heart race.

Starting his truck right away, he drove over to Paige's parents' so he could drop off Trevor. He had to get to Ed's cabin as soon as possible.

There could only be one reason Brian Judd had gone to Lake Granbury, and it had nothing to do with fishing.

CHAPTER TWENTY-SEVEN

"What are you doing here?" Although Sloane had been cold only a moment before, she was burning up, sweating as though she'd just run a mile. She couldn't see what Brian Judd had done with her purse. He didn't seem to have it with him, and it wasn't in the room. But he held her phone in his hand and stood between her and the door as though he was purposely cutting off her escape.

"I needed to talk to you—right away."

She felt for the breakfast bar behind her, wanting to put it between them. "You could've called me."

"No, I couldn't. Then I wouldn't know how you were taking what I was saying, who else was around. I had to speak to you alone, to tell you that you don't understand what's going on."

"I understand you've been lying to me. You said you didn't have sex with my mother, that it didn't go that far, but she was pregnant with your child when she went missing."

"You're wrong! I *didn't* have sex with Clara. It wasn't *my* baby she was carrying—it was your father's. She was upset that she was going to have another baby *with him*."

She could see how desperately he wanted her to believe him, but something about his body language seemed to contradict his words. "My father had a vasectomy after I was born. Besides, my mother told Vickie Winters it was your child."

He threw up his hands while still hanging on to her phone. "Sometimes vasectomies don't take. Clara just wanted it to be my baby so I'd rescue her from the terrible situation she was in."

"A situation you only made worse."

"I tried to help her!" he cried. "But I had no idea that would include leaving my wife!"

"Give me my phone." Sloane reached out, but he shook his head.

"Not yet. We're not finished talking. I need you to listen to me."

He wanted her to do more than listen—he wanted her to believe whatever he said.

The solid granite top of the breakfast bar cut gently into Sloane's back once she'd reached it. "What else is so important for me to hear?"

"Vickie only told you it was my baby so you'd believe your father killed your mother in a jealous rage. She didn't stop to consider what that would do to *me* until she called me late last night, in tears. She wants your father to be punished for the way he treated her all those years ago, and the way he's treated so many people, including your mother. She believes he deserves to go to prison."

Sloane edged slowly around the island. "How did you know how to find this cabin, Brian? Have you been up here before?"

"No. Of course not. Vickie gave me directions when…when she told me you were coming up to search for your mother. She's been here before, with your father."

"If I called her right now and asked if she told you how to get here, what would *she* say?"

"She'd tell you what I just told you."

The rain was coming down harder, pummeling the roof, and Sloane could hear thunder booming in the distance. "Then give me my phone. Let's call her and ask."

He came forward so quickly Sloane scooted even farther around the breakfast bar to remain on the opposite side from him.

"Look, I'm going to level with you," he said. "I *did* sleep with your mother. I admit that. But I didn't kill her. She called me from Vickie's house the night she went missing, and I slipped out to pick her up while my wife slept. She had me bring her here—that's how I knew where to find it. She wanted to get away from your father. They'd just had a big fight, and she was crying. I felt *terrible* for what she was going through, but I couldn't divorce my wife, couldn't break up my family. Ed would've made our lives miserable, for one. And what about the kids I already had? I couldn't afford to support *two* families, not on a teacher's salary!"

Sloane swallowed against a dry throat. She'd been blaming her father for so long. "So you brought her here—and then what?"

"I couldn't stay long. I had to get back before my wife realized I was gone. So I told her we'd talk later. I thought she was safe, that she'd have some time to recover and work things out with your father. It wasn't as if that was their first fight. They fought all the time!"

"She was alive when you left."

"Yes!"

"And that's the last you saw of her."

"Yes," he said again, every bit as emphatically. "That's why I never accused Ed of harming her. I didn't know if she hitchhiked out of here and left, if someone broke in and killed her or if he came up here and killed her himself. But I knew better than to push the issue. If it *was* him, he'd only twist everything that happened that night to make *me* look like the guilty party, since I'd also been with her. And the police would believe him over me any day. I was just a lowly teacher, and he was the wealthiest man in town!"

Vickie had told Sloane her father had taken the boat out that night, which led Sloane to believe he might have come up here after Brian left. But she now understood that Vickie had her own agenda, so was she any more reliable than Brian?

"There isn't enough evidence to convict *anyone* of her death," Sloane said, trying to reassure and calm him so she could retrieve her phone and get safely out of Granbury.

"But if you tell anyone she was pregnant with my baby, word will get back to my wife. She knows a lot of people in Millcreek. We lived there for years. And she's still resentful over the affair. If it goes public, she'll be humiliated and so will I. Not only will it wreck my marriage, it'll get me kicked out of my church—and I can't allow that. I've worked too long and too hard to earn the respect of those around me to have my life fall to pieces because of a mistake I made twenty-three years ago."

Sloane didn't dare do anything to antagonize him. He was already on edge, looked as though he hadn't slept since she first contacted him. "I won't tell anyone. I'm not out to ruin your marriage or get you in trouble with your church."

Instead of relaxing, as she'd hoped, he narrowed his eyes. "You haven't told anyone?"

"No, I—I haven't." She hated that she'd stuttered, but her heart was pounding so hard she was afraid he could hear it. And he was coming toward her in such a purposeful way. With the storm raging outside and the neighbors so far off, he could get away with anything.

"Then give me your password so I can take a peek at your text messages and call history. If everything looks good, maybe I'll believe you."

And if it didn't look good? What would he do? When she'd stopped for gas this morning, she'd been texting with Randy—the same old argument—but the fact that their mother had been pregnant when she went missing had been a big part of their exchange. She might even have texted something to Micah over the past few days. She couldn't remember anything specific, but he was a cop. What would Brian Judd make of that?

Almost as soon as she had those thoughts, she realized Judd wouldn't let this all boil down to what was in her phone, anyway. Just because she hadn't texted someone so far didn't mean she wouldn't or that she hadn't told someone in person. Judd needed her password for other reasons, and she was afraid she knew what those reasons were. If he had access to her phone, he could attempt to throw off any investigation that followed by pretending to be her. He could text Micah, her father or anyone else saying she was leaving Millcreek—for good this time—and they'd assume it was her. Then no one would even look for her.

Brian Judd was far more dangerous than she'd ever dreamed. This whole thing—everything he'd said so far—had been an act. He'd already made up his mind about what had to be done.

She eyed the door, trying to gauge whether or not she could make it past him and out of the house before he caught her.

"Don't." He lowered his voice in warning. "*Please.* Don't make me do something I'll regret, because I *can't* let you wreck my life."

Letting her live would wreck his life. She knew the truth, could talk at any time. "Hurting me will only make things worse for you," she said. "Do you really want to spend the rest of your life in prison?"

"If my wife finds out, my life will be over regardless. So what difference does it make? At least this way, I have a chance of salvaging everything that matters to me."

"Because my father will get the blame..."

"*If* there's an investigation. No one bothered to look for your mother."

And this situation was frighteningly similar. Her father wanted her gone, would be relieved instead of concerned if she disappeared and would squash any investigation for fear it would focus on him and dredge up the suspicion surrounding him for the murders of his parents and brother—just like when Clara disappeared.

"You're making a mistake, Brian," she said, trying

to stall until she could figure out what to do. "*Another* one."

"I have no choice," he responded.

Where had he stashed her purse? The keys to her car were inside it. So even if she got out of the cabin, where would she go? "Is that how it was with my mother? You felt cornered? As if you had no choice?"

"*Yes,*" he admitted. "That's exactly it!"

"So what'd you do to her?" She motioned to the rest of the cabin. "Where'd you put her body?"

"Not in here. We didn't even come to the cabin that night. This is where she *wanted* me to take her. We'd been here before—twice. But this night was different. Everything was about to come out—the affair, the pregnancy. I had to do something. So I drove her out in the middle of nowhere and left her."

Sloane caught her breath. "Without the means to get back? *That's* how you killed her?"

He winced as if it wasn't a pleasant memory. "It's not something I'm proud of. I was desperate. I'm sorry I ever got involved with her. I only did it because I felt sorry for her."

"If you regret it, don't make what you've done even worse."

"I'm committed now. There's no going back. So unless you want me to drive you to the same place I took her, and leave you with no phone or purse or shoes—not even a jacket—you'll tell me the password for this damn phone."

"Oh my God! You let a pregnant woman—my *mother*—die a slow, horrible death!"

He glanced around, saw the kitchen knives on the

counter near him and grabbed one. "I've told you, I only did what I had to do!"

That was what he believed he was doing now. So what was she going to do? Sloane had no better choice than to run to the closest cabin and hope someone was home. If she could get help, she *might* be able to save her own life.

Slumping as though she was giving in, she said, "282328."

He had to put down the knife in order to enter those numbers. The minute he did, she swiped at it, managed to knock it to the floor and darted around the island. She *had* to make a break for it, couldn't wait any longer. The second that password didn't work he'd know she'd been lying to him.

Too bad she wasn't as quick as she'd hoped. She didn't get halfway across the living room before he grabbed hold of her hair and yanked her down.

The drive to the lake seemed interminable, especially with the weather making Micah go slower than he wanted. He wasn't even sure he'd be able to find the cabin after he arrived. Before leaving Millcreek, he'd called the police in Granbury and asked them to check on the McBride place. The sergeant he'd spoken to said he'd send someone, but the same sergeant had also said there'd been a big traffic accident due to the sudden change in weather and because of some flash flooding, the road might not yet be clear.

Micah hadn't heard anything since. He didn't know if anyone had been able to get through or if he'd be able to get through when he arrived. Even if he wasn't held up, he still didn't know the address to the cabin. The lake was located in Granbury, a town small enough he felt he could ask around and probably get directions, but the sergeant on the phone hadn't been willing to give him that information. The sergeant *couldn't*, in case Micah was the problem and not Brian Judd. Micah hoped a regular citizen wouldn't think to be that cautious. In his experience, they normally weren't.

While Micah pushed the speed limit as much as he could, given the terrible weather, he kept trying to reach Sloane. He was fairly certain she'd turned her phone back on, since it now rang four times before transferring to voice mail.

So why wasn't she answering?

Right in the midst of his panic and frustration, he received a call from his mother. She'd heard the news of his suspension.

"Paige is claiming you held a gun to her head?" she cried.

The news was spreading fast, just as he'd expected. By the time he returned, everyone he cared about would know.

He explained that it wasn't true and hung up knowing his family would stand behind him. Although he'd asked his mother not to call Chief Adler, he had the sneaking suspicion she was already on the phone to him. She was too outraged to resist. But she wouldn't get anywhere. Nothing would or could change until Paige retracted the lie, and he still couldn't reach her.

He was only five minutes outside Granbury—*at last*—and still hadn't heard from the police or Sloane when Paige's father called.

"You son of a bitch!" he yelled the second Micah picked up.

Apparently, the Pattersons had heard, too. "I didn't do it," Micah said simply.

"You better not have done it! I'll kill you with my bare hands if you did."

That was a ridiculous thing to say. Burt wouldn't be able to do anything to Micah, especially with his bare hands—not if Micah knew he was coming. But Micah understood the sentiment behind those words and, after wrestling with an upwelling of rage himself, he managed to keep his voice calm. "Take it easy."

"You want me to take it easy when you threatened my little girl—the mother of your child—*with a gun*?"

"I never threatened her, not with anything!"

"You're saying she's lying?"

"That's exactly what I'm saying!" His own tension, and the fear he felt for Sloane, were beginning to ratchet ever higher. This wasn't a conversation he wanted to have right now, but he was curious whether Paige had finally shown up or at least called someone, so he stayed on the line, hoping to find out.

"Why would she lie after you've been divorced for a year? No," he said. "It's just coming out now how bad your marriage was, what my daughter put up with. And to think she never even told me! That's what kills me. I would've been there for her. Hell, I still liked you, even after you broke her heart!"

"I never harmed Paige, Burt, never even threatened to harm her—with my gun or otherwise. Have you talked to her today?"

"I haven't. She's at a trade show—"

"She can talk on the phone at a trade show, Burt. She's done it before. She's just not picking up. Think about that. If what she's saying about me is true, why won't she defend her own words?"

"Do you know how much she still loves you?" Burt countered. "How hard it must be for her to come forward with this, given what it will do to you?"

Micah gripped the steering wheel so tightly he thought he might rip it off. "You're wrong! I have no idea what this is about. I can't reach Paige, either. But I hope to find out soon."

"Don't you dare call her. Don't you come within twenty feet of her! And that goes for Trevor, too. If we have our say, you'll never see him again!"

"Your daughter's lies had better not cost me my son!" Micah growled, but it was too late. Burt had hung up and wouldn't answer when Micah called back.

Thankfully, Brian Judd hadn't had time to retrieve the knife Sloane had knocked away before he came after her. He'd had to move instantly, grab her before she could get away. But it didn't matter. He was stronger than she'd imagined. After dragging her to the floor, he used the weight of his body to pin her down, and now he had his hands around her throat.

She felt helpless as he squeezed, cutting off her air. She had only a few seconds—a minute at most—before she passed out. Then Brian Judd could do whatever he wanted. He could keep choking her until she was dead or use something else to kill her—the knife, perhaps—before burying her in the yard or throwing her body in the lake.

She could hear her phone buzzing. He'd dropped it somewhere between the breakfast bar and the living room floor. It was probably Micah, trying to get hold of her to be sure she was safe.

The mere thought of Micah made her wish she'd waited until he could be here with her…

She needed to answer that phone, to tell him what'd happened to her mother and what was happening to her so that someone would know, so that Brian Judd wouldn't get away with another murder.

"I don't want to do this." Tears filled his eyes and began to roll down his cheeks, but he didn't back off. "*Why* did you force me into this?" he railed. "Why did you ever come back?"

Her mind raced as she stared up into his eyes, which were filled with a madness she'd never dreamed could exist inside a person who otherwise seemed so functional, so normal. She had to figure out how to save her own life, but there was nothing she could do. He was too strong, and he had all the leverage. As much as she tried, she could not break his hold. She couldn't knee him in the groin, either—not with the way he was stretched out on top of her. Although she was fighting as best she could, she wasn't making any impact, and against so much weight, her energy was dwindling fast.

I'm going to die. She almost couldn't believe it—that this would be how it all ended for her. The same man who'd murdered her mother was going to murder *her*.

But if that was going to happen, she was going to leave her mark, at least, she decided. His face, if nothing else, would tell the tale of what went on here this day.

She stopped trying to break his hold or wiggle out

from underneath him and used her nails to gouge his cheeks.

He cursed when she drew blood but didn't let go. He knew he had to hold on for only a few more seconds.

But then she went for his eyes.

He tried to turn his head and didn't do it soon enough. She felt something wet right before the crushing pressure on her windpipe gave way and he covered his face, groaning in agony.

The big gulp of air she sucked in gave her a surge of fresh energy she used to twist and buck, knocking him slightly off center. He lifted up, trying to catch his balance with his knees, but that only gave her the opportunity to use hers. She brought her right leg up as hard as she could, hitting him squarely in the groin.

As he cried out and fell to one side, she started kicking frantically, like a woman possessed. *Escape. Escape. Do anything you have to do,* she ordered herself, and kept kicking until she was free.

After scrambling to her feet, she grabbed the lamp on the side table and swung it at his head like a bat. He was just trying to get up, so he wasn't prepared for the blow, wasn't expecting it, and the sound it made—as well as the sound *he* made—told her she'd done significant damage. When he fell this time, she thought maybe *she'd* killed *him.* He had blood oozing from his temple, staining the carpet in an ever widening pool. But she didn't stop to see if he was okay. Her legs felt like rubber; she had to use what strength she had left to get away.

She saw her phone lying on the carpet. It was only a few feet beyond him, but getting to it would mean putting him between her and the door, and she wasn't going to do that. She wasn't going to take any chances, wasn't going to stay in the cabin to look for her purse or her keys or anything else, so long as there was a chance he might get back on his feet and come after her again.

After grabbing hold of the nearest table for balance, she left him behind and dashed out of the cabin.

CHAPTER TWENTY-EIGHT

Paige hadn't answered a single text or phone call, hadn't been on Facebook or any other social media. Once she'd found a motel room in San Antonio, she'd closed herself up in it with some sandwich makings and a couple of bottles of wine from the convenience store on the corner and had been drinking and watching TV ever since. Although she was doing her damnedest to avoid reality, what was happening in Millcreek was never far from her mind. It hung over her like a dark cloud—oppressive, upsetting, ominous.

If Ed released those pictures, her son would hear of the scandal. Millcreek was small enough that he wouldn't be able to miss it. Even if he didn't understand the full import of what she'd done—God forbid anyone ever showed him those photographs—that wasn't the image she wanted him to have of her. And with the internet being what it was, she'd never be able to put it behind her. Those pictures would, no doubt, surface again and again.

They would destroy her life…

So she was going to destroy Trevor's father's life instead.

She cringed at the thought. But Micah had more options than she did. He could leave town with Sloane; she couldn't go anywhere. Not only did she own a business in Millcreek, she needed her parents and sister now that she was divorced. And she couldn't imagine it would be good to drag Trevor away from his school, his friends, his grandparents and cousins.

She was doing the right thing. She had only ugly choices, but *this* was the path that would impact her son the least. That was why she had to take it. She just had to stay the course.

Finally, after hours of shoring up her determination, she turned on her phone. Micah had tried to reach her dozens of times. Sloane had, too. Most recently, however, it'd been her parents. Considering how many times they'd called, they must've heard what was going on and were freaking out.

She felt bombarded from all sides. Even Ed came up under her recently missed calls. Just seeing his name made her shudder. She'd never hated anyone quite as badly as she hated him. He was so nonchalant about crushing her in order to save himself!

"You son of a bitch," she muttered as she stared at the symbol that notified her he'd left a voice mail. Sloane had tried to warn her about the kind of man he was. But she hadn't listened, which meant she had only herself to blame.

Sick with anxiety and regret, she was tempted to

shut off her phone again and spend another few days hiding out in the motel. She couldn't face what was going on at home.

She ignored Ed's voice mail message along with all the others, didn't even listen to them. But a text she'd received from Trevor, which she spotted as she scrolled through, stopped her dead in her tracks.

Mom, why won't you answer your phone? I need to talk to you. I almost cut off my finger.

The lump that rose in her throat nearly choked her as she dialed her parents' number.

Micah had no trouble finding the cabin, despite the rainy weather. As soon as he reached Granbury, he'd stopped at the hardware store, where the sales associate, bored from how slow it was, informed him that he'd detailed Ed's boat over the summer and told Micah exactly how to find the cabin.

Although Micah had to slow for traffic in two different places where water encroached on the road, the accident he'd heard about must've been cleared because he saw no sign of it.

When he arrived, he expected to find the police at the cabin—or Sloane, at the very least. That he saw no vehicles parked out front made him uneasy.

What was going on?

Fortunately, the front door wasn't locked. He walked right in. "Sloane?" he called.

No answer. He hurried through the dining room to the kitchen and saw a large knife lying on the floor. That caused him to gulp, but it was nothing compared to finding the blood on the carpet in the living room, and Sloane's cell phone lying not far away.

No wonder she hadn't answered. He shoved a hand through his wet hair as he left everything right where it was and called the police again.

The same sergeant answered. "I sent an officer out there. He had to call an ambulance."

"Is she okay?" he asked. "What hospital?"

"It wasn't a she who was injured. Officer Birch found a white male on the floor, unconscious, with a head injury."

"What about the woman? Where's Sloane McBride?"

"I don't know," he said. "She wasn't there when the officer arrived."

"Did he look for her?"

"That's what he's doing now. Last time he checked in, he said he was driving around that side of the lake, canvassing the other cabins, but he wasn't finding a lot of people at home."

Where could she be? Micah wondered. What'd happened here?

Micah turned toward the windows. He couldn't see much, just the wind bending the trees and the rain hitting the glass. Was she out in the storm? And did that blood only belong to Brian Judd or was *she* hurt, too?

He was just about to go outside, to start searching the property in case she'd staggered or stumbled out of the house and then passed out somewhere in the wet and cold, when he got a call from a strange number.

"Hello?"

"Micah?"

"Sloane?" She was speaking so low and with such a

rasp that he could barely recognize her voice. "Where are you?"

She began to talk but even after plugging the ear that wasn't pressed to the phone, he couldn't make out what she said. "Can you speak up?"

"I'm trying! My throat is killing me."

"Why? What happened?"

"I'll tell you when it's easier to talk," she managed to say. "I'm at a cabin by my father's. I had to break in. No one was here to answer the door, and I don't have a coat. I'm shaking so badly I couldn't keep going."

He had no idea what'd happened, but it was obviously not good. He feared she might be in shock. "It's fine. We'll pay for the damage. Are you hurt? Do you need an ambulance?"

"No. I think… I think I'm going to be okay."

Thank God. "Good. Give me the address. I'll be right there."

"How? I'm in *Granbury*," she clarified.

He could tell she was rattled and possibly crying. "So am I," he said.

She told him she'd wound her way around the lake, looking for help and, after giving up about five cabins down, she broke a window.

"What's the address?"

He had to wait several seconds while she found it.

"Got it," he said when she gave it to him. "Hang on, okay?"

"Brian Judd killed my mother," she said, suddenly bursting into tears.

"The police have him in custody."

"He's alive?"

She didn't know? "I can't say for sure. He's hurt.

The police are going to want to talk to you, but I'll be there with you, so you have nothing to worry about."

"Okay. I love you," she said as she attempted to choke back a sob.

He'd thought he'd never hear her say those words again. Closing his eyes, he let his head fall back as he drew a deep, calming breath. "I'm on my way," he said and started for his truck.

Ed was dead asleep when his phone started ringing, but the noise disturbed him enough he cracked open his eyes. There wasn't any light glowing around the edges of the drapes covering the windows, so it wasn't morning.

He rolled over to check the time on his alarm clock. It was at least three hours before dawn. Who was trying to rouse him at this hour?

Immediately, his mind went to Paige. He hadn't been able to reach her to make sure she was saying and doing what she should, so he stretched across the bed to snatch his phone off the nightstand, just in case.

Caller ID indicated it was Micah.

Shit! If Paige had gone to him, if she'd told him that Ed had blackmailed her into signing that complaint, she was going to pay dearly and so would Micah. They thought the truth would save them, but the truth didn't matter unless they could prove it, and they had no way of doing that. Ed would make sure everyone in town saw those photographs, and the fact that they looked like some Peeping Tom had taken them from outside his window meant no one could trace them back to him. He'd look like as much of a victim as Paige. But they wouldn't reflect as badly on him. Paige wouldn't be able to lift her head in Millcreek ever again. And Micah would never be able to return to law enforcement. They were fools if they thought they could fight him and win.

He hit the talk button. "Hello?"

His voice came out scratchy. Even to his own ears, it was apparent he'd been asleep. He just hoped it wasn't also apparent that he was already angry and defensive, prepared for whatever Micah might have to say.

It wasn't Micah, however. His caller was female, her voice muffled by tears.

"Daddy?"

He sat up. It wasn't Paige, either. *"Sloane?"*

"Yeah, it's me. I probably shouldn't have disturbed you so late, but..." she sniffed and caught her breath "...but I needed to call you to say I'm sorry."

He blinked several times as he stared into the darkness. Was he dreaming? He'd never had a call like this from Sloane before. What had changed? "What is it, sweetheart? Why are you crying?" he asked. "What's going on?"

"So much. I'm at the hospital."

"Are you hurt?"

"No. Just rattled. I'll be fine. It's a long story, but the bottom line is that I now know I was wrong about you and...and Mom, and I feel terrible about it."

He couldn't believe the sudden shift. It was too good to be true. "What finally convinced you?"

"I went to the cabin to look for Mom's body—"

"You went *where*?"

"I'm in Granbury."

"So *my* cabin. How'd you get in?"

"I broke a window. I'm sorry for that, too. I'll pay

for it, of course. But you won't believe what happened after I got there."

She could already knock him over with a feather. "I'm listening..."

"Brian Judd came and...and tried to kill me." She broke down again on those last words.

Ed threw off the covers, got up and put on his robe and slippers. "He *what*?"

"He tried to *choke* me to death! But I managed to escape. He's in the hospital now but will be going to jail for attacking me and possibly for Mom's murder, as well."

"He killed your mother?"

"Yes. He's confessed. He took her out in the middle of nowhere and just left her. That's what happened to her, Dad. She had no coat, no shoes, no water or money. She didn't even know where she was, and it was the middle of the night. He's agreed to take the police to where he forced her to get out of his car, and they're going to search for her remains, so we might finally get the proof we need."

"I see." Ed rubbed his beard growth as he tried to soak it all in. "That's why you're using Micah's phone. He's there with you?"

"Yes. I owe him so much."

Ed headed downstairs to pour himself a drink. He needed one—and why not? He had plenty of reason to celebrate. Brian Judd would be going to prison for Clara's murder—even if they didn't find a body. And he had his daughter back. Sloane would no longer be a threat to him. All the angst and upset he'd faced because of her was behind him. Everything had changed in one night. He couldn't believe how fortunate he was. But he'd always been lucky. "I'm not sure I understand how everything went down," he said as he entered the living room. "How did Brian Judd know you were at the cabin?"

"Vickie told him."

"My *neighbor*?"

"Yes."

"I didn't realize they were in touch."

"Neither did I. But she's the one who told me…told me Mom was pregnant with Brian's baby. And…and then I learned how unhappy he was about that, how desperate he was to make sure it didn't ruin his marriage."

"He was desperate enough to kill her."

"Yes."

"I'm sorry you had to learn all of that about your mother. I was trying to keep it from you and everyone else, didn't see any reason to ruin her reputation."

"And I thought you were hiding the truth, hiding your own culpability. I feel so bad. I'm sorry for misjudging you. Randy has been right all along. It was just…some of the things I heard that night have stuck with me. They were *so* confusing, but now I see that they were also misleading."

"Of course they were," he said, gentling his voice. "You were only a child when your mother disappeared. I regret she and I ever had that argument. I hate that the mean things we yelled were the last things we ever said to each other. But I told you I didn't hurt her. I wish you could've believed me."

She sniffed. "So do I. It would've saved me a lot of pain. There was so much I didn't know, and I let it drive a wedge between us all these years."

He poured himself a glass of bourbon. "I'm glad we have a second chance, sweetheart. Now that we know for sure your mother is dead, let's have a funeral for her so we can put her to rest and give her a proper goodbye."

"I'd like that," she said.

"We'll move on, start over."

"I'd like that, too. Are you willing to forgive me?"

He couldn't help softening; she was so humbled, so repentant. "Of course. I haven't been perfect. I've made my share of mistakes, especially back then. But we'll get past all that, okay?"

More tears. She was choking up so badly that, at first, she couldn't even answer. "Okay," she managed at length.

"And I'll do what I can to help Micah," he added. "Don't worry about him."

"Help him?" she echoed.

"I heard he's been suspended from the force pending an investigation, but that complaint Paige signed is ridiculous. Why would she accuse him of threatening her life a year after the divorce? It has to do with jealousy, if you ask my opinion. Now that you're back in town, she's so green with envy she can't stand it."

"I don't know what she's thinking, why she would suddenly do something so terrible," Sloane said. "But it isn't fair. Micah would never threaten anyone, especially with a loaded gun."

"That's why I'm willing to step in and speak to the police chief on his behalf."

There was a slight pause. "Actually, please don't get involved," she said at length. "We appreciate the offer, but we're not asking for any special favors. We'll work it out through the proper channels."

"The proper channels don't always get it right, Sloane. Do you really want to risk letting this go on his record? Let me do what I can. He's a good man, deserves the help."

"But I don't want to take advantage of being related to the mayor. I don't believe in that sort of thing."

Was she for real? He didn't understand why she wouldn't avail herself of every benefit, like Randy. But he wasn't going to argue with her; they were finally starting to get along. "Okay. I won't get involved," he said, but he was going to have Micah reinstated, regardless. Now that Micah and Sloane were no longer his enemies, he had no reason to battle Micah's family, all of whom were angry and ready to protect their own. Ed thought he could easily win the fight that was brewing, had planned on meeting that resistance, but now there was no reason to devote the time or the energy. "Would you like to have breakfast sometime this week, when you're back on your feet?" he asked.

"I would," she replied. "And I hope Randy will join us."

He smiled as he sipped his bourbon. "I'm sure he will. Good luck dealing with that complaint against Micah," he said as though he was going to honor his word, as though it was still going to be a struggle for them.

"Thanks, Dad," she said.

"How do you feel?" Micah asked.

The paper covering the examination table Sloane was sitting on crinkled as she handed Micah his phone. The police had taken hers into evidence, since it had been found at the scene of the crime. "Better," she said as she wiped her cheeks. "I know my father is a...a difficult personality. All the cheating he did when he was married to my mother, the lying, the way he's treated women in general... I can't condone any of that, but everyone has issues, so I'm willing to let the past go in order to pull my family back together."

"What about Detective Ramos and his suspicions?"

"He might still believe my dad killed his own parents, but I'm not going to be wrong about him twice. I accused him of murdering my mother, and he's *innocent*, Micah. I owe him some loyalty after that."

He put the *People* magazine he'd been leafing through back in the rack beside the door. "What'd he say when you told him we don't want him getting involved in what's going on with me?"

"He seemed surprised." She laughed. "He doesn't get why there's anything wrong with that. I was born to someone who thinks he should be able to break the rules whenever he sees fit, and he gets away with it. I don't approve, but that's my dad. It doesn't mean we can't love each other in spite of our differences."

Micah came over, slid his arms around her and kissed her cheek. "I agree. It's not your job to police your father. It's time you had what you've been missing for most of your life."

"I have you," she said. "That makes me happy right there."

"Does that mean you're going to stay in Millcreek, at least for a while?"

"It does. It's where I belong."

"At my place?"

She could pay for them to have a much bigger house, but she knew he wouldn't feel comfortable letting her do that. He was too proud. And his house was comfortable enough. "Why not?" She shot him a grin. "Maybe that means you'll finally unpack."

"I can now see my way clear to doing that, yes." He rested his forehead against hers. "Can you believe you have the answers you've craved for so long? There were times when you thought it would never happen."

She gripped his arms. "I'm sad for what Brian Judd did, what it cost me and Randy and even my dad. But I'm also sad for Brian's wife and family. Crime doesn't have only one victim. They will suffer, too."

"True." He ran a finger lightly over her neck where Brian had choked her. "The doctor said you'll likely have bruising here in the morning. I can already see a little discoloration."

"My throat is killing me, but I suppose things could be worse."

"They could be a lot worse." He leaned forward to kiss her. "I can't believe I have you back."

"We'll see if Paige will settle down and not make it such a problem."

"She'll make it a problem if we let her," he said. "We can't give her that much power."

"She has a lot of control when it comes to Trevor. I'm worried about that, so you must be, too."

"I'm as angry and determined as I am worried. I won't let her get away with using him to punish me."

The doctor walked in, so he backed away.

"Okay, Ms. McBride. You're all set to go. I just went over the X-rays of your neck and, as I expected, didn't see any lasting damage. The bruising to the soft tissue should fade pretty fast."

"Thank you," she said and took Micah's hand as they told the doctor goodbye, finished up at the window out front and left.

CHAPTER TWENTY-NINE

It was the maid's knock that woke Paige at her San Antonio motel the following morning. Not only did she have a terrible hangover, she was so filled with dread she almost couldn't bring herself to open her eyes, let alone get up. She had to go back to Millcreek today. Last night, when she'd talked to Trevor to make sure he was okay, she'd promised him—and her parents—that she would. Although she wasn't looking forward to facing all the people who were going to pounce on her and grill her about her accusations against Micah the moment she showed her face—especially Sloane and Micah himself, not to mention her ex-in-laws—she couldn't procrastinate that moment any longer.

Fortunately, Trevor hadn't yet heard that she'd lodged a complaint against his father. Her parents were careful with what they said, since he'd been around when they talked, but they let her know *they* were aware.

She'd promised them a private conversation when she got home, which was another reason she wasn't looking forward to returning. Her father had indicated he'd already told Micah off, which didn't make her feel any better.

She was the one who deserved to be told off.

"Housekeeping," the maid called when Paige didn't answer in time. The woman tried to come in, but the security lock kept the door from being opened all the way.

"I'm checking out today," Paige told her. "Come back in an hour."

"Checkout was at eleven," she said. "You know that, right?"

It was after eleven? Paige sprang to her feet, then swooned and nearly fell back on the bed, thanks to her headache. She'd had no idea she was sleeping so late. She grabbed her phone to call her parents but before she could get that far, she saw she'd missed ten calls from Ed McBride, and her stomach began to churn, hurting even worse than her head.

She'd missed a slew of text messages from him, too.

"I'll be out soon," she told the maid to buy some more time and sank back down on the bed to read them.

Pick up the phone, Paige. You'll be sorry if you don't.

Sorry in what way? Had he already sent the pictures to the paper?

The mere possibility caused her heart to leap into her throat, so she didn't bother to read anything else. She immediately punched the button on her phone that would call him back.

"Did you get my messages?" he asked without any preamble.

"Only the threat. Did you send the pictures to the paper?"

He made a sound that suggested she was being ridiculous to be so concerned. "You really are a Nervous Nelly, aren't you? I can't imagine why you hate those pictures. I love them, look at them all the time."

She grimaced at the images that conjured in her mind. The sick bastard relished the power he held over her. "So did you send them or not?"

"No, I haven't parted with them, and it looks like I won't be parting with them any time soon."

She rocked back and pulled a pillow over her face. "What do you mean? God, you're the worst person I've ever known. You're destroying my life."

He chuckled as though he didn't care. "Jeez. And just when I was about to give you some good news."

She threw the pillow to the other side of the bed. "Good news for who? *You?*"

"No, you're going to like this, too."

Drawing a bolstering breath, she shoved into a sitting position. "What is it?"

"I told Chief Alder he could tear up that complaint against Micah, that you weren't in your right mind when you signed it."

"And he did that? It's done?"

"Not yet. He couldn't do it without hearing from you first, but as soon as you call him, the investigation into Micah's behavior will disappear, and your ex will be reinstated."

Her relief was so profound she felt faint. "Are you kidding me?" He had to be. Now that she knew him better, she understood that he never did anything without a reason, and everything was geared to benefit him.

"No, actually I'm not."

"What about the pictures?" She hoped this whole thing would simply go away, but even if it did, she'd never forget what it felt like to see those photographs and to know that a man who had no affection for her, no conscience whatsoever, had them in his possession.

"I don't need them anymore."

"So you'll destroy them? And the original files, too?"

"Probably not," he admitted. "As I said, I like them. But no one else will have to know they exist, and that's all that matters to you."

It wasn't all that mattered. She'd live in fear as long as they were in his possession. But that was, no doubt, what he intended. If she ever told anyone he'd blackmailed her, he'd use them to get revenge. "Why are you letting Micah off the hook?" she asked.

"Sloane has found the man who killed her mother, so she's no longer out to get me. That means I can give you a break, too."

"*You* didn't kill Clara?" Paige had grown convinced he was the guilty party.

"I'm disappointed you'd even ask. But no, it wasn't me. It was the man she'd been having an affair with."

"Brian Judd."

"I see word is getting out. The fool has confessed and will be going to prison."

The *fool*? That was an odd way to refer to the man who'd murdered his wife, but Ed didn't care about anyone, least of all Clara, who'd been gone so long. Anyway, it didn't matter that he hadn't committed murder.

He wasn't a good guy, regardless. "I bet she's glad to know."

"She is, and now we can begin to repair our relationship."

Paige wished she could warn Sloane to stay away. Her father didn't deserve her goodwill—or anyone else's. But Paige didn't dare, would never be able to get away with saying anything bad about Ed. "So what will I give as the reason I lodged that complaint to begin with?"

"Well, I still have these photographs..."

She balled her free hand into a fist; he was insinuating *something*. "Which means what?"

"It means you can't say anything that'll make Micah look bad. I wouldn't want to cause Sloane any more distress after all she's been through. So I guess you'll just have to tell the truth."

Silent tears began to cascade down Paige's cheeks—just when she'd thought she couldn't cry anymore. "Which is..."

"You were lying, right?"

Admitting that she'd lied would be humiliating in its own right, but it was better than taking Trevor's father away from him, and it was *infinitely* better than having those pornographic pictures immortalized in the minds of everyone she knew.

"You'll blame it on your jealousy," he continued, "on the fact that you can't beat Sloane at anything and should never have tried."

"You have to be the cruelest individual I've ever known," she said, her voice barely above a whisper she was so stunned.

He chuckled, obviously enjoying her pain. "Maybe if

you'd been a little more realistic about your own shortcomings, you would never have tried to steal Micah from Sloane in the first place," he said and disconnected.

Paige hung her head long after he was gone. "You're a monster," she said into the empty room, but she knew, in her heart, he was right in one regard.

Sloane hadn't caused her divorce. Micah wasn't responsible for what'd happened the past ten years, either. She'd known he didn't love her from the start. She just hadn't been willing to accept no for an answer. She'd wanted to believe, given the opportunity, she could change his mind. That was why, after they'd slept together the first few times, when he'd tried to stop seeing her, she'd gotten pregnant with Trevor.

The next few days were cathartic for Sloane. After receiving several stitches in his skull from where she'd struck him with that brass lamp and being treated for a concussion, Brian Judd had been released from the hospital and taken into custody. He would stand trial for the murder of her mother, and the police were certain of a conviction. She'd achieved the justice she'd been seeking when she returned to Millcreek, and she was back in the most fulfilling relationship she'd ever had—with Micah.

But that wasn't all. Everything else was going great, too. She was slowly repairing her relationships with her father and brother, had had breakfast with them just two days ago. For the first time in ages, she and Randy weren't at odds. They'd talked about Hadley and his daughter, the dealership and other aspects of his life. Now her father was planning a big barbecue for when

Hadley returned, which meant Sloane would have the chance to get to know her sister-in-law and her niece. And Paige had returned to town and retracted her complaint against Micah, admitted that she'd made it all up. Thanks to the sudden resurgence of Paige's conscience, he'd been reinstated, but he wouldn't be going back to work until next week. He was taking some time off to help Sloane move in, since she'd had her furniture delivered, and to finish unpacking himself.

Her phone beeped as they were moving his bedroom set into the spare bedroom for Trevor and hers into the master, since it was nicer. It took a few seconds, but once her hands were free, she checked to see who'd been trying to reach her.

It was Paige.

I feel terrible about what I did. I want to make it up to you, if you'll let me. Please believe that I'm sorry.

Although Paige had texted something the day before, equally apologetic, Sloane hadn't responded. She didn't have it in her to forgive Paige quite yet. It wasn't so much about holding a grudge as it was about being unable to trust her. Sloane felt she could no longer rely on her old friend to want what was best for her, especially when it came to Micah, and how could they be friends without that? She didn't need to surround herself with people who might betray her. She was happy, but it was such a new and fragile happiness she felt she needed to bask in it for a while, become whole and healthy before taking the risk of letting Paige back into her life. She wasn't unrealistic enough to believe that she and her father and brother would have perfect relationships when they never had before, but at least they had a chance for peace now that she wasn't opposing them when it came to Clara. She wanted to put her efforts toward making it up to them that she'd ever doubted so strongly in the first place.

"Who is it?" Micah asked.

"Guess."

"Your father?"

"I'd be more excited to hear from him. It's Paige."

He shoved the bedroom dresser down a few inches to center it. "What does she want?"

"She insists she loves me, and she's sorry for what she did to you."

He leaned an elbow on top of the dresser. "What are you going to say?"

"Nothing. I'm not ready to deal with her yet." Paige had apologized to Micah, too, and, for Trevor's sake, he'd accepted her apology. He *had* to deal with her, but Sloane didn't have a child with Paige. She could cut her off indefinitely, and she thought she just might do that.

"At least she retracted the complaint. It couldn't have been easy to admit she lied."

"She should never have made that up in the first place. She almost ruined your career."

He walked over to pull her into his arms. "God, I love you. Other than Trevor, I've never loved anyone so much in my life."

"It's amazing that being apart for ten years didn't change a thing—for either one of us. We were so young back then," she told him, locking her arms around his neck.

When Sloane first came back, she'd told herself that they probably didn't really know each other anymore, that their attraction would wear off once they'd had their fill of sex and the challenges of real life set in, but it was going the other direction. She was becoming more deeply committed to him with each passing day. It was far too soon to consider marriage and babies, but she couldn't quit daydreaming about those things, especially when they were making love.

He grinned down at her. "Some things are just meant to be." He held her face between his hands as he sobered. "But can you really be happy in Millcreek long-term, Sloane? You don't think you'll want to return to New York one day?"

Surprisingly, she didn't think she would. She was satisfied in a way she'd never been satisfied before. "No."

"What will you do with your time here?"

She hoped, at some point, she'd be raising children. "I'm going to start painting," she said.

"You used to talk about becoming a painter."

"I need to take some classes first, see if I have any talent. But I'm still interested in it."

"I have no doubt you'll be good."

She couldn't help smiling. "How can you say that? You've never seen anything I've painted."

He pecked at her mouth. "Because it doesn't matter if it's bad. I'll like it just because you made it, will hang it all over the house."

She laughed as he let go and they returned to unpacking. They'd promised Trevor they'd take him out to pizza later, and Paige had agreed even though it wasn't Micah's day—one of the benefits of Paige being so penitent—but Sloane wanted to at least finish the bedroom before they had to go. The house was beginning to shape up. She couldn't wait to see what it was going to look like when they were done.

"Where would you like to hang this?" Micah lifted the photograph she'd taken from the cabin, the one of her mother holding her and Randy, which she'd set on top of a stack of boxes nearby.

"Over here on the wall by my side of the bed. I just haven't hung it because I wanted to get a new frame. I did that yesterday, but..." she scratched her head as she looked around "...I can't remember where I put the sack in all of this mess."

"I saw it in the living room earlier," he said and went to get it.

While he was gone, she sat on the bed to remove the backing and was shocked when a letter dropped out.

"What's that?" Micah asked as he came back with the sack.

She was just bending to pick it up. "I don't know."

As soon as she opened it, she had to sit down again. "It's a letter from my mother!" she said. "This is her handwriting. What do you think it was doing hiding behind that picture?"

He put the frame on the bed beside her. "I have no clue. What does it say?"

As Sloane started to read the tiny, cramped writing, her smile faded and her pulse began to race. "Oh my God," she whispered.

Micah bent to catch her eye. "What is it?"

She didn't trust her voice. She shoved it at him, and he read it aloud.

To Whom It May Concern:

If you've found this and I'm dead, it was my husband, Ed McBride of Millcreek, TX, who killed me.

I had no idea when I married him that he was the kind of man he is. I was just a young, stupid girl, giddy in love. But I learned soon after. He's a psychopath. He must be. I've never known anyone more callous. He cares only for himself—the kids and I don't matter to him at all. The stories I could tell... You probably wouldn't believe me even if I had room to write them. So I won't bother. I need to keep this thin in order to make it fit in the frame, anyway.

But if I'm dead, please know that it was no accident. He murdered me just like he murdered his parents and his brother before we even met—maybe not in the same way, but he's to blame. He admitted it to me once, when he was threatening me. He said if he could kill his entire family without a problem, he wouldn't even flinch at giving me "what I deserve."

I can't prove that he killed them. He's so damn smart. But I might be able to provide a clue to solving my own murder.

He would never dispose of my body without removing my wedding ring. It's worth over $100,000; he'd want it back. He's arrogant enough to believe he could get rid of me while keeping what does matter to him, have the best of both worlds. He thinks he can have anything he wants and always has. You should hear the way he speaks of his dead parents and brother—the disrespect and lack of feeling.

But, again, I don't have room to go into all of that. I just want to say that the diamond from my wedding ring is registered with the GIA. I've in-

cluded a copy of the certificate with this letter. If you find my diamond, you might be able to trace it back to him. Please try. I know I'm not perfect, but I hope I deserve that much.

And if I've been taken from my children, tell them I will love them through eternity and that I hope they will grow up and be happy in spite of their father.

—Clara McBride

Sloane covered her mouth as Micah came to the end. "This was written the year she disappeared," he said, pointing to the date her mother had put at the bottom.

"She knew things were escalating between her and my father and didn't know how to stop what was coming."

"That's my guess."

"But Brian Judd killed her. He's confessed!"

Micah frowned as he pulled the copy of the GIA certificate out from behind the letter and looked it over. "Four carats. Nearly colorless. Very few inclusions. Wow..."

Sloane stared down at the copy of the certificate, too. "If we find her diamond, we might be able to trace it back to Brian Judd. He could've taken it from her and sold it as easily as my father, right?"

Concern registered on Micah's face. "We should be able to trace it to *someone*. It has a microscopic number engraved inside it. No two diamonds are alike to begin with, so...we'll see."

Just when she'd begun to believe her father was innocent! That she'd misjudged him. She'd apologized to him, and yet her mother was speaking as if from the dead, saying he *was* responsible for killing his parents and brother, and why would she lie? Sloane had always felt that something was missing inside her father, just as her mother said. That was part of the reason she'd been suspicious of him all along—it wasn't just what she'd heard that night. "Micah, I feel sick."

He slid his arm around her. "You believe her."

"I do. That easily. In spite of how nice my father and I have been to each other this week. In spite of what Brian has said. Does that make me a bad daughter?"

"No. Intuition is a funny thing. Sometimes you can just feel when something isn't right."

Tears welled up. She didn't want to go through this again. She'd been trying so hard to forgive her father and believe in him. But if her father killed her mother—or his parents—he needed to be put away so he couldn't hurt anyone else. "Regardless of whether Brian killed her or my father did, her ring probably wasn't reported as stolen," she said. "My father would've had the original paperwork. He was the registered owner. So he could easily have gone to LA or New York or somewhere else where there's a big diamond industry, away from here so the sale wouldn't trigger any memory of my mother's disappearance."

"Doesn't matter if it was reported as stolen or not," Micah said. "If it's registered, it's registered. The recovery network for diamonds is surprisingly big, and the diamond business itself is surprisingly small. If it's out there, and not buried with her somewhere, we'll be able to find it."

Her phone rang. After dashing a hand across her cheeks to dry her tears, she looked down at it. "No way. My father's calling."

Micah tapped the letter. "I bet he never saw this coming."

"*I* didn't even see it coming."

"Are you going to answer his call?"

She shook her head. "I can't talk to him right now."

Micah took the letter and the copy of the GIA report and stood. "I'll get started on this. The sooner we know, the better."

She was pretty sure Micah kissed her before leaving, but only a few seconds later, she couldn't remember. Her mind had been a million miles away in that moment—and it still was.

"Please don't let it be my father," she whispered, but it took only three days for Micah to trace the diamond to the store where it'd last been purchased.

"I found it," Micah said when Sloane answered his call. She'd been cleaning the house and preparing a salad and some pasta for dinner. But as soon as she heard this news, she had to go sit down.

"Where?" she asked.

"Maine."

"How'd it get to Maine?" She caught her breath after asking that question because this was the answer she'd been waiting for. Although she'd spoken to her father in the past few days, it'd been so hard to pretend as though nothing had changed.

"Your father sold it separate from the setting to a wholesaler in San Francisco five years after your mother went missing, Sloane. From there it was sold to a store in Maine, where a Mr. Rothwell Sturgis bought it."

She only cared about the first part; the rest didn't matter. *Your father sold it...* The words seemed to echo over and over in her mind. "He kept it until he thought the coast was clear."

"That's my guess, too. He held off as a precaution. But when no one really got involved or investigated your mother's disappearance, he felt safe to liquidate it."

"How do we know he didn't take it from her before she left that night? Before Brian killed her? That could be a possibility, right?"

"No. Brian Judd has shown the Granbury detective who's handling the case where he dropped your mother. They've been canvassing the area all day, trying to find someone who might've seen her."

"And?"

"They came across a man who once owned a convenience store at the edge of Rio Vista, a small town of only nine hundred people out in the middle of nowhere. He claims he saw a woman stumble in the night your mother went missing. She was scratched and bruised and didn't have a coat or shoes. He remembers it was that night specifically because it was the anniversary of his wife's death, and he was so surprised by her appearance. Nothing like that ever happened before or since. He was shown your mother's picture, and he confirmed that she was the woman he saw. He said she was beautiful. And he remembers that she was wearing her wedding ring because she had it on when he let her use the phone. He noticed how big the diamond was, wondered how a woman with that kind of money could be out wandering around in the desert and was shocked she hadn't been mugged. He says he asked if he should call the police, but she wouldn't let him. She told him she was just lost, needed to get back to her kids and wanted to call her husband. A couple of hours later, someone in a black Corvette picked her up."

Sloane sat frozen as his words registered in her mind. Her father had owned a black Corvette at the time. "That's why Brian thought *he* killed her. Because she never reappeared—at least no one saw her who knew who she was." Sloane came to her feet. "Wait… Vickie Winters said my father took the boat out that night. He wasn't driving the Corvette."

"That's why I called Vickie as soon as I got this information. She admitted that she made that up about the boat. She wanted to convince you to go after your father. She hates him for what he did to her, and she felt certain he was guilty and going unpunished."

Vickie had seemed so credible. "So what *did* she see that night?"

"She claims your mother showed up, crying and saying she needed to use the phone. After Vickie let her in, your mother called Brian Judd, who came to get her a few minutes later."

"That's it?"

"Not quite. Vickie waited to see if anything else was going to happen and said your father came roaring past her house in his black Corvette several hours later."

"Did she know that the man from the convenience store said my dad was in a black Corvette?"

"No, of course I didn't tell her that. She offered the information when she retracted the bit about the boat. The fact that her story now matches that of the convenience store owner is what gives it some credibility."

Suddenly weary beyond words, Sloane closed her eyes. "Is this enough, Micah? Is it enough to put my father away for the rest of his life?"

"Possibly. With Brian's testimony of the situation, your testimony of what you heard and saw that night, the convenience store owner's testimony, your mother's letter, Vickie's testimony and your mother's diamond being sold by your father, the evidence is piling up. You should finally get the police support you should've had all along. Chief Adler will *have* to take action in order to save his own ass, because I'm going to threaten to go to the media if he doesn't. This is too much to ignore."

"So what will happen to Brian?"

"He'll go to prison on a lesser charge, attempted murder instead of Murder One."

"They'll *both* go to prison."

"That's what they both deserve, isn't it?"

"Yeah." She felt a sadness come over her for all her mother had suffered, and for the loss of what could have been, if only her father had been a better man. But in a strange way, she also felt satisfied that they'd reached the truth at last. Maybe it wasn't the prettier truth she'd wanted to believe—that Brian, someone who wasn't related to her, had killed her mother. She didn't get to think of her father as an innocent man, didn't get to put her family back together, but she cheered the fact that her mother had overcome her abuser at last. Without the note Clara had thought to hide in that picture, Ed would've gotten away with her murder.

"I guess Randy's going to lose all the perks he's received for being my father's son after all," she said.

EPILOGUE

Eighteen months later...

Sloane stretched her aching back as she examined the produce at the grocery store. She wanted to make some fresh salsa. Since she'd been pregnant, she couldn't get enough tomatoes. They were all she wanted to eat. But she had to be careful to select peppers to go with the tomatoes that weren't overly hot. She'd made that mistake last time.

She'd just put a plastic sack containing four small yellow peppers in her grocery cart when she heard the signal for an incoming text and started digging around in her purse to look for her phone. She was picking Trevor up for Micah, since Micah had to work until late, and taking him to a movie after her doctor appointment, and she wanted to be sure it wasn't Paige saying he couldn't go.

Her relationship with Paige still wasn't the strongest. Paige didn't like letting Trevor spend time with her, and although Trevor was thrilled he would soon have a little sister, Paige was having difficulty accepting Sloane's pregnancy. She had come to the wedding ten months ago, however—with her folks—so they were all making the effort to be flexible and forgiving, to somehow get beyond what they'd been through. But that attempt had been seriously tested when Sloane had packed up her father's house following the wedding to get it ready to sell after he went to prison—a difficult thing in and of itself, especially since Randy was still so angry with her he refused to help—and found some shocking photographs of Ed having sex with Paige.

Sloane winced as she continued to dig for her phone. Sometimes she *still* thought about those pictures. She wished she could erase those images from her mind, but it'd been months since then and they hadn't faded a bit. That it was her *father* Paige had slept with explained a great deal about the night Paige had appeared at the motel crying and upset after having sex with someone she wouldn't name. Sloane couldn't say for sure, of course, but she guessed that man had to have been Ed. For one, she remembered Paige saying her partner had had a vasectomy, which fit. She also remembered Paige calling herself a terrible friend and could better understand why. Paige had never been interested in Ed; she'd always wanted Micah, so that encounter had been about something else entirely.

Sloane had kept those pictures hidden for several weeks, wondering what she should do, but finally destroyed them before Micah or anyone else could see them. As stomach turning as they were for her, she ultimately knew she couldn't do anything else.

Although she'd never mentioned them to Paige, she'd

sent what she'd shredded to Paige in a box. She'd figured if Paige knew what that mess was, she might be glad to know those pictures had been destroyed. And if she didn't know what that mess was, she'd ask.

Apparently, she knew, because Sloane had never heard from her regarding that parcel. They both pretended the incident had never occurred. But Paige had let Sloane take Trevor alone, to spend some time with him and get to know him better, for the first time right after.

Sloane moved her cart to the side to allow someone else to get around her as she finally came up with her phone. It was Micah who'd texted her. How's my beautiful wife?

I'm good, she wrote back. Getting the stuff to make salsa.

More salsa? I thought pregnant women were supposed to crave pickles. Or ice cream.

I'm getting more ice cream, too.

Only three more months and our daughter will be here.

I can't wait to meet her.

You still picking up Trevor?

Far as I know. You don't think Paige will back out on me, do you?

Probably not. She's been so much better lately.

It was only a few months ago that Sloane had sent Paige those shredded pictures. Sloane had a feeling that was why. Paige knew she'd done her a huge favor. Maybe she's finally coming to terms with everything.

If that's the case, it's only because you've been so great to Trevor.

Sloane smiled. She was happy to let him think that was what had made the difference. I love Trevor.

He loves you, too. Everyone who knows you loves you.

She was so busy texting with Micah that she didn't at first see her brother. She was just moving her cart again to get out of the way of someone else, when she caught sight of him. Since Ed had been arrested, she'd become friends with Hadley, which meant she'd been able to see Misty, too, but they'd had to keep any interaction on the down low because her brother still refused to have anything to do with her.

She was tempted to smile at him or reach out to him in some other way. He was all she had left of her original family. But she'd tried so many times already, and she was so much more emotional while she was pregnant. She didn't want to give him the opportunity to hurt her again. So she quickly averted her gaze and turned away.

She was in the next aisle, trying to forget that she'd even seen him, when she glanced up to find him coming toward her. She couldn't turn around and hurry off again, not without looking as though she was running from him, so she pretended to be ultra-absorbed in choosing a bag of tortilla chips. She'd thought he'd ignore her as he went by, as he had every other time they'd bumped into each other around town. But this time he stopped.

"Sloane?"

A wave of anxiety drew her nerves taut. She hoped this wasn't going to turn into a shouting match in the middle of the grocery store. Detective Ramos had finally convinced Sammy Smoot's sister to talk and, thanks to the information she'd provided, the police could now trace the money Sam had been paid to murder their grandparents and uncle back to their father. Ed had just been charged with three more murders and would probably never get out of prison. Sloane could only guess her brother had heard the news and that was why he'd approached her. "Yes?"

"You're aware of the latest..."

She gripped her shopping cart a little tighter. "About Dad paying Sammy Smoot? Yeah."

"If you hadn't come back to Millcreek, if you hadn't started everything, our father would still be mayor."

"I know, and I'm sorry, Randy. I didn't do what I did to hurt you—"

"I realize that," he broke in. "Now, anyway. I also realize that I'm the one who should be apologizing to you. I didn't want to believe Dad killed Mom. He still insists he didn't do it, and I wanted to continue to believe him, to believe it was Brian Judd. The police had a confession, after all. And accepting that Dad was guilty meant I was wrong to have trusted him all along." He looked a little uncomfortable as he ran a hand through his hair. "But with this latest development..."

When his words dwindled off, she understood that

he'd finally had to face the truth, finally had to accept what she'd accepted months ago. Their father had murdered several people. They'd been raised by a psychopath. One who was still attempting to lie, who wouldn't even give them the satisfaction of coming clean at last.

"It's hard to believe someone you love could do such horrible things," she said. "You were being loyal to Dad. I understand that."

He hung his head for several seconds before looking at her again. "But you were willing to see the truth, which is even harder, and I was mean to you for it."

She offered him a smile. "It's okay, Randy."

He seemed surprised by her response. "Is it?" he asked. "Can you ever forgive me for being so blind and stupid?"

She'd always wanted to reconnect with her brother, but his resentment had been so great she'd given up. It was hard to believe she might suddenly have the opportunity. "Of course I can forgive you," she said and reached out to draw him into a hug.

"I loved him so much."

She felt his chest jerk and knew he was crying. "I know. What happened was his fault, not yours. We'll heal together," she said and started crying herself when his arms tightened around her.

* * * * *

Questions for Discussion

1. What would you do if you suspected your father had murdered your mother? Do you think Sloane handles the situation in the best possible way?

2. Sloane makes the statement that crime doesn't have only one victim. Myriad people can be hurt by one person's criminal behavior. The family of the victim obviously suffers. But what about the family/friends of the perpetrator? Do you think they are victims, too? Why or why not?

3. Jealousy can cost us relationships we truly value. It's what came between Sloane and Paige, two women who would've maintained a lifelong friendship otherwise. Do you blame Paige for what she did with Micah as soon as Sloane left town at eighteen? What about what she did with Sloane's father once Sloane returned to town? Would you say it's possible to get past this level of jealousy?

4. No one is all good or all bad. Even psychopaths have some redeeming characteristics. Name a few of the redeeming characteristics of the worst character in this story. Name at least one negative characteristic of the other characters.

5. Sloane and her brother, Randy, view the same situation in two totally different ways. Why do you think Randy was so resentful and defensive?

What often stands in the way of us seeing our own "truths"?

6. Micah didn't love Paige, and yet he married her to be a father to the baby they were having together. Do you feel as though he should have done this? Or do you believe he should've been more realistic about his limitations from the beginning? Why do you think he wasn't?

7. Brian Judd is a character whose life would've turned out completely different had he never met Clara McBride. How do you feel about this character? Do you have any sympathy for him?

8. Do you see Paige as a character who could be redeemed? Why or why not?

9. The relationship between parents and children is extremely complex. Do you feel it's possible for people to both love and hate someone who is in their own family?

10. Clyde died before the story opens, and yet he was an important figure throughout. How do you think he impacted everything that came after his death?

If you liked this story, you won't want to miss
Brenda Novak's acclaimed Silver Springs series,
set in a picturesque small town in
Southern California where even the hardest hearts
can learn to love again...

Turn the page for a sneak peek at Brenda's
upcoming novel, Christmas in Silver Springs,
available soon from MIRA Books!

After Tobias ordered his coffee, someone stood up to leave, enabling him to snag a seat at a small corner table near a window that had a Christmas wreath hanging in the middle of it. The guy who'd just walked out had left his newspaper behind, which was lucky. Tobias wanted to take a look at the sports page and hadn't thought to buy one on his way over, but before he could even turn to that section, he heard the barista call out a name that made him look up.

"Harper!"

He'd only ever heard of one Harper.

A quick glance at the faces lingering around the counter confirmed it *was* Harper Devlin, the woman he'd noticed at the Eatery last night.

What were the chances that he'd run into her again, especially so soon?

She didn't hear the barista. At least, she didn't react when he called her name. Standing to one side, out of the way of the line that snaked out the door, she stared off into space, obviously a million miles away.

That was when Tobias realized there was a song by

Pulse playing on the sound system. He could hear Axel Devlin singing, "I will always love you." Had he written those lyrics for her?

"Harper?" the barista called again.

Still no reaction. She was completely lost in thought.

Dropping the newspaper, Tobias got up and claimed her drink for her. But even as he approached, she didn't seem to see or hear him.

"Hey, you okay?" He gave her arm a slight nudge as he held out her beverage.

Startled, she looked up and, as her eyes finally focused, he noticed the shimmer of unshed tears—which she immediately blinked away. "You," she said, recognizing him.

She took her drink, and he shoved his hands in the pockets of his sweatshirt. "Yes, me. But don't worry, I'm not following you. When I heard the barista call your name, I looked up and there you were."

She didn't so much as smile. "Thanks."

"Are you okay? Because it looks like you could use a minute to sit down and relax, and I just happen to have a table." He motioned to where he'd left the paper.

She seemed as lost or bewildered as she'd been last night. "Do you know my sister or my brother-in-law?"

"I've only been in town for five months, so I doubt it. What are their names?"

"Karoline and Terrance Mathewson. He's a podiatrist. She's a housewife who gets involved in about every good cause that comes along—even helped out with the tree-lighting ceremony downtown a week ago. They have two twelve-year-old daughters, identical twins—Amanda and Miranda."

"They sound like stellar citizens, so I'm sorry to say no, I've never heard of them."

She narrowed her eyes. "You have no frame of reference where I'm concerned. I'm a *total* stranger to you."

"Last night the waitress told me you were Axel Devlin's wife. I guess that's a frame of reference."

Glancing away from him at the crowded coffee shop, she took a sip of her drink. "Is that why you bought me the rose? Because you thought I was married to someone famous and that makes me more desirable by extension?"

She wasn't wearing makeup. She had on a pair of yoga pants and a parka with ear warmers and looked as though she'd just rolled out of bed. But he couldn't see how fancier clothes or makeup could make her any more appealing. He loved her golden, dewy-looking skin and the cornflower blue of her eyes. He could all too easily identify with the pain he saw inside them.

Actually, that was what drew him more than anything else.

"Your connection to Axel had no bearing on it whatsoever," he said. "I just thought you were beautiful, and it seemed as though you could use the encouragement."

Tucking the fine strands of blond hair falling from her ponytail behind her ears, she stepped back. "I'm sorry. I'm—I'm not open to a relationship."

The compliment had spooked her, as he'd known it might. But he was only being honest. "That's good."

She seemed taken aback. "It is?"

"Yes—because I'm the *last* guy you should ever get with even if you were."

Her mouth fell open. "Why's that?"

"Never mind. Now that you have your drink, I'll leave you alone."

She caught him by the sleeve as he turned away. "You're leaving?"

"Isn't that what you want me to do?"

She bit her bottom lip. "I don't know. You're...confusing. I don't think I've ever met anyone like you."

He couldn't imagine she'd associated with many ex-cons. No doubt she'd be horrified if he were to tell her he'd done time. Chances were good she wouldn't even be willing to talk to him.

He'd met other women like that, who thought he must be the devil incarnate, especially here in Silver Springs where so many people knew Jada's family. Some women were drawn to the "danger" of associating with a "bad boy" like him but, sadly, those who *were* drawn to him were often a mess themselves.

"That's probably a safe assumption," he said with a grin.

She seemed further confused by his response and the fact that he not only accepted her words, he agreed with them. "So let me get this straight—what, exactly, are you offering me?"

He gestured at the table. "A seat."

"That's all?"

"What more do you want?"

"I don't know. I don't know *anything* right now. I feel like I've just been put through a meat grinder."

He'd never experienced heartbreak on the level she seemed to be experiencing it—not the romantic kind. But pain was pain, and he was well acquainted with that. "Well...I'm a good listener, if you need to talk."

She kept her gaze fastened to his as she took another

sip of her drink. "A man who looks as good as you do is never quite *that* harmless."

He heard the barista call his name above their conversation and that of everyone else in the shop. His coffee was ready. "How long will you be in town?" he asked.

"Not long. Just a few weeks."

"How much damage could knowing me do in such a short time?"

"I'm already a wreck. I doubt knowing you could do *any* more damage," she admitted.

"Then what do you have to lose?" He held out his hand. "Can I see your phone?"

She pulled her cell out of her purse and, somewhat skeptically, let him take it, watching as he added his name and number to her contacts. "I'll leave you alone for today. You can even have my table. But if you need a friend while you're here, you've got someone to call," he said and claimed his drink before walking out.

Christmas in Silver Springs—
now available for preorder.

The countdown to Christmas begins now!
Keep track of all your Christmas reads.

September 24

- ☐ *A Coldwater Christmas* by Delores Fossen
- ☐ *A Country Christmas* by Debbie Macomber
- ☐ *A Haven Point Christmas* by RaeAnne Thayne
- ☐ *A MacGregor Christmas* by Nora Roberts
- ☐ *A Wedding in December* by Sarah Morgan
- ☐ *An Alaskan Christmas* by Jennifer Snow
- ☐ *Christmas at White Pines* by Sherryl Woods
- ☐ *Christmas from the Heart* by Sheila Roberts
- ☐ *Christmas in Winter Valley* by Jodi Thomas
- ☐ *Cowboy Christmas Redemption* by Maisey Yates
- ☐ *Kisses in the Snow* by Debbie Macomber
- ☐ *Low Country Christmas* by Lee Tobin McClain
- ☐ *Season of Wonder* by RaeAnne Thayne
- ☐ *The Christmas Sisters* by Sarah Morgan
- ☐ *Wyoming Heart* by Diana Palmer

October 22

- ☐ *Season of Love* by Debbie Macomber

October 29

- ☐ *Christmas in Silver Springs* by Brenda Novak
- ☐ *Christmas with You* by Nora Roberts
- ☐ *Stealing Kisses in the Snow* by Jo McNally

November 26

- ☐ *North to Alaska* by Debbie Macomber
- ☐ *Winter's Proposal* by Sherryl Woods